LOVE SO LOVELY BORN

Love So Lovely Born

A Novel

Ken Fulmer

Treerise Press

For my Family

A Woman's Love

—The brazen gates ground sullenly ajar,
And upward, joyous, like a rising star,
She rose and vanished in the ether far.

But soon adown the dying sunset sailing,
And like a wounded bird her pinions trailing,
She fluttered back, with broken-hearted wailing.

—John Hay

ONE

Psalm 41:9

Even my best friend, the one I trusted completely,
the one who shared my food, has turned against me.

February 2008

Vickie Morrison sat on a pink flowered couch in the White House lobby. Her tapping foot inadvertently bumped into a mahogany table with thin legs and a glass top as she looked about the room. Unable to keep still, she stood and peered at the painting over the couch, wondering what the settlers in the covered wagon would think of her plight, stuck as she was within and without, in the past and the present, unsure of her path. She'd seen photos of the curio cabinet to her right when it held replicas of birds that sat about brightly and filled the space with cheer. It was a far cry from the thick books that now filled the shelves, accusing her of failing in her earthly duties, much as everyone else had done of late. She would, of course, perform much better if she could only get six hours of sleep.

She told herself the rape was not her fault and that Logan Meson was a madman bent on his own destruction, but the voice inside her head would have none of it. She had considered herself a divine creature but had become a devil in disguise, bitter, battered, and impossible.

A heavy door revealed Todd Reynolds, the president's chief of staff. Vickie inhaled deeply and steeled herself for the conversation.

Todd gestured for her to sit, and he took the red leather chair to her left. His eyes rose to meet the receptionist, who sat at the end of the room at a cherry desk. She found her purse and closed the door behind her.

"Tell me what happened," he said to Vickie. "We'll go from there."

"I've been in tough scrapes, but this one shook me to my core."

"I can imagine. You almost lost your life."

The blood rushed from her cheeks. "Yes, he wanted me dead."

She paused.

"Afterward, I drank and went without sleep. I'm happy to say the booze is no longer an issue, but my nights remain an adventure." She hesitated. "I need to show my network I'm on my feet and I've still got what it takes, and the president needs an ally with a global platform."

Vickie wanted to squeeze Todd's hand, as they were old friends, a rare and valuable commodity in D.C., but he was too far from her, and he might be startled if she did. There was too much history between them, too many cameras in the room, and too many gossips on the prowl.

Todd eyed her with suspicion. "Early primaries haven't gone as we'd hoped, and Preston sees blood in the water. He'll want the kill."

"I'll stand up to Preston Spiro. He doesn't own me."

Todd's serious face took on greater animation.

"No offense, but you just said he did. Isn't that why you're here?"

"Give me an approved script and I'll help you win the great state of South Carolina." She grinned. "You, of all people, know I can deliver."

He laughed. "Still the rebel after all these years."

Vickie caught Todd's eye as she felt Logan's cool, diabolical breath on her neck and the clutching fingers of his embrace. His psychopathy had given her night terrors for months, and she suspected his apparition would haunt her forever as he burned her into a mingled heap of ruins.

Her flip phone rang in her purse, and Todd's eyes flashed restlessly as it faded to voicemail. The jury had gone out, but his verdict would soon arrive. He sat silent, looking at the sun over the covered wagon.

His eyes lingered on the painting, then he turned to her. "All right, Vickie, I'll cut you a break." He held up a palm, interrupting her gratitude. "This only means I will take it to the president."

"It means you will convince him on my behalf."

Todd cut in sharply. "He'll dislike the idea, so there's no guarantee."

"The president likes me. I charmed him long ago."

"So he said." Todd smiled. "You're a lovely temptress."

"Hey, it's how I've gotten this far, so don't knock it."

His face closed as if guarding their secret, one that had lasted for a very long time and could never see the light of day.

"Both our wives hate you, so you were never here. Understand?"

Vickie sighed. "I care only about redeeming myself in the eyes of my producer and my executive vice president. Everything else is secondary."

She needed more, but the walls inside her heart kept out intimacy and had done so for years, ever since she read the letter at eighteen, the one that presented her not as a debutante to be cherished, but as the product of a mother's rape, forever a misfit and eternally on the run.

Like mother, like daughter.

"I'll ensure you return to the top of the ratings," Todd said.

He stood and drew near to her, taking her by surprise.

"And you'll owe me a big favor."

She smiled coyly at him. "Which you can claim anytime."

They both knew it to be untrue, but the sentiment mattered.

"Someday." Todd returned her smile.

"But not now?"

"I think you would fade into the darkness if I did."

"Few would miss me. I've left too much scorched earth, remember?"

"Some of us recall the challenging woman you were, the one who always led and never followed, a journalist of renown, a powerhouse."

"Yes," she said, his words lifting her soul.

He kissed her hand and stepped to the door, leaving her alone.

A rush of warmth flushed through her body, recalling the months that had passed since they'd last bantered, both civilly and uncivilly.

She retrieved her phone and checked her inbox.

Julie's voice sounded frantic. "Helen had an accident on Seneca Road near the violin studio. They wouldn't say much, other than they took her to Rose Sanders. Please hurry. I know she'll want to see you."

Vickie rushed to the Metrorail station and considered her options.

She could ride the Red Line to her downtown office and collect her car from the parking garage, or take the Silver Line to the Reston station and exit near the hospital. It was late on a Friday afternoon, and the traffic on the bridge and Dulles Access Road would be a nightmare.

She bought a pass and hopped aboard the Silver Line.

As she searched for a vacant seat, an elderly woman looked up and her eyes gladdened. She patted the spot beside her. "You can sit here."

Other passengers threw blank looks as Vickie accepted the offer.

"I don't care what people say, dear. I have always loved you."

"Thank you, ma'am. You are kind."

"My name is Alice Harding. Please call me Alice."

It would be a long ride. "All right, then."

"Are you going to the airport? You journalists go everywhere."

Vickie shook her head and smiled. "I'm visiting a friend in Reston."

"Oh, well, that's nice too. Are you close with your friend?"

"I don't have many, so I've tried extra hard with this one."

Alice nodded as if she understood and approved.

Vickie looked at the floor, considering what had transpired earlier.

Todd would follow through, and she would ask President Ambrose softball questions during the interview. Keith's poll numbers would rise, as would ratings for her show, *The Steps We Frame*, which was all Preston cared about anyway, despite his proclamations to the contrary.

A cool draft ran the length of the train, shivering her neck.

Her fingers gripped the wool fabric of her coat and pulled it tightly about her. She would lock out thoughts of the past until Reston.

"I like what you're doing with those girls," said Alice politely.

Vickie nodded at the implication. "We've helped a few."

"Helen Dunstan seems headstrong, if you don't mind my saying so. Have you had much luck with her?" Alice seemed to understand the travails of a disfigured teen. "It must have been difficult to cope."

Vickie gave Alice a faint smile. "I think we'll make progress today."

"Oh, good. I'm so glad to hear it. She has great potential."

Vickie's eyes rose to meet the burly man who sat across the aisle.

"I've never liked you." His scowl drilled into her.

"Please don't be rude," said Alice in rebuke.

Vickie patted Alice's hand. "I see all sorts on the Silver Line, but I've never cared much what other people think of me, which helps."

Alice's face clouded with unease. "You're braver than I am."

"I do whatever it takes to win. It's the only way to survive."

A thickset, flanneled man across the aisle stared at the litter on the floor. His eyes met hers, and he blurted his words with annoyance.

"I like the younger one better. The girl on the weekend."

"Well, you're in luck, because she'll be working tomorrow."

"Good." He turned from her and gazed through his window.

The next forty-one minutes passed in quietude, for which Vickie was thankful. Her blood sugar fell, fogging her mind, and her eyes closed. She drifted into a netherworld and was awakened by Alice, who said it was the Reston stop and she should probably make ready.

Vickie grew alert again as she crossed the Metrorail parking lot and made a beeline for Rose Sanders Memorial. She entered through the Emergency Department's automatic doors and paused, her eyes searching for Ron and Julie in the crowded lobby but finding only unwell people who seemed horribly distressed. A young woman sat in the corner and held a crying baby. She begged the boy who bounced in front of her to play quietly while she tried to soothe her infant.

He instead picked up a magazine and slammed it to the floor.

Vickie approached the desk and asked for information while attempting to disregard the overwhelmed mother, but soon she shared the feeling, as the indifferent nurse refused to answer questions about Helen Dunstan other than to acknowledge her unwelcome presence.

Vickie turned, unsure of what to do, hopeful for an ally.

Ron and Julie appeared, pale and shaken, wiping wet tears.

Julie's feet stopped, and her good left arm reached out and sought Ron's durable shoulder. Once secured, her eyes widened in disgust.

"You should leave right now, before I call the police."

"Is Helen all right?" Vickie squinted as she looked past them.

Ron's voice broke. "Our baby girl is on the third floor. Those people placed her on a stainless steel table as if she was a display in the window." His fists clenched. "I wanted to knock out someone's teeth."

Vickie gasped. Her hand covered her mouth.

"The nurses left a door open on each side of the room, and the staff walked by the entire time we stood with Helen. Some poked their heads inside and gave us a condescending nod. We had no chance to grieve."

"I'm so sorry, Ron."

"I stood there and watched her on that table and thought she looked like another person, someone who had experienced a great deal of pain when she died, and this strange shell was all that was left." Julie stepped toward Vickie. "I'll never get Helen's death grimace out of my mind, no matter how long I live." Her voice raged. "You are the one to blame!"

Vickie's hand pressed against her chest. "What did I do?"

Julie turned to Ron. "Help me get out of here."

"Wait, please. Won't you at least tell me what happened?"

Julie swiped at her tears. "So you can put it on your show?"

Vickie followed them to the exit, unwilling to accept responsibility.

"I can't believe this happened. She was such a joyful light."

Julie wheeled as the double doors opened, and a group passed beside them. She threw a look of contempt at Vickie as the doors closed again with a bang. "I know what you did, so you can stop pretending!"

The lobby fell silent as Vickie took a step backward.

"You're hurting, Julie. I get it, but please let me help."

Vickie reached out her hand, attempting to comfort her friend.

Julie drew away from her. "Don't you dare touch me!"

She turned to Ron. "I need help with my coat. I don't want to get sick on top of everything else. There will be arrangements to make."

He stared into the parking lot. Seconds grew into hours.

"Please, Ron. I won't last much longer in this hospital."

His eyes moistened. "All right, my dear."

Julie's eyes fell on what was left of her right arm, and then she smirked at Vickie as Ron helped her on with her coat. "You know, I lost half my arm trying to protect my child on that tragic afternoon, but you've done more damage than the poor dog, who also lost his life. You must be the most textbook example of a narcissist I've ever seen."

"I asked Helen to stop drinking and to stop speeding in her car."

"And the great Victoria Morrison gets what she wants, right?"

"Please be reasonable. You know I cared deeply about her."

Julie grunted. "You cared?"

"Yes, I did, and still do."

"Then why is my daughter dead?"

This was going downhill fast. Vickie must regain control.

"Let's go to your house and we'll talk."

Julie retrieved a letter from her left pocket. "Look familiar?"

She pushed it hard into Vickie's face, leaving her little choice but to evade. "Please stop. You're a bully, and I won't stand for it."

"Oh, you think I'm a bully? A childless mother with one arm?"

Vickie relented. "All right, I'll play along. Tell me about the paper."

"Helen wrote a journal entry last night, where she recorded your suicidal notions, how you couldn't bear to live and how you dreamed of a life spent in a better realm, somewhere out there in the abyss." Julie's eyes scanned the page. "It says you spoke to her two weeks ago."

Vickie had no choice but to admit the truth. "Yes, I was sad then."

"We all get sad, but we don't corrupt others with our meditations on death." Julie's hand crumpled the page, and her eyes welled. "Helen was my child, Vickie. How could you?" Julie shook her fist and let out a wail. "You should be ashamed, and I hope you burn in the Lake of Fire!"

Ron placed his hand on the small of Julie's back and said they had to leave. Vickie again followed them but stopped inside the hospital foyer. Her shoulder pressed against the wall as they continued to the sidewalk.

He stopped and spoke over his shoulder. "This isn't over."

"I know."

After they disappeared from her view, Vickie slid to the floor.

The tears would not fall, although she wanted to cry.

A guard told her she must leave or the police would be called. He had overheard their conversation and cared little about her status.

She picked herself off the floor and stepped to the same spot Ron and Julie had just occupied, wondering if she should get a cab to their house, take the Metrorail downtown, or lie in front of a bus.

Vickie instead rode the Silver Line in a different direction: west to Dulles and a flight to parts unknown. She was at her best when people hardly knew her, and she loved to explore fresh and exciting places.

At the Delta desk, she bought a ticket for a Caribbean island, one of the few she'd never seen, and told the attendant there would be no luggage. The woman smiled and tapped the keyboard with long painted nails that reflected light like polished diamonds in the sun.

"Here you go, ma'am. One ticket to St. Christina Island."

She found a wooden bench and called her producer, Mitch Dolan. "I won't make tonight's broadcast, so put Nellie in my place."

"What?"

"Look, something terrible has happened and I need solitude."

"How long?"

Vickie considered.

"A month."

"Have you lost your mind? For good this time?"

She smiled dimly, realizing she'd almost forgotten how.

"Just be my friend, Mitch. I could really use one today."

He sighed. "I hope you know what you're doing."

"Me too."

"Did you get the interview with the president?"

"He'll do it. I always get what I want."

"Except today?"

Vickie pushed back her head and looked about the airport lobby.

"She's dead, Mitch."

"Helen?"

"Yes."

"Oh, no. I'm so sorry."

He paused.

"You two were close."

"That's the problem. I let her in, and now I don't know what to do."

"Keep breathing, Vickie. It will work out if you keep breathing."

"Thanks. I owe you one." She hung up the phone.

Dawn's early light caressed Vickie's face, and the satin sheets slid easily against her skin. She rolled over and clutched the pillow as if it were a man. A loud knock at the door startled her, and she sat up in bed.

"What is it?"

Another knock.

She threw off the plush duvet, grabbed her spa robe from a chair, and stomped from the bedroom to the front door, passing the kitchen.

Vickie half expected Julie and Ron as she flung open the door.

"Do you have any idea what time I got in last night?"

A handsome man with dark hair and a flowery shirt grinned.

"Sorry, ma'am. The desk said you requested a guide."

She retreated to a barstool and put her cheek on the granite counter. Her hand rubbed its surface in a circular motion, right and then left.

"There's orange juice in the fridge. The desk sold it to me."

"I've had breakfast." Her guide stood his ground.

Vickie's eyes arched as she raised her head. "You may enter."

"I'm good, ma'am." His arms crossed at the waist, and he smiled.

He checked his watch. "We must hurry."

"Not me. I plan to sleep for seventeen hours."

He chuckled. "It will cut into our sightseeing excursion."

A warning voice of panic whispered in her ear, the one that sounded in the presence of troublesome men, the kind who hurt her.

"Please excuse my appearance," she said nervously.

"I hadn't noticed." His expression was friendly but serious.

"I arrived last night in my work clothes, and there was only this hotel robe, so I've been wearing it ever since." She sat up with a desire to shock him. "I have nothing on underneath. Care to see?"

Her voice had drifted to a hushed whisper as she pictured his muscular arms sweeping her effortlessly into the bedroom.

The guide laughed louder, and his response confused her.

Vickie's fingers grasped the robe's lapels and snatched them shut as she threw him a look. "Keep laughing, pal. I'm going back to bed."

He shifted his weight again and held up his watch.

"We really must go if we wish to avoid the crowd."

She kicked away from the stool, marched to the bedroom, and plopped onto her soft sheets. She felt like an adolescent in full rebellion.

"My name is Raul. I am originally from Mexico."

Vickie yelled her reply. "How nice! Now leave me alone!"

"Will you be long? The sun is perfect, and it will be a beautiful morning on Gibraltar Bay. I would hate for you to miss such scenery."

She rolled onto her back and stared at the ceiling. Coffee would help her function, and perhaps the cool water would soothe her aching soul.

"What's your name again?"

"Raul, ma'am. I was born and raised in Monterrey."

"That's cartel country." She sat up. "You did well by leaving there."

He withheld a reply, which further piqued her interest.

Vickie returned to the barstool. "I need something to wear."

"The hotel has several shops." He looked her up and down.

She liked the way Raul flirted without effort, and he was so gorgeous she trembled in all the right places. "I can open the robe."

He offered her a smirk for her trouble. "It won't be necessary."

She took a heavy breath and exhaled. "All right, then. What's next?"

"Bring your purse, but leave your work clothes. The maids will collect them for the dry cleaners, and we'll dress you for island life."

Afterward, he showed her his jeep, and its condition appalled her.

"These tires are bald," she said.

Vickie scowled as she looked about the area.

"We won't make it a mile."

Raul grunted. "Ma'am, are you always this annoying?"

There was little choice but to trust in his local knowledge, but he seemed plain and rough and wholly unaccustomed to her demands, a problem she would soon rectify, as she always got what she wanted.

"All right, but I'm getting into this contraption under protest."

"I have a feeling you live every day against your will," he said.

She shrugged. "Who doesn't?"

They drove to Gibraltar Bay along a two-lane highway that rose from the village near the harbor to the mountains, which curved along the island's length. This stretch ran around the western side and offered several pristine lookout spots for young lovers to kiss and take selfies.

The jeep descended into a jungle, and they stopped while chickens passed from right to left. Raul smiled at her, and she was happy for the first time in years, as she'd forgotten how much fun and how liberating field assignments could be when accompanied by swarthy men.

The roadway ascended once more, and Raul parked beside a wall.

The sign read: "Gibraltar Bay. Home of the Caribbean Rock."

Vickie turned to him. "Seems odd to call it Gibraltar, since we're a long way from the Mediterranean. Did someone from Spain name it?"

His laughing response carried a tilt of agitation, which she viewed as unnecessary, as she was a customer and he had accepted his role as guide, unforced and well paid. Fury mounted within her, and soon it would boil over, and there would be little she could do to stop her wrath.

"You know," she said, "you're getting on my nerves."

"And your lack of appreciation for anything good has the same effect on me." Several island safari trucks arrived. Cruise ship passengers spilled about their position and formed a military line that progressed down a set of steps to the beach. "We should have gotten here earlier."

His palm landed on the steering wheel as he grunted his displeasure.

Vickie exited the jeep and stretched. "Just find me a spot off to one side and in the shade, and I'll sit on a blanket and read a novel." The last few stragglers disappeared into the trees. "I don't wish to be a bother."

"Too late," he said playfully.

She smirked. "If you knew me, you'd say this is me on a good day."

At the water's edge, she stared at the Gibraltar rock to her left.

Over her shoulder, a blonde-haired woman blurted sound bytes from a megaphone to drone-like people who congregated in groups and moved to the next station when she announced the end of each period.

Raul weaved through the desperate but gleeful melee and approached Vickie's blanket with snorkeling gear from his jeep.

"I already know how," she said. "There's no need for a lesson."

He sat beside her. "I'll bet you know many things."

She shrugged, and her eyes absently scanned the horizon.

"A teenager is dead because of me, so I wouldn't be so sure."

He nodded and kept his silence as a cruise ship couple passed.

The woman stopped and elbowed the man as she turned toward the blanket. "Are you Vickie Morrison?" She spoke with an English accent that Vickie struggled to place, but it sounded upper crust. Vickie grew irritable and unhappy with herself, as she was just in the clothing store and should've bought some kind of hat and a pair of dark sunglasses to hide her appearance. The last thing she needed was attention.

"I am, but this is a much-needed break. I'd like to avoid autographs."

The woman grinned. "We have one of those smartphones that came out last year, the kind with the cracking camera and the brill apps. Can we get a picture?" She hesitated. "It would only take a moment."

Vickie glanced at Raul, who seemed oblivious as he rested with his eyes closed and his hands clasped behind his head. She gently kicked his leg and told him to sit up so they could take a photo together.

"Oh, no," the woman said. "Just us and you, if it's quite all right."

Vickie's lips puckered, but she held her tongue and smiled as the woman and her husband leaned in much too close and snapped four pictures from various angles for thorough measure, overkill in Vickie's estimation, but the matter was promptly settled, and then they left.

A few minutes later, she observed them in the shade, away from the other passengers, reviewing the images on their phone like fussy editors.

Vickie's likeness would likely end up in the British tabloids with a caption that read: "A lousy journalist who believes herself a legend."

She grabbed the fins and attached them to her feet, adjusted the mask's strap, and put its form over her face, but she waited to attach the snorkel until she reached the azure water, where she eased into its embrace, flickering at the initial cold and then feeling caressed by its luxuriant stillness. She took a last look at the mysterious Raul, who lounged peacefully on the beach and smiled, and then she kicked out to the reef, which lay just off the massive Gibraltar rock to their left.

Time slowed, and the portentous world faded from her thoughts.

The water felt pleasant against her skin, and a cadre of green-dotted parrotfish, deep blue surgeonfish, and cyan-striped grunts delighted her visual perception. The sounds of the cruise passengers faded into the background. Underneath her position, a barracuda lingered for a casual moment and then turned as if bored by her presence. She stifled a gasp and followed him instinctively as she might pursue a dictator for an interview, but then she detected a brawny hand that grasped her right leg and stopped her forward momentum as if she were a child's doll.

Vickie surfaced and removed her mask.

Raul did the same.

"Why did you do that?"

He gestured at the beach. "We are all alone."

"So?"

"You can mourn in peace now. There is no need to compete."

"I was enjoying myself until you stopped me."

"No, you were trying to prove yourself by following the barracuda."

This man tried her patience, which had become paper thin of late.

"I was curious, and it was only a fish."

"One with very sharp teeth and a temper to match your own."

He kicked away from her and made his way to the shore.

She returned the mask to her face and dropped her head into the water, trying to forget his interruption. Again, the fish mesmerized her and took her back to Helen and the many late-night talks they had shared, including their last, which was a mistake Vickie would like to take back but knew she could not, as some mistakes were permanent.

She screamed into the water. "It was all my fault!"

Vickie spent nine days with her guide before an epiphany took hold in the spot where she had screamed on the first morning. She would start over with a new teen, and this time she would get everything right.

With renewed vigor, she looked about as she sat on the blanket and wondered after the hill-covered island. There must be more than the tourist-filled dungeon known as Gibraltar Bay, a hopeful place that might bridle her wayward mind and renew her willingness to dream.

She called Raul over from his repose in the shade.

"Yes?"

"I want to see where you go. Don't say it's here."

He smiled. "When I first arrived, I went to the far end of the island."

"Tell me about it."

"There is a rocky beach and another Gibraltar, one that sits in the water and is much smaller than this one. Varieties of fish congregate on the reef in front of the rock. It is a good place to snorkel."

"I want to go there." She gave him a suspicious look as he hesitated. "I'm paying you well, so you must take me where I want to go."

"Gladly, ma'am, but I have bald tires, as you mentioned."

Vickie leaned back and shifted her weight to her hands.

"You're hiding something."

Raul considered.

She sat up and snapped her fingers. "Let's have it."

"I haven't snorkeled in some time, not for a long while."

"What does that mean? You're talking in riddles."

He sighed, clearly exasperated. "There is a camp."

Her eyebrows arched. "And?"

"It is filled with the homeless, those who ran from New York or Paris or London or some other urban environment not to their liking. Each of them tried to find paradise in the Caribbean, one that does not exist and never has, but one that is continually promised."

"Take me to see it."

"So you can kill another with your news coverage?"

All the happy parrotfish in her mind scattered, leaving her alone as Helen had done. She recoiled at his accusation and her flash of memory.

"That's a low blow. I thought we were friends."

"You are persuasive, but I will never expose their world."

"Why not? Public sympathy brings money to a cause."

"Make the authorities nervous, and they will disband the camp. My friends will have nowhere to go, as other islands will not take them."

"They could go home," she said, knowing her words were futile.

"Those doors have been shut for many years."

She sighed. "I must speak with them."

"I will stop the jeep at the top of the hill, and you can look down on their encampment. It's the best I will do. Their fates are in my hands."

She stood, took his hand, and pulled him to his feet.

"Let's go."

***

Multicolored tents had strewn themselves along the beach and underneath branches. The men wore long hair like hippies, and the women sported braids and smiled at their men as they sat near the tents.

From atop the hill, the scene seemed like a Peter Fonda movie from the late 1960s, and Vickie desperately wanted to interview each person.

"No," said Raul, anticipating her thoughts.

She slammed her hand onto the dashboard.

"Watch it," he said angrily. "It may not be much, but it's all I have."

"Sorry."

He rubbed the dash with a clean towel and inspected for damage.

"I didn't hit it that hard. I'm not King Kong."

"Perhaps, but you think you are bulletproof, which is worse."

"You would know, having lived in cartel country."

"Yes, I would."

"Have you ever killed a man?"

His silence said more than words ever could.

Her back pushed into her seat. "Please tell me about it."

He rubbed the wheel with the cloth as if wiping fingerprints.

"I am not like most men you've known."

"I see that, and I like it, but still you won't accept my advances."

He shook his head. "My heart belongs to another."

His words struck Vickie, but she knew them to be sincere.

"Before I leave, will you let me meet her?"

He pointed. "She's down there. The one near the green tent."

Vickie gestured. "That one?"

"Yes, she's the blonde woman with blue shorts."

She seemed young, maybe a few years older than Helen.

"What's her story?" Vickie longed to know details and hoped Raul might share with her. She sensed there was much more than met the eye.

"Like the rest, she lives day to day. I help them with food and water and extra money I make from my spoiled clients." He hesitated. "No offense, but you are a wealthy client, and I am at work."

Vickie shook off his comment. "None taken, and I am spoiled."

If Raul only knew the horrors she'd seen around the globe and in her personal life, he would be less quick to disapprove.

"Has her family deserted her?"

"Her name is Irene."

"All right, does Irene have family somewhere?"

"A grandmother in Boston who is now in a nursing home."

"Irene must have grown up with her grandmother."

"Perceptive. And yes, the two were very close until life intervened."

"It always does."

He smiled. "Do you see why I would not let you interview them?"

Vickie returned his smile. "I wouldn't hurt Irene for all the world."

"Good, then we can remain friends."

Raul cranked the engine and backed out of the space.

As he shifted into drive, she placed her hand on his.

"Help her, Raul. I mean, really help her."

He pointed the jeep to the roadway, and they descended a steep hill. "The problem is, most people think of this island as a utopia, but there is a drug problem here, and many of the homeless are heroin addicts."

"I suspected as much. I've seen the same in L.A. and San Francisco."

"People who get involved with them often end up dead."

Vickie nodded her understanding. "Same as in Monterrey?"

Raul's eyes focused intently on the road ahead of them. She again put her hand on top of his and squeezed. "You've forgotten one thing."

"Which is?"

"I know the president of the United States."

"There's someone I know who is above your president."

"A world leader?"

Raul shook his head. "Jesus Christ, the King of Kings."

"Oh, Him." The wind blew her hair. "We don't talk much."

"Remember Psalm 41:1-3 when your thoughts sink low."

Her focus turned from Raul as she gazed at the jungle foliage. They descended a steep hill, and he pressed the brake pedal, stopping the jeep completely. They waited for two donkeys to pass in front of them. The trees and the underbrush mesmerized her thoughts, helping her keep safely distant from God, the one whom she could never again trust.

Raul turned and placed his hand on her leg. It was the first time he had touched her since they met, and she hoped it meant something nice.

He spoke suddenly and cheerfully, which set her on edge. "Oh, the joys of those who are kind to the poor! The Lord rescues them when they are in trouble. The Lord protects them and keeps them alive. He gives them prosperity in the land and rescues them from their enemies. The Lord nurses them when they are sick and restores them to health."

"I'd like to believe it's true."

"But you don't?"

She wiped tears from her eyes, surprised at their flow.

"I don't think He likes me very much. I'm an awful person."

"May I recite more verses?"

"Raul, I'm not the Bible type. I didn't grow up in the church."

"I was a good Catholic in Monterrey until they killed my family."

Vickie gasped and caught herself. She'd suspected as much.

"You should be as bitter and rebellious as I am."

He nodded.

"I was for a long time, and then the Lord found me."

He paused.

"Now I have a calling, a reason for leaving my bed each morning, and I don't mean to snorkel. May I speak more verses to you?"

"If you must, Raul, but they won't have much impact."

"'O Lord,' I prayed, 'have mercy on me. Heal me, for I have sinned against you.' But my enemies say nothing but evil about me. 'How soon will he die and be forgotten?' they ask. They visit me as if they were my friends, but all the while they gather gossip, and when they leave, they spread it everywhere. All who hate me whisper about me, imagining the worst. 'He has some fatal disease,' they say. 'He will never get out of that bed!' Even my best friend, the one I trusted completely, the one who shared my food, has turned against me." Raul parked in front of the hotel. "This is our last moment together, Vickie. I must say farewell to you now." He hesitated. "It's time you went back to your life."

"Why, Raul? We've become such good friends."

He smiled. "Yes, and our relationship will soon take on another dimension if we continue at this pace. My heart belongs to Irene, which is why I showed her to you today. I don't wish you to be hurt."

"Oh, plenty of men have done it before you. I'm numb to it now."

"There's a man out there, someone chosen by the Lord."

Vickie abandoned all façade. "Ever since I was a girl, I've known there was something different about me, which is why I wasn't surprised when I learned about my reckless mother and my murderous father who raped her. But ever since I read my mother's letter, I've given myself over to evil, allowed it to cover me, and I have lived with obsessions and vexing oppressions. Sometimes I think I might be demonically possessed." She hesitated. "Once I even went to an exorcist."

"I'm no different," Raul said. "I've done many bad things."

Vickie looked away and then returned his gaze. "You did what you had to do to survive, which I admire, although I'm sure it got bloody."

She gestured at herself. "I am exactly the same as the men you fought. I may hide it better than they do, but I am every bit as vile."

"I will never believe it, Vickie. There is good in you."

She sighed. "Only you see me that way, so I guess I have one friend."

He squeezed her arm. "Remember the verses I quoted."

"I won't." She shrugged. "Hey, I'm just being realistic."

"Then look them up in your hotel Bible. Verses 4 through 9."

In the eventide, Mitch called her into work, and her grave spirit, which had been raised by the rush of death and adventure in the Caribbean, fell crashing down about her, halting the renewal of her garden and the abstract music of her gaze. She wept into her pillow, the extra one that substituted for a man, and her entire body shook.

Three times she got out of bed and took a knife from the drawer and sat on the balcony with her arm over the railing, but in each instance there was an unmistakable pull back to her bed and the soft satin sheets and the man-sized pillow. Perhaps she was not ready to die and might yet find hope on the horizon, as the axis powers of prattling voices and bored anxiety and unbearable loneliness fell to life's charms once more.

She opened a drawer when the night had fallen quiet as a tombstone and rubbed her palm across the Bible she found there, but she could not broach its cover nor could she peruse its pages. Years had passed since her last confession, and her sins piled themselves higher than the ziggurat of Babel. Like the Babylonians, the Most High would soon scatter her vain ambitions to the wind, as she knew not how to love.

Vickie closed the drawer and recalled the fear in the priest's eyes when she presented herself to him. A seer had phoned to say a devilish woman would soon arrive on his doorstep, and a malaise would cover him, even priests and nuns, with God's permission, were not above its powerful grasp. He tried each exorcism prayer to no avail and later said her voice grew sinister as a legion of spirits spoke through her, reticent at first as demons always were, but eventually they declared his efforts must cease, as her ancient purpose would be revealed at the appointed hour.

There was a great and terrible malevolence within her.

It lay dormant, gnashing and seething, waiting to erupt.

Wise and relentless, with teeth sharpened over centuries, this force cunningly hunted by night and meandered in the daylight hours, unconcerned with the trivia of men or the desperate tears of women.

Victims offered barren cries as they uttered their regrets on pain of death, but never before, as the fallen world's delights were their interests before its arrival. Evil would soon consume Vickie Morrison, along with every poor soul in her path, either from within or from without. Once satiated with the bloodshed and the deception and the torments, her end would follow, and her soul would descend to the Lake of Fire.

Two

Psalm 42:7

I hear the tumult of the raging seas
as your waves and surging tides sweep over me.

John Breyer sat atop the Mayfield Acres arena as he watched Rachel Daniels test shoes he'd crafted for her all-world jumper, Lexington, a sixteen-hand blood bay chestnut who'd put more equestrian trophies in her case than any other Thoroughbred. Rachel laughed and gave John a look that said he knew more than she ever would. The sparkle in her crystal-blue eyes confided a deeper secret, one born from the scarcity of a violent past, as some men hit and enjoyed dispensing pain. She viewed John as her misfit counterpart, a man equally put upon in this life. His decency and strength and love for God astounded her, or so she said with a frequency that created an awkwardness between them. Her bright golden hair, pale skin, and slender form made her an exquisite beauty, but his heart had bound itself to another.

"Lex loves them!"

John hopped to the arena's dusty floor. "I'm glad."

Rachel giggled as she dismounted. She dropped the reins and her helmet and ran to him, throwing her arms around his neck and drawing herself close, locking herself in his masculine embrace.

"I've missed you so much!"

He pushed her back slightly. "Rachel, please."

"It's time, John. I want a family, and you're the one."

He grabbed her wrists and peeled her arms from his neck.

She fought against his strength but relented as he overpowered her and moved toward the rail. He leaned against it and stared vacantly at the ground as she asked, "Am I not good enough?"

His eyes rose to meet hers, and a gamut of emotions assailed him, each clamoring to be heard. Vickie had left to pursue her career at eighteen, leaving him to fend for himself in matters of the heart. For a while, he'd charmed gracious women into the bedroom, enjoying the delights of each one, both in private and in public. He genuinely liked the feminine spirit and sought to cultivate its expression and explore its many fineries. He was aware then that his behavior would not win him favor in Heaven, but his wounded soul deemed it a necessary wickedness.

Time had changed him for the better, at least in his estimation. He was today a sinner reformed by the resurrected victory of Jesus Christ. He would not lead on another woman nor sample her wares outside of marriage, no matter how magnetic her personality or admirable her beauty. His phone rang, interrupting his determined thoughts.

He held up a finger to ward off Rachel's impatience and greeted his cousin, Missy Weldon, who looked after the girls while he worked as a farrier. She was a rash woman by nature, but she rarely called.

"What's up?"

"Sorry to interrupt your work, but Katie's gone missing. I was busy with the new horse, Chief, who survived the bear attack. Ever since this one arrived, he's had a rough time, and I thought Katie might help."

Missy paused.

"I looked away for only a few minutes, and she'd disappeared. Help me find her, John. I won't forgive myself if something happens."

He sighed. "Did she take one of your trucks?"

"All my vehicles are here."

"Well, that's good. Doubt she made it far on foot."

Rachel moved nearer to John. "Ask Missy to visit this afternoon."

He removed the phone from his ear. "Why?"

A hint of fear sparkled in her eyes. "I need her to check a horse with a cough. It's probably nothing, but she should have a look at him."

There might be an explanation for the horse's distress, but it could also be something serious that neglect would worsen. "Rachel needs you out here later," he said with concern. "There's a sick horse in the barn."

Missy sighed heavily. "There always is, and I've got no time."

"Can Lee have a look?"

"He's out with the trailer all day, tending to dogs and cats."

John shook his head at Rachel. "Today's no good."

Rachel swallowed. "Tell her it could be serious. I need her."

His eyes met hers in disapproval. "What are you hiding?"

He looked about the area. "Should this farm be under quarantine?"

"I don't know, honestly. A horse arrived that wasn't properly vetted before getting on the plane, and now some others are sick."

"What do you mean, 'others'?" He hesitated. "At its former farm?"

Rachel gave him a sheepish look. "I swear, John, I didn't know."

His voice hardened. "She may have to isolate all her horses."

Missy yelled an obscenity in the background.

She stepped away and returned a minute later.

"Better?"

"Yes."

"So how do we deal with this situation?"

"Tell Rachel to keep everyone away from Mayfield."

"Does that mean you'll be out here soon?"

"I don't have a choice, but you'll have to take Abbie with you."

"Be there soon." He closed the phone. "I have to leave."

He turned and started for his truck.

Rachel called to him. "I'm not through with you, Mr. Breyer."

John wheeled and threw her a sly grin. "Never thought you were."

His Chevy Silverado meandered along a back road that rose and fell and curved as it neared Missy's farm. He expected to find Katie trekking along the side of the highway, desperate to find a place for herself. Though he craned his neck and squinted his eyes and turned on the defroster for a clear view through the windshield, she was nowhere to be found. After several conversations with Missy, he finally realized where Katie might hide, and it should have been the first place he looked.

Dear Lord, please give me the right words.

He drove to Bluecreek Stables, angered by his foolishness. It was the site of Red and Michelle's deaths, but also Katie's former home. The property represented both a refuge and a battleground, as the losses had seared themselves into her psyche, unrelenting and bitterly abrupt.

"Will we find her soon?" asked Abbie helplessly.

John scanned to the right and to the left as they neared the driveway.

He pointed at the far side of the pasture. "There she is!"

Abbie stiffened in the passenger seat. Her eyes widened.

Katie stood near Michelle's horses, sure to catch her death of cold.

John parked the truck in front of the house and wiped the glass on his driver's side window. He peered at Katie and wondered about her.

He spoke over his shoulder as he cracked open his door.

"Stay here." His voice held deep authority.

"Yes, sir."

Abbie had hardly said a word since her mother's death, and her response surprised him. He turned up the heater. "Everything all right?"

She shook her head.

"I'd like to get more words from you this morning." He gestured at the pasture. "Katie is out there with the horses. They're all safe."

"I don't like it when she runs. It makes me scared."

A heaviness centered over each of them as he thought of Vickie.

"I've felt the same in my life," he said.

"Will you help her feel better? I don't want her to be with Mom."

"Figured as much, but I don't think that will happen."

He paused.

"Your mother rode Wildfire before he was ready, and when he reared on her, she fell and broke her spine." He touched the back of Abbie's neck to illustrate. "Michelle held on for as long as she could."

Abbie peeked through John's foggy window.

"Katie's with him right now. He might hurt her like Mom."

Abbie's fears suddenly became clear. She couldn't rationalize why her older sister would dare work with the horse that killed their mother.

"Katie's not just with Wildfire. She's also with Hero, whom Michelle loved very much. She rode him in the mountains, and he always loved her more than anyone else." John prayed for the correct words. "Wildfire had warmed up to Michelle, and she thought they'd formed the same bond she shared with Hero, but something happened and he reared."

"Is he still dangerous?"

John shook his head. "I don't think so. Remember, many of these horses went through an ordeal. Some were neglected, left to starve or rot in a stall. In other cases, mean men beat them half to death."

He wouldn't mention the kill buyers to her, as they were dangerous men who murdered people as well as horses.

"Missy said she heals them, so why did Wildfire hurt Mom?"

"Good question. It shows how smart you are, especially about horses and people. Missy is a veterinarian who works with large animals. She takes care of their outside problems, like when they run through a fence or eat rotten food or pull a muscle in their leg, but she can't help them on the inside, where their feelings live. Michelle picked up where Missy left off and tried to help Wildfire get back to his old self."

He glanced at Katie, ensuring she was still present, and turned to Abbie. "I need to go out to the pasture and stand with your sister."

Abbie stiffened again. "How come?"

"To let her talk like you just did. It might help her get some things off her chest, things she might have held inside for a long time. I want her to know she can come here when I check on Michelle's horses."

"I'll bet Grandpa would like it if she did."

John smiled. "He sure would. Red loved you both very much."

He cracked open his door. "Would you like to come with me?"

Abbie shook her head.

"I'll be right back, so don't worry."

She shivered as air flooded the cab and rubbed her hands together.

He left the truck running and told her not to touch anything.

He then made a beeline for Katie, hopping the fence.

"I won't go back to Missy's, so you can save the speech."

"Well, glad to see you too, Katie. How are things?"

"You're not funny, although you think you are, which makes you kind of pathetic if you think about it." She rubbed Wildfire's back with a gloved hand and soothed him. "Go away and leave me alone."

He shook his head. "Can't do that. Missy would skin me alive."

"She's mean, and I won't stay there."

"My cousin is not mean, and I won't have you saying so."

"She won't let us come here and see our mother's horses."

Katie moved to Hero, and he whinnied at her touch. She rubbed his neck and said summer would be here soon and they would ride the trails up in the mountains. "Mom may be gone, but I'm still here."

"Tell you what. You can come with me every day when I check on them. They get fresh water and hay and a blanket when it freezes."

Katie gave him an angry look. "Why didn't you say so before now?"

"I thought it might be too difficult with Red's funeral being so recent and these horses being Michelle's. I didn't want to bring up bad memories and cause you more pain." He took a step toward her, but she backed away. John glanced at his truck and knew Abbie watched their body language closely, monitoring for harm.

He rubbed Wildfire's back. "Maybe we can work them together."

"Do you think Vickie will ever come home?"

"Wow, that question came out of nowhere."

"Will she?"

John took a heavy breath and exhaled. "I doubt it."

"Why not? We need her now that Mom and Grandpa are dead."

The starkness of Katie's words struck John, and he stifled a rush of emotion. She could be insistent like Michelle and just as unkind.

"Vickie built a career in the corridors of power in Washington, D.C., and we can't ask her to give it all up and return to Addison."

"She's worse than Missy, and I hate her. She wouldn't even come home when Mom broke her neck and couldn't get out of bed." Katie looked about, as if seeking support from the horses. "Who does that?"

"I know, honey, but those two never really got along, different as they were." He rubbed Hero's back but kept his distance from the changeable Wildfire. "I'll keep things going here as long as I can."

Katie went to the pasture fence and leaned against a rail.

John joined her. "Can we go back to Missy's now?"

She looked over her shoulder and waved at her sister.

Abbie gestured slightly and then ducked out of view.

"I'm worried," Katie said. "She's hardly spoken since Mom died."

"She talked to me in the truck."

"Yeah, but not much, right?"

"I suppose. Give her time to get used to things."

"We both feel like orphans."

"You two are orphans."

Katie gave him a shocked look. "Thanks."

"Missy and I will take care of you girls for a while longer."

"And then what? Will we go to a group home?"

A thought occurred to her, and her eyes welled with tears.

"Please don't separate us. We couldn't take it."

He pulled Katie close and gave her a hug. He drew back and clutched her shoulders. "Missy and Lee won't let that happen."

"Do you promise?"

John knew there were no guarantees, but he had to be optimistic.

"I sure do."

Katie's eyes rolled. "It's exactly what will happen, and you know it."

John let his gaze drift to the road. There was little left to say.

John slept fitfully and dreamed of Vickie for the first time in years. She dressed for her cable news show and fled her apartment and stepped through the streets toward her building, which extended high into the clouds above Manhattan, a strange place for her to be, since she lived and worked in the nation's capital. A dog barked loudly and incessantly, as if he'd just been attacked by a sound that was inaudible to humans but caused him pain. Vickie fell to the ground and writhed in agony. When she arose, she continued forward, but her walk had changed. She was larger and more muscular, and as she attacked her first victim, fangs descended into their neck and blood flowed from them.

John recoiled in the dream and drew away from her, as she was without mercy. He awakened with a start and resolved to inspire courage within the girls, for the Lord would keep them from evil.

On the drive to Missy's farm, he recalled Paul's teaching in Corinth, his admonition to live a life worthy of Christ and to set the example for others. John pulled the truck to the side of the road and removed a worn Bible from his center console, one that had renewed his faith.

He turned to 2 Corinthians 6 and read verses 3-11 aloud. "We live in such a way that no one will stumble because of us, and no one will find fault with our ministry. In everything we do, we show that we are true ministers of God. We patiently endure troubles and hardships and calamities of every kind. We have been beaten, been put in prison, faced angry mobs, worked to exhaustion, endured sleepless nights, and gone without food. We prove ourselves by our purity, our understanding, our patience, our kindness, by the Holy Spirit within us, and by our sincere love. We faithfully preach the truth. God's power is working in us. We use the weapons of righteousness in the right hand for attack and the left hand for defense. We serve God whether people honor us or despise us, whether they slander us or praise us. We are honest, but they call us impostors. We are ignored, even though we are well known. We live close to death, but we are still alive. We have been beaten, but we have not been killed. Our hearts ache, but we always have joy. We are poor, but we give spiritual riches to others. We own nothing, and yet we have everything."

John stopped reading as his thoughts fell again to Vickie.

Her departure had been cold and heartless, and she'd displayed a similar level of cruelty twenty years ago as she showed her victims in his latest dream. He wondered after the Lord's intention. Was she beyond hope? As his restless thoughts stilled, verse 11 made itself known to him on the page. "Oh, dear Corinthian friends! We have spoken honestly with you, and our hearts are open to you. There is no lack of love on our part, but you have withheld your love from us. I am asking you to respond as if you were my own children. Open your hearts to us!"

In 1988, they'd shared one blissful night at summer camp, where they worked as counselors, and then she departed for college. She later refused to return when her sister needed her the most. Michelle took the news hard and died soon afterward. Red Morrison had a habit of blaming Vickie for all of life's ills, but this was a special case and she should've come home, for Michelle, for Red, and for Katie and Abbie.

John parked his truck near the barn and stood peering over Missy's shoulder as she examined a horse. Abbie whimsically floated about her sister, who sat nearby on a feed bin, reading her leather-bound Bible.

He turned to Katie. "Have you learned anything useful?"

Her eyebrows arched in defiance. "Not really."

"What's the problem?" He sat beside her on a bale of hay.

"I don't get all the fuss over tents in the desert."

John smiled, recognizing his own difficulties with the subject.

"They were made from curtains of finely woven linen," he said.

"What was the point? I get lost just thinking about it."

He patted her knee. "Keep reading. It will make sense in the end."

Back at Missy's side, he asked to be of use. She said to soothe the horse as she examined him, as he liked to shift his weight and position.

"I'm bored," Katie said, closing her Bible.

She got up and left the barn.

The front door to the house slammed shut behind her.

Abbie stared after her sister for some time, and her face grew pale.

"Will she come back?"

"I'm not sure, honey, but I think she's a little frustrated."

John considered.

"Your mother used to sit out here with the horses and read her Bible. She had a curious mind and liked to know things." A portrait of Michelle formed in his mind, her kindness and her ability to persuade others. She moved too fast for anyone to keep up, but it was part of her charm, and he missed her. "She would have been so proud of you."

Tears coursed down Abbie's cheeks, and she shook as she wept.

Missy gave John a harsh glance of disapproval. "Nice job."

John wasn't sure how to proceed. He struggled to keep his thoughts from drifting to the disturbing vision the Lord had shown him.

What does it mean, Lord? Please help me understand.

Missy finished with the last horse and turned to him with her hands on her hips. "Are you going to comfort the poor girl or not?"

A portrait of children playing in the schoolyard formed in his mind. He smiled and thanked Jesus, then his eyes met his cousin's.

"You know what I miss?"

"Abbie needs you, John. You're all she has left of Red and Michelle."

"I miss hide and seek," he said. "We should play it."

"What's that?" Abbie wiped her eyes.

Missy looked astonished. "You've never played hide and seek?"

"No, ma'am."

"What about duck, duck, goose?"

Abbie wiped her eyes again and shrugged.

"Here's one you'll like." John approached Abbie like a monster, which caused her to shrink. His hands extended and his fingers curled and opened again, as if he intended to grab her. Then he rushed forward and tickled her sides. She fell over on the hay, giggling with joy.

Afterward, they played hide-and-seek while Missy typed at her desk, which lay next to the barn's only runway. Every so often, she called out to be quieter, as she couldn't concentrate on her notes while they playfully cavorted. Then she relented and joined their fun.

Abbie covered herself with a tarp and hid on a storage room table. The memory of her mother's body returned, making her cry again.

She retreated to the loft, which rested lazily above the barn.

John followed her, unwilling to let her withdraw from the world.

He told her fun stories of his youth and how happy Michelle and Vickie had been together, and Abbie seemed to feel better. They climbed down the ladder and resumed their lighthearted game, but then an ornery horse nipped at John and hurt his right shoulder.

He recoiled and heard a word from the Holy Spirit.

Vickie hurts like this horse, and she often hurts others.

A truck and trailer appeared, carrying a pregnant mare and a gelding with a ligament problem. Abbie grew excited and ran outside to see the arrivals. She bounced excitedly as the driver opened the trailer door.

John turned to Missy. "Do you have room for two more?"

"I do, but only for a while. If this keeps up, I'll be out of space."

The gleam in Abbie's eyes must be protected at all costs. She would soon give the horses names, and she would fall in love with them.

He spoke over his shoulder, his voice filled with worry.

"I shudder to think what it might mean for these new horses and the two in the front pasture, not to mention Katie and Abbie."

"It bothers me to think about it, but I'll tell you one thing, and I mean this with all my heart. I will put down a horse before I let it go to auction. Too many kill buyers still linger and lurk, waiting to strike."

"Can't say I blame you there, but I'm working on the rest."

Missy sank into her seat and gave up on her notes. "You'd better be careful, John. The girls can't lose you like they lost Michelle and Red."

He exhaled a heavy breath. "Impossible, and you know it."

"Remember what I said. Their mother and grandfather are gone."

"And I'm not their father."

"You're the closest they've got."

Three

Vickie pushed through the studio doors on the Twelfth Floor of the Planar building in downtown Washington, D.C., and did her best to avoid her producer's reproachful look. She was glad to have disentangled herself from him, as he was a grim and soundless automaton, consumed with his own desires, caring little for her morose thoughts or the way the late afternoon sun had dipped behind passing clouds, leaving a mist of snow in its wake. Without an explanation for her lateness, she marched to the news desk, the vastness and impersonal nature of her surroundings making her insignificant and completely alone, a feeling worsened by the swarm of crew members who surged about the set, stopping and starting amid a flurry of scattered praise and harsh curses, their lack of grace recalled her innocent and more defenseless years.

She glanced at her reflection in the monitor and saw a gifted imposter, unblinking and unnatural, one whose lies hurt people and caused their untimely deaths, most often when the victim was worthier than she would ever be in a thousand lifetimes. The image shifted to that of another, a girl with a gnarled, leprous face who flashed her eyes as death claimed her in the spring of life, the barren and indifferent journalist she trusted and loved nowhere to be found, caught up in the chase for money and status.

An assistant accidentally bumped Vickie's chair while bringing Mitch fresh coffee. He apologized, and she regained her composure by absorbing herself in pages of show notes. She tried to clear her mind of Helen, a haunting figure who tormented her hours and fragmented her dreams, reminding her this world was not for the living but for the dead, and the whir of the Reaper stopped only when Heaven's light broke above the snow-capped mountains and the flat-valleyed rivers and the evergreen grass. Vickie sighed and wished she remembered the Lord's Prayer.

As she had made her way through the streets and into work, a lunatic on the opposite corner held an apocalyptic sign and stood on a box, staring at her as she approached his unsteady position. His gaze mesmerized her, fueled as it was by fervent rage and glowering insanity and the revelations of doom beyond the horizon. Vickie knew not how she discerned the voices in the man's head but she understood them all the same, just as she sensed what the audience felt as she delivered the day's worst possible news, the aftermath giving her a sense of ghoulish pride, as evil lurked within her flesh, lying asleep in her blood, waiting for the precise signal to activate and wreak havoc on the masses.

Mitch nuzzled Nellie's chair forward.

"Too much?"

Nellie smiled at him. "It's perfect. Thanks, honey."

Vickie narrowed her eyes, squinting. "You never did that for me."

"She's nicer than you were."

Mitch leaned over Nellie's shoulder, and his palm lay flat beside her papers. His eyes scanned the room briefly, and then his lips whispered sweet pleasantries into her ear. The twenty-year-old former intern smiled and wrapped her left hand around his neck, pulling him nearer, nibbling on his devoted ear in playful jubilation, all while grinning at her former mentor and latest nemesis, who sat flatly unamused.

He stood and straightened his shirt.

"You'll pop a button, grandpa." Vickie placed her head into her hands with fluttering eyelids. "What will our young starlet think of you, then?" She sat up and straightened her papers, tapping them aggressively on the Formica. "When New York calls, this one is on the first plane."

"You should have married me while you had the chance," he said with a resolute grin. "Big changes are coming. You heard it here first."

Vickie shuffled her papers, trying for a sense of security, finding less and less with each passing second. Something was about to happen; she could feel it in her bones, and her gut instincts were usually accurate. She looked about, interpreting the tone and the mood of the crew.

Her chair rolled backward, and she considered a retreat.

The key light shifted to brighten the features of her face.

From the booth, Mitch's assistant director counted three, two, one.

Vickie slid her chair forward, turning off the spigot of emotions which threatened her survival. She made herself appear fair and strong and perfectly virtuous and then addressed the camera as a trusted friend.

"Hello, and thank you for returning to The Steps We Frame. Tonight, we have a special guest, a former protégé of mine, someone you may know from our weekend broadcasts, Miss Nellie Michaels."

The camera shifted to the rising star, whose lack of experience was no match for her ambition, nor for her beauty. "Hello, Vickie. So glad to see you tonight, and thanks for having me on your wonderful program."

Vickie addressed the camera with a smile, suppressing her combustible mood, repellent and broken as it was, worn from the tears of a teen who died on the highway in a stranger's arms. "As many know, our show tried to help a young woman, Helen Dunstan, mauled by her mother's Rottweiler, who literally ripped off Helen's face and almost severed her mother's arm when she tried to save her daughter from an even worse fate. When our show learned of this tragedy, we wanted to help, not for publicity, but for the sake of a family. For three years, we documented Helen's reconstructive surgeries, helped organize relief efforts, and asked our audience to contribute much needed funds." Vickie hesitated. "Asked is too weak a word. The proper word would be begged. We pleaded with our audience for aid and our audience stepped up, donating record amounts to a special account set up in the family's name." Sorrow overwhelmed Vickie, and her eyes fell to the news desk. Her mind distracted itself with a review of the notes, but the words blurred themselves on the page. She swiped tears from her eyes and tried to complete her report. "Two weeks ago, Helen Dunstan..."

Tears gushed forth. Vickie dropped her head below the desk.

She froze motionless as Nellie assumed command of the segment.

"While Vickie takes a moment, I'll continue in her stead. Two weeks ago, Helen Dunstan wrecked her vehicle at a high rate of speed and died at the scene. This news devastated our cast and crew, as you can see by Vickie's reaction. Our hearts go out to everyone involved, and if this show can help the Dunstan family in any capacity, we will find a way."

Vickie sat up and reluctantly faced the camera, hoping for kindness.

Nellie's heels clicked as she glanced at Vickie, and then she listened to her headset for instructions from the booth. "Alright, we are shifting to the next topic." Nellie turned toward her co-host. "It may surprise our audience to discover the next segment involves Vickie Morrison."

Vickie pointed at herself. "Me?"

Nellie nodded.

"New information surfaced last week regarding your background. There are pertinent details which might impact how the public feels about your credibility and, therefore, how they evaluate your dealings with Helen Dunstan and her family over the last few years."

Vickie leaned back in her chair and tapped her fingers on the desk.

It all made sense.

She glared at Mitch, who stood off set in the unshapely shadows, moving heavily like an old man who had reached the winter of life, his steps heavier than in his springtime.

She whispered into the microphone. "Mitch, this is an ambush."

He motioned for her to go with the flow.

Nellie's eyes rose to meet the center camera. "I'll just lay it out for the audience. A convicted felon named Price Brewer raped Valerie Morrison and nine months later Vickie was born. This means she was conceived by rape, and her last name is not Morrison, but Brewer."

Nellie held up a piece of paper for the viewers.

"This is her birth certificate, and the last name reads Brewer."

Her back pushed into the chair. She wore a look of pride.

"How does this revelation make you feel, Vickie?"

"I'm still Valerie Morrison's daughter, and Red Morrison raised me as his own, so I'm not sure what you're trying to prove here today."

"You lied to elevate your position at this network. Red Morrison, the visionary who created Planar, the man most responsible for your unearned entry into the cable news industry, and a dear friend of our executive vice president, Preston Spiro, was never your real father."

Nellie turned to the camera and offered a wink. "Yet you used Red's connections for your benefit and never spoke a word to anyone."

Vickie had climbed uphill for decades, the rocks and trails and trees providing no path to safety, and her heart threatened to explode inside her chest with every hungry word spoken by this haughty rose, but she once again stuffed her feelings deep inside and gave Nellie a blank look.

"My mother died young, and Red asked me to make her proud."

Nellie feigned shock. "Proud? From the grave? Who would you say is more or less delighted by your accomplishments, Valerie Morrison or Helen Dunstan?" Nellie euphorically snarled, aware her blow would land true. "From where I'm sitting, they are both equally dead."

"That's a cheap shot, Nellie, and you know it. More to the point, it's unfair to Helen's mother and father, not to mention my own."

"Do you have an answer?"

"Red enjoyed my success and, as I mentioned, he raised me as his daughter, no matter what you claim to the contrary."

Nellie studied Vickie, scheming her next tactical offensive. Vickie's fingers wrapped around the arms of the chair and slowly squeezed.

"Precisely one year ago in the coldest salvo of winter, you assisted the FBI in its failed attempt to apprehend Logan Meson."

"I would hardly characterize it as a failed attempt."

"Is he in prison somewhere?"

Vickie rolled her eyes. "Nellie, let's not play games."

"Oh, that's right. He couldn't be in prison since he's no longer alive." Nellie picked up a piece of paper, which displayed a headline. "POLICE CHASE TURNS DEADLY." She dropped the note. "This article refers to the perpetrator, Logan Meson, who led federal agents and local police on a thirty-mile chase in a stolen cruiser which ended when he ran the car through a locked gate, along a stretch of woods, and then careened from seventy feet into the waters of a quarry." Nellie caught her breath. "You had been in the cruiser with him, correct?"

"Yes, counselor. Where is this line of questioning going?"

Nellie looked at the camera. "If Logan Meson wanted to take you to the frigid depths of the quarry, then why did he let you out of the car?"

"He didn't let me out of anything. The FBI found a side entrance to the quarry and used it to sneak a white Tahoe to the edge of the road. It had been snowing for some time, and snow covered everything in sight, so the vehicle blended into the surroundings. When Logan and I entered the drive, heading for the cliff, an FBI Tahoe rammed his police cruiser, slamming it into a tree and freeing me from the backseat."

"This is when he let you go?"

Vickie took a heavy breath and exhaled. She had a sudden desire to hand Nellie the show and return to Addison where things once made sense. "It's not so simple, Nellie."

"I think it is."

Nellie's family was reportedly of means and noble in character, but this upstart behaved as if she came from the gin-soaked gutter. Thoughts swirled, jumbled, and twisted inside Vickie's head, scorching her heart. She was ashamed of her hostile apprentice, who goaded until there was little left but to tell the story and hope the audience empathized with her outrageous burden.

"Without hesitation, Logan shot both agents, killing one and injuring the other. Then something very odd happened which I cannot explain. Watching him commit murder jarred him and slowed his reflexes and willingness to kill again. At that point, I think he was ready to go quietly, but there was no one else around but me and the agent who was fighting for his life. The impact threw me when the cruiser slammed into the tree, and I was still in a kneeling position when he shot those men. I wanted to run away as fast as I could, but I knew he'd shoot me in the back for cowardice. Scratching that idea, I wondered if I could get over to the officer in the passenger seat of the Tahoe, maybe help him to the ground, where he could rest until help arrived. Logan seemed lethargic and out of the fuel necessary to do any more damage, but he pointed the gun at me and asked me to get back in the car. He wanted us to perish in the quarry together. I told him to kill me on the spot. I wasn't going anywhere." Vickie gazed beyond the cameras into the glittering white memory of a snowy day in the woods, flooded with the light of condemnation and the suspense of death. "Logan's face registered deep sadness, as if he expected me to join his cause." She shuddered at the notion. "As I told the agents and detectives, the man was clinically insane, and it's a wonder I survived the encounter."

"He drove off the cliff without you?"

Vickie crossed her arms. "You know he did."

"What I don't know is if he actually raped you, as you've claimed many times in interviews since the chase occurred." Nellie signaled, and a video montage of Vickie's comments played on the monitor.

Afterward, Nellie seemed confident in herself.

"What the audience most wants to know, and I think this gets to the root of the matter concerning your credibility, is this vital question: were you and Logan Meson involved in a romantic relationship? Keep in mind before you answer, this is the man who brutally murdered Lena Lambert, your former mentor at this network, and her husband, Richard, yet another father figure in your charmed but troubled life."

Chills ran through Vickie's body as Nellie leaned forward, readying herself for the kill. An indulgent smile formed across the attacker's face.

"How could you betray your friends so bitterly?"

As the venomous question lingered unanswered, the crew seemed to crowd themselves about Vickie with the bulging eyes of executioners.

She glared at her producer and gestured sharply. "I will not sit here and take abuse from this pompous intern. You've gone too far."

Nellie spoke soothingly to the camera. "Millions of viewers are out there, and they've placed their trust in you. They would like an answer."

Vickie wrinkled her brow while she calmly placed her headset and battery pack on the chair. She stopped and took a last look at the set.

Nellie would finish the show alone.

At the elevator, Vickie mumbled to herself as she pressed the button for the executive floor. Hosts must engage for the duration of a debate, the hotter and more contentious the better, and it mattered little whether her adversary was young or old, male or female, kind or unmerciful. Vickie had broken the cardinal rule of cable news: do nothing that might impact advertising revenue. Her throat throbbed as her mood shifted from hopefulness to loathing. She stepped inside the elevator with a frown and thrust her fists into her pockets. As the steel box rose to Preston Spiro's floor, she felt trapped and alone, but she reminded herself millions of women envied her, and perhaps she should act like it. She would wrangle with Preston, and he would battle with her, adamant as he was in his dislike for renegades.

Minutes later, she stood at the executive desk, tapping her foot.

She glanced at the receptionist, Monica, and gauged her reaction while she bit her lip. She wanted to ask for advice, but the phone rang endlessly, and Monica talked while bouncing a fancy pen on a notepad.

Helen had grown attached to Vickie as a new best friend and wanted to be her roommate. When the reply was a firm no, she dropped the subject without an argument. Vickie played her part and never revealed the request to Helen's parents, nor did she tell them about a subsequent conversation where she shared her suicidal fantasies with Helen as a means of atonement. The confession made Vickie feel dirty and abnormal, so she allowed the distance between them to lengthen until barely any ties remained. Helen ended her life two weeks later.

A security guard strolled past and tipped his hat. He paused and wheeled around, now facing her. "Ma'am, would you mind if I quoted a psalm?"

"I wouldn't mind," she said. "It might do me some good."

The guard straightened his shoulders and read aloud Psalm 43:1-4. "Declare me innocent, O God! Defend me against these ungodly people. Rescue me from these unjust liars. For you are God, my only safe haven. Why have you tossed me aside? Why must I wander around in grief, oppressed by my enemies? Send out your light and your truth; let them guide me. Let them lead me to your holy mountain, to the place where you live. There I will go to the altar of God, to God, the source of all my joy. I will praise you with my harp, O God, my God!"

Vickie met his contented smile and the kind hand he offered.

He said things would work out as God intended, and then he left her alone with her thoughts. When he rounded the corner and vanished from sight, her eyes rose to the ceiling, and she wondered why the Lord would use this ordinary man to communicate a vague message.

He had better things to do than encourage her villainy.

Suicide's allure had captured Helen in a pool of inexorable light, and there were nights when Vickie had narrowly escaped the siren call of the grave while alone in her apartment. For a time she helped Helen escape the cell that imprisoned her, but the thickets and the rocks and the hills encumbered Vickie's path, and she worked too hard until her last ally abandoned her. If only she could have offered advice to her friend one last time, but Helen would not have accepted it, as her desire for recompense was too great and the call of death too powerful.

Preston rang the desk, asking why Monica buzzed his phone. "Miss Morrison needs to see you, Mr. Spiro. She says the matter is urgent and time sensitive." Monica listened to him speak while staring at Vickie, and then she rolled her eyes as Vickie had done to Nellie. "Yes, sir. Will do."

She hung up the phone and pointed to her left.

"Mr. Spiro will be with you in a few minutes."

Vickie slumped onto a leather-bound chair and waited, her endurance reaching its limit. What transpired was new territory for a woman who controlled others for her own ends, and waiting to learn if she still had a job was surreal. She had seen the assault coming but did little to stop it, which made the damage to her reputation even worse.

The grief Vickie suppressed had weakened her aggression.

Nellie should have demurred, but she chose otherwise, and now the ungrateful brat had formally humiliated Vickie live and in color on national television, blaming her for everyone's death, including Logan's.

Monica interrupted her thoughts. "Mr. Spiro is free now."

Preston opened his door and invited Vickie inside his office.

"Please, have a seat on the couch." He made them each a whiskey and soda at his bar and turned to her with a smile and a gleam in his eye.

"Nothing for me, Preston."

He held the drink out for her, shaking it, and the ice in the glass clinked, making a strange and horrible sound. "You know, Vickie, I didn't always view you as the logical choice to replace Lena, but I admired your work ethic and your long-term ambition from the start."

Her eyes arched. "Meaning I should take the drink?"

He handed it to her and took a seat at the far end of the couch.

"You'll burn yourself out if you continue at your current pace."

Preston paused.

"You've done so much in this business and at this show, there's nothing left to prove. Sturgis asked me to give you this message."

She looked about, hoping Sturgis was in New York and not watching and listening from the next room. "He's unhappy with me?"

"I wouldn't say so, but he's not completely happy either."

Vickie set her drink on the end table and paced the floor.

"I feel guilty about Helen's death. I thought she was under control, would do what I say, when I say it, and she was a boon for ratings, but she slipped from my grasp, and I lost her." Vickie rushed her speech, and with two fingers she tapped the mantle over the fireplace, a move she had observed Paul Newman do in movies as a child. It seemed masculine and intentional, as if Paul knew what to do in any stressful situation.

"You must let the girl go, Vickie. We have a show to run." Preston poured himself another drink. "You haven't been yourself lately."

Vickie's throat tightened. She ran a hand through her hair.

She mouthed the words "let the girl go" while Preston turned his back, finally realizing the truth. She used a carefully controlled tone, hoping to disguise her mounting anger. "I cannot believe you'd stoop so low."

"Did something happen?" His question suggested surprise, but hidden in his words was a sinister unkindness that paled her cheeks.

She went to the end table and grabbed her drink, downing the contents. She threw the glass against a marble wall, shattering it, and glared at him. "I see what's happening here. Sturgis is pushing me out."

Preston's hands clasped. He seemed reserved but projected a raw and pointed wrath. "Not today, my dear, but if you don't pull yourself together, you'll be looking for a job." He sat at the end of the couch, and his voice dropped an octave. "Take more time for yourself, a month, maybe two. Then come back ready to earn your inflated salary."

Vickie steeled herself. "Lena and I built this show from the ground up. You cannot take it from me, Preston. It's all I have in the world."

He waved at her dismissively. "I can handle your melodrama, but the public is fickle, and they will soon grow tired of your antics. Take a few weeks and think about who you really want to be when you grow up."

She hated his mocking grin. "Only a few weeks?"

He nodded.

"Once you've rested and cleared the cobwebs out of that pretty head of yours, you'll be good as new. We can then shuffle Nellie into her own time slot, and The Steps We Frame will once again be your show."

He stood, and a stony expression settled on his face. "Fair enough?"

After she left his office, Vickie broke down in the elevator's rear corner, knowing full well she was fired. She gave others a fake smile and avoided eye contact as she recalled the adversities endured, the danger confronted, the homesickness surmounted along her path to becoming a bright and charming star. She pushed further into the corner as the steel box descended, weeping over Helen, her imploding career, and the profound loneliness that never faded, even when she called on the name of God in the late hours of the night, a time when vain regrets made themselves known, their nocturnal natures more atrocious than her infrequent and insincere prayers or the entities asleep in her blood.

Silvery metal doors opened at the parking deck level.

The Christian security guard smiled at her with warmth.

He was to be her escort in this humiliation. Thankful her employee badge unlocked the door to the ghostly parking garage, she marched to her 2007 Ford Expedition with its Carbon Clearcoat Metallic paint and its factory sound system and its four-wheel-drive capabilities. She took a lingering look at the Planar building and the smiling guard, who told her to read each of the psalms, as they were the gateway to the Bible.

On the drive home, she mulled over the guard's comment and asked the air what he might have meant. She waited, but the air remained still and withheld a reply. A lengthy span had elapsed since voices answered her queries, but she hoped for something from them, as the spirit of insomnia often made its way into her bedroom, it being so very different from the utopian world of the Caribbean, no matter what Raul might believe.

Inside her apartment, she tossed her keys onto a magazine that rested on the coffee table and checked her voicemail. The day's betrayal rocked her senses, and she needed an affable voice, even if it was from last month. There were three saved messages from her father and an unheard message from John. "Hello and long time, no talk. Red passed on Tuesday, and you missed his funeral yesterday. I have no idea what went on earlier, but he desperately wished to see you before he died."

The message ended, and she moved to the next in line, rubbing the back of her neck as she listened to John's voice. "Michelle's two girls are at my cousin's foster farm. Keep them in your thoughts and prayers."

Vickie played the last message. It was always the most difficult.

"This is Katie Morrison, Michelle's oldest daughter. We met when she brought me to Washington for a fourth-grade field trip. Do you recall meeting a smart-aleck kid who gave you a hard time for three days?" Sounds emanated from the background as Katie put down the phone and whispered to someone, and then, just as suddenly, she returned to the one-sided conversation. "You probably don't, but I hope you remember your sister, who is or who was my mother. Anyway, we need you to come back here. Missy can be mean but sometimes she is nice, and she lets us do neat things with the horses, and we throw the ball for her dogs, but we had to leave our rooms and our own horses behind. Can you come back home and say you'll be our mom?"

Vickie screamed, and in her mind she was submerged in a sunny Caribbean bay, where language was free and the reef fish cared little for fear, anger, and sadness, the latter proving the most debilitating of late and the hardest to understand. The upstairs neighbor banged on her floor, rattling the chandelier over the dining room table while Vickie observed her gaunt appearance in the mirror, realizing she seemed older than thirty-eight. She rushed into the bathroom and knelt in front of the toilet and threw up for a couple of minutes, and then she got a case of the dry heaves, as if she'd eaten contaminated restaurant food.

The heaving finally subsided and she fell against the tub; the cool porcelain surface felt good to her hand as she rubbed it with care.

Vickie went to the kitchen and hugged herself as she played the last message several times, her numbness deepening with each repetition.

There was something wrong with her, a defiance, a refusal to be caged by anyone or anything, even Katie, who merely craved love and solace. The depravity within caused Vickie's failure with Helen, and she could never make it up to Julie and Ron, or anyone else from the grief-stricken Dunstan family, some of whom now threatened civil action.

She looked at a calendar on the wall to her right, noting the date.

Chelsea's death day was on Saturday, a moment Vickie dreaded each year, as it arrived on the heels of Valentine's Day and she rarely had a man in her life to reassure her she was a good person despite one ruinous mistake. God had already condemned her lust and her greed, and so would church groups across the nation once they learned her secret. Henry David Thoreau said the true cost of anything was the amount of life one sacrificed toward its attainment, and at eighteen, Vickie took a sensual risk and afterward gave herself over to ambition at her daughter's expense, locking the sorrow inside, never to be examined by the mind nor felt by the heart. But for the last few years and, most especially, the last week, portraits of cradles and laughter and flesh fallen cold breached her defenses. Her pleading eyes lifted to the ceiling.

Dear Lord, why not take me instead?

Jesus kept silent, so her fist beat against the counter until the pain made her stop, and then she rubbed her fingers on the soft surface, sliding them to the right and then to the left, considering what remained of her dwindling options. The security guard's kindness prompted her to open a dusty Bible, one given to her by Michelle in the waning months of high school. She flipped to Psalm 43 and read the last verse aloud. "Why am I discouraged? Why is my heart so sad? I will put my hope in God! I will praise him again, my savior and my God!"

Vickie went into her bedroom and opened a nightstand drawer.

She retrieved a pistol that Red had given her for protection and sat on the bed, eyeing the weapon, knowing with certainty she deserved to join Helen and Chelsea in their lonely abyss. Perhaps she might actually rest in peace for once. Vickie glanced about the room, loaded pistol in hand, and considered a trip to a nearby cemetery, as a cable news host's indelicate corpse might prove a Valentine's Day gift to the world.

Vickie listened for advice from the room as her eyes moistened.

None was proffered, so she took it upon herself to decide.

Some in her circle had considered Lena Lambert a highly connected dragon with fiery words and vicious eyes that burned those in her line of sight, but she was one of the few in D.C. who had been nice to her apprentice, and Vickie owed Lena more than a suicide, if not by keeping her news program afloat, then in some other yet unknown capacity.

Vickie unloaded the pistol and laid it beside her on the comforter.

Not long after Red's death, she had received a mysterious packet from his attorney that provided a map with directions and keys to the house in Addison. The least she could do was appear in town, remove any legal obstacles, and get the estate ready for sale. Vickie could then return to Washington, D.C., armed for battle with Red's money, wholly unbeholden to weasels like Preston Spiro and Sturgis Faulkner. Many ideas for documentaries still occupied her mind, and an ample infusion of cash would fund their development over the next two decades.

Vickie scanned the sparsely decorated room, looking for any tokens she must remember or keep near her side, finding instead artless walls and bland shelves, a synthetic plant near the window that she rarely noticed. Vickie had no pets, no friends, and no man. Her reality was like this Church Street apartment, void and without form. Her fingers tapped the pistol. She would forge a genuine life for herself once she returned to the D.C. political circuit, but for now she would pack her clothes, grab her keys, and abandon her newly orphaned residence without a goodbye. It was exactly what her mother would have done.

Four

Psalm 44:6

I do not trust in my bow;
I do not count on my sword to save me.

John's white Silverado carried him and his father through miles of hills that bordered Route 15. As the truck neared Bluecreek Stables and its sprawling front pasture, the tires swerved onto gravel, forcing John to correct. Each glance at Garrett's pallid form sparked greater concern for his condition. His father demanded they share a cross-country golf outing before the inevitable embrace of the Reaper, and he spoke so loudly and trembled so violently that his lungs hacked up phlegm that might return him to the hospital. Recent cancer treatments had made the trip impossible, at least for the time being. John disengaged from conversation on the topic, aware his father would coerce him with notions of adventure, unable to accept his son as a farrier and horse trainer with clients spread across three counties.

"Chris won a major, but I miss the ball entirely."

Garrett threw his youngest son an annoyed glance. "So?"

"It's too late, Dad. We're past worrying about golf."

"Who's worried?" A pause. "I just want us to be together."

"It might have happened last year; I'll give you that much."

His father would spoil their last months, enticing John to play a game he hated, one Garrett had so genuinely enjoyed with his favorite, the brother who had taken everything from John since childhood, including his wife.

"We took a trip after he retired." Garrett allowed the portrait of a proud father and receptive son to paint itself. "Do you think I liked playing with a guy who hit perfect shots?" The question lingered between them in the cab. "The answer is yes, because he was my son."

John stared at the roadway with accusing eyes and spoke firmly. "You chose him over me and made sure I knew it every day, so you can save your Norman Rockwell speech about family bonds."

Garrett gazed quietly through the passenger window. He returned to John. "Norman Rockwell painted Americana."

"I know that, Dad."

"I'm just saying. He didn't make speeches. He only painted."

A tall man in a faded army jacket emerged from the woods and walked across the highway. He stopped and addressed the truck with a menacing presence. From three hundred yards away, John sensed a yearning for warfare and a need for love. He instinctively understood the man, although he didn't know why, but there was a connection between them, body and soul, each dismissed as a blend of beast and vagrant. For John, it was caring for horses rather than shuffling papers at his father's company. For the graying nomad who blocked his path, it must have been the thrill of seeking blood and death, either in-country, as people referred to the theater of war, or in some other violent domain.

John's boot pressed the brake, and the truck slowed. His muscular arm restrained his father, who sat stiff and guarded.

The horizon blended into the familiar stretch of highway as Route 15 enveloped the truck like a scowling, open-mouthed inquisitor, shoving the stranger front and center. There he posed and broiled and led a charge into the underworld or out from it, with ghouls and goblins at his side, alert and aggressive, fists shaking to beat back resistance.

"I recognize him." Garrett's voice hinted at contempt.

"Who is he?"

"The rapist, Price Brewer."

"How do you know?"

"I never forget a man I hate."

Garrett rolled up his sleeves as if preparing for a fight.

"Dad, keep quiet, and this guy will leave."

"No, Son. There are days when a man needs a beating."

Price peered into the windshield. His form was immovable.

Garrett cracked open his door and yelled for Price to get out of the way or else. As the situation unfolded before him, all John could see was his father and Chris at Pebble Beach, enjoying their final round.

His eyes fell on the steering wheel in shame.

He felt on display like an animal at the zoo. Carlie's affair with Chris, her abandonment of the marriage, and their subsequent deaths from a freak accident two years ago had shattered John's life and rendered his soul joyless. For a time, he hid himself from anything that required intimacy, opting instead for the numbness of booze and sex.

Red had come to his rescue. He would save the horse that paralyzed his daughter, along with others bound for Texas kill pens and Mexican slaughterhouses. Red recruited John for his horse sense and his network of influence, but most importantly for his inclination toward risking harm to himself, as retrieving stolen horses could often prove fatal. John fell in love unexpectedly with the idea, having been viewed as an orphan most of his life, a trait he shared both with the wounded horses and with the fractured shell of a man who now stood before him.

Garrett flung open the door and approached. John followed, half in anticipation, half in dread.

Price slammed his fist on the truck's hood, rattling the sheet metal, and then he stepped back two paces, readying himself for battle.

"Don't try that one, mister." Garrett drew his pistol and racked the slide, then aimed. "Now get out of here before I start firing downrange." He tipped the muzzle up slightly. "Just so you know, this is a 1911, and I've got seven rounds." A fierce look of determination broke over Garrett's face as the muzzle dropped again; any mistake would be fatal.

"You'll go to prison. Trust me, it wouldn't go well for you there."

The words seemed to suit Garrett. "This is where you've got me all wrong, mister. I won't be going to prison. My cancer will see to it."

"Sick or healthy," Price said. "It's all the same to them."

Garrett grinned. "Take a step forward, and we'll find out together."

John stood in front of his father, who lowered his weapon but held onto his fury. Garrett's behavior astonished him, but he knew it shouldn't, as the old man had long mired himself in bitterness.

His eyes rose to the tall man, and he threw a fragment of a smile at him, hoping to receive the same. Price stood stoically in place.

Garrett looked upward and recited Psalm 44:1-8 from memory. "O God, we have heard it with our own ears, our ancestors have told us of all you did in their day, in days long ago: You drove out the pagan nations by your power and gave all the land to our ancestors. You crushed their enemies and set our ancestors free. They did not conquer the land with their swords; it was not their own strong arm that gave them victory. It was your right hand and strong arm and the blinding light from your face that helped them, for you loved them. You are my King and my God. You command victories for Israel. Only by your power can we push back our enemies; only in your name can we trample our foes. I do not trust in my bow; I do not count on my sword to save me. You are the one who gives us victory over our enemies; you disgrace those who hate us. O God, we give glory to you all day long and constantly praise your name." Garrett's countenance grew triumphant.

Price sized up his adversary as he retrieved a handkerchief from his jacket and wiped his nose. He returned the handkerchief with care, displaying an unexpected warmth, both in tone and gesture.

"Are you a praying man?"

"I've prayed the psalms all my life, not that my son would care."

John let the comment pass. The two men must reach terms.

Price spoke tentatively, as if testing the other man's response. "I found Jesus in prison, where the Catholics taught me to pray the psalms. It's where I learned to wait for Jesus. He will manifest Himself in grace to those who cry after Him as David did so many times."

Garrett nodded. "I've known men who laid down their burden only to pick it up again, which is poor business and the wrong way to go about it."

"Which is the right way?"

Garrett's eyes widened at the question's sincerity. "To overcome sorrow, we must pour it out to God with a pure and genuine heart."

Price looked upon Garrett's feebleness and smiled. "On this point, we agree, and it is my earnest hope you do the same before He calls you to your place of rest, for His peace awaits us all."

John's stomach clenched, and it was impossible to calm his pulse.

"Come on, Dad." He eased Garrett toward the pickup and spoke over his shoulder as they neared the door. "It's time we part company."

"You'll get no argument from me," said Price gravely.

John pushed his father into the seat. He started the engine and waved congenially as the truck pulled around the tall man. Soon Price Brewer's image in the rear-view mirror washed into the background of frosty trees and rolling highways and mountainous uncertainties.

Thank you, Jesus, for keeping us alive on this rural stretch.

Winter blustered as the truck progressed toward Bluecreek Stables. After he checked on the horses, he would drop off Garrett and hear no more talk of golf excursions nor witness any more threats, having experienced them all too often as a boy, his mother's mental illness causing chaos and police interventions and frequent stays at the asylum.

Vickie arrived at the ice-covered gate, stunned by the magnificence of her former home. After she double-checked the address, she entered the four-digit code, and the gate creaked open with a moan of displeasure.

Two horses milled about in the front pasture as they munched on clumps of hay and eyed her through a three-rail fence. There was a reddish one and a spotted one, which she faintly remembered as an Appaloosa, trivia that Michelle had taught her in high school.

She fought the urge to flee as her Expedition continued along the driveway. After what seemed an eternity, she parked in front of the house and caught her breath. The place differed from what she recalled; the gracefulness and sophistication of the property both mesmerized and startled her, making her feel as if she were on the first day of school. She had spent high school summers at the television station and on field assignments, forever pursuing the dust and haze of Red's approval while Michelle whispered to the horses in the barn and in the pastures, keeping them comfortable in the knowledge they were loved. As she looked about the house and land that she once called home but that now seemed foreign, Vickie wondered why the two horses stood isolated. Sadness overwhelmed her, and she gripped the wheel for support.

Michelle should not have died so young and so forsaken.

With Chelsea's memorial imminent, Vickie was incapable of being in charge of the estate or making important decisions about anything. She held onto the wheel for dear life, and her eyes glanced about, noting through the driver's window the serenity of the horses. They lazily chewed on what must be good hay, as they seemed content with its flavor. She sighed heavily, understanding the truth of her situation.

Addison, North Carolina was known far and wide for its criticism of anyone who strayed from the norm, the community having organized itself around God and horses and the mountains in no particular order. The town's scrutiny would be unbearable once folks discovered how she had gone about furthering her career. One thing was for sure, Vickie dodged a bullet in getting fired by Preston, as her withdrawal from the limelight lessened the chance her story would reach local ears. The national audience would move to someone new, a gossip artist named Nellie Michaels, whom Vickie hated with the heat of a thousand suns and wished to see murdered by a horde of howling pirates.

She rested her forehead against the steering wheel and suppressed the churn in her stomach, and then she rolled down her side window.

John Breyer approached from the barn and cast a charming grin. "Happy Valentine's Day. I guess I can say it, although it's been a long time since we were together." His eyes radiated contentment.

A shock ran through her body, forcing a shaky hand to her forehead. "What's all this about?"

"Before he died, Red planned a special surprise."

Her eyes narrowed. "For whom?"

"For you, apparently." John smiled again. "It wasn't for me. That much I know for sure."

Her body stiffened, and her breathing stilled. "Do you live here?"

John shook his head and gestured at the front pasture to their left. "Red recovered Michelle's two horses from a nearby farm."

They both grew silent, as they understood the ramifications of taking on Michelle's horses, one of them having reared and paralyzed her. Vickie's glance lingered as she observed the sorrel and the Appaloosa. Somehow, the equestrian vernacular had come back to her.

"The operators ran into hard times and couldn't care for them, but Red wanted to restore them to health for you and the girls. I helped him out as needed." He hesitated. "There are still good people here, Vickie, and these are excellent horses. All they need is the right owner."

"Front door open?"

"It auto-locks when you leave. I can open it for you."

She retrieved a set of keys from the attorney's packet and jingled them, half hoping he would snatch them from her and take charge. "Let's see if these work."

He took a step back from her car door as she opened it.

Vickie dropped her bags inside and, with John's help in locating the proper supplies, she made coffee. They sat on the porch and talked about old times: the depressing difficulties, the relationships that tainted their virtue with age, the career ordeals that were suffered and withstood, and the devastating losses of those few they had truly loved.

Garrett glared from John's truck as he'd done in years past, and she dropped the lawyer's letter onto her lap and twisted her watch. Why must he be so agonizingly furious with her, as if her mother's taunts and jeers were carried over to him and he delighted in their continuation?

She gazed across the pasture in front of the house, the two-lane highway, and the secondary pasture on the other side to the far bordering woods. It was gorgeous land, and she now owned every acre.

"Are you surprised Red left it all to you?"

Her eyes welled, but she resolved to keep her composure. She snatched the letter and neatly folded it and stuffed it inside the crumpled envelope. "Not really. There's no one else around."

He smiled. "You haven't been around for twenty years."

"You know what I meant."

Another envelope revealed a handwritten note. Red said his heart would soon fail, which was why he'd contacted her by phone. He begged her to raise the girls for his beloved daughter, Michelle. It was the least she could do after abandoning her sister in her most desperate hour.

Vickie ripped the note to pieces and wiped tears from her cheeks.

John calmly rubbed her arm. "You'll get through this."

She drew away from him and sneered. "Everyone expects me to raise Michelle's children, but I don't know how to be a mother, and they're not mine to raise." She stood and glanced at Garrett in the truck.

John rose with her and pointed at the stables. "You should see what your father did with the place."

"Why?"

"It's much nicer than you remember."

"Another time, maybe. I'm exhausted."

He grabbed her shoulders and turned her body, unwilling to accept her refusal. "Now is the perfect moment. You won't be sorry."

They toured the renovated runways, and an eon passed before her eyes. She hardly recognized the tack room and the hay barn, much less the shiny round pen and the frozen pond on the other side. She felt unsafe on this property and in her hometown, as if she belonged to everyone and no one, forever dressed with nowhere to go and not a soul to see. Vickie peered into a stall and realized she lacked direction, a sense of meaning. Could she find such a thing outside of Washington?

She caught herself glancing uneasily over her shoulder at John. "Did you send Michelle's horses to the pasture?" she asked.

He placed a feed bucket on a top shelf. "Those two were at the other farm, so they can share a field with no problems, but once more arrive, integrate them into the herd with care." He locked a feed bin, snapping shut the latch with force. "Otherwise, someone might get hurt."

His eyes sparkled as they met hers, and a pall fell over her. "Someone always does when I'm around."

She moved toward the front porch.

John caught up and stopped her progress. "Hey."

Vickie turned. "What is it now, John?"

"Leave me alone."

"Katie and Abbie don't know how to be your daughters, either."

"Fair enough." She looked up at the blue sky and took a breath.

Her eyes fell to the secondary pasture on the other side of the road, where she caught a flash at the far line of woods, freezing her in place. She strained her eyes but found only a motionless landscape.

"Does Red still have a rifle?" she asked cautiously.

"There's one in the gun cabinet. Just so you know, it's loaded."

They stepped onto the porch, and she sat in an Adirondack chair, feeling its form against her lower back. She remembered Bluecreek's nooks and crannies, the wondrous smells of dandelion and rain and earth in summer, the eerie creaks that made themselves heard late at night or at dawn or at random intervals throughout the day, and the waterfall that everyone in Addison knew about but few ever visited, as Red had deemed it off limits to all but the Morrison family.

John's jaw tensed, betraying a deep and abiding resentment.

She placed her hand on his arm. "I've missed you."

He leaned in and they kissed for the first time in twenty years.

Vickie realized the preciousness of her chances, which she had tossed thoughtlessly to the wind, assuming more would present themselves at every turn. His hand on the back of her hair and his lips intertwined with hers and the smell of his male sweat lessened the hurts of her past, if only for the briefest of moments. She wanted madly to fall into his embrace and to weep for hours, but she needed a quiet spot to think.

Garrett exited the truck and pounded his fist on the hood. "Can we leave now, or do you two lovebirds plan to make out all morning?"

She glanced about, seeking to understand. "What have I done wrong this time, Garrett?"

He looked away. "Nothing."

"What then?" Vickie waved a hand as she spoke.

John stood. "Dad, you are exerting yourself. Get back in the truck."

"Don't tell me what to do. You're not my caretaker."

She turned to him. "Is there anything I should know?"

Garrett threw her a look. "I've never liked the Brewer clan. They're always up to no good." His eyes scanned the house's dimensions. He stuck out his chin, and his countenance grew harsh. "I don't care how much money you throw at them or how thick they wear their makeup."

Vickie brought a quavering hand to her forehead. "I am Red Morrison's daughter. I am not a Brewer!"

Garrett gestured with disgust. "You can stop with the pretense of glamor and fame because the good folks of Addison know all about you. To us and now the world, you'll always be a Brewer, and it would be just like one of their clan to hop into bed with a no-good murderer like Logan Meson and then claim rape when you get caught."

He recovered his breath. "Trust me, I'm old and I'm a fool, but I'm not an old fool."

Garrett climbed into the truck, slammed the door, and glared at them.

He had put the finishing touch on an already trying day.

She stood and her eyes met John's. "Can we do this another time?"

"Sorry for my father," he said, grinning. "He's a handful."

"I remember all too well." She turned, readying herself for a retreat.

John drew near and his strong, calloused hands dropped to the small of her back and pulled their bodies together. Her form molded against his.

"Let's try this again, shall we?"

His touch felt so good, and it had been so long.

"It's nice to see you, John." Her thoughts scrambled themselves.

He bent down slightly. "So Michelle's horses in your field, good idea or bad?" His eyes penetrated deeply within her, to the marrow of her bones where some said the soul lived. "You need them as much as they need you." He rubbed his fingers through her long black hair.

"Leave them here until I can decide what to do with the place." Vickie paused. "It's the least I can do after being gone for twenty years."

"What about the girls?"

She smiled coyly and slipped from his arms.

The doorknob clicked behind her as she entered the house.

FIVE

Psalm 45:3

Put on your sword, O mighty warrior!
You are so glorious, so majestic!

Vickie switched off the lamp and succumbed to sadness in Red's bedroom. The height and hardness of his bed caused her discomfort and worsened her grief. She stared at the ceiling, unable to sleep, and counted starlike bits that skipped above her eyes. As she drifted toward sleep, she said a prayer, hopeful for relief. Her mind surrendered to the glide, and as the mist around her cleared, she found herself on a rocky hill in Israel, walking with Jesus.

He said to focus on Him continually, so she might overcome the persecutions and temptations of the fallen world, made so by Adam and Eve, whom the Most High created in His likeness to spread Eden's abundance over the earth. But they ate of the fruit, wishing themselves cast from the garden on the mountain, reborn to wander until Jesus returned.

Over the course of history, they would know some good and much evil. It was the latter that would captivate the hearts of men and women, as good would always seem dull. The adversary would remind them of his fascinations, until he forgot his many promises of glorious youth and the universal electric force that bound them as one.

"Lord, I am fearful of my nature, what smoldering madness lies within my flesh, ready to awaken and devour those around me."

"My daughter, read Romans 12:2 and other Scriptures. They provide spiritual food for those in crisis. I am your only haven."

"Will you forsake me as others have done?"

"I have been with you all of your life, and I have suffered with you."

"Will you, Lord?"

"I will always be with you, but you must reach out to me every day."

She awakened with a start and sat up in bed, soaked in sweat.

In Red's office, she found several Bibles, each coated in dust. She turned to the New Testament and located Romans 12:2. "Don't copy the behavior and customs of this world, but let God transform you into a new person by changing the way you think. Then you will learn to know God's will for you, which is good and pleasing and perfect."

Vickie went to the bathroom and dipped a towel in water, then returned to the office and wiped the covers of the leather Bibles. Her eyes fell on Red's chair, the location of his death, and she pondered the fate of his soul. She hoped his latest declaration of faith was sincere, as his sins over the decades had sharpened her into a dreadful weapon.

She left the first Bible open to Romans 12:2, and flipped to Psalm 45 in the next, reading aloud verses 9-11. "Kings' daughters are among your noble women. At your right side stands the queen, wearing jewelry of finest gold from Ophir! Listen to me, O royal daughter; take to heart what I say. Forget your people and your family far away. For your royal husband delights in your beauty; honor him, for he is your lord."

Vickie showered and sat on the porch in reflection. Had the Lord selected John Breyer as her royal husband? Could she become a new creation and honor him as her lord? She would like to think it possible.

Mitch called, interrupting her troublesome thoughts.

She sipped coffee while listening. A squirrel ran along the railing in front of her, then stopped briefly at the steps. It looked back before bounding to the grass, nose to the ground, sniffing for a morsel. Vickie took a wary breath and blinked as she watched the furry creature, bracing for it to repeat its steps and leap crazily at her.

"Are you paying attention?"

"Believe it or not, Mitch, it hurts when you scream into my ear."

She lowered the phone and looked for the squirrel, which now hid from view. She raised the phone again. "Guess I'm back."

"I said Nellie is doing well. She scores across all demographics."

Vickie held her stomach as if pained. "Preston said I should take a few weeks, but I'm doing better than expected here. I've changed my travel plans and I'll be back next Wednesday to co-host with Nellie." There was no way she could get her affairs in order and be at Planar next week, but she would feel Mitch out and confirm her suspicions. "If you want a fireworks display, it's exactly what I'll give you."

"Yeah, well, about that..."

Her lips trembled. She slid to her knees on the concrete and sank her face into the seat cushion. It calmed her breathing, and she returned with a vengeance. "I can't believe it, Mitch! How could you?"

"You'll receive an exit package in the mail. You can sign your approval at the online portal. There are instructions, so don't worry."

Although they'd once been close, Mitch's heart had become a desolate land.

"I'm not supposed to worry?"

"It's the way we do things nowadays, Vickie, so take it up with HR."

"You didn't answer my question, so I'll ask you again. How could you do this to me?" She leaped to her feet and paced the length of the porch, seeing no sign of the squirrel. "We interned together, Mitch!"

His voice wavered. "Something better will come along. You'll see."

"Great, so you refuse to respond! I have a long memory, and I will never forget your nasty betrayal." She tugged at her hair with her free hand and fought against a barrage of suicidal thoughts, more powerful than her night on the balcony in the Caribbean, when the knife and the grave had beckoned her into the great unknown.

"Our show is a relic, Vickie, and we're dinosaurs fighting extinction. These kids are true believers who think they're saving the world, but they can't use a can opener without a struggle and a crowd to film their achievement. It's little wonder. Our network creates an existential crisis every other day, which perfectly aligns with their notions of grandeur."

He paused.

"When you and I came of age, all we wanted to know was where to find the best party or who made the most money. But these kids are all about ideology, which scares me quite frankly, but it's a reality we can no longer avoid. Both Preston and Sturgis believe it's time to let a fresh young voice take the reins. What's the worst that can happen?"

"The show will tank. That's what!"

Mitch sighed. "If you feel so strongly about it, I'll find you a spot as an assistant producer on some hip new program. But I must warn you, twentysomethings are everywhere, and they see you as obsolete."

"You're pushing me back down the ladder, Mitch."

She paused.

"It was too hard to climb it the first time. I won't do it again."

"Does your father still own the station in Addison?"

She shook her head. "I own it now."

"Even better. Lie low for a while and focus on local stories."

Her heart raced. This couldn't be happening.

"Still friends?"

Her sable eyebrows pushed together as blood flushed her cheeks.

"Are we friends? You must be kidding me!"

"Come on, for old times' sake. We almost got married once."

"Is that why you're doing me dirty right now? You think I left you at the altar?" Vickie shook the phone above her head and cursed.

She calmed herself, brought the phone to her cheek, and forced a smile, praying it would carry through the wires and change his mind.

"It felt that way to me," he said sharply. "I was in love with you."

Movement caught her eye from beyond the secondary pasture.

Mitch's last sentence lingered as she hung up on him.

The distant man turned and vanished into the woods.

Vickie went to the gun cabinet and tried to open the door, but it was locked. She discovered a key on top of the unit and asked the empty room for answers, but heard no reply. Vickie was alone, having shut out everyone for so long that few cared if she lived or died. This knowledge was the hardest to bear. She had been more concerned with the opinions of others than with her own best interests or the welfare of her daughter. Her life had been one of inconsequence and inexhaustible chatter, over the airwaves, in boardrooms, and in what passed for love. Each fling had failed more impressively than the last, each taking apart her soul bit by bit, leaving only a shell.

A voice inside her head delivered commands and rebukes as if it had authority over her life, leaving her dark and cold and uncivilized. Her eyes closed tight, and she fought the urge to crumble. She retrieved Red's rifle from the cabinet and held the weapon in her hands, feeling its weight and bearing, noting it was loaded. The frigid quarry had ended Logan's life, and if she had found the courage to get back in the car with him, it would have ended hers. Now the frozen pond behind the barn, the summer waters where mallards once swam, would align her murderous fate with his.

All she needed was a long stick and the wherewithal to do the deed.

John's truck arrived, pulling a trailer. As she peered through the curtain, the sounds of horses filled the air. "What in the world?"

He hopped out of the truck and approached the house.

Vickie stepped outside and pointed the rifle at her former flame.

He stopped abruptly and held up two gloved hands, grinning.

"Don't shoot. I come in peace."

She rested the rifle against her left arm with the muzzle aimed at the ground. "What do you think you're doing? This isn't a horse hotel."

He pointed at the massive trailer. "After police confiscation, Missy kept this group in quarantine on her farm to confirm they weren't contagious. She's treated them for starvation and other problems, but with more banged-up rescues coming in every week, she finally ran out of room. Now she needs to rehome them somewhere safe, at least temporarily. These horses have recovered well enough to move."

He pulled off his leather gloves.

"You'll be saving their lives, and I'll owe you one," he said.

"What exactly are you asking me to do here?"

"Give them refuge."

"Refuge?"

He smirked. "How about sanctuary? Any better?"

"Not really."

"What they need is a place to stay."

She frowned. "How long?"

"It could take a few months to find homes for all of them."

She planted her feet wide apart, and her nostrils flared.

"A few months? Have you lost your mind?"

"Possibly," he said, grinning. "It depends on who you ask."

Vickie smirked. "You're not funny."

"Well?"

She took a deep breath and exhaled. "You're in luck because my schedule just cleared." She hesitated. "I have little sense of direction or any real purpose in life other than to cater to your every whim."

He stood his ground but gave her a quizzical look.

She scanned the trailer's length. "How many are in there, anyway?"

"I thought you still had your show. Has something changed?"

"For me, there is no show, since I've been fired." Vickie shifted her weight and kicked at the porch slats, wanting to hurt someone, to see their blood flow onto the ground. "Not officially, since they haven't sent me the separation package, which I'm supposed to sign through an online portal. It's all driving me to madness."

"There must be something worth going back for."

John had always been insensitive.

Vickie could take the butt end of the rifle and charge him, perhaps catch him off guard, and beat him senseless. She looked away and cleared the terrible imaginings from her mind. "There's nothing for me in D.C. but a sparsely populated apartment and unpleasant memories. But I'll create a real life for myself once I return with Red's money. I've learned a lot recently, and I plan to build on those lessons."

"I sincerely hope you do, Vickie. You deserve to be happy."

She wiped away a tear. "I wonder if I'm worthy of love."

"I'd say you are, when you're not flashing that evil temper of yours."

She pointed to herself in mock disbelief. "Who, me? Temper?"

"I must be thinking of another foul-mouthed, raven-haired beauty."

"They run in packs these days."

He smiled. "I hear they carry rifles."

She looked at the ground, then raised her eyes to meet his.

"Most men can't handle my spirit."

John grinned at her, as if he knew her plan to leave this world. His awareness filled her with anticipation. When her emotions descended to their gloomiest depths, he had a knack for reserving all judgment and, in so doing, turning her back toward the light.

"I'm not most men." He tipped his hat. "As you know."

He led each horse to the barn as she studied him from the porch.

Her right hand scrubbed over her face, and she fought the urge to follow and beg him to save what was left of her miserable existence.

Movement again caught her eye from beyond the secondary pasture, interrupting her thoughts. Her fingers squeezed the rifle stock firmly as she sat up straight and peered at the far tree line. The gray-haired man stepped into the open and eyed her across the expanse. She sensed his mood was dark and lonely and violent. If she did not go to him, he would eventually come to her. Only one man could be so bold.

With rifle in hand, she marched toward Route 15.

John called to her. "Where are you going?"

Vickie pointed to the far woods. "A creep showed himself to me earlier, and I'm going to find out who he is, although I already know."

John yelled for her to wait, but she stubbornly continued.

64

Vickie bared her teeth and swore under her breath as she made her way across the two-lane highway, climbed the fence to the secondary pasture, traversed its depth, and trekked through woods to a clearing with a trailer and a driveway that led to another back road to nowhere.

Price Brewer stepped from behind a colossal oak tree.

This would be no lighthearted excursion.

She aimed Red's rifle at Price. The weapon and the land were once possessions of the only father she'd ever known, and she would not let this interloper steal from her. "What do you want with me, rapist? And what are you doing on my father's land? You have three seconds."

He frowned wistfully. "After Red passed, I'd hoped you might know me as your father. We are blood, you know."

She lowered the muzzle. "You'll never be him."

"So be it." He shrugged. "To answer your question, Red felt bad about what transpired between us years ago. I think his conscience got the better of him, and it was about time, if you ask me. But at any rate, Red allowed me to live in this trailer and even gave me an allowance."

Price spoke as if prompting her forgiveness.

She gestured with the rifle. "What did Red regret?"

"It's a topic best left for another time."

"When you're drunk, I'll bet no one can get you to stop talking."

"I haven't had a sip of alcohol in many years, not since I discovered Christ while I served my time in Baldwin Correctional Center."

Vickie pressed her lips together and kept still.

John arrived from the woods. "Are you all right?"

Price cocked his head. "I recognize you from the highway. You should watch where you're headed, if you don't mind me saying so."

Vickie took a step backward and covered both men with her rifle.

"Do you outlaws know each other?"

"I almost ran him over while driving Garrett home from chemo."

Price shook his head and looked at the clouds. "I guess hatred really eats at a man's insides. He's always despised me, that's for sure."

"With good reason," John said flatly.

"Maybe so."

Vickie dropped the muzzle. "Do you have handyman skills?"

"I'm better with horses."

John snorted. "This is your lucky day. We have a lot of those."

"Yes, and they are cast-offs," Price said. "That no one wants."

Vickie eyed him dubiously. "You know this how?"

"Your boyfriend drove by here earlier."

Price gave her a moment to process his subtle accusation.

"For the record, I worked with quarter horses at Baldwin. If it's acceptable, I'd like to work with this batch and see if I can help."

He paused.

"You may be surprised."

"Surprised by what, the horses or a rapist such as yourself?" she asked fiercely, raising the rifle and squeezing the stock with all her might.

He shrugged. "Why don't we find out together?"

She cast a skeptical glance at John and slowly lowered her weapon.

John nodded. "Another hand is always a good thing. Some of these horses may have deep issues, and I don't want to see anyone hurt."

She examined the rapist for several moments.

"I'll trust you because my father trusted you to live on his land. There's a loft apartment over the barn that Red fixed up for me in high school. If it's still livable, you can stay there, at least until I leave."

When the sunlight shifted and fell on Price's face through the trees, he looked decidedly older and more jaded. "You offer me shelter and a job, although I do not deserve your kindness or your trust. Vickie, you have an honorable heart and a kind soul." His voice lowered. "I never meant to hurt your lovely mother or you, my darling daughter."

"I've shot Red's guns since I was a girl." Vickie pointed the rifle at Price and cocked it. "I know how to use this thing, and I won't hesitate."

His palm raised. "You have nothing to fear. I've killed enough for three lifetimes, and I don't plan to start again. Jesus taught me to love my brothers and sisters and to pray for those who wish me dead."

She lowered the muzzle and searched her soul for a warm feeling or some kind of reassurance she would make the right call.

"Did you become a pastor in prison?"

"I taught men about grace and truth while I served my sentence."

Her grip tightened, and she aimed at him again. He would prove himself or die, and this time Vickie would follow through. "Lay some verses on me, old man. Let's see what kind of minister you've become."

"Now?"

She nodded.

Her body tensed.

She was on the verge of firing. Afterward, there could be only one fatal outcome, both for her and for Price Brewer. A cell on death row might be the best place for the murderous Victoria Morrison.

He looked at John and then at her. "The law was given by Moses. Grace and truth came from Jesus Christ. The law showed what man ought to be. Christ showed what man is and what God is."

If she couldn't shoot him, Vickie would humiliate him.

"All right, I'll play along. What is man and what is God?"

"You have no faith?"

"Monsters like you snuffed it out. Answer my question, rapist."

"The first word of law is 'Thou.' The first of grace is 'God so loved.' But it is grace through truth. He knows everything about you, and nothing has been overlooked. The greatest sin any man or woman might commit has already been committed, the murder of the Son of God."

"I knew you wouldn't answer me directly."

"Vickie, the greatest grace of God was manifested on the cross."

She turned and marched through the woods.

John spoke to Price and then caught up with her.

He snatched the rifle, unloaded it, and chastised her fervently as they walked through the secondary pasture on their way back to the highway. She would never go off on her own again, or so John declared. But what did he know or control in her world or anywhere else? Vickie's biological father had reappeared just as her adopted father had passed from this realm. She understood the synchronicity and how marvelous she should feel about the great and mysterious cycle of life. But she only wanted one thing, to lie down in a grave beside Helen Dunstan. Perhaps there all would be made clear to her.

Vickie made breakfast on the loft stove and struggled to clear Chelsea's death day from her mind. Yet another year had gone by without confessing her sin to a priest or receiving a word of comfort for her grief. She had paced the floor in the main house since dawn, and if she allowed herself to go there for another minute, she would collapse. So she turned to Price, surprised to be thankful for his presence.

"I don't understand the bad blood between you and John's father. I get why Red hated you, but the whole Garrett thing baffles me."

Price stood at the window, staring into the unknown.

Vickie snapped her fingers.

"Hey, over here. I asked you a question."

He sighed and eased into a chair at the table. He put a hand in his pocket and calculated his answer. "I had never spoken to the man before the other day, so I do not know why. But sin makes enemies."

"Do you have any friends from the old days?"

He shook his head. "All are dead or disowned me long ago."

She smiled. "We're both strangers in our hometown."

He chuckled. "I have your friendship, so I'm a contented man."

"You have no such thing," she said. "It's a miracle you're here at all, especially after they fired me for your heinous rape of my mother."

He blushed and sat up straight. "See what I mean? God is already hard at work, bringing father and daughter back together."

"There never was a first time, so you can save it."

"Fair enough. I'll stop pushing you." Price gave her an unhappy look. Then his entire body tensed and he placed a hand over his chest. A few moments later, his shoulders slumped, and he settled into his chair.

She grew worried. "Is everything all right?"

His grimace faded, and he forced a smile as he sat up straight. "For the last year, pressure in my chest has come and gone. It's nothing."

"It could be something. You're not getting any younger."

His face took on more color, but he looked apologetic and ashamed.

"Speaking of younger men, I have a roommate in the trailer. I suppose you might call him a friend. We seemed to hit it off when we first met."

Vickie switched the stove dial to off and scraped eggs, ham, and toast onto a plate. She handed it to Price and arched her eyebrows.

"Details?"

"His full name is Lewis Samson."

"Why would you say it like that?" She studied Price and then tossed her head. "Wait, don't tell me. He's in trouble with the law."

"Afraid so. He's in jail for a bar fight."

Yet another outlaw. "I swear, you guys could star in a B-movie."

Price let her insult pass. "He's a veteran of Afghanistan who's had a rough time since he lost a portion of his right leg. Red knew about Lewis through the VFW and wanted to help a fellow soldier."

Vickie needed to end the conversation, it was about nothing and everything. She gestured at the plate, and his eyes followed her movement. "I'll collect the war hero after you finish breakfast."

***

Vickie entered the police station and spoke to the desk clerk. He told her the bail amount, which she posted, and then he sent someone to collect Lewis Samson. The concrete walls presented a dreary mood she hoped never to experience again, though she had a premonition this would be the first of many moments spent within them, as her nature bent toward trouble and it found her effortlessly and without fail.

Lewis collected his things. His blond hair and youthful face struck her as handsome, but she resisted her attraction to him.

As they walked to the door, she looked back at the clerk.

"Officer Taylor said you were treacherous and I should be careful."

Lewis chuckled. "Takes one to know one."

He pushed open the door, and a cold breeze greeted them.

"Is that remark aimed at me or the officer?"

He smiled. "Guess we'll find out."

In her SUV, she gripped the steering wheel and sighed.

"I've been called treacherous so many times I've lost count."

"Is that so?"

"I'm sorry I said that to you. I've had a difficult few weeks."

She paused.

"I'm tired of being treated like a criminal."

He sat back, and his expression grew serious. "Vickie, you seem like an okay woman, so I'll give you some free advice. Stop caring about what others think and learn who you're meant to be in this world."

It was her turn to laugh. "If it were only so easy."

As they drove through the countryside toward Bluecreek Stables, the hills rolled and tumbled along with her thoughts. She liked the fact that Lewis was a veteran and could hold his own in a fight. But there was John to consider, and she didn't know what went on in his head.

She took the long way, which ran past the golf course and looped back to the east. Lewis didn't seem to mind the diversion.

Her Expedition passed Bluecreek's front pasture and four lanes narrowed to two. She braced for the curves that would soon appear.

Lewis looked up through the windshield at the glorious majesty of the mountains that rose above them, then gazed out his side window at the gorge that fell below their eye line.

The terrain leveled, and a creek ran beside the roadway.

She pulled into a tiny parking area and shut off the engine.

They walked to a bridge and stared into the rushing waters of the creek. She felt compelled to share her pain with this man, a stranger who gave her comfort but also made her sad at the gloomy implication.

"I've reached a point," she said, "where nothing seems to matter anymore. Each morning I lie in bed and wonder if I should get up."

He nodded his understanding as his eyes fixed on the water.

"I've felt the same since I lost my leg." He chuckled. "You should've seen me as a recruit. I was so gung-ho it was ridiculous, especially when no one cares about military sacrifice or the reasons we fight."

"I thought I would make my father proud if I became the face of cable news. But he never really cared about my accomplishments. Red always favored his birth daughter, Michelle, which really hurt."

They walked back to her car. Vickie fought the urge to kiss Lewis.

She started the engine and pointed the Expedition west.

"Will you go back to Washington soon?"

She tapped the steering wheel. "There may not be a place for me anymore. I feel sad and depressed when I think about what happened."

"If they make a place for you again, will you go?"

"Probably, since I live in a state of denial. But there are two girls to consider, and I know I just can't up and leave them stranded."

Lewis locked eyes with her, and his face grew serious. "Sounds like you've reached a conclusion you won't allow yourself to admit."

Her pensive expression gave way to a smile.

"Oh, really? You already know me so well?"

Vickie was attracted, but he was a young man with a hard past and anger issues. She must be careful to live the way Chelsea needed her to live, as a mother who made her daughter proud rather than ashamed.

Her affinity suited him. "A woman like you isn't hard to figure out." He rubbed her arm, and it felt good. "You've reached a certain age..."

She drew back. "Hey, I might be cursed and I might be tainted, but I'm not an old lady. Millions of people watch me every night."

He laughed, playing along. "I was about to say you've reached a level of success, and there's little beyond this point, nothing out there waiting to satisfy your needs. Then you look around and notice there's no man in your life, no children, no home to tend. And the idea of baking cookies at Christmas doesn't sound so ridiculous, does it?"

"It did when I was twenty," she said. "You've got me there."

They pulled into Bluecreek's driveway and parked in front of the house. Vickie glanced at Lewis. They smiled at each other, then found something else to focus on as a distraction. Vickie gazed through the sunroof at the overhanging trees and the clouds that floated overhead. Lewis turned and scanned the length of the house.

"I could get used to this place," he said.

He opened his door and then turned and drew her near. Vickie closed her eyes and awaited his kiss. A portrait of Chelsea flashed across her mind, and she swiped at the tears that coursed down her cheeks.

She drew back from him. "Me too."

"Then don't leave." He leaned over and wiped her tears.

She smiled. "I won't if you won't."

Lewis shut the door and leaned against it, studying her. "So, is this a thing? I thought you had the other guy wrapped around your finger."

"We'll see," she said. "I'm impossible, and men don't stick."

He pointed to the metal rod that had replaced his right leg below the knee. "If I took off right now, I wouldn't make the gate by noon."

His joke eased the awkwardness, and she laughed freely.

It was high time she considered life on her own terms. She couldn't have wished for a better companion. Lewis Samson would teach her to value more important things than which party controlled Congress or which candidate might win the presidency in November.

Vickie playfully pushed his arm. "Then we'll drain the moat."

He chuckled. "You're all right, Vickie. I could enjoy it here."

Through the sunroof, a single light popped into her view, emanating from behind her house and shining brightly halfway up the mountain. Just as quickly as it arrived, the light extinguished itself, reigniting the gloom that lived inside her. Although the temperature was frigid in February, soon summer would show itself and folks would ride horses along the mountain trails. Stones and boulders dotted the landscape up there, with trees that peaked mightily above the tops of winding cliffs and low-hanging clouds that often misted over the mountaintop. She'd camped by herself along the trails and streams in years past. When the air was cool at first light, the canopy of clouds beckoned her forth for a swim in a floating lake. Perhaps she would climb the mountain when the weather warmed and her life made sense.

She gave Lewis a heartfelt smile. He might become her next mistake.

Vickie and Price leaned against a fence rail as the chilly afternoon turned into a bitter evening. Michelle's horses meandered across the pasture.

"Should we bring them inside? It's cold out here."

"They're a hardy pair like you and John."

"I'm serious. It's unkind to make them stay outside in this weather."

"John put blankets on them earlier."

She looked away and tried to think of something else.

Her arms crossed, and her nose wrinkled. "Tell me about prison."

Price spoke as if in mourning, but also expectantly.

"Isolation was the worst part. As an older man who appreciates the preciousness of time, I grieve over the loss of my son, Tink."

"You have a son?" she asked incredulously.

"He was from a different mother, and he passed years ago."

Vickie reflected.

"I'm sorry for your loss and that I never knew him."

"Tink ran in different circles and lived in another town."

"Michelle mentioned a guy in Walton County when we were in high school, but I never heard his name again. Was he my brother?"

"It was a different time, and we were all different people."

She turned to Price in anger. "Why did you rape my mother?"

He stiffened and pushed himself from the fence as if preparing to leave. He hesitated for a moment, then turned toward the barn.

She grabbed his arm. "Wait. I need you to say something, anything."

"Vickie, it was so long ago. I'd rather not revisit the past. I am a changed man since Jesus Christ found me, and it should be enough."

"I don't understand you yet, but I'm going to eventually." Vickie gazed into the distance. The barren trees sat still and lifeless and bleak.

"Most people would assume I've lost my mind by talking with you. But the only father I've ever known now lies in the grave." She hesitated, then nodded solemnly. "You claim to be some kind of holy man after forty years in prison, but I don't buy it. I'll say this, and you'd better hear me. If you prove unworthy, I will yell it from the rooftops."

"That would be your right." He spoke with grace and stepped toward her, grabbing her shoulders. "I know it's hard to lose Red. He was your rock after Valerie died." Price wore the sad smile of a clown.

Memories surfaced, compelling her penance. "It's not like we had a great relationship, though. I hadn't laid eyes on him since I bailed at eighteen. We were like oil and water, better apart than together."

"Even so," he said thoughtfully, "this is a difficult time for you."

Price had a nice way of talking to her, light and confidential.

"You would think I'd be a wreck."

She frowned and kicked at a rock, then put her boot on the lowest rail. "There's something terribly wrong with me, something wicked inside. I've been through ordeals that would kill most people, and it would be easy for me to believe Logan Meson was the one who crushed my soul. But I was broken inside well before the quarry."

"I'm listening."

"It's not every day a woman born from rape gets raped. I'm sure I won a blue ribbon for that one." She hugged herself. "I envy those who live normal lives. Their biggest worry is what's for dinner."

She wiped a tear, and her eyes fell to the ground.

He lifted her chin so her eyes met his. She felt safe in his presence.

"I don't know those people," he said. "The only world I know is a brutal place, and folks do the best they can to survive its violence."

"Thing is..." Her eyes fell to the ground again, and she peeked up at him like a little girl. She held up a boot and kicked at the post, chipping the wood. Price arched his eyebrows as encouragement to continue.

"I think whatever's wrong with me was there all the time, asleep in my blood. Maybe Garrett is right when he says the Brewer clan is no good and every one of us should be shot. At this moment, I find it hard to refute his claim." She hesitated. "I am a greedy woman who drifts through life, unable to find happiness or satisfaction, and I hurt others."

"I felt the same while in prison. We had little time outside the cell, so reading became a cherished activity. I tried the literary classics, but most were nihilistic, and I was already depressed. It took me about two years into my second stint, but I finally found the Lord's Holy Bible, and it has made all the difference." He took her hand and squeezed it. His enormous paws were calloused and strong, but gentle as a teddy bear. "If you'll allow me, I'd like to share the Word with you. It will surely help you deal with the pain and uncertainty you're feeling, as it did for me."

"All right, but only a little. I get bored easily."

Price retrieved a worn but well-cared-for Bible and recited Ephesians 6:10-20. "A final word: Be strong in the Lord and in his mighty power. Put on all of God's armor so that you will be able to stand firm against all strategies of the devil. For we are not fighting against flesh-and-blood enemies, but against evil rulers and authorities of the unseen world, against mighty powers in this dark world, and against evil spirits in the heavenly places. Therefore, put on every piece of God's armor so you will be able to resist the enemy in the time of evil. Then after the battle you will still be standing firm. Stand your ground, putting on the belt of truth and the body armor of God's righteousness. For shoes, put on the peace that comes from the Good News so that you will be fully prepared. In addition to all of these, hold up the shield of faith to stop the fiery arrows of the devil. Put on salvation as your helmet, and take the sword of the Spirit, which is the word of God. Pray in the Spirit at all times and on every occasion. Stay alert and be persistent in your prayers for all believers everywhere. And pray for me, too. Ask God to give me the right words so I can boldly explain God's mysterious plan that the Good News is for Jews and Gentiles alike. I am in chains now, still preaching this message as God's ambassador. So pray that I will keep on speaking boldly for him, as I should."

Price's eyes found hers as he closed his Bible. "This passage always comforts me when I'm restless."

"Did you first read it while in prison?"

"Yes, and now I read to my daughter so she might escape her own prison, one not of her own making, but of others who led her into sin."

"I suppose you include yourself in that group?"

"I do, and now I seek to right your path." He ran his fingers along her hair and kissed her on the forehead. He gambled with her patience, and his carelessness filled her with unease. She drew back from him.

"God has no use for me. I'm a wretch who somehow became a star."

"May I teach you the Word, as I taught other men at Baldwin?"

She placed her hand on the top rail and shook her head. "What you can do for me is instruct Lewis Samson about horsemanship. He needs a valuable skill outside the military, or he will not make it as a civilian."

She sighed and let go of the rail. "I sense he feels lost and alone."

Price nodded his agreement. "I've thought the same."

"Back in D.C., I tried to help a young girl through her many horrible ordeals. But in the end I was selfish, and she committed suicide." A pause. "Now Helen's ghost wants to break me, but so far I've resisted her." Vickie swiped at her tears with a gloved hand.

"Perhaps you should cease trying."

Her eyes widened as she squeezed his arm. "Listen, good or bad, I know you and Lewis are tough men who think you don't need any help. But in this case he honestly needs someone to step in or he'll end up like Helen Dunstan. And if that happens, I won't bear the weight."

"Are you attracted to him?"

She recoiled. "What? It's nothing like that."

"I've seen how you look at him. You should be careful."

"Why?"

Price's tone hardened. "Lewis is a powder keg waiting to explode, and you'll do well to steer clear before he takes you down with him."

"I'll take it under advisement."

"See that you do."

He turned and walked toward the barn.

Vickie stood alone and watched Michelle's horses fade into the night, as she had done. Then she wondered about her future. A portrait of Valerie's final weeks flashed, the all-day drinking, the pill popping, the taunts and jeers while dancing to one album after another in the living room, the vomit and the rags and the tears. Each day had built more impassioned momentum, leading inevitably to the wreck of her station wagon.

Because of the political climate of the late sixties, Valerie couldn't abort her daughter. So instead she aborted herself. As the thought struck her, Vickie wasn't sure whether to laugh or cry, to be gracious or petulant. She put a boot on the rail, thankful to have made it this far, even though her rise to fame had destroyed lives, including her own.

Vickie looked up at the stars, which twinkled merrily. "I'm sorry I was so hard on you, Mom. I know you would have aborted me if you could, but I'm glad you didn't. Maybe one day I can hug your neck. I would like that, because this world hasn't been the same without you."

Vickie looked around for another person, then stared into the night's grim oblivion. "Just for the record, I envy your circumstance, resting peacefully until Christ returns. I haven't yet decided whether to join you, but it grows more likely every day."

Six

Psalm 46:1

God is our refuge and strength,
always ready to help in times of trouble.

Wednesday afternoon, a northerly wind swept hard and fast across the county, blasting the truck as it parked in Missy Weldon's driveway. Streaks of clouds topped the mountain range beyond the foster farm, and Vickie's breath fogged as she followed John to the barn. She recalled a golden summer spent as Michelle's assistant, the briefest of moments when her will, her love, and her soul coalesced into something fine. Michelle's sudden paralysis, her devastating death after a year, and the lack of a father in Katie and Abbie's lives had combined to ruin their fragile innocence. They could not bear any new revelations of family shame. Vickie would keep her wicked secrets hidden at all costs, and in so doing, Missy would assume her role as their mother's unworthy replacement.

A terrier mix with fluffy fur observed from the barn entrance, where an adolescent girl addressed him as Basil. She glanced at Vickie and threw a ball toward the open grass, where it skipped and bumped and rested invitingly, but Basil refused its allure. He instead ran smiling to Vickie and pawed her leg. She stepped back and cursed his mangy form, but Basil snuck between her knees, wagged his entire body, and then danced about with a beaming grin. She kicked at him, and he slunk over to Missy, who grabbed his collar and threw a mean look at Vickie.

"Do not hurt my dog!" She stood with hands on her hips.

Basil wore a sad face until the teen knelt and hugged him, then his eyes gladdened and his body wagged. He clearly loved the girl, who must be Katie, but she and the dog should learn to behave.

"Tell your filthy mutt not to jump on me. My clothes cost more than your house."

"He's nice." Katie rubbed Basil's ears. "You don't have to worry."

"Who's worried? I just don't like dogs, alright?"

Katie turned to her caretaker. "Is he okay, Missy?"

"He's fine." Missy glared at Vickie and clicked for Basil to follow.

Basil happily trailed her into the barn, his furry form disappearing from view as quickly as Vickie's goodness had departed from her own.

The teen drew near to Vickie. "I have valuable information."

Vickie's anger rose as she searched the area for John. He was nowhere to be found, so she turned to the girl. "You are Katie, right?"

"Yes, and you are my mother's sister, the one who doesn't exist."

Vickie's eyes fell on her Christian Louboutin stilettos, which were now ruined, the red veneer would never look the same. She kicked at the ground and wondered why she was in the middle of nowhere.

"Red told me something about Lewis you should know." Katie spoke with gravity, as if the subject had slightly embarrassed her.

Vickie bit down hard, her teeth almost cutting into her lower lip. There was mud on her Rag and Bone jeans from Basil, the dog everyone believed was friendly and wonderful. "Alright," she said while brushing off bits of clay before finally giving up. "Let's have it."

"He was a brilliant soldier before he got hurt."

"Any idea how it happened?"

"A training accident. I think they were about to come home from the desert." Katie seemed delighted to share a newsworthy item.

"That's usually how it goes. One minute you're riding high, about to go home, and the next, you're lying in a pool of your own blood."

A whinny from the barn drew Vickie's thoughts to her summer with Michelle. She dragged a hand through her hair and tried to forget, but it was of little use, her sister plagued her night and day. Vickie grew unsteady and again searched for John, but he was inside the barn.

She returned to the conversation, hoping to restore her balance.

"Did my father have plans for Lewis?"

Katie shook her head. "Red was about to set him up with a job at the station, but then he had a heart attack and died. Since then, Lewis has been doing random work around the farm and for some neighbors."

Vickie's phone rang from inside her purse, and she held up a finger.

"It's my boss. I have to take this."

She fumbled for the phone and almost dropped it.

"Get your scrawny rear end back here this instant!"

"Hello, Mitch." A sheen formed on Vickie's neck. "So happy to hear your voice." She gave Katie an exaggerated eye roll and turned away from her, seeking privacy. "What seems to be the problem?"

"I'll tell you the problem. You refused to mentor your protégé when you had the chance and instead walked off the set. Nellie has folded since the last time we spoke in a manner unparalleled in cable news history, which is an achievement, if you ask me. Our overnight ratings have nosedived, and I hope you're having a jolly time down there because I am not happy. In fact, I am very far from happy. I would say I am so far from happy that no one can even see happiness from where I sit, and they never will again!"

"Did Preston put you up to this?"

"I was going to call earlier. The show doesn't work without you."

Vickie rubbed her freezing hands together. Even with gloves, she was a cold-natured city girl, and it was a bitter February day.

"Serves you right, Mitch, for raking me over the coals." She paused. "You made me a laughingstock on live television."

"For old time's sake, let go of the past and come back to the show."

"Nellie's your whiz kid and your puzzle to solve." Vickie shrugged as she paced to the round pen and back to the barn. "Hey, she seemed like a great kisser, which should make up for her other deficiencies."

Mitch demanded she stay on the line, but she hung up on him.

She grinned at Katie. "Now that was entirely satisfying."

"I guess."

John approached with a distracted countenance. His voice was firm. "I have to take Dad to his appointment."

He walked over to his cousin and hugged her goodbye.

Abbie stood at Missy's side, clinging to her and staring at the road. Lewis and Price arrived in one of Red's old farm trucks. They got out smiling and waved to her. Had she known they were about to appear?

John started to leave but stopped himself. He went over to Abbie and squatted, then grinned and drew her to him like a father. He threw a look at Vickie, but her eyes averted. She would keep her distance from the child, as Michelle had requested before her death.

John then whispered funny quips into Abbie's ear, and the girl's smile moved across her face. He laughed heartily and tickled Abbie's sides, causing her to giggle and fidget. Vickie felt a warm rush of blood to her arms and legs, and whatever pain she'd experienced from the wintry morning, she forgot. She eyed a metal pipe on the ground and once more considered a sprint toward John with a weapon. She could inflict blunt trauma on his skull and she might even be justified, there was little reason to put her and the girls in such a position. Katie and Abbie were Michelle's daughters, not Vickie's, and she hardly knew them. There would be little love lost or gained from this encounter, and his attempt at manipulation infuriated her.

John whispered in Abbie's ear, and the child ran forward.

It was too much to handle, so Vickie glanced about, looking for an excuse to leave. With seconds ticking, she sighed heavily and waited for Abbie to crash into her legs, but the child halted halfway and looked back at John. He encouraged her with his voice and gestures. Vickie's eyes narrowed as she discerned a vague but familiar deadliness in Abbie, her look, her smile, some nameless evil, which she found most worrisome. Abbie was the offspring of gloom just like her, a born villain who belonged in prison where those she hurt could visit her each day and tell her what a vile creature she was and how they wished she had never existed. Vickie somehow discerned this knowledge as Abbie turned from John and looked at her, and it was clear the two shared a need for vengeance and a desire to inflict pain. Vickie wanted to run and hide from this hellchild, but she somehow knew the urchin would scour the landscape for her whereabouts. The girl's eyes shifted from light to dark and mocked her relationship with John Breyer, he had brought her here to inflame Abbie's rage and her devilish need to destroy all those with the capacity and desire to hurt her.

Price took advantage of the situation and drew near to Vickie. Although she hoped he might remain silent and give her space, it was of little use, he must speak his mind. He let a minute pass before he pointed at the girl, likely a kindness, but it rekindled the fires of hatred within her, inciting them to an unnatural temperature.

"Abbie seems nice. Why not accept her into your life?"

Vickie turned to him. Her face fell scarlet and her voice blazed. "What do you know about anything, rapist?"

"I know about regret and a desire to make amends."

"It's too late."

He retrieved his Bible and recited Psalm 46:1-10. "God is our refuge and strength, always ready to help in times of trouble. So we will not fear when earthquakes come and the mountains crumble into the sea. Let the oceans roar and foam. Let the mountains tremble as the waters surge! A river brings joy to the city of our God, the sacred home of the Most High. God dwells in that city; it cannot be destroyed. From the very break of day, God will protect it. The nations are in chaos, and their kingdoms crumble! God's voice thunders, and the earth melts! The Lord of Heaven's Armies is here among us; the God of Israel is our fortress. Come, see the glorious works of the Lord: See how he brings destruction upon the world. He causes wars to end throughout the earth. He breaks the bow and snaps the spear; he burns the shields with fire. 'Be still, and know that I am God! I will be honored by every nation. I will be honored throughout the world.'"

She smirked. "This applies to me how?"

"God says the faithful have no reason to be afraid, as the Lord is always ready to deliver us from our travails and He is invincibly armed."

"Oh, really?"

"You may believe otherwise, but Jesus has always been with you."

He read the last verse. "The Lord of Heaven's Armies is here among us; the God of Israel is our fortress." Price closed his Bible. "You see, the Most High repeats this statement twice, reminding us believers that we have been separated from the fallen condition of the other nations, those who worship lesser gods, and therefore our faith may rest truly and persistently in Yahweh, who holds immeasurable power but who dotes on us with fatherly love, which He manifests in His Word."

Vickie could endure this man no longer. She bent down beside Katie, who sat on the ground, and picked up a rock. She stood and turned it over in her gloved hand several times, then tossed it. Price walked to the barn, dejected and murmuring, ending their conversation.

Katie observed him, then her eyes rose to Vickie. "She doesn't bite, you know."

Caught in her own thoughts, Vickie took out her phone.

Katie tugged on her jeans. "My sister doesn't bite. Abbie's a nice kid, like Price said. If you gave her a chance, you might actually like her."

Vickie offered an annoyed look. "I'm sure I would, but your sister isn't the problem." Vickie's voice trailed as she searched her contact list.

"Then what is?"

"Abbie reminds me of someone."

She waited for Katie to ask the obvious follow-up question, but it never came, so she toed the ground with her stiletto and kicked at another rock. Katie flinched as the stone bounced off her jeans.

"Sorry about that." Vickie swept the rock away from Katie. "Did you hear what I said a minute ago about Abbie reminding me of someone?"

"Yes."

"Don't you want to know who the person is?"

"It's you. I'm not a dummy."

Vickie chuckled and smiled at Katie. "I can see that, and I'll keep it in mind the next time I need someone smart to solve a riddle."

Katie looked at the horizon. "Whatever."

John grunted in Vickie's direction and turned his back on her. He seemed sullen while he walked to his truck, as if he had given up on her humanity. She reached him as he opened the driver's side door.

"Please wait."

He turned to her in anger and took a while to speak. "Why are you upset with me?"

"These are nice people who are not out to get you, especially those two girls. You might find you have a lot in common with them."

She had to make him stay and fill the hollowness inside her. "Oh, really?"

John slammed the truck door. "Yeah, really."

He must understand her or she would die. "John, you cannot expect me to handle this much scrutiny and this much responsibility. I never signed up for any of this, but everyone around here expects me to waltz in and play the doting mother as if I was born for the role. Well, I have news for you, buddy. That woman isn't me, and she never was."

"You were pretty terrific back at summer camp."

"It didn't make me a mother then, and it doesn't now."

He sighed. "I'm saying you could have been one."

"I papered over a lot of fresh pain when you met me. It was easier to pretend I had myself together back then, when we were younger."

John considered. "You've got me there because it certainly was."

He eyed her for several moments, as if weighing his verdict. "You're doing fine, and you seem like a natural when you aren't faking your emotions." He climbed into the truck and rolled down the window. "I won't be gone all day. Try to feel more comfortable."

As his truck faded into the horizon, Vickie turned from him. Her bleak insecurities threatened to overwhelm her senses, and she had to follow him to the hospital and do anything, say anything, to be near him. She was indebted to him for showing her love so many years ago, one of the few men who'd ever seen all the way to her core and accepted what he found there, both a noble heart and a corrupted soul, each portion clamoring to be cherished and to be truly known.

John sat in the hospital lobby and observed people as they floated about the area. Vickie plopped into an adjacent chair, startling him.

He gave her an irritated look. "How did you find me?"

"I'm a reporter. We chase people down in hospitals."

She made a face at him and looked about the lobby. Her eyes followed a group of nurses who stopped at the floor station and chatted.

He chuckled at her tenacity. "Insane is what you are."

Vickie turned and gave him an intense look. "I think they know more than they're telling you."

"About what?"

"Your father." She glanced at the station and spoke with an edge. "One of those nurses noticed me just now, then she dipped her head and wrote in a chart. When they do that, it's a bad sign."

"You're paranoid, which is what I remember most about you."

"Stop calling me crazy. I don't like it."

He grinned at her reaction, he could always get under her skin and loved it. "If you behave like a good girl, you'll get an ice cream later."

Vickie's shoulders slumped and her voice took on a more desperate tone, as if she had grown fearful. "You've got to help me with the horses and the girls and the two losers above my barn. I haven't been to Red's station yet or contacted a real estate agent." She looked at him nervously and took her time before speaking again. "I'm about to explode."

John smiled. "You mean implode."

Vickie grinned and playfully bumped into him. "That, too."

Garrett looked pale and gaunt as he exited the doctor's office.

John patted her leg. "I have faith in you, Vickie Morrison."

He escorted Garrett to the parking lot. The day had drained him and he was ready to put up his feet, maybe watch some television.

"Don't throw me down, John. I know you've thought about it."

John blushed as he spoke in a harsh tone. "Sorry your perfect son isn't here, Dad." He hesitated. "Chris would never do such a thing."

Garrett snorted. "The heck he wouldn't. My perfect Chris would throw me into the meat grinder tomorrow if there was a dollar in it."

John laughed. "I thought he could do no wrong in your eyes."

"I enjoyed living through his exploits, but you were the one with the most potential, the one who most resembled my personality." He paused. "Chris was like your mother, and I'd lost her at a young age, so I suppose I felt a kinship to her through him." He shrugged. "Maybe I was wrong all those years, but I thought you knew I loved you."

John cut in sharply. "I didn't."

Garrett rubbed his chin. "We'll have to fix that while I'm still alive, now won't we? It's the reason I wanted us to take a trip together. I thought if I taught you the game of golf like I should have done when you were a boy, maybe we could reset and give each other a clean slate."

"There's not enough time, Dad."

A look of anxiety twisted Garrett's face. "We don't know that yet. Stop being pessimistic."

John frowned. "Alright. Fine."

Vickie appeared beside the truck. "Sorry, but I'm now stalking you."

John smiled at the decency hidden within her stubborn nature. "I could've used some stalking years ago. Now, not so much."

"I get it." She drew herself from him. "I should back off."

He reached over and pulled her nearer. "I didn't say leave."

"What then?"

"Just don't act like a creep."

"Noted," she said, smiling.

She stood near Garrett while John unlocked the passenger side door. Garrett coughed, startling John, who clumsily dropped the keys.

As he bent down to retrieve them, Garrett's legs swayed, and he slipped from John's grasp. Vickie ducked under Garrett's shoulder and supported his frail body as John opened the door and helped his father inside. She put her hand on his back as he settled Garrett into his seat.

"Should I let Lewis work at the television station?"

"Mary Bishop works there. Maybe she could show him the ropes."

Vickie bristled at the mention of Mary's name. "How do you know her?"

John smiled, enjoying the jealousy in Vickie's tone. "Addison is a fishbowl. Everyone knows each other."

There was still love in his heart for her, but he suppressed it, she was no good for him, and he could not trust her to stay in town.

Her cheeks flushed red. "Mary Bishop is too young for you, John."

"Turnabout is fair play. Lewis is way too young for you."

He slapped the side of his truck through the open window as the wheels rolled forward. "Don't worry your pretty little head about it."

Vickie smirked at his obvious joke, but she looked sad. "Worrying is what I do best. Please don't leave."

"Got to go!" He gave her a cheerful yell and hit the accelerator.

As his truck exited the parking lot, he eyed her through the rearview mirror. She stood motionless, watching him, probably hoping he'd turn around.

He instead turned right at the stop sign, and her form disappeared.

Vickie Morrison had come home. The notion made him smile.

John dropped by the station early Friday morning. He swung open the pressurized glass door, which caught the wind, making it difficult to open, and he trekked his way to the break room, searching for coffee and whatever was left in the fridge. With a warm mug and a stale biscuit, he meandered along the seemingly endless hallway and finally turned right into a virtually deserted newsroom. He stopped and surveyed the scene.

Mary Bishop sat at her desk, perusing a story. She looked up at John with parted lips and a soft expression. "Where have you been, stranger?"

"I had to take care of grouchy Garrett for a while."

"Are you two getting along?" Her eyes lingered on John.

"I can't please him, so it's about the same."

"It sounds like me and Eudora. Been anywhere else lately?"

He nodded and arched his eyebrows. "Vickie Morrison's ranch."

Mary's face went pale. "Are you two already an item?"

"It's been twenty years." He took off his coat and hung it over the back of a vacant chair. "Besides, she'll be gone in a month, maybe two."

Mary smiled. "Mom says you two were in love once." She sighed. "You know what I want from you, John, but you never give in to my teases. I've accepted your brush-offs because who can compete with Leslie Carter?" He tried to look away, but her hunting eyes found his. "The woman is about to become our next governor, so there was no way I could win your heart with her in the picture, not to mention Rachel Daniels, who never had a chance with you in the first place, but now there's yet another one, and she's someone special from your past." Her face contorted, and he thought Mary might cry. "I've hoped for so long, John, but still you refuse to love me."

This would soon become a cross-examination, so he must change her tone. "Mary, you only feel this way because I'm older and there's no one else you like around here, but trust me, I'm not the man for you."

She drew nearer to him. "Then who is?"

He put his hand on her shoulder, and she squeezed it.

"You're still young. There's plenty of time for love and marriage."

"And kids. I want a pile of kids."

"Them, too."

Mary went to the window and opened the curtains. She gazed at the two-lane highway. "I'll climb the corporate ladder like Vickie, and when I'm famous, I'll marry someone important." She nodded. "We'll have a fairytale wedding for the ages."

He grinned and sipped his coffee. "That's the spirit."

She returned his grin over her shoulder, but spoke curtly. "Are you here to rub my nose in the glamorous spectacle that is Victoria Morrison, or is there another reason? Please say there is one."

"A guy named Lewis Samson helps with Michelle's horses, but

apparently, he needs a more substantial career." John pointed at his jeans and she briefly glanced at them. "He lost part of his right leg in the war. Vickie wants you to mentor the guy, so he doesn't go insane."

"Well, you'd know all about that, wouldn't you?"

Mary grinned and, as he stiffened, her face grew serious. "Sorry, bad joke." A pause. "I'd have to clear it with my boss."

"Vickie owns the station now, and she goes way back with Laura."

A flush crept across Mary's cheeks. She clutched the curtains with both hands and then impatiently let them go. "I guess it's settled. My mother used to be best friends with her in high school, but they haven't spoken for many years." John noted the discouragement in her voice.

"Do you know Vickie?"

"I met her in fourth grade. We went to Washington for one of those field trips and we stopped by her apartment before we came home. I barely remember what she's like in person, but I've always admired her." Mary turned to John and smiled apologetically, as if ashamed to admit the truth. "She's my inspiration, the reason I joined the news business."

"So you'll work with Lewis?"

Mary lifted her chin and seemed more confident. "Reggie, our cameraman, wants to retire soon, and he pesters Laura about his replacement every day. I'll ask him to train Lewis." She considered. "I'll need a favor from Vickie. Something more valuable than gold."

"You'll have to take that up with her."

"Don't worry, John. I will."

SEVEN

Psalm 47:5

God has ascended with a mighty shout.
The Lord has ascended with trumpets blaring.

The 2007 Ford Expedition with its Carbon Clearcoat Metallic paint, factory sound system, and four-wheel drive rolled to a stop in front of the station. Vickie's fingers grasped the steering wheel as regrets worked within her, binding her to quietude until a storm of emotion struck, sweeping like a hurricane, slow and deafening. Her eyes searched for refuge in the oaks that occupied tracts of Baldwin County. She looked about, heeding the glory of the onward sun and the serenity of the road behind her. There was virtue in this town, a simple honesty, and here she could learn her authentic path, one that might grant her access to the heavenly realm, its unutterable and infinite beauty granted from the sorrow of truth and grace. Both would be revealed once the sword of the Spirit found her.

She had discerned the existence of the Lord in girlhood, when all believers expressed a childlike faith, but traumatic experience stifled all willingness to share her rage with Jesus. If He knew her fully, all the way to the cellular level where her baseness dwelled, He would cast her into the Lake of Fire, so she hid herself from Him as she later fled from John after summer camp, immersing herself in career. But soon this town would expose her sins, and the thought of confronting her hidden torments was more than she might tolerate. Vickie should tread softly, but she knew she could not, as both fire and candle were in her blood and she stood poised with a lighted match and a willing hand.

John arrived in his truck, interrupting her fearful speculations. She exited her car and stood in the cold once again, this time wearing a new outfit purchased from the feed and seed store, along with durable boots.

As John approached, she grinned and flashed open her coat.

He seemed astonished but pleasant, which bore promise.

"I like your style," he said. "Those clothes fit you perfectly."

A flush of embarrassment filled her cheeks, so she toyed with him.

"While in Rome, do as the Romans and all of that prattle."

He chuckled. "The posh reporter in her native dialect."

"Always," she said confidently. "And don't you forget it."

Vickie was glad to have met the British couple in the Caribbean.

A dusty Toyota Camry pulled into a space on the other side of his truck, and soon the driver's door opened, revealing a gorgeous but unkempt woman of about twenty-five. She smiled at Vickie as she approached and almost stumbled to the ground as she stepped onto the sidewalk. "Hello, I'm Mary Bishop." She extended her right hand.

"You're late," said Vickie, now in a dark humor.

Mary's arm dropped to her side. "What?"

Vickie spoke as if the reporter might be hard of hearing. "You'll never make it in this business if you drag into the station looking like you do." She removed her gloves and tucked a wisp of hair behind her ear, noting the shock on Mary's face. This was a tedious person whom others rarely tested, an unhelpful practice that would end today.

"Sorry. I was out until three o'clock with a guy."

"Never kiss and tell, honey. It reeks of indecision."

A man opened the heavy glass door at the front entrance, grimacing as he battled against the building's vacuum effect. He made it through and then turned to Vickie. "Are we going or not? I hate to sit around."

Vickie smiled. At last, someone she could admire.

"You must be Reggie." She extended a hand to him.

"Yes, ma'am, and you are the fabled Victoria Morrison."

"It's Vickie to my friends."

"All right, then." He nodded to John, who nodded back at him.

"Just so you know, I'm not a sitting-around type of gal."

Reggie smiled. "Then we should get along just fine."

Mary slung her purse over her shoulder as beads appeared on her brow. She wiped the sweat with one hand and smiled at the group.

Vickie gestured at the van. "We need to get your blood moving."

Mary held up a palm of surrender. "Please, wait."

She grabbed her stomach and then hurried to the open field behind the station. Retching sounds reached Vickie's ears, and she grinned.

While he drove the county roads in the news van, Reggie relayed his desire for retirement, as his wife, Susan, was desperately ill and required a home health nurse. Susan had supported his exploits for three decades, and he must be there in the horrible and helpless moments.

"I'm sorry for her suffering," said Vickie from the passenger seat.

Reggie nodded his appreciation. "It's in God's hands now."

Mary cleared her throat from the back, where she sat beside John.

"When will this Lewis character appear? I've waited, but so far, he's been a no-show. Reggie needs to train someone, for Susan's sake."

Vickie craned her neck and addressed John.

"You spoke to her about Lewis?"

"We move fast in these parts," he said lightly.

Vickie addressed Mary like an inquisitor. "Tell me about this guy of yours." Her eyes narrowed. "Does he look anything like John?"

"Don't worry." Mary rolled her eyes and looked away.

"Meaning?"

"John is a big boy who tucks himself into bed."

Vickie's face flushed crimson once again.

John smiled and feigned ignorance. "Hey, what did I do?"

Mary sighed heavily. "I had a boyfriend a while back who left for a job in Atlanta. He popped into town last night, and we had to party."

Vickie tried to hide her envy, but it filled her voice, as she had been the one all men wanted. "That's your age talking. No one has to party. You agreed to meet us at eight o'clock, but you failed to satisfy your commitment." She gestured at Mary. "Don't let it happen again."

"Aye, captain!" Mary saluted her newfound nemesis.

Vickie turned and looked through the side window, seeing little.

"While you're at it, take a shower. Your hair is greasy."

She craned again. "Did you hear what I said, Mary Bishop?"

Mary was embarrassed, but she withheld a response.

"She apologized for her mistake." John stiffened. "Let it go."

"All right," said Vickie, shrugging. "Don't be so sensitive."

She faced Mary again and gave her a look of suspicion.

"Are you sure there's nothing I should know about you two?"

Mary threw her an awkward glance. "There are others."

"Others?" Vickie looked at John. "Do I really want to know?"

"Well, there's Rachel Daniels. She's been after him for years."

"Like you, I imagine."

It was Mary's turn to blush. "I suppose."

"Who else?"

Mary glanced at John, but he shook his head.

"None that I can mention. It wouldn't be right."

"Fine."

Vickie faced the road with clarity. She took a breath and exhaled, and gloom overtook her as she gazed at the trees, seeing them pass in a blur, recognizing their vague form while thoughts overwhelmed her senses, telling her she was worthless and no one could ever love her.

Minutes passed in silence, and finally her self-scorn and bitter panic subsided, though her losses remained dark and cold and irreparable.

"I was sorry to hear about the show," said Mary in a hopeful tone.

"My selfishness caused a girl's death. I have to live with the fallout."

Vickie hoped the truth might mend their broken fences.

"And you lied about Price Brewer all those years." Mary flustered, as if she knew her comment was inappropriate. She hesitated and then grew sincere. "I shouldn't have thrown that in your face, but I'm ashamed about how I look and a little bummed about my boyfriend."

Mary would soon redirect, as there was a purpose in her voice, the same ambition that had driven Vickie for the last two decades.

"Your success makes me jealous," she said presently.

Vickie snorted. "Are you joking?"

"You are the face of cable news."

"That's a wretched line if there ever was one. Try again."

"I want your fame, your set of experiences, your wealth."

"I see."

"What do you see?"

"You are too simple to follow your dreams."

Mary embodied defeat. "It's true, Vickie. Maybe I'm not you."

"You might be someday, but you have a long way to go."

"Will you help me? I'll put aside my jealousy, if you will."

Vickie offered a dim smile as she ran her coat sleeve across the foggy window. A small-town reporter envied a washed-up fossil whose name was now tied to rape for eternity? It made about as much sense as anything else of late. When Vickie considered her background, her chest tightened and her reserves drained. She hadn't slept well in weeks.

Reggie happened upon a kill buyer farm ahead on the right.

"Find a side entrance and sneak up to the barn," Vickie said.

"You must be crazy." He gestured and threw an angry look at her. "Those guys have rifles, and they'll drop us from fifty yards out."

Vickie's eyebrows arched in indignation.

"Then let's just sit here and stare at them like fools."

"Sounds about right," John said. "We'll live longer."

Reggie idled the van on the road, and the group watched those who entered and exited a tattered horse barn. To their left, a monstrous truck pulled up and a burly, sneering man tapped his window with a pistol.

Reggie glowered at Vickie. "Can we leave now?"

"Floor it," she said flatly. "Before we're shot to pieces."

Each member of the group periodically spied over their shoulder in hopes the burly man and the immense truck would not follow, and each member breathed a sigh of relief when the highway curved out of sight.

John leaned forward. "Will you drive us to my cousin's farm?"

"Why must we go there?" Vickie tried to keep a neutral face.

"I should check on the girls. They don't have anyone else."

She leaned over and faced him. "What about Missy and Lee?"

"Their clients overwhelm them with work, and I have more time."

Her eyes widened. "There's more, so let's have it."

John set his jaw. "The girls never knew their father, so I'm trying."

"To replace him?" Vickie pushed her hair back in frustration. "You never married Michelle like she wanted, nor did you marry me, but like a fool, you chose that nasty woman, Carlie Hill, who cheated on you with your own brother." Vickie had reserved support after his divorce; they hadn't spoken for years and a call seemed inappropriate. "Look, I'm sorry for my bluntness, and I don't mean to hit below the belt."

"You do a good impression of someone who does, Vickie."

"And I'm sorry they both died. It must have been hard on you."

"It hasn't been easy, but it's why I should focus on the girls."

Vickie weighed the danger of her next comment but proceeded.

"You think you owe Michelle for breaking her heart, but you don't."

He smirked. "Look who's talking. The selfish sister."

John needed kind words and a soothing tone, so she would offer them, even if he was a brute. "You are a good man. Do you know that?"

His eyes moistened, and he looked away, and then he returned to her. "They need you, too, Vickie, and you know I'm right."

"I'll grant they need a mother."

"But you won't be one for them?"

Vickie stiffened. "Trust me when I say I'm no good."

"You're no monster, either, and they don't need a perfect mother."

"A monster is exactly what I am, John, and if you knew me better, you'd agree and you would look for some other woman to please you."

John glanced at an anguished Mary and squeezed her hand.

He turned back to Vickie and spoke with renewed determination.

"I don't want anyone else. Never have, never will."

Vickie gave him an incredulous stare. "You've been with others since me, as our good friend Mary has already stated, so don't play games."

"I'm talking about love, not sex, and I don't do that anymore."

"What, have sex? Did you become a monk since we last met?"

She chuckled to herself, as if the notion was inconceivable.

"Where you and God are concerned, yes, I am now a monk."

She rolled her eyes. "Men say things, but they never stay."

"I'm not most men, and you know it."

An image of Raul flashed across her mind, and she missed him.

"Look, you tend to the girls and I'll work out the details of my father's estate, and then I'll go back to D.C. We'll both be happier."

John crossed his arms and looked past Mary at the passing scenery.

"Whatever."

"Good. I'm glad we got that settled."

Vickie followed his lead and gazed through her window.

He spoke over her shoulder. "The horses need you as much as the girls, if not more, but you'll abandon them like you run from everyone else who matters." He fell silent, and she braced for the worst. "You've always been predictable, but I hoped this time you might be different."

"I'm not, John. I'm the abominable snowman you need me to be."

He leaned forward, and with a rough hand, turned her chin.

"You'll keep those horses at Bluecreek, or there will be hell to pay."

He sat back and stared at her with a look of disgust.

She faced him with her entire body and with fire in her eyes.

"What does that mean?"

"It means try me and find out. Now turn around and fume."

Turbulence lingered, disengaging Vickie from the group, taking her back to the winter of 1987, when Red purchased a horse farm on Route 15 and named it Bluecreek Stables. He expanded the barn to three runways, each with twenty stalls, and bought sixty horses for Michelle to train, in hopes the experience she gained would establish her name in the area and place her career on firm ground. It was a good plan for

Michelle, as she had dreamed of working with horses since childhood, and she got along well with the horses and their owners. Ranchers would visit her clinics, take home tips, and they would ask her to help them with their horse problems in the future. Vickie understood Red's reasoning, and she forced herself to admit a need for a new and exciting venture in her own life, but Michelle and the herd needed her to remain in Addison.

She had lowered her eyes and avoided her father's probing look.

When he demanded a response, she asked to work with Michelle, but Red shook his head. Vickie had argued with her suicidal mother before Valerie took the keys, and then she failed to deter her mother from weaving along the highway at a high rate of speed, and now she owed a debt. In Red's estimation, it was Vickie who should have died on that fateful day, and to make amends, she must live the life Valerie would have wished for her, the one Red could provide through his contacts. Michelle tried to interrupt her father's rant, but Red sent her to bed. He then drew Vickie near and spoke peacefully and said she would enter the world of network news and his contacts would make her a star.

With the recent death of Jessica Savitch, which some called murder, network executives searched for the next face of the nightly news.

"No one will dare question your pedigree, nor your potential."

He drew back from her and looked into her eyes.

"We owe it to Valerie to make the most of your life, don't we?"

Vickie sighed. "I suppose."

She paused.

"Mama said to make you proud."

He squeezed her shoulders with both hands.

"We'll both make her proud, which is even better."

Vickie wiped a tear. "I'll give it all I've got."

As the gray chill of morning advanced to bright afternoon, the sun thawed the roads and bridges that passed before them, and at last they pulled up to Missy's farm and eased into her welcoming driveway.

John slid open the side door. "How's the pregnant mare?"

Missy cast a frown and glanced at the barn.

"Savannah's stable for now, but she has a weak heart."

"Savannah?" John looked at Katie, who shrugged.

She pointed at her sister. "Abbie named them when they arrived."

He grimaced, knowing these horses would prove troublesome to the child, as she grew attached in an instant. "How about the foal?"

"He seems okay, but his mother may not make it to delivery."

"That's a real shame, Missy. I wanted a good life for her."

"There's another horse named Dash with a hurt back leg who could use some attention." Missy gestured to follow her. "I'll show you."

Abbie took Vickie's hand and squeezed it as they walked to the barn. Vickie glanced behind her at Mary, who gave her a knowing look.

Mary's face shined. "She likes you."

"Who wouldn't?"

John's anger mounted at Vickie's arrogance toward Mary, who was no threat to her, and for her unwillingness to help Michelle's children.

Inside the barn, he stared into the stall and considered his options.

He turned to Missy. "We'll take the mare."

"Her name is Savannah." Abbie's look noted her displeasure.

"I'm sorry. We'll take Savannah, the pregnant mare."

Abbie raised an eyebrow and gave him a shy smile.

Missy rubbed her neck, and her gaze bounced from the horse to John and back to the horse. "Did you hear what I said about her heart?"

"I heard you. I also want Dash, the horse with the leg."

Vickie stepped forward. "With whose money?"

"Yours, of course. Don't you want to help them?"

"It's not about money, but I don't have an unlimited supply."

"You have more money than you could ever spend."

He pointed at Missy and told himself to keep calm. "My cousin has limited resources, and these two horses no longer need her care."

"I understand if you'd rather not." Missy looked Vickie up and down. "It's better to be alone than with people who don't want you."

John held up his hand, silencing Missy, who wanted to say more.

He rushed at Vickie with a threatening look. "We've got many horses in the area, and that means kill buyers. There's more going on here than you understand, so you'll have to trust me, but soon there will be even more horses who need Missy's care, and it would be best if we funneled them through her farm for treatment and then to Bluecreek for training and re-homing." He caught his breath. "Once we find stable homes for the healthiest, we'll let them go, and the cycle will repeat."

Her nostrils flared, and her feet planted wide.

"How long?"

"Why is it always about time with you?"

"I'm going back to D.C. once I sell Bluecreek."

"You hated it there, and you had no life."

"I'm smarter now, and with Red's money, I can get back to the top."

"The top of what?" He sneered and tried to level his voice. "Why do you care so much about things that won't matter in a thousand years?"

She swallowed hard. "You have me all wrong."

"What then? Stop playing games with me, Vickie."

"I will make documentaries, the kind that expose the Washington political scene. More goes on there than you can imagine, and I will bring it to the light of day." She hesitated. "It may kill me in the end, but I already have the first subject in mind. Her name is Irene."

John rubbed his temples and considered letting her go.

He squinted. "Documentaries no one cares about?"

"I will make them care, John."

Her words infuriated him. "We need you here and now in Addison. Are we not good enough for the great Victoria Morrison?"

Vickie threw up her hands and groaned.

He grabbed her arms and brought them down to her sides, and then he squeezed her shoulders. "I've had enough. You will do what I say."

She spat in his face and marched to the van as he recoiled in shock.

The love of his life had cast a great weariness upon him for years.

Vickie and Reggie traveled along the winding roads, with runs of farms on the right-hand side and beyond, as rolling hills gave way to forested earth that ascended to lofty heights, blending curiously with another and still another ridge, as the chain crested and toppled infinitely.

She recalled her after-school internship at the television station and the way people treated her during her formative years. She could never make it up to her mother nor to Red, who blamed her for Valerie's death, and she believed she did not deserve to be happy. Daily Red told her she was a terrible daughter for missing what had unfolded in Valerie's psyche. Vickie saw her life as a great big awful falsehood, since her mother didn't want her as a daughter or even to live on this earth as her mother, and the result was a mix of love and anger and disappointment.

Over time, Red got over his grief and then pressured Vickie to let her mother go, which of course would never happen in a million years.

Some in town saw Vickie as a bad seed. When first asked about her mother, she feigned ignorance, as if she wasn't sure what happened that tragic afternoon, but then she talked openly about her mother's suicide and the grownups ostracized her. Circulating gossip benefited a rival girl at school, Haley Johnson, who used it to her advantage, mocking Vickie as trash whom teachers should throw out the back door.

Vickie felt betrayed, but she still loved Valerie and wanted her to land on the porch, alive and happy and ready to once again become her mother, this time with love, but the moment never arrived and she fell adrift and unable to trust anyone, especially God, who let it happen.

Her suicidal thoughts alarmed Michelle and annoyed Red, so he sent her to the television station, where she would work after school and on weekends, without dissent or excuse or compensation.

At his insistence, the staff gave her no breaks, nor any leg up, nor much encouragement, and she became a dutiful errand girl.

The manager, Laura Henagar, took notice of Vickie's potential and put her with a journalist, Ellen Myers, saying she could make it all the way, but Ellen was honest to a fault, and men didn't like those traits in a woman. Vickie made a mental note to push as hard as possible without ruffling too many feathers, especially among her insecure male cohorts.

The work isolated her. Few gave her any attention or respect.

After a year, she grew adept at cutting field footage into broadcast segments, and she earned esteem as an editor, a rare reputation for even the most hardened of journalists, much less an intern. Every so often, Red would stop by, ask Laura about Vickie's progress, and then leave the station without a word, and each time he left, his abandonment broke Vickie's heart, as she knew he would praise Michelle for the slightest of accomplishments and chastise Vickie for her mistakes.

Laura saw Vickie's hurt and offered extra support on those days, becoming like a mother so the teen would feel less abused by her father.

Several months later, Laura placed Vickie on a field assignment, one that no one else wanted, as they viewed the story as pithy and having little chance of making the air, but Vickie took her break seriously and won over the best cameraman by forming a friendship with his wife and within a week, she had sorted their marital problems. Together, they turned in a solid piece on local kill buyers, exposing documentary-style the process by which families bought prize Thoroughbreds for eventing or Quarter Horses for barrel racing, and once the child's equestrian phase passed, the family sold the horse at auction, unaware of kill buyers who fabricated stories of a happy home life on a farm that never checked out, and the horses suffered until their horrifying death in a rancid Mexican slaughterhouse. After the news segment aired, the sheriff closed a kill buyer farm out in the county, and Vickie received a pat on the back from the mayor and from Laura Henagar.

Red had little to say about her win, but at least he wasn't furious.

John arrived with Dash and Savannah while Vickie sipped coffee on the porch. She regretted their argument the previous day and how awful she had acted. She felt like a petulant child more than an adult.

"I'm sorry, John."

He hesitated and then smiled. "Bet that hurt to say."

"You do not know."

She squeezed his arm. "Seriously, I won't do that anymore."

"Good, because it was a first for me and I'd rather not repeat it."

Vickie considered.

"We kiss, so what's the difference?" She grinned innocently.

"One comes from love and the other, hatred."

"I love you, John. That isn't the problem."

John turned toward the barn without glancing down at her. When he faced her next, a strange concern shone in his eyes and he seemed to look through her to the future. "Yet you have to leave me again?"

She nodded.

"What's pulling you back is obvious, and it might as well be twenty years ago when you couldn't get out of here fast enough, so you ran."

"You don't have any idea, but you think you know everything."

"Whatever." He smirked and faced the road.

His silence was torture, but at last he gave her his blue eyes.

"You need a break from your addiction."

"What addiction? I don't get drunk or stoned."

"You used to do both, so don't lie to me."

"I stopped those, and I no longer have sex, same as you."

He drew back a little. "Fine."

"We're both recovered addicts. How nice." She turned away to hide a smile, as she grew tired of watching him timidly, begging for his love.

"You can't get enough fame, Vickie." There was an unforgiving tilt to his voice, which spoke of an ancient wound, unhealed and open and with a waning hope. "These horses can help you leave it alone."

His observation shook her, and she wiped the tears that had formed and now threatened to give away her desperate love for him.

She stammered, unable to form a coherent answer; she wanted to scream foul obscenities but only murmured unintelligible words.

John scanned the house from top to bottom and then looked at the barn and the pasture. His appraisal of her had somehow fallen lower than ever, and it was more than her fragile heart could endure.

Vickie slammed her mug on the table.

"What else is wrong with me?"

"Did Red actually leave you this estate?"

She recoiled. "If you're after my money, buddy, let me reassure you, I'm no pushover, and you won't get one cent from my bank account."

He drew nearer, and she stood, unsure, as his hand passed across her brow. She paced backward, and he followed her, pointing a finger.

"My father owns a shipping company, and he will soon pass. With Chris and Carlie gone, I'll inherit everything, so I don't need your wealth, but I do need your help in rescuing these wounded horses."

A turn of fate had brought them together after twenty years, but today John seemed wild and discouraged, and he bore such animosity.

Vickie considered how best to address him.

"Why not build your own operation after Garrett dies?"

John seemed ready to hurt her. "It's a harsh question, don't you think? I might miss my father, unlike you, who hated Red."

Her cheeks burned. There was something about John that stole her self-confidence and replaced it with shame and uncertainty. She clasped her hands in front of her body. "You and Garrett had no love for one another in the past, and I assumed it was the same today."

She could no longer resist.

He bewildered her and wore her out.

He nodded coldly, and his voice fell flat. "Our relationship was strained at best, but I'm trying to be a good son in the end."

Her heart beat fast, and her ears buzzed, and the grimness of his mood consumed her. "You did great with Garrett at the hospital."

"There's more." John's eyes grew moist. "I'm supposed to take over the company after he dies and run it as he did, perhaps even expand our shipping routes." His face paled at the notion.

"You never followed Garrett's wishes before, so why start now?"

Tears coursed down John's cheeks.

He allowed her to see them with a passionate masculinity. "I'm not sure what the future holds for the company, but I will help these horses who have no one else, and I can't do it without you."

Katie exited the truck and loitered near the porch.

Vickie waved for her to come up and sit on the glider, and the teen complied. "I know you listened to our conversation," said Vickie in a soft, motherly fashion. "You might as well offer your opinion."

Dark circles had formed under Katie's eyes, as if she slept poorly most nights. "Things are good at Missy's farm, but it's not the same."

Vickie resolved to speak in a firm tone as she stroked Katie's hair.

"You girls should understand reality, as Bluecreek Stables won't be in my possession for much longer. I'll help John because it's the right thing to do, and believe it or not, I care about the horses and about you and Abbie, but once everyone is okay, Bluecreek goes up for sale."

"Why? You could stay here."

"Addison has never been my home. My life is in Washington."

Katie shifted in her seat, the picture of youthful unease.

"I should confess something," she said.

"What in the world could you confess, honey?"

"I'm the reason you got fired."

An hour later, John brought Dash to the tie-down area so they could have a look at his hind leg. John stood still and observed the horse, but Vickie's perfume distracted his wonderings and made him anxious, sending him back to his teenage years. Then, as now, he had tried to extricate himself from his father's wealth and influence, but Garrett made him feel ungrateful for each attempt at independence.

Once his father's diagnosis went from difficult to unfathomable, John had planned to leave. Vickie soon arrived and changed everything.

Her eyes grew suspicious. She wouldn't last much longer.

"Why are we staring at a horse? Don't play a joke on me, John."

"I've seen Missy do this, so be quiet and follow suit."

They both gazed for another minute as Dash withheld his

answer to their silent query but chose instead to stand peacefully motionless in the face of what passed for a careful and scientific observation.

"What has gotten into you, John? You're driving me mad."

He rubbed Dash's back. "That's your problem."

"What problem? I don't have any problems."

"Oh, yes, you do."

She crossed her arms. "All right, enlighten me."

"You have no patience. At all."

"I have plenty."

"Then stare at Dash and try to sense where he hurts."

She massaged her temples and seemed perplexed by the fuss.

"Is it what you're doing?"

John took both her hands and placed them on Dash's back.

"Try it."

"Well, if you'd tell me what's going on instead of acting like a weirdo, I might join in, but don't tell me I have no patience."

"Can you be quiet or not?"

"Watch me." She stepped back from both man and horse.

They stared at Dash, who swished his tail. The air had grown thick in the tie-down area. Vickie leaned over and flicked on a fan.

"Interesting." John rubbed his chin.

"The fan?"

He leaned slightly forward and gave her a conscientious look.

"The noise could have startled Dash, but he remained calm."

"Is it a good thing?"

"We don't want a half-crazed horse who's terrified of fans, so yes."

"Is that the extent of your knowledge? He's not afraid of fans?"

John crossed his arms. "You're right. You are hard to please."

"I am a journalist, and we gather facts. What are we doing here?"

He grinned. "Do you want the truth?"

"Of course."

"I don't have a clue."

She gave him an exaggerated shrug. "Now you tell me."

"Here's the deal. These horses have above-average intelligence and volatile tempers from being mistreated by their previous owners."

He gestured in her direction, and his annoyance showed.

"Like you, they're a misunderstood lot, but if you'll take the time to really get to know them, I'm sure you'll find much in common."

Vickie pointed at Dash. "With a horse?"

John rubbed Dash's back and ran his hand down the leg, toward the pastern, locating the spot where he hurt. Dash looked at her and his eyes flashed. "See? It's only a matter of time before we develop an empathic bond with the animal. When that happens, he'll tell us where to look."

"Communication without words?"

He smiled. "Otherwise known as E.S.P."

"Now I know you've gone bananas." She took a step back and looked about the barn. "So you fancy yourself some kind of whisperer?"

"Me? No way. I'm talking about you."

She laughed. "So I'm the guru with all the answers? I can't keep a job in the news business, but I cure horses with the touch of my finger."

"Not cure, but diagnose, and not with a touch, but a connection of your spirit with theirs. Mankind has been doing it for thousands of years, and not just with horses. I knew a guy once who connected with his cows, and you read about shepherds in the Bible having the same sort of empathic bond. It's why Jesus taught about going after one lost sheep, even if the day is the Sabbath. The shepherd is so attached, he can't bear to let even one sheep go, no matter the difficulty."

Vickie threw her hands in the air. "Am I the sheep in your scenario?"

"You're resisting. When you accept your gift, this will come easier."

"Whatever." She went outside, leaving him standing with Dash.

John led the horse back to his stall and found her on the porch.

"I thought you wanted to help them, not convince me I'm a healer."

"I want to do both at the same time." He looked about the area and then turned to her. "This facility can do much good, but it means little without someone empathic at its center. Otherwise, it's just a building, and these horses have seen plenty of those. They need someone like you, a sad woman whom people have hurt, someone who shares their pain, a woman who understands what it's like to be abandoned, and worse."

"While we were with Dash, I felt nothing." Vickie swiped her tears. "You think I'm a decent person, but you are way off the mark. I read the news of the day to an unsuspecting public, and I feel nothing while I do it." She hesitated. "Other than glee. If you want the truth, there are moments when I'm proud of myself for hurting people. If they were having a nice day, and I ruined it for them, then all the better." She pointed at the barn. "You want someone like me to help these animals?"

"It's why you're the perfect fit."

"You make no sense." She stood, but John pulled her back down.

"Like everyone else, you dislike grace and truth. You're not satisfied with justice, as in Price paying his debt to society, or goodness, as in your ability to communicate with these horses. When John the Baptist arrived on the scene in righteousness, people said he wasn't human like a normal man, and a demon must have possessed him because he was too harsh, and when Christ came after him, people accused Him of being a friend to sinners. Ministers speak of God's righteousness, but the people turn and say the law is too strict. They plead with God to allow their imperfections, but He makes no provision for the fallen flesh."

"What does all of that nonsense have to do with me?"

"Price served his time and now seeks life as an honest man, but you won't allow it, as you see only the criminal who stole your innocence, the man who raped your mother." John suffered with Vickie as he spoke to her. "Price has hidden nothing from you, but he's come to you in truth and has asked for your grace. Why not forgive him in love and become the woman God meant you to be?" He pointed sharply. "These damaged horses need you. Price and the girls need you. And so do I."

"I don't get you, John. You've lost your mind."

"Don't you see? You've been in the wrong business, the career Red sent you to conquer, the one meant for someone else, but not for you."

He gripped her chin and turned it toward the barn.

She resisted for the briefest of moments, but it was little use.

"This is where you're supposed to be, not in D.C. telling off the public. Here you can make a difference, not just in the lives of horses, but in Katie and Abbie's upbringing, and in my own lonely life as well."

Vickie locked eyes with him, and the anguish overwhelmed her. She couldn't take much more. "What are you saying? You love me?"

"I'm saying I need you to stay. Let's see what develops. After twenty years of being apart, I think we should investigate the possibilities."

His right hand gripped her hair, pulling her head backward as his left hand caressed her cheek. He drew into her and his lips kissed her deeply. He drew back and smiled. Vickie thought she might faint.

"All right," she said. "When you put it like that, who am I to argue?"

Eight

Psalm 48:1

How great is the Lord,
how deserving of praise,
in the city of our God,
which sits on his holy mountain!

March 2008

Katie and Vickie toured the tack room, where the teen pointed to buckles, ropes, and harnesses and explained the function of a western saddle, how styles varied across activities such as herding cattle, racing barrels, or riding trails. Two six-foot wooden bins caught her eye near the doorway; one held sweet pellets for energy and the other grain pellets for stamina. Horses really liked to eat, so John regulated their portions, but in the spring, when winter's death gave way to life and birds chirped amid the budded trees and deer stirred from their slumber and the green grass grew with abandon, they filled their bellies without restraint, as the world abounded and delighted.

Katie glowed as she spoke. "Alfalfa hay offers more protein than any other feed, and it's good for neglected rescues who are usually starving." She took a breath and spoke gravely. "They're like people with Type II diabetes, and if we gave them too much at first, they could die."

"How did you learn all of this?"

"Mom read horse books, but she tried new things all the time to see what worked and what didn't. She said mistakes teach great lessons."

"I'm impressed," Vickie said. "With her and with you."

Katie grinned and crossed her arms. "Thanks."

John, who had been observing from the tack room, went inside to open the envelope Vickie had left for him. On the cover, she had scrawled, "Please read my mother's letter and help me cope, because very little works anymore and I fear myself. Since my arrival, and especially when we're together, I am a little girl." He laid the letter flat on the counter.

To my daughter,

I sit here at my desk and wonder about tomorrow.

You are playing in front of the television in the living room, a funny label if there ever was one, as hardly any life occurs in a room where entertainment dominates.

Red controls me and this town. He has the sheriff in his pocket, along with attorneys and judges. There's no going against him here or anywhere in America, as his reach extends farther than you can imagine.

As I sit here, I can no longer be his wife.

You are the product of a rape at the hands of a man named Price Brewer, and I see him in you, bits and pieces, which makes me ashamed of the role I played in giving life to a monster's baby.

I look at my walls as late afternoon sunlight filters above the curtains and I consider my great losses.

I have endured too many since girlhood and as I sit here at my desk, there are too many reminders of an innocence which will never return, and I can no longer cope with the passage of time as I once did.

Red knows I slip deeper into madness and soon he will have me committed to an asylum, so I will take the keys which burn in my pocket and I will venture to an unknowable land, hopeful of a kind welcome. Be the monster Red needs you to be, for it will justify him and it will make me proud, for I am every ounce as monstrous as you, my child, the purveyor of doom.

Your departed mother, Valerie

John carefully folded the page and slipped it inside the envelope.

Vickie leaving such a hurtful keepsake was a test, and he would show her love with his actions rather than words. He grabbed a rubber curry and a dandy brush and called her to Dash's stall. She followed him but smirked and asked if he would play a joke on her. He held up the curry. "Rub clockwise, and when you're done, whisk dirt from his hair with the dandy brush like this." His other hand illustrated an upward flick. "Return these when you've finished and grab a soft body brush and follow the flow of the hairline." John slid his palm from Dash's withers to his ribs and belly. "See how it runs down and back?" He pointed to the hip. "Here it runs up and over and then jogs down the thigh."

He paused.

"Piece of cake for a smart journalist like yourself."

"Cake? I have no idea what you just said."

"What do you mean?" He moved the curry in a gentle circle. "Start like this." He handed it to her. "Seriously, you can't go wrong here."

She hesitated and took the curry as if it were a deadly weapon.

"I have a bad feeling about this, John."

Dash turned his head and snorted.

"He's getting impatient, so go ahead before he stomps on your foot."

She laughed. "How hard should I rub?"

"As hard as you would your own hair. How's that?"

"Depends on my mood. Some days I'd rip out every strand."

He sighed, and a smile broke across his face.

She took his cue and groomed Dash, who liked her touch. A glow enveloped her, which warmed John's heart, as she seemed at home.

His eyes fell on Katie, who sat on a feed bin, reading her Bible. He left Vickie in the stall and sat beside the teen to her right. "What's up?"

"Not too much." Her eyes rose to Vickie. "Is she getting it yet?"

He smiled. "Sort of, but not really."

"Is that why you didn't take her to the tie-down area?"

He nodded.

"I wasn't sure if she'd take to grooming or run away, since you never can tell how she'll react to new things, but she seems to like Dash, and once she started working on him, I sensed a peace come over her."

"It will take time to learn," Katie said. "Don't expect miracles."

"I know, but we'll keep working with her and she'll get there."

Katie sighed. "Until she leaves."

"I suppose."

Katie closed her Bible with a thud. "So, what's going on between you and Leslie Carter? Is she your girlfriend, your fiancée, or what? Missy said Leslie didn't want you on the campaign trail."

"That's one way to put it, but not very nice to say out loud."

"Sorry, but I'm direct."

Katie's eyebrows raised in anticipation of a straight answer.

"If you must know all about my love life, it hurt my feelings when she said I should stay home, and we haven't spoken since she left."

"Are you still a couple?"

He grinned. "Who knows?"

Katie seemed uneasy. "I'm serious, John."

He glanced at Vickie in Dash's stall and knew she was listening.

"Let's just say we're seeing other people."

Katie's eyes moved to Dash's stall and back to John.

"Are you in love with Vickie?"

A voice reached him from across the runway. "Yeah, John, tell her."

Vickie stood with brush in hand and a smirk on her face.

"Are you in love with the great Victoria Morrison?"

The air thickened between them. "We were in love a long time ago."

Vickie seemed disappointed. She returned to grooming Dash.

Katie's eyes widened in astonishment, as all intimacy had fled the barn and what remained seemed more like stone, weighing them down to some deeper depth, stifling their oxygen, refusing a restorative breath.

"Why wouldn't you tell her? Vickie wanted you to say the words."

"I told her I don't want anyone else. Does that count?"

Katie nodded, but still seemed reticent. "It's not the same, though."

He shrugged. "Guess not." He glanced at Vickie, who now ignored him. "We might get there in the end, but there's history to overcome."

"Does her fame scare you?"

Her question annoyed him, but he would be honest to a fault.

"Probably a little. Millions of people know her name and hardly anyone knows mine, twenty years removed from high school and working in this small town. I have little to show for my life but these calloused hands." He raised his palms and noted their rough texture, made from decades of work and bar fights and mornings in the rain.

Vickie completed her tasks and returned the tools to the tack room.

When she passed them on the feed bin, John's heart skipped.

Katie gave him an admiring look. "Vickie's eyes sparkle when she's around you, John. There's something there, no matter what you say."

"For me, too." The notion left him an insecure wanderer.

"Don't mess it up like you normally do. We need her."

Vickie's boots descended the tack room steps.

She offered a coy smile and sat on the bin to Katie's left.

"What schemes are you two planning?"

"I read my study Bible when I'm bored."

"Why?"

"It helps me deal with life and I learn things."

Vickie chuckled. "I've never been very religious."

Katie gave her a look of rebuke, so Vickie caught herself.

"What are you reading about, specifically?"

"Water baptism and why it's important."

"Would you teach me?"

"It depends. Do you really want to learn, or are you being mean?"

Vickie put her arm around Katie. "Teach me, professor."

Katie stood in front of the bin and Vickie leaned on her hands.

"The word comes from the Greek and means to dip or to immerse, and there are four types. The first is Baptism into the Body of Christ, which is the church. The second is Baptism into Water, which is the first step of obedience to the Lord and His call to the church body. The third is Baptism into the Holy Spirit, which fills the believer with the Holy Spirit's presence and power. The fourth is Baptism of Fire, which is baptism into sufferings, as believers must follow in the footsteps of Jesus, who suffered on the cross for our wickedness."

"Once again, I'm impressed."

Vickie patted her hand on the bin.

"Come sit by me so we can talk some more." She waited as an eager Katie complied. "The priest poured water over my head three times and anointed me with oil. I was only a baby, so I don't remember much."

"It's all right."

"Do you miss your mother?"

Katie nodded.

"Is it why you told Mitch about Price?"

Katie nodded again and wiped a tear. "I was angry about not having parents because it wasn't fair, and I resented you never coming home to see Mom after she fell, or even for her funeral." Katie took the Bible and placed it on her lap. "You wouldn't go to Red's funeral either, and then you made us go live at Missy's farm. Do you care about us at all?"

Vickie rubbed Katie's back and gave her a faint smile.

"I don't know you, and I barely knew Michelle or Red. Once I learned who my father was, and how I had entered this world, the knowledge crushed my spirit, and I left Addison. The only reason I came home was because I got fired and had to handle Red's estate."

"I'm sorry for what I did, but please let us live with you."

Vickie sighed. "The problem is, I see myself in you and Abbie."

"I thought you didn't like her."

"Valerie died when I was her age, and the portrait of my mother's body on the side of the highway still haunts me. Whenever I look at Abbie, or at you sometimes, when you smile just right, I see me as a kid, wondering why God took my mother." Vickie hesitated. "At eighteen, I learned my father was a rapist, and I was the product of his rape. Suddenly everything made sense." She swiped at her tears. "I was a beast just like him, and I had driven my mother to suicide. I had no right to expect happiness, and my only prospect was a gloomy career delivering bad news to an unsuspecting public, so I attacked my job with relish."

"There's more if you want it," John said. "I know you think love is conditional, but we're right here." He gestured at Katie. "You're the one talking about leaving, not us. We're in it for the long haul."

A door to his heart fell open, and he hoped to draw Vickie inside and show her the love which was denied her, the love she deserved.

"John, everyone says those things, but no one sticks around."

Her fingers clutched at the feed bin. "Even Mitch betrayed me with Nellie, live, in front of millions, and only because I wouldn't marry him. We lived together, and he had dreams of us becoming a power couple, husband and wife hobnobbing with the rich and famous, but after a while, I couldn't stand being with him. I felt like a fraud."

"Then do something real for the summer," John said. "In the fall, if you still want to leave, we'll understand and get out of your way."

His eyes met Katie's, and he spoke with deep feeling.

"Who knows? Maybe I can take these girls after my father passes. Missy would be glad to help, since she's head over heels for them."

"You'd do a better job as a father than I'd ever do as a mother."

He sighed. "That's probably true."

Katie burst into laughter.

Vickie frowned but forced a laugh. "Jerk."

He feigned innocence. "Hey, you started it."

"So I'll end it." Vickie ran over to him and tickled his sides.

Katie jumped up and joined her aunt, as he tried unsuccessfully to block their attempts, giggling like a schoolboy having the time of his life.

John was glad the girls and Vickie could experience some normalcy, as neither had known a real family life, and neither had he, when he really thought about it. His father was unavailable and his mother, Nicole, was unstable. To make matters worse, he grew up in the shadow of his brother, who was good at everything and seemed born for this world in a way John would never understand. He was considered stupid and clumsy, while Chris was the consummate athlete, good at everything, even ping-pong and swimming. The pressure to live up to his brother grew unbearable, making him feel he had little to offer.

He had to distinguish himself but he didn't know how, and his low expectations coupled with his brother's pity drove him to take an interest in horses, as they were also prey. He worked with them from an early age, much as Abbie was now doing. When John met Carlie Hill and fell in love, she refused to marry him but wouldn't say why or even call their relationship exclusive, preferring to keep her options open. She made jokes about sharing a bed with him and said if they ever got married, they would need two houses, two cars, and two beds, as she wouldn't sleep with him. John wanted to respect Carlie's fears of marriage and so he tried to love her unconditionally, but he resented her unwillingness to return his love, as it touched a sorrowful nerve from his childhood, left there by a schizophrenic mother who checked out on him without hearing the words "I love you" one last time, words John had wanted to say to her, as she was his mother and such things were eternally true, no matter how much pain she might have caused.

After Nicole perished tragically in an asylum fire, John wrestled with questions of right and wrong, as he was both happy and sad, but her death left him flawed and less popular than other guys his own age.

Past failures paralyzed him, but the joy exhibited by the cool kids motivated his conventional side, and he hoped to rise in social standing.

However, bullies took advantage of his vulnerabilities and soon pressured him to cheat on an exam and lie to the principal when confronted. John's life spiraled downward from there, but he denied his relationship problems with Carlie until the bitter end. As a bright college student with eyes toward the future, she told him to give up the farrier life and help his father run Skyline Shipping. John listened to her and quit working with horses for a while, going to work in the bowels of the company, ensuring he knew what went on from the bottom to the top. He developed a dislike for the operation and left in early summer for a wrangler job at Horseshoe Lake dude ranch summer camp. Garrett grew livid and asked what in the world John thought he was doing with himself.

"Living," John said.

"Well then, you can live somewhere else other than my house."

John went to work at the camp, and their relationship reverted to normal, but after the summer ended, she returned to Brockton University and broke up with him in a letter, one which confused him, as it held him up for ridicule. No matter how much he might implore her to change her mind, she would not be deterred, as there were important people to meet and grand pianos yet to play.

Thursday afternoon it warmed, and John brought Garrett to the farm so he could observe the horses from the porch. John sat beside his father on the glider. "Who's tending to the company while you're sick?"

"My vice president knows the business. He does a phenomenal job in my absence because he knows my motto: if you're not first, you're last." Garrett winced as if in pain, but regained his boldness. "If you decide to keep up this charade instead of running my company after I'm gone, it will be all right. You can sell or let Jim keep the operation afloat."

Garrett reflected.

"If you do the latter, offer Jim a quarter stake."

Vickie walked Dash in the front pasture to exercise his leg.

She approached the gate, which opened inward, careful to avoid Wildfire and Hero. She seemed agitated and unsure when near them.

Lewis stood nearby, watching her as he leaned against the pasture fence. He climbed the rails with ease, but fell when he landed and grew embarrassed. Price had observed the scene unfold from the barn. He strolled over to the pasture with an encouraging countenance and perched himself at the top of the fence. He recited Psalm 48:4-7 loudly. "The kings of the earth joined forces and advanced against the city. But when they saw it, they were stunned; they were terrified and ran away. They were gripped with terror and writhed in pain like a woman in labor. You destroyed them like the mighty ships of Tarshish shattered by a powerful east wind." Lewis dusted off his pants as he listened.

He gave Price a confused look. "What does it mean?"

"Kings assembled to attack Jerusalem, but its marvelous beauty struck them and they would not attack it for fear of their safety."

"I wish it had worked out in Afghanistan, but it didn't."

Price smiled faithfully. "Your war isn't over yet."

John sauntered over and hopped the fence, infuriating Lewis, and made a beeline for Vickie and Dash in the field. "Let me show you."

She stepped back from him. "I can do it."

He shook his head. "There's a right way to do everything."

"Fine." Vickie relinquished the lead rope.

John kept Dash's head near as they walked side by side to the gate. He snapped the latch, and the gate creaked as it swung inward. John stepped backward and held the lead rope tight so Dash would follow his movement, which he did. Once the gate opened all the way, he and Dash moved through and stopped on the other side, and then John turned his horse to the right and they moved in unison back through the opening. He and Dash stepped forward, and John pulled the gate shut.

He nodded and grinned sarcastically as Vickie leaned against the fence, watching him. John waved his free hand. "Something like that."

"I see."

"Don't be defensive. You need training and you know it."

"Will you help me? I don't want to look like an idiot."

He then showed her how to tie Dash to a rail and how to turn him when he was bound to one spot. He illustrated how to lead Dash through the pasture, how to back him and turn him, and how to fit a halter. She then returned Dash to his stall, as his leg was likely tired.

She emerged from the barn with a gleam in her eyes and sat beside Garrett on the glider. Wildfire pawed at hard dirt, and the clamor from his hooves reached their ears as a thud, which sounded more like an axe head cementing itself into solid oak than a whimsical gesture. The horse aligned himself perfectly with Vickie, nose, eyes, and raised tail.

An image of her paralyzed form flashed through John's mind.

"Wow, there's a lot to learn about horses," she said. "Who knew?"

She took several gulps from a water bottle as John drew near her.

Price appeared with an enthusiastic air but without Lewis, who had disappeared. Price took out a handkerchief and coughed into it, then precisely folded the cloth and stuffed it into his pocket with a smile.

"Will Lewis be okay?" Vickie threw him a concerned look.

Price smiled. "Oh, yes. The fall merely hurt his pride."

She pushed into the glider. "It must be hard on him as a veteran."

"Our war hero will be all right," said John coldly. "He's seen worse."

"So have I, but it doesn't mean I like to be humiliated."

"You must, since you set yourself up for it continually."

She playfully slapped his arm. "That's not very nice."

"But oh, so true." John's chiding seemed to suit her.

He put his hands on her shoulders, and she squeezed one of them. "We're done for today. Dash is tired and the mare's heart is too weak and the other horses are too much for you, especially Wildfire."

"I might surprise," she said. "I used to help Michelle."

"Pity," said Price thoughtfully. "I can help her with the fierce ones."

"Did you see many in prison?" asked John, who sat on the steps.

Price nodded.

"All were rescues who'd been through hard times. It was a good alignment for us inmates, as we'd seen our share of brutality."

"Another day." John spoke kindly but with firmness.

Garrett leaned forward and sneered. "There's nothing here for rapists, so I guess you'll have nothing to do. Yes, what a pity."

"Dad, quiet down." John rose to his feet.

"Don't shush me. I'm just getting started."

She interrupted. "Why do you care so much? Price is my father, and it's my decision to let him live here and work with our horses."

"I'm not surprised. You Brewers stick together like molasses, and it's why I never wanted John to have anything to do with you."

Vickie stiffened. "You allowed him to date Michelle."

"She was a real Morrison, not a pretender like yourself."

Price smiled wanly. "I'm so glad you called me father."

She crossed her arms. "It's who you are, no matter if I dislike it."

"It's a wonderful thing for me to hear at this age, and I thank you."

"Whatever." She looked past him to the highway.

Price wiped his moist eyes and turned to Garrett. "Please stop attacking my daughter. She needs serenity, not your criticisms."

"The folks you murdered have it in bunches, now don't they?"

"Why must you repeat the same tired line?"

Garrett struggled to his feet, and John rushed up the steps to help.

"I'll tell you why, you dirty, old reprobate, a man who has done nothing worthwhile in his entire worthless life. I followed Valerie Morrison on a two-lane stretch the afternoon she died. You victimized the poor girl so badly she became a raging alcoholic and a pill popper who committed suicide in a station wagon. I parked on the side of the road and ran up to her door and pulled her bloody body into my lap, where she whispered your name with her last breaths, begging you to save her." Garrett hesitated. "I was a man of God before that day, but since then I've wanted nothing to do with Him, and I blame you for killing that innocent girl, along with the remnants of my faith."

Price openly wept and excused himself to the barn.

Vickie trailed behind, clearly irritated by Garrett. "Is there more to the story? Why did Valerie whisper for the man who raped her?"

Price waved his hand. "Stop right now and give me space."

"I need answers."

"Get away from me!"

John bolted toward the barn.

He reached Vickie before father and daughter broke into a tirade.

He marched her toward the porch, where he sat her on the steps.

She glared at the barn, seeking answers but finding none.

John held her, and she wept against his chest, shaking as the tears coursed down her cheeks. Minutes fell into hours, and after a time, her tears withdrew. Vickie wiped her face and thanked John and casually stepped up to the porch, where she again sat beside Garrett on the glider. She bumped his shoulder with her own and gave him a knowing look.

"Are you Mr. B?"

"Thought you'd never ask."

"Thank you for being so kind to me that day. It meant a lot."

"She wasn't much of a mother, I'm sure."

"Valerie was my world at eight years old. I didn't know any better."

"Now it's time for you to be better. Can you do that?"

"I don't know. I'd like to believe it's possible."

"Believing's the hardest part. Trust me."

Vickie patted his knee. "I always have."

Nine

Psalm 49:5

Why should I fear when trouble comes,
when enemies surround me?

Vickie took the girls to Thompson Cemetery to see Red's, Valerie's, and Michelle's graves. The day was warm and full of promise, and it seemed the right time to get past the visit. But the names carved by workers in the granite were sorrowful, and they uttered a low cry, their owners' deaths had come too soon, without love in their hearts or a relationship with Christ or blessed hope for eternity. Each pillar of the Christian faith had been lost along the way: Valerie to rape, Red to greed, and Michelle to a year of paralysis, a cross which proved unendurable even for her children, two girls who had once been her everything but now reminded her of an untraveled future.

Memories surfaced of camp, where Vickie was more a misfit than at home, as she was shy and better suited to introspection than gossip.

Interruptions from the dull routine of summer flashed before her: van trips to a medical facility, men and women in white lab coats who studied and comforted her and stuck her with needles, some hurting and others making her sleep, only to awaken changed in her bunk. Something terrible was now inside her, seeking expression.

Those flashes had occurred throughout Vickie's teenage years, and they made her reluctant to become a camp counselor. But she ran to John for refuge, uncaring of what might beset her, as he was her only friend.

At the end of the summer, she left Addison, intent on building a life for herself in the nation's capital, both as a freshman in college and as an intern for Lena Lambert, the dragon lady of cable news with a fiery personality and a well-earned reputation for getting the story at all costs.

It was there Vickie discovered her pregnancy, and it was also there the flashes stopped, gone from her life until her visit to the cemetery.

She made friends with Mitch Dolan and Logan Meson, two interns who joined Lena's staff on the same day as Vickie, a coincidence which would prove troublesome in the following years. Both men held her in esteem but pushed her in different directions: Mitch toward career and politics, and Logan toward marriage and family. It was Logan who advised Vickie to confide in Lena about her pregnancy, as she would offer wise counsel.

Lena took the news in stride and said career was everything, the only course of action was abortion, a path she had taken twice in the late 1970s, a road which made all the difference.

Vickie took her suggestion to heart but needed support, so she asked Logan to accompany her to the clinic, which he did under protest.

She waited with Logan in the lobby, her foot tapping on the tile floor amid frightful sounds which emanated from a back room, sobs which were undeniable and everlasting and filled with regret.

Logan asked her to leave, but Vickie could not face Lena on Monday, and so she went through with the procedure. There were complications to the saline abortion, and the doctor seemed nervous.

The baby stayed alive as he delivered her, but died soon afterward.

Vickie's tortured psyche conjured a name, Chelsea, for the departed as she waited in a large room filled with beds and weeping girls.

Some curled in little balls like roly-polies.

Vickie rocked in place on the side of her bed. She clenched and unclenched her fists and told herself there was something horrible in her blood, and ending Chelsea before her life began was good for everyone.

She cried for a week, missing work, but when she returned, all was well. Lena never spoke of the incident but gave her preferential treatment over the others, saying Vickie would become a star, it was her destiny. And so she did, honoring her commitment to Red and to Valerie and to Lena Lambert, a mother figure in a shark-filled business.

Logan's reappearance as a cult leader years later surprised Vickie about as much as anything else she'd witnessed to that point. When she interviewed him, she pulled no punches, doing her best to make him seem a fool on national television. He lost the debate and his status, and it was this, more than Chelsea's death, which caused his insanity. Or perhaps it was there all the time, hidden under the surface, its dormant form waiting for just the right moment to massacre his victims.

He appeared near her desk late one Friday night and attacked, leaving her bruised but undaunted in her ambition. Not long afterward, he murdered Lena and Richard in their home, crossing a line, never relenting until his own destruction. It was then he raped Vickie, appearing from the shadows in her apartment, sparse as it was and unforgiving of spirit, and took her after a shower in her bathroom, leaving her in the tub corrupted and broken and meant for perdition.

In the months which ensued, she looked over her shoulder often and spoke to investigators and dredged up every conceivable clue to his whereabouts. But he found her again and took her in a police cruiser on a joyride for the ages, almost convincing her to join him in the quarry. But the entities asleep in her blood would have none of his plan, as they had not begun their work and the appointed hour was still to come.

John spent the next two weeks working with the horses, including Savannah, and he grew concerned over her pregnancy, so he called Missy to discuss her weakening heart. Missy said Vickie should help deliver a foal in the county and see a horse die up close and personal. It wouldn't be a pretty sight, but the experience might convince her to change her mind and keep more horses from the Mexican slaughterhouses.

"She's evil," Vickie said. "That's all there is to it."

"We both need you here to make this work," he said.

Vickie gestured impatiently. "See? I'm just the wallet." Her hands found her hips. "Bet you wouldn't want me if I was broke."

The sound of a nicker and a wall kick arose from the runway.

John investigated.

"Leave me standing here alone. That's just great!"

"Come here."

"What?"

"You heard me. I said come here."

Every fiber in her being said don't go, but still she went.

They stood in front of a stall as John peered into the gloom.

"See this bay? His name is Chief."

"Why should I care? It's just another horse."

John drew her nearer to the door so she might see inside the stall. Chief was a thoroughbred who stood sixteen hands. The bay turned his head toward Vickie and John, revealing hideous scars on one side of his face. Vickie recoiled and tugged against John's grip, breaking free.

"That wasn't fair."

"Since the cemetery, you've regressed into a brat," said John angrily. "Bring Chief to the tie-down area and give him a proper grooming."

"I want nothing to do with such a monstrous creature."

"Why? Does he remind you of yourself?"

She stuck her hand out, and Chief snapped at her. He lunged at the door, then raised his front legs, kicking at the wood as she fell back.

John grabbed Vickie and pushed her away from the stall. He closed the top half of the door, shielding her from the beast. "Chief can wait."

She gazed into the stall and sensed alarm, shame, and a hatred of the grizzly who hurt Chief all over his body, and then she visualized the attack which had killed his beloved owner while on a Montana trail ride.

John squeezed her shoulder, and she almost leaped out of her skin.

"Sorry," he said, stepping away from her. "Will you try later in the week?"

She nodded.

He led her to the barn office, where they sat, him behind the desk with his boots propped on one end and her in a rickety wooden chair.

"Don't get too comfortable, cowboy. This is my office."

"I know, and someday soon you'll be the boss around here, but today I'm the one telling you what's what and how things will go."

Vickie had to admit the truth. John had a way about him.

"What now, boss? Any cows to brand? Chickens to decapitate?"

John broke into laughter. "With your sense of humor, I can see why you succeeded in the corporate world. You must have been a sight."

"You're more right than you know. It's a dismal bunch in D.C."

"Well, one thing is for sure, you're different from most women."

Vickie pursed her lips. "I'm guessing you don't mean Mary Bishop."

He shook his head. "She's a nice girl. Just not the type for me."

"Who then?"

"You'd laugh if I told you."

"Try me. I'm a reporter, and you know I've seen it all."

He cocked his head sideways and arched his eyebrows. "You've seen nothing this crazy, I assure you." He dropped his boots to the floor with a loud thud. "You ever hear of a woman named Leslie Carter?"

She had heard the name during Dash's first grooming, when Katie quizzed him while she and John sat on a feed bin, but Vickie shook it off as misunderstanding, as no woman of elegance and style and a desire for political power would stoop so low as to wed a country farrier.

"You mean the Leslie Carter, the one who's running for governor?"

"The same. I did some shoe work on her farm, and I must have impressed her because she asked to see me. Leslie grew up on the eventing circuit. You know the type, having a sister who was a jumper."

Vickie nodded and frowned. "Michelle was obsessed for a while."

"Here's what's so remarkable," he said. "Leslie is less pretentious than any socialite I've ever met, so we get on like Bonnie and Clyde, as long as we hide ourselves from the public, and deep down in her heart, she's just a horse-crazy girl like Michelle was in high school and like you would've been if Red had allowed it, except she doesn't have your gift."

He paused.

"Neither did Michelle, by the way, which is why she got hurt."

Vickie tried to let the comment go, but felt compelled to respond.

"You like to compare women, which we all hate, so stop."

"I'm being honest, Vickie. It's my curse."

"No, that's my department."

"Funny and true at the same time."

"Does Leslie have a gift, something I don't possess?"

"Maybe," he said with a slow smile.

Vickie frowned. "Like what?"

"I could tell from the start she's a political operative, savvy at parties, addresses crowds without breaking a sweat. Again, you know the type."

Vickie despised the sort, although she had often encountered them.

She gave him a worried look. "Do you love her more than me?"

"Who couldn't love the great Victoria Morrison?"

Her cheeks flushed. "I'm serious, John."

"You don't have to worry. Leslie is a predator, and horses sense it. They tense up when she's around, unlike you, who calms them."

"Glad for once I'm not the monster you must overcome."

John stretched in his chair and smiled. "Me, too."

Vickie considered.

"You represent the horses who will never love her."

He reflected and then nodded graciously.

"Perceptive, and probably accurate."

"Why not travel with her? If she becomes the next governor, she'll have powerful connections who could help you save more horses."

"Leslie sees them as buildings to be renovated rather than a calling, as dollar signs blind her to the truth. Horses are empathic animals who need our care and attention. They're not widgets on a balance sheet, and her leadership would destroy my efforts, which is why I need you."

Vickie regarded John with a friendly eye. "Here's the real question, the one you hope I won't ask. I must warn you, it's provocative."

He smiled. "I know what it is, but go ahead."

"Is Leslie Carter ashamed of you?"

"It's what my father thinks."

"But what do you believe?"

"It's a definite possibility."

"Then you really do need me."

"That's what I've been saying, Vickie."

"I'll listen more intently from now on."

His blue eyes bore through her. "See that you do."

"Will you kiss me again?"

John eased around the desk. "Thought you'd never ask."

———

Vickie tried to cook a grilled cheese sandwich but burned the bread, so she aired out the house by opening the front and back doors and then went out to the pasture and climbed the rail to watch John work.

Riddle had become depressed like her and needed attention.

Eudora Bishop arrived from nowhere. She opened the gate and took a position near Vickie, who gazed at John and Riddle. "That horse looks as thin as you do," Eudora said. "Are you two on a hunger strike?"

Vickie smirked and dropped to the ground.

She hugged Eudora's neck. "You're hilarious."

"I aim to please."

The dryness of Eudora's reply caught Vickie's attention. Something was wrong, and she must ferret out the details. "Some say I look starved and beaten, as if the devil himself has been after me at night. What do you think?" Vickie drew back and made eye contact. "I need honesty."

"We all have problems," said Eudora flatly. "I know all about yours."

Vickie's eyes fell, and she considered joining John, as she hadn't slept well since the cemetery and was in no mood to argue with a friend.

A train of shared memories swept her backward with a friction which crackled and threw sparks, and she stood looking at Eudora for a moment before speaking again, as yesterday had slipped from her grasp.

"I see you're the same curmudgeon you've always been."

"You're one to talk."

"What does that mean?"

"Mary told me about her day in the van."

Vickie hugged Eudora a second time, both as a gesture of affection and as a firm warning. "I wasn't too hard on the precious Mary Bishop, but I'll tell you what, Eudora, you can stay here with us and watch the handsome John Breyer work his magic with Riddle, or you can leave and start a fight somewhere else. Maybe you could haggle over expired coupons at the supermarket or throw shoes at the bowling alley."

Eudora suppressed a smile and crossed her arms in defiance.

"I should have called when you first got into town."

"You'd better believe it. Where have you been?"

"Where have you been? The phone works both ways."

Vickie gave Eudora an astonished look and waved her hand.

"I can't believe this. You know I've been dealing with Bluecreek."

"Well, I've been sitting with my husband in the hospital."

Vickie gasped and put a hand over her mouth.

"What? I'm so sorry."

Eudora looked away. "Thanks."

"What's wrong with Craig?"

"They say he's battling cirrhosis, but he's already lost."

"He's going to die?"

"Yes, soon."

"Oh, no." Vickie's hand found her heart. "Again, I'm so sorry."

John stopped lunging and coiled the rope. "Me, too, Eudora."

"Craig is going to hospice, and he cannot die in our home." Eudora glanced at Vickie's house. "Would you allow him into one of your bedrooms? I hear you're about to sell Bluecreek Stables and leave town for good, so you wouldn't have to live with the memory of his death."

Vickie ran her fingers through her hair, unable to believe Eudora would make this request after years apart. She held her breath and then exhaled. "Girl, my ghosts haunt me every day." She broke into a smile.

"You know what I meant, Vickie Morrison! Don't play games!"

"Eudora, you show up without a call and tell me Craig's dying and then you demand I give him a bedroom to do it in, as if it's my duty."

"We go back a long way, and that should count for something."

Eudora's bitterness and her machinations shocked Vickie, but she would acquiesce to her old friend's demands, as there were sins to atone.

"Craig can die here. I owe him for helping me in high school."

John waved an aggravated hand and grunted.

"You two be quiet and let me corner this horse."

Eudora's eyes fell to the dirt in front of her. Her hair had tangled itself into knots, and her nails were too long. She smelled a bit, as if she hadn't bathed, and her eyes were red from sleep deprivation.

Vickie refocused on John. "I thought lunging worked on horses."

"We haven't had our come-to-Jesus meeting yet, so Riddle's still skittish."

Her distraction fractured the shaky bond between horse and trainer. John went left, but Riddle went right. John stepped, and Riddle bolted through the gate which had swung wide and now rested against the fence. "Vickie, shut the gate like I've taught you a thousand times!"

Riddle bounded straight for the house, and once there, he barreled through the doorway. Three frazzled humans ran after him, screaming bloody murder, finding no sign of a horse. Vickie noted the back door had flung wide, so they traced Riddle's footsteps through the side yard to the front pasture, where he stood waiting with a sly grin on his face.

"I'm sorry for yelling," said Eudora with a lethargic smile. "It's been an awful decade." Her eyes filled with tears, and her voice trailed off.

Vickie put up a finger as she bent over and caught her breath.

She straightened, and her eyes met Eudora's.

"Don't worry, honey. We'll make it work."

The following Monday, Vickie rode with John and Garrett to the hospital, where Garrett had been called to meet with his oncologist.

As they entered, John and Garrett turned left, while Vickie went right for what seemed like a mile of halls and elevators and open doors.

She almost bumped into a nurse as she found Craig's room.

"Sorry," she said politely, unsure of herself.

Craig's eyes flickered when she drew near. He removed his oxygen mask, which scared Vickie and caused her to draw back from him.

"Sorry you have to see me this way," he said in a raspy voice.

Eudora put a hand on Vickie's back. "I'll step outside for a bit."

Vickie smiled, but Eudora closed the door without a word.

She took Craig's hand. "You know what I remember about us?"

He lifted his oxygen mask again. "I think so."

"I was terrible at algebra in high school."

"You were absolutely abysmal."

They both laughed. Craig replaced his mask and wheezed into it.

Vickie had known many men in her thirty-eight years, but none like Craig Bishop, and she would never regret their flirtations or their friendship, no matter what Eudora might think of their warm banter.

His eyes seemed swollen as he removed the mask.

"You overcame your deficiencies, which spoke of your character."

"It was your patience when I continually blew the word problems, Craig. You showed so much encouragement, I couldn't let you down."

"It was my honor to tutor you, Vickie, and my privilege to call you my friend. I'm sorry we lost touch, but I would've been bad for you in my condition." He hesitated. "I became a drunkard, just so you know."

"So was I for a time, which makes us even."

"Still, we'll always have our algebra sessions," he said, smiling.

She drew near and squeezed his hand. "Even though you were only five years older, you displayed a brotherly maturity, and in my dysfunctional and bizarre life, I desperately needed it, so I thank you."

He tried to lift a frail smile to her but couldn't, and she knew this would be their last encounter, the one she would remember the most.

"Please care for Eudora when I'm gone and be patient. She'll have a hard time working through her grief and her anger, and she'll need you to take her abuse for a while. It may prove a lonely job."

"I'm honored you thought of me. It's the least I can do."

He stared at the ceiling and took several relaxing breaths.

Melancholy overwhelmed Vickie. It confirmed her decision.

"The doctors are about to place you into hospice care, so I'll provide a spot for you in one of my bedrooms where you can watch the horses through your window." Her eyes moistened. "I wish I could do more."

He squeezed her hand. "Thank you, my old friend."

The nurse stood over him with a concerned look. "Ma'am, you'll have to leave. He's struggling to get enough oxygen into his bloodstream."

Vickie stood near the door as the nurse injected something into Craig's IV. He fell asleep as the nurse read stats from a machine.

A solitary desolation settled upon the room.

"I'm sorry, Miss Morrison, but you must let him rest."

Vickie grabbed the door handle. "I'm going. I'm going."

She stood in the hall, flooded with emotion, guilty for being alive, and a compulsion to die washed over her soul and the soul of everyone she had ever known or would ever know, for if they knew her, their life would surely end. Her fingers tapped the sheetrock as Paul Newman had done, and a group yelled to clear the way as they rushed past with a gurney, their thunderous blur sending her fast in the opposite direction.

She found John and Garrett and strolled with them to the parking lot, and at last they reached the truck. "What did the oncologist say?"

John exchanged a glance with his father, who waved his hand, giving permission. "Dad's cancer has spread everywhere, and there's nothing more they can do for him. They've promised to make him comfortable."

Vickie hugged Garrett. "I'm so sorry."

"It's just my time. That's all."

As they climbed into the truck, she felt a resurgence of loneliness.

She went with her impulse. "You'll come to my house, Garrett, so you can join Craig Bishop, who will be set up in a front bedroom. There's another bedroom next door with your name on it. You can watch us work with the horses through your window, just like I promised Craig, and on your good days, you can sit on the porch."

"From what I hear," he said, "you'd rather play than work."

"All right, fine. Give me lessons from the porch."

"That's John's area. I'll be content to sit and watch you fail."

She smiled. "Does this mean you'll stay at my house?"

"Sounds just peachy, but I'd rather play golf at Pebble Beach."

She smirked and tossed her head, unwilling to let him win.

"You'd keel over on the first green. You'll live longer my way."

He laughed and gestured at her in the back seat. "I'm liking this one." He faced her. "You're better now than you were in high school."

"How was I then?"

"You were a conceited jerk, full of yourself, always trying to be the smartest, coolest person in the room. You were not, by the way."

"And now?"

He settled into the seat. "You might actually be a good influence on my son. Lord knows, other women have put him through the wringer."

"He means Leslie Carter," said John with a grin.

"Yeah, I do." Garrett struggled to face Vickie again. "She has some cowboy infatuation with John and won't let their relationship end."

Vickie glanced at Garrett as if he'd said something appalling.

"She has money, so it can't be about his inheritance."

Garrett gazed through the window. "Leslie sees John as an outlaw and likes the portrait she's painted in her head, but her people will have none of it, and they won't let him anywhere near the campaign."

"Do you think she's ashamed of him?"

"It's crossed my mind, and I've said as much to John, although it makes him mad, but something is off with her, and that's all I'm saying."

He waved a hand. "You shine by comparison, which baffles me."

Vickie crossed her arms. "You know what? I'm liking the new Garrett, a fact which surprises me. It's a shame you're about to croak."

He laughed louder than before and then coughed deeply.

She leaned forward, hopeful he would survive her morbid sarcasm.

"Sorry for the joke, but you walked into that one."

Garrett wiped his mouth with a handkerchief and drew it to his lap.

"I did." A pause. "You got me good."

"So it's a deal?"

"Deal," he said. "Are you ready for a silly old codger and a no-account drunkard in your home? I warn you, we may be a handful."

She nodded.

"My father is also there, so that makes for three pirates."

"Don't speak his name. If I die early, it would be all your fault."

Vickie's face flushed red.

Garrett pointed at her and grinned. "Got you."

———

Vickie placed Craig and Garrett in bedrooms near the front of the house, and hospice sent nurses to watch the patients around the clock.

She stuck her head inside Garrett's door. "Everything okay in here?"

"Craig's room is bigger. I won't stand for it on general principle."

A slow smile broke across Vickie's face. She winked at the nurse.

"They are the same size, Garrett."

"Then clear out the furniture in here, so I have more space."

"Why do you care? It's not a competition."

"Everything is a competition. You remember what I said."

Later in the evening, the group sat in the living room, and Vickie paced the floor while talking to Mitch. He begged her to return and said his job was on the line. If Preston fired him, he would have nothing, as he had saved little money. Vickie said he should have thought of his future when he ambushed her. As Vickie paced, the nurse whispered she should get off the phone for an announcement, one which would change things. She hung up on Mitch and refocused her attention.

"Mr. Bishop has taken a turn for the worse, and he doesn't have long. I suggest you say your last goodbyes as soon as possible."

Eudora went outside and sat in the glider. Her head hung low.

Vickie glanced at John and then followed Eudora to the porch. She sat beside her and spoke in a soothing tone. "It will be all right, honey."

"Get away from me," said Eudora sharply. "I don't want you here."

"I'm just trying to help."

Vickie had often wondered just how much Eudora knew.

"Don't act so fake, Vickie. No one is buying it anymore."

"What do you mean?"

John sat down. "Can I be of service?"

"Everyone should just leave me alone!"

Eudora stomped down the steps and marched toward the barn.

John hopped onto the grass and followed. Vickie called out for him to let Eudora grieve, but he continued. Vickie huffed and did the same.

Eudora plopped onto the tack room steps and wept to herself.

Price descended from the loft with a concerned look on his face.

"What's the matter, Eudora?"

"Everything is fine, mister, so go away. I don't even know you."

John approached. "You know me, Eudora."

Price sat beside her. She tried to push him away, but he grabbed her in a firm embrace, and she melted in his arms, weeping uncontrollably.

Lewis descended the stairs and sat beside John on the feed bin.

"I'm sorry for your loss, Mrs. Bishop."

"Craig hasn't died yet. Everyone can stop worrying about me."

Lewis tapped his metal leg with a yardstick. "When I got this, my buddy Roger died, so I was the lucky one, or at least it's what they said."

"Were you close friends?" John asked.

"We survived BUD/S, which was no easy task. Roger and I thought we were invincible warriors." He snapped his fingers. "Poof, he was gone, and I was a helpless cripple. Life plays funny jokes sometimes."

"I want to give up," said Eudora through tears. "It's too hard."

Lewis reflected.

"I visited Roger's grave and broke down, feeling exactly the same."

He gave her a moment to process and then continued. "My family was never close, and I joined the Navy to escape. I met great people, especially my SEAL brothers, but even they found it tough when I lost my leg. I suppose it leaves a person in limbo, not knowing what to do."

Vickie had been standing several feet away, listening. She sat on the far end of the feed bin. "Is that why you get into bar fights?"

He grinned. "Warriors need a battle."

Eudora's expression fell grim. "Craig drank every day. He beat me and screamed obscenities at our daughter. I put up with the abuse, and it became all I knew or expected. Mary left at seventeen and lived with a boyfriend whose family accepted her." Eudora stretched. "Then the doctor said Craig had cirrhosis, and everything changed. He found God and became a husband. Mary forgave her father; how I will never know, but I've been unable." She pointed at the house. "Everyone expects me to play the dutiful wife during his last hours, but it's what I've done for twenty years, and I'm weeping because I can't bear the thought of being relieved when he's gone, but I know I will. It's already crept into my heart, telling me life will get better when my husband is underground."

She faced Vickie. "How awful am I?"

"You're a human being, Eudora, and it's only natural." Vickie didn't want to ask the tough question, but knew she must. "What happened to Craig? He was never an abusive drunkard before I left for Washington."

Eudora sneered. "Could you actually be serious right now?"

"What did I do?"

"He was in love with you, Vickie, and his pining for you destroyed our marriage. Why didn't you two get married and leave me out of it?"

"I didn't marry Craig because I wasn't in love with him, and because he was your man, Eudora. I thought of him as a big brother like you are a big sister to me. That was the extent of my involvement with him."

"Maybe so, baby girl, but he felt differently about you."

"And you paid for it," Vickie said matter-of-factly.

"Along with our child."

"I'm here now, Eudora, and I will make up for it. He will die in my house, and we'll bury him together. Then you and I will move forward as strong women, and I'll do everything possible to help Mary's career."

Eudora groaned and shook her head. Her eyes once more fell low.

"You'll leave us again. It's what you do, Vickie."

Vickie cupped Eudora's chin and made eye contact.

"Not this time. I will get the girls soon, and we'll be a family."

Price shifted on the steps. "Are you sure? It's a big change."

Vickie surveyed the group and smiled. "I am now."

TEN

Psalm 50:3

Our God approaches,
and he is not silent.
Fire devours everything in his way,
and a great storm rages around him.

April 2008

Hardly anyone from Addison attended Craig's funeral on Saturday, which was surprising since he was once a math teacher at the high school. But in Vickie's absence, he had become an abusive drunkard whom few claimed, including his wife, Eudora, who stood silent and sorrowful and secretly glad while his casket sank into the dark and gloomy earth. Mary trembled and grimaced and closed her eyes at her mother's side, squeezing her hand for all it was worth. John supported Mary as she turned and wept into his chest, an intimate moment between devoted friends which should have stirred Vickie's ire but made her thankful to know such a man.

Afterward, Vickie asked Eudora to help her walk Dash, but she wanted only to lie on her bed. Vickie knocked at her door and begged her to come outside, as he needed exercise, and it was all she knew to do.

"I don't think so, Vickie. I'm tired."

"Please, Eudora. For me?"

The first years as an intern, an era before Vickie had impressed Lena Lambert with her inexorable ambition, were the best and most charming, and they helped take the sting out of her abortion of Chelsea. But regret came round again, and there would be no release through clenched and unclenched fists nor rocking on the side of her bed. Fire was now upon her, and she must rise to put out its flames, as a little girl danced both within and without, internal and external, her frivolities and her princess dresses and her whimsical reflection mirroring a naivety lost on the side of the road. But like a comet returned on its elliptical path, renewal was here once again, presenting itself as a trusted advisor, and Vickie would not lose another loved one to the throes of sorrow.

"Put Dash in the pasture so he can run around and play with Hero and Wildfire anytime he wants. The other horses could join them."

"It's not that simple, Eudora."

"Why not?"

"John hasn't taught me how to integrate horses into a herd."

"Then get him to teach you. I need to sleep."

Vickie pounded on Eudora's door. "Get outside this instant!"

"Okay! Don't get so mad at me."

When they reached the front pasture, which was green with new grass, Eudora would only rub Dash's back. She resisted all efforts to lessen her depression, even though the breeze tossed her hair with abandon and the air smelled of lilac, and a field dotted with pink and orange and red beckoned her attention. Wildfire and Hero munched in silence, watching keenly from a safe distance, understanding more than they let on, as the troublesome woman would soon approach with disorderly intentions. Vickie discerned their thoughts as she neared, unsure how or why or when her telepathic powers first beset her, but their restless eyes told her to have a care, as they would not kindly nor patiently nor willingly receive her wrath. She had told John her horse knowledge had returned, which was a lie meant to impress him and buy her time to learn on her own, so she would put aside her fears and tread into the unknown, bypassing the sane route which went through Hero. Putting on her coat of bravery, she went straight for Wildfire, her sister's killer, who kept his ground and then reared against her.

Vickie stumbled backward and fell to the ground.

John parked and approached her with a look of fury, which said she'd ruined his afternoon. "You lied about your experience, Vickie, and it shows." He pointed in a sharp motion. "You know nothing about horses, tack, or how to handle yourself around the stables."

"I didn't exactly lie."

"What then?"

"I stretched the truth a bit, but it was for a good purpose."

John turned from her and grunted and gazed at the road.

"You make me question whether we should be together," he said, turning to her. "One thing I cannot stand is a liar."

She marched to the gate in a huff and wheeled, pointing her finger at him and then jabbing it into her chest like a knife. "If you knew half the things I've done, John, you'd want nothing to do with me!"

He covered the ground quickly and stood in front of her.

"Be honest. It's all I ask."

She grabbed the gate. "You want too much."

"Fine." He shoved her out of the way and left the pasture.

He stopped at his truck and faced her with flushed cheeks. "When you're ready to speak your truth from the heart, come see me."

She weaved in place as her balance fled, but when she called after him, he dismissed her with another grunt and vanished into the barn.

Garrett raised a summoning hand from the porch and asked her to join him, promising not to bite. She smirked and mouthed the word "great," but he patted her leg as she sat beside him on the glider and said he understood her situation better than his son, which she found highly doubtful. His eyes shifted to the barn, and he seemed reflective.

"I multitasked at Skyline, which is what it takes to succeed in the corporate world, but John believes people should say what they mean and mean what they say. Unlike Chris, he's got a touch of the pastor's calling in him." Garrett smiled. "He thinks men can live by the Word."

Vickie's eyebrows arched. "Nice sentiment. I'll give him that much."

"It sounds good to say, but it's not very practical." Garrett gestured toward the horses with a weak hand and spoke with contentment. "What else makes no sense is giving up when you've made so much progress in so little time. Learn from today and keep your momentum."

She shook her head. "I made a fool of myself, which I hate."

"People will remember very little about today once you're proficient with horse rehabilitation and training. The rest is up to you."

Vickie considered this.

"Do you know anything about Price's son, Tink Brewer?"

"There's not much to tell. He ran a criminal ring after Price went to prison. They were running drugs through kill buyer trucks, the kind which transport poor, unwanted horses to Mexican slaughterhouses via kill pens in Texas." He shook his head. "There must have been a falling out because suddenly Tink came up missing, and no one knew where he'd gone. Some said he was tired of crime and wanted a new life, but I knew his type, and those men never change. I figured he hid from the law and would surface on the run from the FBI or some other agency."

"Katie said he was most likely dead."

Garrett spoke between his teeth. "Oh, he's dead, all right. They found his body in the lake, and he wore a gold watch which belonged to Red." Vickie put her hand over her mouth as the portrait painted itself. "Apparently Tink had it out for Red, so he snuck in and stole the watch from his office. I don't know what significance it held for Tink, but it must have meant something. He went to great lengths to get it."

"How was he connected to Michelle?"

Garrett winced. "You'd best let sleeping dogs lie."

She smiled. "Garrett, I'm a reporter. We dig up dirt."

He stiffened slightly, and his eyes seemed more bloodshot.

"Be careful. Folks around here don't like outsiders who dredge up the past. Small towns are full of secrets which can get a person killed."

Vickie rocked side to side, tuning out her flawed mentor, as he would soon gasp his last breath, a casualty of this realm, and the stray segments of her life had yet to coalesce into a unified whole.

———

Vickie dreamed of a serpent man who promised her everything her heart might desire if she would worship him. When she refused, a section of woods enveloped her, and she stumbled upon seventy grizzly bears who fought one another at a garbage dump, clawing and scraping for their feast. Vickie backed away and searched for Abbie along the trail, but growling sounds reached her ears and sent a chill down her spine as she progressed until finally she came upon the serpent man, who stood with Abbie in front of a colossal oak. The bears surrounded her with red glowing eyes and frothing fangs and thunderous hatred, and she awoke in a cold sweat. Grief and shame overwhelmed her, and she cried, although she would not talk to God because the pain was too great and her sins were many. She fell adrift from her family after they broke her trust when she was a girl, and the letter on her eighteenth birthday nearly ended her life, as she took pills and landed in the hospital. It was there the serpent man first appeared in her dream, promising her the entire world without asking for her soul nor demanding she worship him. Red came to see Vickie but didn't stay long, as her vain trivialities did not bother him. Eudora and Craig kept vigil with her and showed her an unforgettable kindness, which saved her tormented life.

Over the following years, Vickie had worked at tearing out the root of bitterness so she might forgive her family for their many betrayals.

Forgiving herself was another matter and would never happen.

"Good morning," John said, calmer and happier than yesterday.

"Is it? I wouldn't know."

He sat beside her at the table. "What's wrong?"

Vickie put her head in her hands and cried. "I don't know."

"Something must be bad for you to be so morose."

"Don't let me pull you into my despair. It's a grim spectacle."

He rubbed her arm. "Confide in me, Vickie. I'd like to help."

"I'm torn over the pull to stay here and my need for fame."

She looked up and forced a smile. "Dark, huh?"

He squeezed her hand. "I'm glad you can finally be honest about your need for validation, but you should do something about it."

She sat up in the chair. "Like what?"

"Well, the first thing is to choose where you want to be."

"I already said I'd get the girls and stay here."

"Right, but is it really what you want, Vickie?"

"People expect me to be in both places, so it's not so easy to say I'll go back to D.C. or even to stay here with you and the girls. Mitch and Preston and the people who work on the show need my help, even Nellie Michaels, who might be decent one day, which sounds crazy, but I have a feeling about her." Vickie gestured toward the room and tried to check her emotions. "Here in Addison, there's you, there's Katie and Abbie, there's Eudora, not to mention Garrett and the horses." She felt betrayed, although she wasn't sure why. "I can't just up and leave my father's horse farm to rot, can I?" She thought of Price, her real father, and put her head in her hands once more. "Then there's the rapist."

"You're stalling. If you want to leave, find a job in D.C. and go."

The obligations which went along with motherhood stifled, and she summoned all her courage to run from John, as he would leave her once he discovered the truth of her abortion, Chelsea being his child, the result of a horseback ride to his tent and a hushed night of bliss.

The pills had almost killed her, and she needed an intimate release.

"I put out feelers early on, but no other network ever responded, and now I feel even more toxic. It doesn't matter now anyway because I've committed to staying here for everyone's sake but my own."

"Have you taken your problems to the cross?"

"As if it would help anything."

"Vickie, you must come to God in truth and supplicate for His grace. The Lord knows what He's doing and with whom He's working, even the chief of sinners like you and me, as the whole truth is out about us. God's grace saves and gives us a fresh nature, and He places us before

Him in the highest places of His confidence. Someone as wicked as Price got converted, and those who knew him back in his criminal days might wonder at the boldness of his preaching. They think if folks knew what he did, they would refute him, but God knows us better than we know ourselves, and nothing surprises Him. This is the source of our blessed confidence, Vickie, and you must take your regrets to Jesus, because once you do, He will reward you with an outpouring of His grace."

"I've spent twenty years telling lies for my own gain."

John sighed and then opened his Bible to Psalm 50. He ran his index finger down the page and paused for a few moments, clearly pondering his message. After what felt like an hour, he cleared his throat and recited verses 16-23. "But God says to the wicked: 'Why bother reciting my decrees and pretending to obey my covenant? For you refuse my discipline and treat my words like trash. When you see thieves, you approve of them, and you spend your time with adulterers. Your mouth is filled with wickedness, and your tongue is full of lies. You sit around and slander your brother, your own mother's son. While you did all this, I remained silent, and you thought I didn't care. But now I will rebuke you, listing all my charges against you. Repent, all of you who forget me, or I will tear you apart, and no one will help you. But giving thanks is a sacrifice that truly honors me. If you keep to my path, I will reveal to you the salvation of God.'" He closed the Bible and smiled.

"I can't give thanks for what He allowed." She turned and wiped tears from her eyes. "Even if I could forgive, my sins are too great."

"It's what every man and woman says at some point in their lives."

He leaned over and kissed her forehead. "Think about what I said."

She squeezed his hand. "I will. Thank you."

John left for the barn to work with Riddle in the round pen.

A vision took hold of Vickie as she sat by herself in an Adirondack chair on the porch, and she gripped the chair's armrests for support, as the dreamlike state filled her soul with terror. She and Abbie walked a limited visibility trail in Montana, where aunt and niece topped an incline and encountered a mama grizzly and her cubs. Enraged, the mama charged and was on her in a second, ripping her face and biting her body. Vickie resisted but then gave into death and fell to the ground. The mama bear left her and went for Abbie, who kicked at the beast and resisted, but within seconds, she was dead. Vickie observed Abbie's body after the monsters left and wondered at the entities which released into the air like fireflies in summer, swirling about Abbie's form. Vickie pressed her punctured face with a handkerchief and eased farther up the trail, careful to stay downwind. She found the bears and gazed at them as they dug for food, marveling at the protective instinct of the mama, hating herself for ending the life of her daughter.

The vision left, and she sat up, aware she would become another Lena Lambert if she went back to Washington, or worse, another Logan Meson, a man who let pride crush his sanity and end his existence. If she made the wrong choices now, it might lead to more loss of life, but to stay here she needed a big picture understanding of horse training and riding, and she must begin somewhere. Although he might get annoyed with her, she sought John in the barn and asked for his help. He agreed but said she must learn the fundamentals, which involved working with a horse in the round pen and the correct use of saddlery and tack.

"Sure, but I don't have time to waste, so let's get on with it."

As John led an angry Chief toward the round pen, images flashed of the mauling of horse and owner in Montana. Droplets of sunlight had filtered through the canopy of trees, brightening the blonde curls in the woman's hair, and she spoke kindly and lovingly just before the attack, which left her as a discarded, broken carcass on the side of the trail.

Vickie realized the serpent man was real, and he used her bond with Chief against her, which neither she nor the horse could afford.

She took the lead rope from John and led Chief to the front pasture.

"I don't think it's a good idea, Vickie."

"Let me handle this," she said, waving for him to leave.

As she closed the gate, Vickie looked for John, but he had heeded her call, which made her glad and frightened all at the same time.

She tried to latch the gate with the lead rope in her other hand, but Chief tugged against her like a petulant toddler, so she allowed the gate to swing open as she turned and struggled with her aggressive horse, who seemed to believe his wretchedness was her responsibility to heal.

Price stepped near to the fence and watched for several minutes.

He finally spoke. "The horse knows something is wrong."

"Really?" She smirked. "Thanks for the insight."

"You must be clear, as you must be honest with yourself and with God. Horses like Chief will tolerate little else from their owners."

John approached from the barn and perched himself on the fence.

He called down to Price. "I have things under control here."

"Doesn't look that way to me." Price's expression seemed strained.

The horse and the men frustrated Vickie, so she dropped the lead.

"What are you doing?" John landed on the grass and went for Chief.

She marched to the gate, and Chief charged past her and ran down the driveway. He crossed Route 15, which was void of traffic, and jumped the secondary pasture fence like an eventer. Vickie asked John to let her handle it, as this was her mess. She and Price searched the woods near Price's trailer, and they heard growling about them in the trees and undergrowth, and Vickie shook with the knowledge her dreams had become a reality. Just then, Chief set upon her and charged wildly like the bear and demanded her attention, and she calmed him with her hands and a voice filled with reassurance. The win was nice, but she wished John had followed and could see her victory, as he did not believe in her.

An exhausted Vickie fell asleep in the barn office and had another dream, where she happened upon the serpent man and Abbie at the oak tree. Bears surrounded, but the serpent man pointed and grinned, and she became a monster who terrified the grizzlies, causing them to flee. The serpent man roared with delight and said Vickie must prepare, as there were grand tasks ahead and these hicks interfered with his plans.

She awoke with a start and stared at the horse pictures on the wall, her feelings shifting between confusion and anger at being persecuted for Valerie's death, as she was just a little girl who needed her mother's love. Sometimes she believed she was born a mistake, and the world would be happier without her taking up space or harming others for her own gain. Vickie had made little progress with the horses, none of whom seemed to like her except the horribly damaged Chief, who seemed connected to her past and to her future in unacceptable ways.

Abbie bounced into the office, interrupting her thoughts.

Vickie wiped tears from her eyes and the horrible grizzlies from her bedeviled mind. She turned to the excited girl and cast a faint smile.

"Hi, Abbie. What are you up to this morning?"

"I'm supposed to make you leave." The eight-year-old smiled at Vickie and took her hand, which Vickie allowed with reservation.

She stepped lightly outside into a sunny day, where John appeared from behind his truck with Dash and Riddle, who were tacked and ready. "It's time to go," he said, showing no sign of compromise.

"Where?"

"We'll picnic at the falls."

Vickie peered at the horses, seeing no basket attached to anything.

He smiled. "I packed a saddlebag on Dash, so don't worry."

Abbie pulled at Vickie. "You need to go now and have a wonderful day." She was a sweet kid who needed a mother, which forced Vickie to relent, and they left the girls with Eudora for the afternoon as they rode behind the barn and through a gate which led into the deep, dark woods and along the winding and ascending trail which led through a steep cut in the mountains. Along the way, she caught him watching her, which made her nervous, as she knew he would criticize her technique.

"Stop being a creep," she said, hoping he might go easy on her.

He laughed. "What's creepy is your posture, which is nonexistent."

"What do you mean?" She looked about, right and left.

"Slumped shoulders, torso tipped forward, reins way too high, which is a big problem. Who in the world taught you to ride?"

"Michelle, but it was twenty years ago, in case you've forgotten."

"Who could forget Vickie Morrison, the big shot news anchor?"

"Hey, my Logan Meson exposé, which almost killed me, I might add, broke records, and then there were the dictators, musicians, actors, athletes, and politicians, including the president of the United States."

"Did you sit like that when you interviewed the president?"

Vickie looked down, bewildered. "Like what?"

His words washed over her. "Like you're about to slide off his back, one minute to the right and the next to the left. I'll bet your spine was straight as you sat with the most powerful man in the world."

There was something about John which enchanted Vickie, as he'd lived a rough life, the same as her. He enjoyed the freshness and beauty of women without being taken in by them, as they were often viewed as pottery which must not be broken, but he inherently understood their pieces had already been shattered long ago, and his decency undertook to put them back together. In such a sense, he was a man of nobility.

"Well, yeah, when you put it like that, I would agree."

"Realize you sit on a stronger animal, one who could rise up and kill you at a moment's notice, but before you get upset and want to jump off his back, he won't want to do such a thing if you treat him right."

She called to him. "Sounds like a man I know."

He smiled as he craned his neck, and his blue eyes fell on her.

"Nothing wrong with being treated right, is there?"

"I wouldn't have a clue, because no one has ever done it."

"Well, it makes two of us, so maybe we'll balance out."

"Or we'll commit hara-kiri with a butter knife."

His laugh came from his belly, and its sound reverberated off nearby rocks. He pointed. "The falls are through the break in the ridge, which forms an alleyway of sorts. You'll hear the roar of the falls soon."

His use of the word "roar" recalled the serpent man. She shuddered.

They passed between two high walls which formed a passageway, and for the first time since she was a girl, Vickie felt claustrophobic, like the world closed in on her and Riddle. She tried to hide her nervousness while she craned her neck, looking behind her at the gloom and hoping it would soon open up. Just then, she heard the falling water.

As they arrived, John tied the horses and pointed to a grassy spot.

He spread a blanket and opened his pack and placed items on the cloth. Vickie sensed John brought her here for an intimate conversation, one he'd wanted to have since she first arrived, so she braced herself for the worst, believing whatever he might say would be bad for her.

"Let's get this over with," she said.

He smiled and sat on the hard rock which jutted beside the red plaid blanket and gestured for her to enjoy its soft and thick comfort.

She took his hand. "You're always telling me to be honest with you."

"Yes." His eyes fell to the falls below them, and then he made eye contact with her, and she steeled herself for the misery to follow.

"All right, I will. You should've come home sooner."

"As I said earlier, it wasn't any simpler than it is right now."

"It's been hard on the girls, especially Katie, without Michelle."

"I can imagine."

She paused.

"What happened to Carlie? You two were on and off for years."

"It's a story for another day." His back leaned against a rock. "What about you? Were there any passionate romances in Washington?"

She sighed. "I almost married my producer, Mitch Dolan, who thought we'd make a power couple, but when I evaluated the situation, I couldn't see spending the rest of my life with him. It was nothing personal, just the same analysis any woman must make when choosing a man as a husband, but he took it as an affront to his value as a human being and set about to make my life miserable, taking up with my intern, who was still in college. He pushed her timetable forward much faster than Lena pushed mine years ago, and much more quickly than the young woman could handle, which is evidenced by the lack of ratings since my departure." Vickie stopped talking for a moment and caught her breath.

He laughed.

"When your story gets rolling, there's no stopping you."

She sipped water and smiled. "I got carried away for a minute."

"Does Mitch still love you?"

She shrugged. "Who knows with him? He's an emotional guy."

"Go on," John said. "I'm listening."

"He and I wanted different things from life. I think it started my shift away from politics and toward something real here in Addison."

"Mary might take your place someday. People say she's good."

Vickie thought of her lack of attention to the television station.

"I've received reports of Lewis acting abusively toward Mary and Reggie, but he's probably frustrated from trying to learn the business."

"When he worked at the farm, Lewis watched you from the barn most days. I must admit, your friendship with him makes me jealous."

She smiled and then leaned over and kissed John. "I hadn't noticed."

He gently stopped her. "I need to know how you feel about him."

Vickie jingled her plastic fork and spoon as if they were leather reins and corrected her posture. "Is this how I should sit in the saddle?"

"You're changing the subject."

"Someone had to before things got too serious."

He smirked. "All right, we'll talk about something else."

"Thank you. Much appreciated."

"So why stay gone for twenty years? It would have been nice to see you at some point over the span of time, to know you were still alive."

"My past is a sordid mess, and you wouldn't like my explanation."

"I have nothing but time," he said, smiling.

"If you want to know the truth, I feel disillusioned after being loyal to Red and sacrificing so much, and often I think of what might have been if I had stayed here. I have trouble bonding with Katie and Abbie, although they're great, but guilt eats me alive most of the time." He gave her a quizzical look. "Michelle needed me to work the horse business with her to take some of the load off her shoulders, and after her fall she and Red needed my help, but I didn't have the whole story back then, and I wouldn't allow anything or anyone to derail my career."

"Michelle's paralysis was very hard on Red, and he tended her day and night, only to lose her a year later. I felt sorry for him and for you."

"For me?"

"You lost a sister and a father, and I'm not talking merely about

Red's death, but his furious anger when you refused to return and help him through it. I thought it might kill him and, in some ways, it did."

She recoiled as she realized her role in Red's heart attack. "He never needed my help with anything before, so why start with her accident?"

"Vickie, this was different, and you know it. Michelle was paralyzed, unable to move a muscle below her neck. Red rarely left her side, and when he did, it broke him." John frowned. "Did you love them at all?"

Vickie connected the serpent man and her abortion of Chelsea, who was John's little innocent daughter, as she now believed she had sold her soul to Lucifer years ago and signed the contract with a blood sacrifice, which destroyed any chance for her happiness in marriage or a family which might be formed from her union with John. In so doing, she sealed her eternal fate. She was no good for Michelle or Red and could never be for John. She stood and fervently dusted off her pants.

"I need to leave. The past makes me sad."

"I'm sorry," John said. "It wasn't my intention."

As they approached Dash and Riddle, Vickie took John's hand and drew him in for a kiss. "I know we need to talk about these things, but I've made a habit of denial, and I want to keep all my trauma buried for as long as possible." She drew away from him. "I see you disapprove."

"You've got to work through your issues, Vickie."

"For our future?"

He nodded.

"What if we don't have one? Would that be okay with you?"

A rifle shot cracked, and a bullet missed John's head, landing in a tree to their right. They grabbed the horses and ducked behind a rock.

John retrieved a pistol from a saddlebag and made ready for a fight.

"What are you doing? You'll get us killed!"

"Whoever shot at us barely missed, so I can't make things worse."

An engine revved, and tires flung dirt and rocks as a truck sped into the distance. John spied for a few moments, ensuring their safety.

On the trail down to Bluecreek Stables, Vickie tried to understand what had transpired. "Why would someone want to hurt you?"

"Could be Tink's men who are unhappy with my kill pen raids. Since the coroner tagged his body, I've been snagging their horses."

"Isn't it illegal?"

"Not any more than the criminals who stole them or bought them at auction from good folks who thought they were doing the right thing."

John paused.

"Law enforcement around here is part of the network, so nothing is likely to change soon. This goes higher than you realize."

Vickie's love for John drove her to help as atonement. She couldn't have wished for a better father for Chelsea, and she wanted to die rather than admit her mistake to him, but he would raise Katie and Abbie as his own, and Vickie must see he made it all the way to their adulthood.

"So you took things into your own hands?"

"Someone had to do something."

"I admire your courage," she said.

He tipped his hat. "Thanks."

As they rode, Vickie asked how she'd progressed with the horses.

"Great and terrible at the same time."

"Wow, really let me have it, John."

"You know almost nothing, but you have great instincts."

"Then you should teach me what I don't know."

"If you're serious, I'd be willing to try."

"I really need your help and as soon as possible."

"Okay, then. We'll start tomorrow."

ELEVEN

Psalm 51:3

For I recognize my rebellion;
it haunts me day and night.

Vickie lunged Chief in the pasture while John observed her form. She wandered in a circle, lost in the depths of her thoughts, tired of the whispers and the losses and the bloody sadness of it all. When she had first come around a bend in the woods and met Price Brewer, she had discerned a kinship beyond inheritance, he was a creature of death like her, but his decency and his love for Jesus and his preaching from the Bible conflicted with the entities in her blood. Now she was unsure of what to think or say, and her second tenure in Addison felt more like a sentence than a respite, although it had proven itself a better home than she'd ever known. Loneliness overtook her wherever she went, whether in a group or by herself, and John was the one man who had ever broken through her hasty and desolate defenses.

"Move Chief's feet." John grew agitated. "Push him harder."

Her fingers gripped the lunge rope as she paused for a breath.

She must snap a whip or use the inflection of her voice, saying "get up," or press her body within Chief's drive line, the space between his withers and the top of his tail, to send him in a circular motion either right or left. Lunging was the best way to win his respect and his obedience and, ultimately, his friendship. John helped her start Chief's feet to the left with the wave of an arm and a press forward into his drive line. Man and horse worked up to three circumnavigations without prodding, and then John explained how to turn the horse inside and outside.

"You'll have to repeat these lessons, or it's wasted effort."

"I have all the time in the world, John. I'm not going anywhere."

"Are you sure about that? Don't want to cramp your style."

A knot rose in her throat as their summer rendezvous in the tent flashed hot in her mind, and she hid her impulse to let him take her, just as he expected her to command Chief against the rope's taut length.

She wished he would marry her and turn her into an honest woman, as they say. Her tortured psyche painted a portrait of a future wedding night, blissful and enduring and circular as their bodies moved about the plush and elegant room like a dirty round pen, returning to the place of origin, the satin-sheeted bed, never ending and never full.

From his bedroom window, Garrett observed her and Chief, and as the horse orbited her in the pasture, Vickie's eyes met Garrett's. She wondered if he needed her or was in pain, as little time remained for him. She refocused on Chief for three more laps and then said "whoa" and tried a join-up like Michelle with her rescues, but Chief turned and pawed at the ground. She dropped the rope and disobeyed John's order to pick it up as she walked inside and sat by Garrett, asking him to help her understand the Breyer family and what went wrong with Nicole.

Garrett reflected on Vickie's question and then asked for his son.

"A golf trip would've been a disaster," said John, sitting down. "I'm terrible at the game, and if you want the truth, I'm bad at everything except horses and women, and only the former ever does what I say."

"The latter should be your concern. This one right here." Garrett gestured at Vickie. "Your great love has come back to you."

John glanced at her. "Yes, after twenty years and a rape."

Vickie recoiled, unable to believe what he had just said.

"You shouldn't throw that in my face, John. It was awful."

He crossed his arms. "You haven't mentioned the rape once to me."

"Why should I? Do you talk about your deepest pain?"

"Not with anyone but you, Vickie, and I do little of it because you never want to discuss important things, like how that man raped you."

She got up and paced. "What do you want, details?"

He snorted. "I want the truth, which you hide from me."

"It's too much, John. I won't even let myself think about it."

"It? You mean the rape?"

"Yes. Please leave it alone."

"Maybe you should get out of denial, because I'm tired of the wedge between us. You won't let yourself get close to me or anyone else."

"Logan asked me a horrible question, one I will never repeat, and since then I don't feel worthy of love. It's not like I was feeling good about myself before it happened, being the product of rape and having everyone in this town blame me for my mother's suicide, as if I could've stopped her from doing what she wanted." Vickie rolled her eyes. "No one could get through to Valerie, not even Red, who loved her."

"You're repeating her mistakes, Vickie, because you won't let me love you or get through to you, and you won't let those girls in either."

"That's different, John, so let it drop."

A voice of warning screamed in her head, and she wished to escape.

"I don't know what you want from me." She sank into her chair. "But you'll watch while I say a tearful goodbye to my father?"

"Of course, John, because I love you. Is that so wrong?"

"You don't know the history, and you think the only person who's suffered in life is you, and you believe you're entitled to a good time."

"I've asked you to share it all with me," she said, "but you refuse."

He smirked. "You don't want to hear about my past any more than I want to discuss it with you." He gestured at Garrett. "Or with him."

Garrett grimaced as he tried to sit up, and the nurse helped.

"Stop feeling sorry for yourself, John, and forgive those of us who've hurt you. My father wasn't exactly a loving man, but we got along."

John gave Garrett a half sneer. "I guess you're better at that, too."

"Son, learn to take the best from your parents and let the rest go. It's what I tried to do, and I wanted more for you and Chris, but after Nicole died, I was both a mother and a father, but I didn't know how."

Vickie placed her chair between them to mediate their angry disagreements. She rubbed John's arm and spoke gently, calming his mood. "May I ask how Nicole became mentally ill?"

The subtle question dismayed Garrett. His voice cracked slightly.

"She fell into a depression when the boys were little. I would come home from work and find her on the couch, enveloped in darkness."

"I'm sorry, Garrett. How did you cope?"

"I went upstairs to my office and sipped whiskey at my desk." Garrett considered. "Instead of booze, I should have invited God into my life to work His perfect will. If I'd done such a thing, maybe she'd still be alive."

He asked the nurse for his Bible, and she brought it to him. He read Psalm 51:4-6: "Against you, and you alone, have I sinned; I have done what is evil in your sight. You will be proved right in what you say, and your judgment against me is just. For I was born a sinner, yes, from the moment my mother conceived me. But you desire honesty from the womb, teaching me wisdom even there."

"We didn't read the Bible much when I was a girl. As Catholics, we listened to the priests who instructed us in the catechisms."

"I imagine you had a field day in the confessional."

Vickie smiled. "My specialty was shocking Father Thomas."

She tapped John's arm. "Did Nicole grow worse over the years?"

He looked away, but she stared at him until he turned to her.

"Mom heard voices and talked to people who weren't there."

"Schizophrenia?"

He nodded.

Vickie held his hand. "Why was your mother committed?"

"She attacked Chris after one of his matches and tried to choke him to death. He could be sarcastic and he lashed out at Mom, just as he did with me and his peers, which helped make him popular in high school."

Vickie tensed. "Are you like your mother?"

"John is like me," Garrett said, "but he suppresses his personality because he thinks I'm an abuser who ruined our family. Chris was like Nicole, temperamental but skilled at everything and very charming."

"The Scardell fire has always confused me. How did it start?"

"Old wiring sparked, and her ward went up in minutes."

"There was nothing they could do?"

Garrett shook his head. "She was in an older wing, which ironically was set for remodeling the following year. It was just bad timing."

"No, you mean it was God's perfect will," said John angrily.

From what Vickie had heard over the years, Nicole was a tall brunette who enjoyed the piano but found sorrow in between the notes. As her fingers caressed each key, tears pursued down her cheeks in bleak strands, which both romanticized the music and gave it a nebulous quality, as if the bell tolled only for her. Her weeping grew legendary, as she often performed in front of others, drawing outward with each lyrical note and withdrawing inward by her intolerable despair, which choreographed every day, there could be no respite, save the little boy who sat with her and ate ice cream. He was her special child, the one who shared her insights about the fallen realm, noticing when others didn't, and he would never leave her as others had done. They could not see inside her soul nor like what they found there, the darkness and the fire and the distance from saving grace.

"John, do you blame Garrett for Nicole's death?"

Vickie knew the answer, but he must speak his truth aloud.

He shook his head. "She was insane, and I was glad he sent her away because she talked to herself and waved her hands as if someone was in her face, and she said delusional things to me when I played outside. The other kids assumed I was a freak who lived in a haunted house."

Garrett wiped his eyes. "John blamed Nicole for losing her mind and me for not saving her." He glanced at his son, who looked down, and then stared at Vickie with kind eyes. "I couldn't save her any more than I could Valerie, who died crying out in agony in my arms."

"Nicole must have been every bit as terrified, knowing a fiery death approached." Vickie turned to John. "We share a tormented history."

"The difference is I stayed home while you ran to Washington."

Vickie grew uneasy under John's scrutiny. Logan's wicked hands groped her skin, and she shifted in the chair to create distance from him, but it was of little use, his evil would forever remain inside her.

"That's not fair, John." Vickie hugged herself and tried to avoid tears. "Red expected me to learn from Lena Lambert and to become a superstar in cable news, which I did, but it was never enough for him."

"You craved fame and fortune. Don't lie now and blame it on Red."

Garrett cleared his throat. "Children, let's get along, shall we?"

His attempt to lighten the mood fell flat, as they each gave him a blank look. His head pressed into his pillow, and his face went gray.

"Garrett, are you alright?" Vickie stood and summoned the nurse.

"I see Nicole all day in my mind, and her screams haunt me."

John went over to the window and gazed in silence.

Garrett blocked the nurse's attempt to administer high-flow oxygen.

"Son, please forgive me. I didn't know she would die at Scardell."

"This goes back earlier than the fire," said John with feeling. "You taught Chris sports, which made him popular, but no one was there for me except a lunatic mother who refused to bathe and who talked to herself. She gave me ice cream so I would stay with her, but once I gained weight, the other kids picked on me. Even you and Chris joined in on the fun, but you didn't teach me about exercise or nutrition and certainly nothing about sports, so I had to learn for myself and I made mistakes, which turned me into a clown." He glanced at Vickie with a perplexed expression. "Chief needs me in the pasture. I'll be outside."

Vickie watched John through the window as he climbed the tack room steps. He wanted to be left alone, possibly to weep over his father.

She followed him and opened the door. "Will you be alright?"

He held his head as he paced.

"Now is not a good time, Vickie."

"I'd like to help if you'll let me," she said, unsure of what else to say.

He stopped and glared at her, and she tensed.

"Do you know what I was doing when you arrived?"

"Just now?"

He pursed his lips. "No, before you came back to Addison."

"You had all the women in town jumping when you said jump."

He placed his hands on the counter and dropped his head.

Ever since Valentine's Day, when John said hello at her window, he hadn't spoken much about his plans, other than that he desired to rescue unwanted horses from their fate. Now she must encourage him to share with her, as her heart had opened itself just enough to let a faint hope for love creep inside. She wouldn't easily open it if closed again, so she held onto the door with all her might and did not allow her heart to crumble into vinous dust. Instead, she put on a cheerful face.

"What, John? Tell me."

He rubbed his stomach and straightened. "I may have an ulcer."

"We'll deal with that later. Please tell me what you were doing."

She breathed in air, but it would not fill her lungs.

He turned to her, scrubbing a hand over his face. "Leaving."

"Leaving? You mean Addison?"

John nodded and offered her a languid smile. "I couldn't take another minute in this town, being confronted every day by all the things I'd seen and done here." He hesitated. "Memories of family."

He grew silent, and his eyes fell to his feet.

"John, I'm here and I'm listening."

She held onto the door and longed for his masculine embrace.

Price came up from behind her. "Have you seen John?"

Vickie's hand clutched the handle and her hip pressed the wooden frame, blocking Price's view of John, who paced and swiped at his tears.

She spoke over her shoulder. "He's in here, but he's not having a good morning." Her neck craned. "Come back in twenty minutes."

The door closed, and she stepped into the tack room, concerned.

"Price asked about you. Can I tell him you'll be okay?"

"I'm fine." John grabbed at his neck. "I'll be there soon."

Price stomped up the steps, intent on getting what he wanted.

The knob turned, and the door cracked open, but Vickie rushed over and shoved it against her father, then stuck her head through the opening. "I said to come back later. What part was unclear?"

"Someone's out front."

Vickie sighed. "In the pasture? Speak plainly, Price."

"A limousine arrived a few minutes ago and parked in front of the house. I didn't think too much of it until a classy lady stepped out to the driveway looking like a runway model. She demanded to see John."

Vickie surveyed her country clothes, which were dirty from working with Chief. Her nemesis had picked the perfect moment to strike, a morning when Vickie had ventured to the barn without makeup.

She flung open the door, hitting John, who had drawn near, and they descended the stairs, bumping shoulders as they raced to the front. John shoved Vickie off the path, and she shoved him in response.

As they approached the limousine, a blonde woman with hazel eyes stepped into the light and beamed at Vickie, who was underdressed.

"Leslie, I told you we were done, as in no longer an item."

John marched toward the woman with disgust written on his face, but she brushed past him and extended her hand. "I'm Leslie Carter."

Vickie acknowledged her adversary's strength by speaking coyly.

"The Leslie Carter, the one who's running for governor?"

She stepped back a little, deferring to the powerful woman.

"I'd like to think I'm leading the race, not just running." Leslie looked at John and then smirked at Vickie. "I see you've met my fiancé."

———

Leslie grinned at John as she spoke about herself. "I graduated from law school and eventually became the Charlotte D.A., but I grew up on the eventing circuit and still keep thoroughbreds at my father's estate."

Vickie handed Leslie a coffee and took a seat beside her.

"You met John there?"

"Yes, he worked a miracle with a chestnut Morgan named Prince." Leslie paused. "Prince has won multiple trophies, and I wouldn't dare let him go."

Vickie's eyelids fluttered. "John is such a blessing to you, Leslie."

"I think so, even if you don't." Leslie gestured at John and then placed her elbows on the table and absentmindedly played with a pack of sugar. "Our man has a touch of ESP, wouldn't you say?" Leslie leaned back and straightened herself in a well-calculated motion. She looked about and chuckled, but she appeared sullen underneath her veneer.

"You believe in horse telepathy?" Vickie seemed intensely interested.

"I certainly do, having experienced it all my life. In fact, I'm the one who mentioned the subject to John." Leslie's wicked laugh reminded Vickie of a spoiled princess. "He was ready to send me to the loony bin like Nicole, but then he recalled having had similar experiences, the kind no one can explain and few would care to try. At any rate, we both have an affinity for the equine, which is why I love him so dearly."

"You qualify your words." Vickie gave her a wry smile.

Leslie stiffened. "What do you mean?"

"You say his care for horses is why you love him."

"Well, yes, but it was merely a figure of speech."

"What if he changed? What if he did something else?"

"I would love him just the same."

"If you truly loved John, he would join you on the campaign trail."

Leslie's eyes fell to the table, and her hand rubbed clockwise, as was Vickie's habit, and the recognition bothered both women. "Those with deep pockets and powerful connections wouldn't approve of him. I'm sure you know of whom I refer, having kept their company."

"You are ashamed of John, and it shows."

Leslie's cheeks flamed and her eyes flashed fervently.

"You've lost the fine art of tact, Vickie Morrison. What a pity."

Vickie glared. "I'm not like you, Leslie, and never will be."

"We were together at Horseshoe Lake for three summers. I was the counselor who ran the crafts shed where we made the pretty lanyards to show our parents. Do you remember me in the slightest?"

"I think so, now that you mention it. Yes, I do."

"Good. Do you recall the men and women in lab coats and the needles and the cognitive tests? I watched them take you in the camp van and bring you back, beaten down and tired, ready for sleep."

"You look younger than me, Leslie, so I doubt it."

"I'm a few years older, but my handlers keep me youthful, and I go along with them because what's the alternative, God?" She laughed wickedly. Her face grew serious, as did her tone. "I'm here for John."

"You can't have him," Vickie said. "I don't know what others might have told you about me, but I'm here to stay, and we'll be together forever once we work through our emotional baggage."

"That's quite a speech. Good for you, Vickie."

"I'm serious. Don't test me."

Leslie shook her head. "No, I'm afraid your keeping John is simply out of the question." She leaned forward. "I like money and prestige, so I've gone along with the cabal's plans, because it serves my interests to do so, and I'll be perfectly blunt by saying they can be a nuisance, but I wouldn't cross them, as they are brutal to flesh and bone and sinew."

"You've seen what they do to people?"

"I have, up close and personal. One doesn't get over such things."

"I know the president of the United States, Keith Ambrose, and he would never be a part of some nefarious group, nor would his chief of staff, Todd Reynolds, who is a friend, not to mention my producer, Mitch Dolan, a colleague I've known since my first day in Washington."

Leslie tapped her finger on the table, and her hazel eyes pierced her adversary, who seemed lethargic and confused and suddenly frightened.

John tried to stand and tell his former lover to leave, but his flesh refused, and he wondered if their coffee was laced. Before his death, Red had relayed threats against Vickie and the girls, as they fit like puzzle pieces into an agenda. He repented of his sins, hoping to break out of a self-imposed prison, but someone gave an order and his heart failed.

"You're scaring me," Vickie said. "Who are these murderers?"

Leslie smiled. "Oh, you know, those who ran the camp." She paused. "They call themselves the Consortium."

Vickie's eyes flickered at John and then darted to Leslie.

"Were all the kids at Horseshoe Lake from cabal families?"

"Those like John were there for cover. Some of us were the offspring of well-connected bloodlines, yours being the Morrison branch."

Vickie uttered a confused sigh. "I'm a Brewer, not a Morrison."

"Yes, but they do whatever they want, and they chose you."

"For what, the cable news business? I was disgraced and fired."

"They have something else planned, but I wasn't told what."

John again tried to get up from his chair, and his body obeyed his will this time, but weakness overwhelmed him and he sank into his seat.

"What did you do to us, Leslie?" He gave her a pleading look.

Vickie's cheeks flushed and her thoughts seemed to crash into one another, and her home suddenly seemed off-limits to them both, more the cabal's than theirs. Her resistance wouldn't last much longer.

"I'm glad John can see who controls your actions," she said wearily.

"They control yours, Victoria Morrison, as you've done their bidding for many years, both at the station and at Planar."

Vickie turned sluggishly to John. "Did you know about this?"

"Not until recently, and I broke with her once I learned the truth."

Leslie's face brightened. She squeezed the pack of sugar on the table opportunistically, which surprised John and made him angry.

"He was your first love, and those can be difficult to forget."

Vickie regained some strength. "You'll have to kill me to take him."

"If it were up to me, you'd be dead. Sorry, but it's how I feel."

Vickie scraped a hand over her face. "Please stop this, Leslie."

Leslie seemed sure of herself, as if the fix was in and her opponent was the last to know, and every word spoken by this vulture who would claim high office made the future vague and impossible and urgent.

Eudora appeared from the hallway and frowned. "Look, lady, Vickie owns Bluecreek Stables, not you, and she wants you out of here, so leave." She gestured at John with a pained but tolerant face. "This man said he wants to move on from you, so take the hint and let him."

Leslie raised her palms in surrender. "How much did you overhear?"

"Enough to know you are not welcome in this house."

Leslie closed her eyes and reopened them. Her lips pinched, and she mumbled a word and then she grabbed Vickie's wrists as she addressed her, making direct eye contact. "Others will follow behind me, and they won't be as nice to you or to John. Let me have him now and get on with your mission." Her head tilted. "You two can never be married."

John's erratic pulse would not calm. He hoped for a quick death.

Eudora rushed over to Leslie and dragged her by the back of the hair from the table. Leslie's knees hit the floor with a thud, but Eudora held onto Leslie's hair and pointed toward the front entrance.

"Get out of this house and off her property this instant!"

Leslie fought against Eudora's grip. Her eyes cut to Vickie.

"Is this what you really want? Think about your family."

Vickie's eyes fell, and she whispered. "Please leave us alone."

"All right, but you will not like what comes next. I assure you."

Eudora released her prey and pointed. "Get out!"

Leslie straightened her clothes as she eyed Eudora. "Feel good?"

Eudora gave her a sneer. "I've never felt better, but you'll be sore."

"Oh, I'll soon return the favor." Leslie threw her a callous grin.

Eudora shoved the woman forward, and she complied, eyeing John as she walked through the door and onto the steps and across the grass.

She paused halfway to her limousine and wheeled.

"John, this is an unfortunate mistake. Please let me help you."

He led her the rest of the way, ending their encounter. "My father is in hospice, and Vickie graciously offered to let him die at Bluecreek. I can't commit to anything with all these horses who need my help and with Garrett's health worsening each day." He glanced at Vickie, who crossed her arms and glared at him. "After he's gone, we'll talk."

Leslie drew near and fixed his collar like a mother.

"Fine. I will let you play cowboy a bit longer."

"Thank you."

"But after my election, I want us to spend Christmas together."

"Why?"

"To announce our engagement."

She would hold a press conference on a cabin porch overlooking a gorgeous mountain lake, most likely Tahoe, which fit her elegant style, and which represented everything John despised.

"My people will set it up, and we'll share you with the entire world."

His agreement would get her to leave. "I'll think about it, Leslie."

"It's all I ask." She leaned in for a kiss, but he drew away from her.

She opened the door and paused as her eyes met Vickie's across the grass. She kissed John's hand softly and with wet lips, which reawakened Vickie from her slumber and drew her ire. "One more thing."

"Yes?" Vickie lifted her eyebrows.

"You needn't worry about Tink Brewer's men."

"What does that mean, Leslie?"

The next governor smiled. "Just what you think it means."

Eudora rushed toward Leslie, but she ducked into her seat and slammed the door. Eudora searched the grass and found a handful of rocks and threw them at the car, pelting it as it inched forward.

Vickie went to Eudora and squeezed her arm and shook her head.

Leslie Carter's limousine drifted methodically along the driveway and turned right onto Route 15 and accelerated beyond their point of viewing, the sound of her furious engine lingering like a threat.

They checked the mail at the road and gazed, ensuring she was gone, and on the return they examined the lilacs along the far edge of the driveway. Their eyes rose to the hickories and oaks and pines, which ran between Bluecreek Stables and an expanse owned by the power company, a clearing dotted with high-voltage towers and frequented by deer at midnight and the occasional bear in summer season.

Garrett summoned John and told him to leave the toxic woman alone because Vickie was right: Leslie was ashamed of him.

He asked to remove the high-flow oxygen, but the nurse refused.

"I'm sorry for how we treated you, John, but you won't make it right by marrying Leslie Carter. She wants a man she can control, and that man isn't you, or it had better not be you."

"I was wrong to be with her, but I've never had an ounce of status, unlike you or Chris or even Carlie, with her boutique on Adams Street."

Garrett gestured at Vickie, who shifted her weight.

"This one has status, but she also has heart and loyalty."

John sheepishly smiled at her, as he was unsure of their future. "She and I haven't been in a relationship for twenty years. You know that."

Garrett fell back against his pillow and struggled to speak.

"Your mother and I broke off for ten years before we married, so don't act like there's no precedent. This woman loves you."

Garrett's eyes searched the ceiling as if he contemplated death.

The nurse scanned the PERF metrics. His oxygen saturation was low and his heart rate elevated. "You two should leave. He needs rest."

He fought to get out the words. "I have little time left, and I have to know you're okay, John." A pause. "You must rediscover your love."

John turned to Vickie, and a confession broke from her lips.

"I can't live without you. This world has almost destroyed me."

"We must turn to Jesus and repent and ask for His protection."

"Will He save us from them?"

"His grace is enough, Vickie. It will be enough."

Her eyes gazed into his without blinking, and she moved closer and kissed him, and a beautiful bond fashioned itself between them, a renewal of all which the Lord had intended and would ever intend, as a restoration of family was His legacy and the Edenic calling once tainted by Adam and Eve grew within these two tarnished but repentant souls.

John retrieved Garrett's Bible from the table and read Psalm 51:7-19: "Purify me from my sins, and I will be clean; wash me, and I will be whiter than snow. Oh, give me back my joy again; you have broken me, now let me rejoice. Don't keep looking at my sins. Remove the stain of my guilt. Create in me a clean heart, O God. Renew a loyal spirit within me. Do not banish me from your presence, and don't take your Holy Spirit from me. Restore to me the joy of your salvation, and make me willing to obey you. Then I will teach your ways to rebels, and they will return to you. Forgive me for shedding blood, O God who saves; then I will joyfully sing of your forgiveness. Unseal my lips, O Lord, that my mouth may praise you. You do not desire a sacrifice, or I would offer one. You do not want a burnt offering. The sacrifice you desire is a broken spirit. You will not reject a broken and repentant heart, O God. Look with favor on Zion and help her; rebuild the walls of Jerusalem. Then you will be pleased with sacrifices offered in the right spirit, with burnt offerings and whole burnt offerings. Then bulls will again be sacrificed on your altar." He closed the Bible and said a silent prayer.

Garrett raised his frail hands high and repented to the Lord.

They joined his side as he received the salvation of the cross from Jesus, and John thanked the Most High for never giving up on his father and for keeping him alive so he might be liberated from his sin.

TWELVE

Psalm 52:3

You love evil more than good
and lies more than truth.

John and Vickie compared their experiences with horses and shared ideas on how best to work with them. The night before, Vickie had found Michelle's diary entries documenting her equestrian principles, but she didn't agree with the sentiment her sister expressed. Michelle had written that some owners starved their rescues beyond recovery, and it might not be worth the trouble or expense to treat their myriad symptoms.

Vickie's anger toward Michelle flared. She could no longer call to mind the thousand sisterly moments they had shared, and she believed Michelle deserved her fate, the indifference she had once shown those rescues had come home to roost. The thought made Vickie glad.

Unable to bear her heartless nature, John led them in prayer.

"Lord, we repent our many sins and ask your forgiveness."

He held Vickie's hand and asked her to recite the Lord's Prayer.

She held the Bible and read Matthew 6:9-13. "Our Father in heaven, may your name be kept holy. May your Kingdom come soon. May your will be done on earth, as it is in heaven. Give us today the food we need, and forgive us our sins, as we have forgiven those who sin against us. And don't let us yield to temptation, but rescue us from the evil one."

Vickie closed the Bible. "Did I recite the verses correctly?"

"You did very well." He smiled. "You should read them more often."

She smirked. "Monologues of a lapsed Catholic."

John chuckled. "God is no respecter of persons."

Vickie crossed her arms and sighed. "You just lost me."

"Jesus cares only about relationship with you, not ceremonial rites."

"If He knew what I've done, He would want little to do with me."

"He does, Vickie. He knows the number of hairs on your head, and there's nothing you can hide from Him. All He wants is your honesty."

"I can't bring myself to think about my sins, much less confess them."

John left her with a Bible and Michelle's notes. After a few minutes, Vickie grew bored with her lack of love for a sister who seemed more stranger than friend. She rifled through papers in Red's office, looking for answers to forgotten questions.

She tripped over some boxes and discovered a gold watch inscribed to Valerie. It was the watch Tink Brewer had stolen and returned after his death. The inscription read: "To my darling wife, Valerie, a loving mother to our angel, Michelle, and an enabler of her misbegotten, Vickie."

She dropped the watch and fell to her knees, shocked at the hatred both Red and Valerie had felt for her and for Price, as if biological father and daughter were identical. Valerie's taunting once more washed over the illegitimate child who now occupied an adult woman's body.

Moments from a birthday flickered, and she curled into a ball.

Red had promised a special night when Vickie turned eighteen, father and daughter bonding over an expensive meal, celebrating her entry into adulthood and the possibilities college afforded. Red could spin with the best of them, and Vickie doubted him from the start, but still she hoped they could become a real family.

She arrived before him and perused the menu, hardly believing the prices or variety. She picked one entrée and steeled herself for the ordering process, which she intended to do completely on her own, as she was shy about such things. Tonight would be a turning point in her life, she was now an adult, and this is what they did. Or so she thought.

A server happened by with a supportive smile, filling Vickie's glass with water several times before commenting on her dress, telling her she looked very nice and her father would be very proud.

Red burst into the restaurant and sat opposite Vickie.

He seemed bitter and inattentive, his usual demeanor, only this mood seemed different, as if weighty issues occupied his mind elsewhere.

The server floated to the table, but he shooed her away.

He shoved an envelope across the table. "Open this after I leave."

"What? You're leaving?" Vickie nervously scanned the dining room.

"I must get back to the station." His eyes were angry and sad.

Vickie held the envelope and judged its weight. Her fingers squeezed one end, but Red stopped her from opening it until he was gone. She complied and watched as he marched to the exit and vanished.

The server put her hand on Vickie's back and leaned close.

"I overheard your conversation. Sit here as long as you like."

Vickie swiped at her tears. This was supposed to be her birthday.

"Thank you, ma'am." She carefully opened the envelope.

Her body settled into the chair, and her fingers traced the words, circling and riding the cursive letters. She vowed never to write in such a fashion again, typography and newspeak would become her primary forms of communication, curt and reliable as they were.

She took a bottle of pills and almost died in the hospital, fleeing to summer camp the following week, where John worked as a counselor.

As a child who craved home and family, Vickie had tried to hug Red, but each time he drew back from her. His disgust made her cry.

Now, as she wept silently in her bunk at midnight, she waited her turn. When her bunkmates fell asleep, she took a horse to John's tent, which he'd placed away from the others who slept near the fire.

For the first time in her life, a man showed her love and affection.

Afterward, she left John for college at Hosman University and an internship with the Planar network. She regretted her midnight decision four weeks later when tests confirmed her pregnancy, a reality that would sink her cable news career before it even started.

Vickie placed the gold watch on Red's desk and swiveled in his chair, stopping when her head grew dizzy. Preston and Lena had owned her at the behest of a father she never knew, and she became a kept woman, never free to make her own choices. Her little innocent daughter paid the sacrificial price, giving her life for her mother's ambition. Chelsea was as much John's child as hers, and it was high time she acknowledged it to herself and to him, but he would leave her once he learned the truth.

Emotions ran hot. Vickie grabbed the edges of the desk and considered taking her life, as the brutality of her action seemed worse than before and she deserved to join her beloved daughter in the grave.

She reflected on Katie and Abbie, how they waited patiently for the old men to die at Bluecreek Stables, although no one dared verbalize the goal or define the interval they might endure before coming home to their rooms and their horses. They would question her choice of death for her own child, and as they wondered at the permanence of such an act, they would doubt her desire to choose life for them. Why should this murderous woman be different from a mother who claimed to love them but lay on her bed for a year and then dropped six feet under, or a father who never existed for them, or a grandfather who suffered a heart attack and then disappeared into a similar hole as their mother?

Unable to stand another minute in Red's house, Vickie slept outside Chief's stall on a couple of hay bales, clutching the watch as she fell into deep slumber. The motif in her head soon shifted from ponderous to a mist of bony hands and skeletal faces and tattered clothes. She tossed and turned and fell onto the floor, picked herself up, and looked about, noting Chief, who stood at his door, staring blankly. Vickie felt safe in his mangled presence; he would protect her.

She drifted to sleep, this time deeper than before, and dreamed.

The woods enveloped her, and she awakened and then drifted again. She stumbled upon a grizzly who slept over a carcass. He moved slightly, and several birds tried to get at the slain body, but the bear's massive girth blocked their attempts. Coyotes and wolves appeared, arousing the bear from his rest. Vickie tried to back away from the bear and the carcass, but the bear was on her fast, menacing her with growls and sweeps of his arm and claws.

It was then her fangs grew, and her form transformed into another, a beast with greater strength than even the seven-hundred-pound grizzly, if such a thing was possible. She confronted the bear with all her might, terrifying him. After he left, she investigated the blood-soaked carcass, but the bear had crushed the poor victim's face, making recognition impossible. She looked about the area for clues and discovered a well-worn and dusty Bible.

She opened the cover and read the inscription, written in cursive: "To my darling daughter, Katie, whom I love with all my heart."

Vickie jolted awake on the floor and sat up, removing hay from her mouth and hair. Her hands groped for the gold watch, but it was gone.

Katie occupied her mind as she frantically searched through the hay bales and along the floor, unable to discern how she might have lost such a precious and hurtful keepsake. She sat and wept into her hands, uncaring of the scars on Chief's face or the worried look in his eyes.

He discovered the watch in his stall and offered it to her.

Vickie shoved new bales together and slept on them three nights in a row. Chief's behavior improved, but the hay threw her back out of joint. She had trouble sitting at her desk or doing work in the field, and John thought her strange for avoiding the house and a perfectly good bed in the main bedroom, even if it rode higher than she preferred.

On the third morning, a box truck ambled up the driveway and dropped off a casket. The driver said little when asked about the delivery other than "sign here" before leaving for greener pastures. A note inside the satin-lined box declared the sender was none other than Leslie Carter, who presented a "kind and thoughtful gift" for Garrett's last days.

Eudora's earring rested on the pillow as yet another threat.

Vickie laughed to herself as she considered sleeping in the casket, and her thoughts once more shifted to Chelsea. She went to her desk in the barn office and rocked in place, telling herself Chelsea was better off staying out of this fallen world. It might have made her deviant like Valerie, and Vickie couldn't have handled such a horrible outcome. Valerie popped pills and drank alcohol and passed out on the couch with vomit on her cheeks and on the carpet below her sad and wretched body, and that was before she killed herself in a wreck.

Red wasn't her biological father, but she tried to be a daughter to him, as she tried with Valerie before her death. He would have none of it and kept his distance, working long hours at the station even though Laura Hangar ran the daily operations for him and the small market wasn't exactly a challenge to withstand. Michelle wasn't much better, rubbing her burdensome nature in her face, saying she wasn't actually a Morrison but a Brewer, and everyone knew the Brewers were trash. Michelle later found Christ and repented for her sins and tried to teach Vickie about Jesus, but by then Vickie wanted little to do with Him or with her younger sister.

Then Vickie aborted Chelsea for her dream of becoming the face of cable news and blamed Lena for years, but it was her own choice and she must take accountability for her sins, as Michelle did before she died. Katie and Abbie's hearts were pure gold, and they deserved a mother if anyone on earth did. Vickie must preserve and foster and balance the tiny remnants of innocence that remained in their souls.

Vickie put her head on the desk and spread her arms, stretching them across the cluttered surface, knocking papers and books and other random items out of the way. Her childhood abandonment and

Chelsea's abortion and her rape had left her too broken, all hope drained, stealing her resourcefulness and her desire to move a finger.

"What's going on here?" asked John. "More self-pity?"

She sat up straight and got a crick in her neck and rubbed it hard.

"You caught me in the middle of an extravagant pity party."

He seemed restless but played along with her.

"Anyone there I should know?"

"Only the best come to my gala events. We weep into punch bowls."

He smiled and gestured for her to follow him outside, where he would teach her about equine body language and common behavioral issues and how the two often intertwined. If she knew how to read a horse's body language, she could head off misbehavior just as the idea formed in the animal's mind, and the place to learn was the round pen.

She was confused when he led her to the front pasture, turning right instead of left, as she thought he would have her lunge Chief again.

They stood at the fence and watched the herd interact with Wildfire and Hero, whom he'd integrated three days earlier. There was Dash, the light bay with the leg, which had healed nicely; Riddle, a bald chestnut who seemed mysterious, as no one knew a thing about his background; Suzy, a buckskin mare who enjoyed biting humans as they turned their backs on her; Sky, a gray horse whom Vickie named because of his color and her disposition toward life; Ocean, a liver chestnut with a strong presence; Sapphire, an overo with one blue eye and a sparkling radiance; Caprice, a palomino with a playful and unpredictable manner; Breakfast Blend, a pinto mare, named because of Vickie's undying love for her morning coffee and for the color of the horse's coat; and Salem, a pleasant roan gelding. Savannah, the pregnant mare with a weak heart, and Chief, whom a grizzly had mangled, remained in the barn for safety.

Vickie informed John of Chief's progress, but he wouldn't budge.

He opened the gate and beckoned her to join him in the field.

John gave her extra time, and she appreciated his affections, but when he mentioned the signs of a sour horse, how they no longer seem willing to do basic things, frustrating their owners with their defeated spirits, how they resent everything and everyone about them, she grew angry and crossed her arms and defied his attempt to refocus her.

He fell to impatience and marched inside, leaving her to observe the herd. She stood in wrath for ten minutes, tapping her foot, kicking at rocks, glancing several times at the house. Then she tried her sister's techniques, noting each horse's movements, but as she went, she sensed each emotion that caused an external manifestation of behavior.

John stepped to the fence and called to her. "Garrett needs you."

She entered the house and stood beside Garrett's bed.

"Take care of John when I'm gone."

"I promise."

He lifted his frail hand, and she squeezed it. "You'd better, because you're the best thing to happen to him, and don't let Leslie Carter run you off." A pause. "Don't forget what's been missing from your life."

"I won't," she said.

"Other folks let people love them, Vickie. You should try it."

When he coughed blood, she swiped tears from her eyes.

Riddle nickered from the pasture, and Vickie knew he sensed her pain. She went to the window and placed her palm against the glass.

He circled the other horses and looked at the house and sniffed.

"I have to go to my horse," she said.

"Vickie, not now." John's voice cracked.

"It's alright." Garrett smiled at her. "See you on the other side."

"Goodbye, Mr. B," she said. "I have always loved you."

Vickie took his hand and kissed it, and then she left him with John.

Once in the pasture, she rubbed Riddle's back, calming him, and sat on the grass as minutes slipped into an hour. It wouldn't be long now.

John stepped outside, and she stood. "Garrett is gone."

He sighed and looked at the road.

"I have to call the funeral home." He shut the door.

The permanence of Mr. B's death upset her more than she'd expected, and she left Riddle's side on unwieldy legs, somehow moving herself toward the fence. She took a knee in the spring grass, clutching a rail, weeping, feeling completely unprotected, the same emotion she experienced when her mother died on a slim stretch of highway in a bloody, tearful mess. Price approached from the house and dropped to his knees beside her. He hugged her and said he was sorry for her loss.

She pushed him from her. "I don't need your help."

Price spoke through tears. "My absence caused you pain, but you were never an orphan. I'm your father, and I won't leave you again."

She hugged him and wept.

Her body shook with desperate violence.

"I want my daughter, Daddy." Her fingers clutched his shirt.

He held her tighter and whispered into her ear. "Go get the girls."

She drew back from him. "No, I need Chelsea, my baby."

Price wiped her cheeks. "I don't know about her, but I can guess what happened, as you've been distant since you arrived in Addison and I've sensed something was terribly wrong. But there are two girls who need a mother, and you can be one for them, especially Abbie."

Vickie buried her face in his chest and moaned.

"I don't know how, and they won't want me when they find out."

He rubbed her hair. "I don't know either, but I'm doing it."

Her head fell back, and she wiped her tears. "Meaning?"

"You'll figure it out like everyone else."

Vickie pushed the rapist from her and went alone to the barn, where she took her place at the desk, contemplating her memories and her mistakes and what remained of her options. Garrett had been so kind to her on that fateful afternoon, the one that forever changed her life.

Valerie had left a letter on the table and then taken pills with her vodka, and it wasn't long before she played loud music and danced about the room like a banshee. But then her mood changed and she grew sullen and dangerous and unkind, which seemed the usual afternoon routine, or so Vickie thought. She grabbed a washcloth from the hamper and wet it under the sink and wiped the vomit from Valerie's chin and the bits that hit the floor, knowing Red would be angry with her if Valerie disappointed at dinner. But her mother regained consciousness and shoved her daughter and the towel to the floor and grabbed her car keys from beside the letter on the table.

Valerie's dress slipped from her fingers, but she followed her mother to the station wagon and climbed onto the passenger seat and slammed the door.

"Get out of here!" Valerie's voice was a high-pitched wail.

Vickie crossed her arms and shook her head, unwilling to budge.

"Have it your way. We'll die together."

The frightened eight-year-old's back pressed into the seat and her fingers pushed into vinyl upholstery as the car sped wildly along the highway and swerved to the right and to the left. She placed a hand over her mouth and stifled a gasp when Valerie screamed obscenities and threatened to run the station wagon off Watkins Bridge and into the river that meandered and gurgled and called menacingly to them. She was thankful when Valerie pulled over to the shoulder and shoved her to the warm asphalt. As the station wagon sped from her position, she waved one last time.

It was then the kind man arrived in his own station wagon and stooped to ask her what might be the trouble and why a young lady would be all alone on a hot July afternoon. Then Vickie told him of her travails and about the mother who possessed a death wish for the ages. The man introduced himself as Mr. B and said they would catch up to her mother and stop her and get her some much-needed help, so Vickie should not trouble herself with worry. But soon they happened upon the wreck and he rushed up to the disfigured car and flung open the door, which didn't work very well, and let the woman he didn't know fall bloody into his lap, crying out in a whisper for someone Vickie didn't know, nor did the man, because he asked politely and listened hard with his right ear against Valerie's lips.

Mr. B assured the frantic woman she would be just fine and the phantom man would be along any minute to take care of her. This was the moment Vickie knew Mr. B was a liar and all the world was delusion and she would believe nothing ever again, and he knew it too, because when Valerie's tears ceased and her breath left her body, he fell onto the pavement and cried out to God in agony, as if he'd been the one to wreck his station wagon. Vickie knew she would withhold her love eternally and no more truth would pass across her lips, as the whole world was false.

Vickie's eyes rose to the ceiling.

"Goodbye, Mr. B. Thank you for being so kind to me that day."

She paused.

"I was just a kid with a tragic mother who died and a father in prison who was never alive, at least for me, and I really needed your help." She looked about the room and the tears burst from her like water from the falls and would not stop. After several minutes of clutching the side of the desk and falling to the floor and writhing like the women at the abortion clinic, she flopped over to one side and rubbed the slats in the floor, wondering what to do next and dreading the answer but knowing she must bare her soul in honesty.

She sat up against the desk and spoke aloud to the room.

"I will put the wheels in motion and soon the girls will be mine."

Vickie waited for an answer. Sunlight broke through the curtains, and the nickering of horses in the field called to her like a glad song.

THIRTEEN

Psalm 53:1

Only fools say in their hearts,
"There is no God."
They are corrupt, and their actions are evil;
not one of them does good!

May 2008

As early May broke across the county and shadows covered ready cornfields, spring blossomed in respectable fashion, soon to make way for a long, hot summer. John thought of October sea breezes in the Outer Banks, which felt cleaner and softer and more inviting after the throngs of tourists went back home. He hoped Vickie might still be in Addison then, and perhaps they could share a rental house in Avon or Buxton or Hatteras, anywhere near the brush of the ocean and the smell of salty wind and the fineries of a boiled shrimp life-style. Leslie's spiteful threats and Garrett's death had left the reunited couple in low spirits, and a week at the beach would do them well.

After a few turns in the round pen, which they'd barely used in favor of the front pasture, they coaxed Savannah into the barn. But she tugged on the lead rope and, despite John's efforts, pulled free at the gate and ran toward the highway. He waved a hand and let her go, ashamed of his amateur mistake. She stopped at the end of the drive and looked back at them and at the house in a muddled state of confusion, and John cursed himself, which painted a look of concern on Vickie's face.

"Won't we go after her? She might get hit on the road."

"It's bad horsemanship to corner a horse. I should know better."

"That's fine, John, but what about the mare?"

He looked judiciously at Savannah and then turned to Vickie.

"I hope she comes home sooner rather than later." He scowled. "Happy?"

He walked to the barn and sat on the feed bin.

Vickie leaned in for a kiss, which drew a surprised look.

"What's that for? I thought you'd be upset."

"You are a good man, John Breyer."

He ran his fingers through her hair. "Now you're scaring me."

She laughed. "You need my encouragement and support. You've just lost your father, and you're not thinking clearly this morning."

Vickie paused.

"It's all right. I understand."

"Great. I have that going for me, which is nice."

She leaned in again, and this time she tickled him, which he loved.

A nicker sounded beside them, and they looked up to see Savannah, who stood ten feet away, licking her lips. He drew Vickie back and gestured. "Licking is a good sign. Her brain has released serotonin."

"Which means she's relaxed?"

He pulled Vickie to him and kissed her, harder this time.

A few minutes passed, and they looked up to find Savannah standing in front of her stall, waiting for someone to open the door.

John left Vickie at the bin and helped the weak horse inside. Then he went back to the woman he loved, hopeful this wasn't all some dream or a sick joke played on him by the devil. He stood beside her, and she said she loved him, and he said it too, and their kisses lasted longer.

A thought washed over her. She pulled back from him in sadness.

"I wish I could be a mother to your child, but it's too late."

"Not really. Women have babies into their forties."

She bit her lip in frustration, but he wasn't sure why.

Please, Lord. Help her come to terms with what's on her mind.

Suddenly, buying a ring and getting down on one knee sounded like a great idea, and a portrait of Bluecreek Stables filled with love and laughter and children painted itself merrily across his mind.

"I'm not like them," she said. "It wouldn't work for me."

He smiled and kissed her and pushed a strand of hair over one ear.

"You say it so formally and so officially, and it's neither."

She paced slowly in front of him and started to say something.

His head dropped, and his eyes met hers. "It's all right."

She shook her head. "No, it isn't, John."

Vickie clenched and unclenched her hands as if they were sore from overwork, and she continued to pace with a worried look, which passed some of the concern onto him. He looked at her with respect and feeling and confidence. "You have a golden opportunity right in front of you."

Vickie stopped pacing. "How?"

"Katie and Abbie."

Her tears flowed, and he wiped them with his rough hand.

She seemed anxious and taken to some foreign country, but she kept still and sentimental when asked to share what bothered her.

"I've made mistakes, John. It's all I can say."

He kissed her fingers and wished to make love to her but knew they could not, as they were unmarried and the Lord would disapprove.

"Please share your brokenness and your corruption with me."

She looked at the sky, and then her desperate eyes met his.

"Maybe someday, but not now."

After dinner, they talked into the night in the living room.

A dull noise outside startled her, and she left the couch and moved toward the foyer, but John grabbed her, pausing her momentum, and stuck his head through the front door, finding only the hum of crickets and a pulse of breeze against his cheeks and the sweet smell of jasmine.

He guided her to the couch, and she seemed mesmerized by him.

"I can't believe how strong you are and the fortitude you've displayed with your father's death. Most people would lose themselves."

"Is that what you do when someone dies?"

"Yes, and I've often considered ending my own life."

He pulled her legs onto his lap and held them in place.

"We'll have no more talk of suicide in this house," he said sternly.

"Yes, sir." She nodded to him in mock surrender.

He smirked. "I'm serious. Stay with me."

Her legs pushed into him. "How are you coping without Garrett?"

"It's harder than I expected." He hesitated, measuring her support.

Another disturbance arose, this time from the direction of the barn.

On their feet in half a second, they headed for the door, racing in a fast walk, unwilling to concede victory. Chief had refused to come in from the side yard earlier, but now he loudly asked to enter the runway, pounding and screaming. His coat was dirty, as if he'd rolled in dirt.

"What in the world? He's a filthy mess."

She moved nearer to Chief, but John stopped her.

"Give him some space, Vickie. I don't want you getting hurt."

"He needs me. We have a special bond, which I won't break."

Her defiance made John unhappy, as he had her best interests at heart, and her refusals seemed disrespectful, as if she held him in low regard. He paced in front of the barn, biting his lip to keep from blowing up at her. Vickie's rebellious nature and Garrett's death had pushed him to a breaking point, and his eyes flashed at her indignantly.

"I told you to stay back, and I meant what I said!"

She shrank from him. The daylight within her turned to night.

Her fear melted his wrath, as he had become like his father, and he grew mournful. "I'm sorry, Vickie." He drew nearer and held her and kissed her forehead. "You mean everything to me. I love you."

Chief emitted a high-pitched scream, which deafened them.

"Why is he doing that?" She held her hands over her ears.

"I don't know."

John wanted to rush toward Chief and grab him and make him be silent, but he kept his focus on the panic within Vickie.

Abbie leaped from the porch onto the grass and approached Chief before anyone could stop her. She grabbed his halter and led him to the slat that barred entrance into the runway and slid it open, which made Chief flinch, but he stayed with her. She led him into the barn and opened the door to his stall and let him inside, where he pawed the floor.

"That's all he wanted." Abbie placed her hands on her hips.

Katie ran up to the group, breathless. "Are you okay?"

Abbie crossed her arms. "I'm fine. Maybe you should ask them."

John kept his eyes on Vickie as her look of alarm dissipated.

He smiled at Abbie. "Sorry. I've been out of it since my dad died."

"We get it," Katie said. "Now you're in the orphan club."

In the barn office, Vickie allowed Abbie to climb into her lap.

"You know, Chief can sometimes be a furious horse."

"Not with me," said the girl calmly.

"With anyone, even me, and I've slept near him on hay bales."

Abbie perked up at the notion. "Did he like that?"

John saw their dialogue as a hopeful sign. They might actually form a mother-daughter bond if they broke through their awkwardness.

"He did, and I must say I am impressed with your care for these horses," said Vickie with deep meaning. "I saw you in the field earlier, standing between Dash and Riddle, who are friends, and Wildfire, who can be as aggressive as Chief. You helped all three horses form an empathic bond, and it will make a big difference to the herd's health."

Abbie's eyes dropped. "I don't know that word, empathic."

Price stood in the doorway and leaned against the wooden frame.

"It means horses love like people do."

He paused.

"You are a natural horsewoman, just like your mother."

Abbie's eyes moistened. "Please don't say that."

"Why not? You could be as good as her someday."

Vickie's face clouded with apprehension.

"It might not be the best time, Price."

He shrugged. "I was just saying she has a gift."

Words burst forth, exploding the dam of Abbie's restraint.

"Mommy's accident was all my fault!"

Vickie hugged her tightly and fought tears.

"No, sweetie. Sometimes horses rear on their rider."

"Mommy said she would show me how to work with him."

Vickie glanced at John, and they both understood.

She wiped tears from the girl's cheeks. "Wildfire?"

Abbie's head fell in shame. Her silence spoke volumes.

"Was she teaching you when it happened?"

Abbie's eyes met Vickie's, and she cast a sorrowful look.

"I'm so sorry, but please don't leave us. I didn't mean to kill Mommy." Her eyes searched for Katie, who swiped at her own tears.

"Oh, honey, your mother loved you more than anything, and she wanted you to follow in her footsteps as a trainer." Vickie took a breath and exhaled. "Do you know what she told me the last time we talked?"

"What?"

"To stay away from you girls."

Abbie seemed confused. "How come?"

"So she could have you all to herself. Michelle was the best mother in the entire world, and she would never abandon you on purpose."

"Like you do?" asked Katie from the end of the desk.

Vickie smiled faintly. "Yes."

"Do you leave people before they leave you?"

Vickie's face flushed red. "You are a perceptive girl, Katie."

John saw their talk had gone in a negative direction, and he tried to change the tone. He gestured at the house. "What should we do now?"

"We could play a card game at the table," said Katie dryly.

John thought back to a time before Michelle's paralysis and before Red's death, when there was life in the house and the girls were happy and there were fun games around the table and laughter filled the air.

"Like we used to do with Michelle and Red."

Katie nodded.

"It's been too long. The house seems dreary and lifeless."

Vickie's eyes fell warmly on Katie. "I'm game for some cards."

"Are you serious right now? Don't mess with us, Vickie."

The teen's eyes lit up, which tugged at John's heart.

"Sure, but if we play UNO, I'll win every game. I'm the champion."

"Oh, yeah?" Katie laughed. "We'll see about that."

Vickie's arms squeezed around Abbie. "What about you?"

"Me?"

"Do you know how to play UNO?"

The little girl shook her head, and again she seemed ashamed.

"It's okay." Vickie's eyes sparkled. "We'll teach you."

Abbie gave her aunt a kiss and looked at her with amused wonder.

"I wish you had come home sooner. Mommy needed you."

"I know, honey." Vickie placed a strand of hair behind her ear.

Abbie pulled back and considered. "She told me something."

"You mean just before she died?"

Abbie's face went pale. Her eyes darted to Katie.

Katie gasped and moved nearer. "You were there?"

Abbie nodded.

"But we didn't see you." Katie knelt and cupped her sister's chin.

"You were supposed to be upstairs in your room, playing."

"I hid in the closet and peeked through a crack."

Vickie pushed Abbie from her lap, standing her on two feet.

"What did Michelle say to you before she died?"

Abbie's eyes fell to the floor. "She said not to tell."

"Please, Abbie. It's important we know the truth."

"She said our daddy's name was Tink."

The room fell silent. No one said a word for several minutes.

Two days later, they sipped coffee at five o'clock in the morning and talked in the living room, where she confided her faith. It was surprising considering her history, but since she was a girl, she'd known God existed and the Bible contained the only truth in this fallen realm.

"That's wonderful," he said. "But there's a next step."

"Which is?"

"You must confess all your sins to Him and ask for His grace."

"Will it be enough? It seems strange to bypass a priest."

John pursed his lips, as he wanted to criticize the worship of Mary and the archangels, but his disdain would only anger her. "Jesus is always enough. We must confess our sins to Him and those we've sinned against, not some guy in a confessional who thinks he's a god."

"You don't like me as a Catholic, do you?"

"I love you, Vickie, which means I accept everything about you."

She considered.

"I'll talk to God later by myself, but not here in public."

"Am I public?"

"You know what I meant. I'm embarrassed."

He shifted the subject, as she'd clearly grown uncomfortable.

"Can I ask you for a favor in the meantime?"

She nodded.

"Please nurse my heart. I'm having a rough go without my father."

"It's what I'm doing right now and what I'd love to do forever."

The permanence of her comment struck him, and he drew back.

Air between them grew thick as each felt awkward and without oxygen, although each of them desperately needed romance and to share a home filled with love and affection and the validating breath of life.

"Did you know Tink?" she asked. "He was my brother, but I never knew him, and from what Price said, it was for the best."

He shook his head. "I'd heard he was a bad guy who ran with a hard crew, and then I found out about the horses and the kill pens, and that told me all I needed to know. I'm surprised Michelle knew him."

"I talked to Mary, and she said the station is abuzz with gossip about the murder of his men. Two separate crews have investigated and issued reports from various farms that extend over three counties."

Vickie paused.

"He had a serious operation, but I had no clue he existed."

"Me either, until recently, and I've been here all my life."

"Mary said police found his body in a lake six months ago." Vickie retrieved the gold watch from her pocket. "I don't know why, but I've been carrying this stupid thing since I discovered it in Red's office."

She handed it to John, and he flipped it and read the inscription. "Wow, what a heartfelt message." He smirked and mimicked throwing the watch across the room, but she caught his hand and stopped him.

"Please don't," she said.

"I wouldn't throw it, but you should dump it in the garbage."

"I may be crazy, but it was Red's, and I want to keep it."

"Fine, but I think their attitude was horrible. They mistreated you."

"If it makes you feel better," she said, smiling, "I lost it for a while."

"Good riddance, with all that mess written on the back."

He reflected.

"How did it turn up? Did you find it under Red's papers?"

"I lost it in the barn, but it wasn't me who found it."

John grabbed the watch and weighed it in his hands. He returned her smile and tossed the watch into her lap. Her hands fumbled for it, and she held it against her chest like a prize, which amazed him.

"The watch is here with us," he said. "I doubt magic was involved."

"The magician was Chief."

John laughed. "Our resident barn monster?"

"You're quick for a country boy." She chuckled and caught herself.

"Oh, really?" His eyebrows arched as he leaned in and tickled her.

She giggled and then tried to peel his arms away, which he allowed.

"An officer returned Red's watch after detectives recovered it from

Tink's body." Her voice grew grave. She held it up to the light and studied it with narrowed eyes. "With all this thing suffered and how unlikely its travels to reach home, it still ticks and keeps good time."

The watch meant much more to her than a family keepsake. Behind her facade of bravery, she was still an eight-year-old girl on the side of the highway who had watched her unforgiving mother whisper a last word.

He pushed himself to the end of the couch and considered.

She gave him a hurtful look, as if he didn't want her anymore.

"Don't get worried, Vickie. I want to talk about something else."

She shifted her body to face his across the distance and waited.

"I've been thinking about Leslie's threats for the last two weeks."

"Do you think she had something to do with Tink's death?"

"Yes, and all his men."

"If she was involved in their operation, she'd want it cleaned up before the election, or it would end her chances of becoming governor."

"We must take her seriously," John said. "I believe she's a misguided woman who's likely in over her head with some very dangerous people."

"They'll murder you and take me for some crazy agenda."

"I won't let either of those things happen," he said.

"What are people saying in town? Has there been any gossip?"

His voice grew ominous. "Most people either don't know or wouldn't utter a syllable out of fear for themselves or the lives of their loved ones, but I know a few people who trust me enough to share."

"Don't keep me in suspense." She threw up her hands in revolt.

"Leslie and Tink ran drugs between the mid-Atlantic and Mexico."

A look of recognition broke across Vickie's face. "In horse trailers?"

He nodded.

"Kill buyers route horses from the Carolinas to Texas kill pens, and then trucks haul those horses to Mexico. It makes for a handy pipeline."

"And people here knew about it? I find that hard to believe."

"Like I said, I was planning to leave this place when you arrived."

"Addison isn't so bad." Her eyes grew amused. "Odd for me to say."

He spoke in a jesting tone. "Especially since you were adamant about leaving. I thought your tires would sling gravel at me."

"I remember, and I was an idiot."

When he made a mean face, she playfully slapped him.

They both laughed, but then she caught herself and spoke gravely.

"When Leslie said a cabal runs everything from behind the scenes, my mind saw a movie villain bent on global domination. She called them the Consortium, but I have no idea what the word means."

Vickie went into Red's office and came back with a dictionary.

"Looking it up?" he asked, grinning.

"Hey, we're not all geniuses. I had to work for my pay."

She flipped to the correct page. "It says an association or a society or a group assembled for financial, investment, or business activities."

"It's a vague description that could apply to just about anyone."

Vickie sighed. "I imagine that's why they're so easily hidden."

He stretched his legs onto hers, and she pushed against him and smiled and gazed blankly at the room. "Probably not a good idea to get on their bad side." Her eyes moistened. "Will we be okay?"

He slid over and drew her near. "It's why we take our problems to the cross in humble repentance and ask for His grace. When we reach the third step, we inherently trust in the righteousness of Christ."

"In all things?" Her whispered breath warmed his neck.

John drew back from her so he might explain. "We must trust in God's will, even when we don't understand, because it's perfect."

She wiped her eyes. "Even if we die? Why would He allow those people to hurt us?" Her arms dropped to her sides, and her shoulders slumped. "Why would He allow all the things that have happened to us in our lives if He really loves us? Why would He gather us as a mom and dad for Katie and Abbie, only to let the murderers win? I've never understood God's plan because it seems so mean-spirited." She grabbed John's arms and squeezed them. "Look at how Tink's men treated the horses." She hesitated. "Chief's owner screamed in terror as the grizzly ripped open her flesh and spilled her blood, and then the bear turned on Chief and clawed his face. I've seen in my mind over and over what happened when Chief tried to save the woman he loved but couldn't. Her death grieved him, and he still remembers. I think he's ashamed."

"Do you think he still misses her?" John gave Vickie a tender look.

"Of course he does, and I think it's why he's bonded with me."

"And it's why he let Abbie be kind to him," said John softly.

Lord, help me convince her your will is perfect.

"Don't you see? Jesus reunited us for a purpose that has eternal value. We'll help these horses recover, both physically and emotionally, and we'll do the same for Katie and Abbie, who need us to raise them."

"If Jesus lets us live," said Vickie in a cynical tone.

"He will. There's no other explanation."

She buried her face in his shirt. John held her close as she wept.

An hour passed, and the couple moved so they could watch the sun break over the far mountains and see deer scamper into the tree line.

"Do you know much about Leslie's family?"

John had been looking at a stray Labrador retriever that hopped on three legs along Route 15, but the dog passed Bluecreek's pasture and vanished. John gestured at the roadway, seeming resolute and angry.

"Someone should see about that dog. He looks injured."

She smiled. "So get off your rear end and do it."

He smirked. "Frankly, I'm tired, and I'm enjoying this coffee."

"Do you think he'll be back again?" She peered through the thin stretch of oaks and hickories that separated her land from the power company's, and wondered if a black bear might hurt the poor dog.

"How do you know it's a he?"

She settled into the rocker. "You know what I meant."

"Guess we'll see. If he's hungry enough, he'll come back around."

Vickie's voice grew gloomier. "Tell me about Leslie's father."

"His name is Roland, and I've never liked him much, to be honest."

"Does he race horses?"

John nodded.

"Leslie said he's always on the lookout for the next Triple Crown winner, and his horses originate from the Native Dancer bloodline, which goes back to the 1950s. Scientists believe the C-allele accounts for the great speed in thoroughbreds, and all Roland's horses have some of Native Dancer in their blood. He touts it as their mystical weapon."

"The cost must be sky-high," she said in amazement.

John's smile became a sneer. "It's why they're so rich."

Lewis opened the door and sat in an adjacent set of rockers, preparing for work at the station. He spoke little and seemed aloof.

"How's everything going?" asked Vickie cheerfully.

"Not so well," Lewis said. "But I'll see it through."

"Is Mary helping?" Vickie felt a rush of anger. "If not, let me know."

"She's been standoffish, like I'm a criminal." He hesitated. "To be fair, she stays busy with all the fuss lately. Reggie is cool, though."

"How about the others? Do you get along with them?"

He shook his head, and his voice carried a tilt of reproof.

"Not really. I don't think they like the military or veterans."

"Have they been mean?" Vickie rose and peered down at him.

His eyes followed her movements. "You're graceful when you want to be, Vickie Morrison, and I can see why the camera likes your face."

She blushed and sank into her rocker, unsure how to respond.

"Do you enjoy working behind the camera?" asked John firmly.

Lewis eyed Vickie, which made her uncomfortable.

He held his gaze and withheld a reply.

"I asked you a question."

"Yeah, I guess. Whatever." Lewis finally turned from her.

John got up and went over to Lewis. "Vickie is my girl, so lay off."

Lewis chuckled. "She's a fine woman, not a girl. Get that straight."

John recoiled, as if he couldn't believe what he'd just heard.

"You should find someone your own age. That's free advice."

"My age?"

John glanced at Vickie, who shrugged.

He turned to Lewis. "She and I went to school together, and in all those years and all we did after school, working and playing and kissing, I looked around, but never once did I see you. How can that be?"

John paused.

"Oh, right. You were in diapers and a high chair."

Lewis sneered. "Don't you have horses to shoe, old man?"

"Watch who you're calling old." Vickie gestured at John. "As he said, we're the same age, and we've known each other for a very long time."

"Difference is, you don't look your age. He looks about fifty." Lewis looked away, and Vickie steeled herself for what came next. "I see you get your women to fight for you." He stuck out his thumb to start the count. "First, Mary has been rude to me every day since I started. Second, Vickie investigated the kill buyers, trying to shut down her own brother's operation, but all you've done is steal a few horses. Third, your other girlfriend, Leslie, dropped Tink in the lake like you should've done, and then she had his men killed, one by one, like roaches."

Lewis paused.

"You must be proud of yourself, loser."

John stepped forward. "Let's go into the yard, and we'll find out."

Lewis grinned. "Fine by me, but you won't like the outcome."

Vickie got between them. "John, please let Lewis leave for work."

"Nice." John held his head high. "I'll leave you two lovebirds alone."

The tense muscles that rippled under his shirt quickened her pulse. She turned with a smile, and his grief and his despair washed over her, and he stood like someone whom she and Lewis had struck hard in the face. "It's not like that, John, and you know it, but this needs to end."

Lewis nodded and smiled teasingly at his newfound nemesis.

"She'll never have to fight for me. I handle my own business."

Price approached from the barn. He stomped up the stairs.

"I suggest you cool off right now before this gets out of hand."

"I know what I'm doing," Lewis said. "Don't worry about me."

"This man has become my friend, and I won't see him betrayed."

John sighed. "Price, I can handle myself in a fight."

The older man turned and put a hand on his shoulder. "I know."

"I'm sorry about Tink's murder," said Vickie sincerely.

Price sat in a rocker, and his skin took on a grayish color, as if the blood ran cold and sorrowful. "My son was an evil man all his life. He never accepted Christ, even when I wrote of my conversion in prison and suggested he pick up a Bible and read the text for himself."

He forced himself to his feet and stepped closer to Lewis. "This woman is not for you, but for John, and it would be wise to remember my words. I've refrained from murder for a long time, but if you push me, I won't be responsible for my actions or for what happens to you."

An arrogant smile broke over the younger man's face, and he shrugged. "No worries, old codger. Just messing with her boyfriend."

"And now you know not to play with me."

Reggie arrived, and Lewis climbed into the van. He looked at Vickie and cast a flirtatious smile, seemingly unaware of any danger to himself or to her. He stared blankly through the windshield as the van eased along the driveway. It turned left at the road and accelerated out of sight.

John addressed Price. "Thanks, but I can fight for myself."

"Son, you must discern the worthy battles and leave the rest alone."

"I won't turn the other cheek, if that's what you mean."

Price looked at the road and then made eye contact. "We're not all Jesus Christ, the Messiah, although some men try harder than others to follow Him, but some men respond only to pain and death."

"If Lewis keeps pushing me, that's exactly what he'll get."

Just before daybreak and while it was still dark, booms of thunder sounded from the southeast, and rain fell hard as John took his coffee to the front porch and sat in his favorite rocker. He attached little import to the drop in temperature or the increased velocity of wind, but the rain intensified as thunder shifted direction to the northeast and water collected in the gutter and fell onto four ferns that John had mounted on curved hooks the Saturday before last. As he sipped Vickie's blend, he loved the flavor as much as she did, but he grew concerned about the flow of water hitting a fern on the center-right hook. He swapped it with one from the far left end and sat again and sipped his coffee and wondered if the stream off the gutter would drown the replacement fern. He took another sip and noticed the plants in pots to his left and the others that reposed at the opposite end of the porch, and a picture of an old-time water tin formed itself in his mind. John got up and found the tin where Vickie had stuck it, just behind the plants at the far end, and removed an old shoe brush from inside and shook his head at her sense of logic. He held the tin under the quarter-sized flow that ran through the drenched fern and smiled at his ingenuity and his desire to do something pleasant and useful and kind for what was quickly becoming as much his home as hers. He watered the plants at each end and sat in his rocker, his arms and shirt also watered, content as he sipped his blended coffee and considered life's many vagaries.

Vickie opened the glass storm door. "Are you okay out here?"

Her eyes took in the rain. She flinched at the booms of thunder.

"I'm great, but also kind of hungry."

She smiled. "Want me to make a big country breakfast?"

"Sure," he said, perking up. "Need my help?"

She shook her head. "You can sit at the counter while I cook."

Vickie laid out bacon strips on a sheet and cracked a dozen eggs for the crew, cooking them in a pan lined with coconut oil. She woke up the girls and sat them at the table, drowsy as they were, but ready to eat.

She went to check on Eudora and asked John to tend her eggs.

"Yes, ma'am."

She grinned at his mock salute and told him to watch it.

A minute later, Vickie returned with a worried countenance.

"I need your help."

His eyes met Katie's, and he gestured. "Serve these and the bacon."

Katie wiped her eyes and yawned. "Yes, sir."

He had to admit it felt good to be treated like a father.

John followed Vickie to Eudora's bedroom, where she knocked and called out to its occupant, begging her to come out for breakfast.

Eudora cracked open the door and spoke in a shaky voice.

"Let me sleep, Vickie. I'm not hungry."

Vickie traded glances with John. "You've camped out in there for too long, Eudora, and I won't have you depressed in my house."

John broke in softly. "We'd like you to eat with us."

Eudora tried to close the door, but John stopped her.

"Please come to the table. We need to share something with you."

"I don't want to hear about God. Just let me be, all right?"

He pushed on the door, and she resisted, but he was stronger.

"Stop, John."

Vickie pushed with him. "Eudora, you're coming out of there."

Eudora let go and stepped back as they fell into the room.

They toppled onto each other in their disarray. John caught Vickie and positioned his body so it hit the carpet, shielding her as they rolled.

She kissed him. "Thanks, but I know how to fall."

He smirked. "Do you know how to get off me?"

Vickie laughed. "Not really."

He shoved her to one side, and they both stood.

"After that display, you have to join us. No excuses."

Eudora crossed her arms but couldn't stop her smile. "Fine."

At the table, John flipped to Psalm 53:2-6. "God looks down from heaven on the entire human race; he looks to see if anyone is truly wise, if anyone seeks God. But no, all have turned away; all have become corrupt. No one does good, not a single one! Will those who do evil never learn? They eat up my people like bread and wouldn't think of praying to God. Terror will grip them, terror like they have never known before. God will scatter the bones of your enemies. You will put them to shame, for God has rejected them. Who will come from Mount Zion to rescue Israel? When God restores his people, Jacob will shout with joy, and Israel will rejoice." He inserted a placeholder and closed his Bible.

She gave him a tired look, so he continued.

"The last verse asks who from Mount Zion will rescue Israel."

"Yes?"

"Whom might it be?"

"How would I know? I don't look at this stuff."

"I think it's a reference to Jesus as Messiah, although many say it refers to deliverance from an army that placed Jerusalem under siege."

"It doesn't matter because I don't believe in God anymore."

He nodded his understanding. "I know, Eudora."

He sighed and turned to Vickie, who said nothing, so he read the first verse. "Only fools say in their hearts, 'There is no God.' They are corrupt, and their actions are evil; not one of them does good!"

"You're saying I'm corrupt and wicked, after all Craig did to me?"

"I'm saying you are a woman who feels hurt by God."

Her eyes dropped to the table. "Yes."

He opened another book, *Grace and Truth: Under Twelve Aspects*, which William Mackay published in 1872. John had long admired the book and read it often, which is why he felt a sudden kinship to Price, as the veteran of wars also quoted from its worn and dusty pages.

He read aloud. "Man by nature likes neither grace nor truth. He is satisfied neither with perfect justice nor perfect goodness. If John the Baptist comes in perfect righteousness, he is hated, and men say he is too harsh, and not human. He must have a demon inside him. If Christ comes in love, He is taunted with being a friend of sinners. So when the righteous requirements of God's law are preached, many people turn and say the law is too strict. God must make allowance for human imperfections, but Jesus says to make no provision for the weakness of the flesh. If you give the flesh even one thing, it will take all. When a sanctified walk, separate from the world and all its belongings is insisted on, many will call it legalism. On the other hand, when the grace of God is preached, man's wisdom makes it out to be tolerance of evil."

"What does this nonsense have to do with me, John?"

"I've seen you with Price, and he has served two twenty-year stints in prison, paid his debt twice over, and found Christ. The Holy Spirit dwells in him, and he's working tirelessly with our horses as we speak."

She glanced at the window. "In the chilly rain?"

John nodded.

Eudora sighed. "Well, that's his problem."

"If he catches cold and gets sick, he'll need a caregiver."

Panic seemed to riot within her as her face colored.

"My husband just died and took a piece of my soul. I'm not ready for romance with a convicted rapist. I don't care what you say."

John put his hand on her shoulder. "Return to the living, Eudora."

She grunted and left them at the table. Her bedroom door slammed.

Vickie and John sat with the girls, and each was concerned about Eudora's state of mind, as she seemed unable to cope with her loss.

"I'll call Mary later and tell her about this morning."

"Think she can help?" asked Katie like an adult.

Vickie seemed to welcome her concern. "I'd like to think so."

She turned to John and gave him a quizzical look. "Did you study theology at some point? You sounded a lot like Price just now."

"I've read many books over the years, but it wasn't until I met Price that I turned to the psalms for instruction, and I now realize he's right. They are a gateway to the Bible." He held up the other book. "Price quoted William Mackay on the day you confronted him. I recognized it from this book on grace and truth, and I knew he was a learned man."

"Meaning he actually knows what he's talking about?"

"He knows more than me, and I'm impressed by his renewal."

"Me, too." She straightened herself with nobility.

She turned and cast a smile at the girls, who smiled back at her, and then she held William Mackay's book in her hands and flipped it open and rubbed her slender but precise fingers across the frayed edges and the discolored spots. She took in its musty smell and held it close to her.

"You can borrow it if you like."

She frowned. "Maybe some other time, when I know more."

"There are good Catholic books. We can buy them for you."

She tossed her head lightly, as if half agreeing with him.

"For now, would you recite something else from the Bible?"

He flipped to Matthew 1:20-21. "As he considered this, an angel of the Lord appeared to him in a dream. 'Joseph, son of David,' the angel said, 'do not be afraid to take Mary as your wife. For the child within her was conceived by the Holy Spirit. And she will have a son, and you are to name him Jesus, for he will save his people from their sins.'"

"It's powerful," she said, "but it condemns sinners like me."

"Why?"

She looked away, which confused him.

He squeezed her hand. "If you're too scared, or it's too painful to tell me, then come to Jesus in truth and hide nothing from Him."

"I might admit my sins to Him, but never to you."

"Why not? It's obvious I'm in love with you and always have been."

"It will destroy the love in your heart, which I couldn't bear."

"It's time for you to trust me, Vickie. I won't let you down."

She forced a smile. "I'll think it over. It's the best I can do."

<hr>

Later in the afternoon, Vickie knocked on Eudora's bedroom door and dragged her outside and asked her to stand against the pasture fence so they might watch the herd roam and luxuriate on spring grasses.

A breeze kicked up and brought the smell of wildflowers mixed with clay earth and manure from the field. A blue jay cawed loudly, and when he finished, he flew to the other end of the fence and stared at the road.

Vickie turned to Eudora. "I'd like you to do something for me."

"What, honey? You know I'm not up for much right now."

"I know, but this should be easy."

Eudora waited without protest, so Vickie continued. "Live with us."

"Here?" Eudora's eyes flickered, and she glanced at the house.

"Yes, here in this big house where Craig and Garrett died, not to mention Red and Michelle." Vickie took a deep breath and exhaled.

"Katie said it the other night. This place is dead. I'm ready for life."

"Are you? I hadn't noticed."

"Well, you wouldn't since you've been grieving."

"No, I mean you don't act like a woman who wants to live."

Vickie gave her a reproachful look. "And you do?"

"No, but I want to die, and I'm honest about it."

"Look, Eudora, you put up with so much for so many years, but it's over now, and there's life left to be lived and adventure to be found." She hesitated. "Love is out there if you're willing to let someone in."

Eudora stood in silence, considering, and then turned to Vickie.

"Will you marry John and have a child with him?"

"It's what I want, but I'm not sure if he wants the same."

"Have you asked him? It's what people do, Vickie. They talk."

"I know, but I get scared of him sometimes, of what he might say."

"And you need me to be your big sister again, to give you strength?"

Vickie nodded and smiled. "You know me so well."

She placed her hand on Eudora's arm. "Please stay here."

Tears welled in her friend's eyes. "Okay, for a while."

"It's all I ask." Vickie hugged Eudora, and they both cried.

They drew back and wiped the tears from their eyes and laughed at themselves and called each other lame for being so weepy.

Vickie retrieved Chief from the barn so they might lunge him in the front pasture, but she took him through the gate incorrectly and then tied him without a slip knot on the railing and, to make matters worse, she chose the wrong one. As she turned, her eyes fell on a furious John.

He rushed over to her, untied the knot, and tied it properly.

"I showed you how to do this about forty times."

Vickie shrugged.

"I can't remember everything, John. I'm still new to this world."

He untied Chief and led him into the barn without issuing a reply.

Eudora rubbed her back. "Go to him. Don't let this rest."

Vickie called out to John. "Don't get so mad at me!"

His silence inflamed her insecurities and her passion.

"This is why I don't share myself. If you know the truth about me and what I've done, you'll leave me all alone and never come back!"

He stuck his head outside and yelled. "Oh, yeah?"

"Yeah!"

"You're probably right!" He disappeared inside the barn.

Eudora took Vickie's hand. "Let's go inside before this gets worse."

Vickie marched to the barn, bypassing John. She opened Chief's stall, replaced his halter with a bridle, and threw a pad on his back. As she grabbed the saddle that hung on a rope outside Chief's door, John asked what she thought she was doing with this dangerous horse.

"What does it look like? I'm going to ride him."

"In the round pen, I hope."

"Sure, whatever."

She saddled Chief and runway-mounted him to John's chagrin, and bypassed the round pen as she made her way around the pond.

He called out to her from behind. "Where are you going?"

She pointed toward the mountain. "Up there!"

"Vickie, wait! Don't do this!"

She waved a hand, dismissing him and his foolish male pride.

Vickie eased through the back gate and carefully latched it and then meandered along the wooded trail that led to a fork, the right trail leading to the falls and the left up the mountain. At the fork, she turned Chief left with a slight inside push of her right leg. Horse and rider ascended the nearly vertical incline, and Vickie once again saw a bright light halfway up the mountain. She wondered if it might be a fragment of sheet metal or a stray piece of glass that reflected sunlight down to her position. Chief saw the light and stopped. She tugged on his reins and kicked into his sides with her boots, even though she knew it was the wrong set of moves, but her mood had turned to fright, and she desperately needed him to carry her to safety. He grew restless as he nibbled on foliage and pointed his ears ahead and stepped to the right and to the left for better angles and sensory perception. Little creases formed over his eyes, indicating anxiety, and he sniffed loudly in dissent with each tug or gentle kick of her heels. She looked down and caught sight of her arms, which glowed with fluorescence, and she grew terrified of what might be happening. Still, she pushed Chief and herself ahead, her visions notwithstanding. They reached the spot where she thought the light had originated, but there was no sign of metal or glass or anything else in this desolate, remote portion of the mountain, which was in fact quite beautiful and teeming with wildlife.

She dismounted.

Her eyes scanned ahead and behind, and she peered over the side of the steep cliff, noting the tops of trees, their growth stopping about twenty yards shy of the trail where she now stood, unsteady and unsure.

Chief broke free from her.

She called after him, but her voice trailed.

He grew mercurial and shimmied in place, and then he left her alone. Vickie fell to her knees and shared the completeness of her truth with Jesus and offered sincere and humble repentance. She heard nothing from Him, and so she began her descent down the mountain without Chief, but as she talked to God, she suddenly encountered a mama black bear and two cubs, who had each climbed halfway up a sycamore tree while the mama positioned herself between them and glared at Vickie, who heard a word in her spirit for the first time in her life. It startled her and made her step back, as if in fear of the mama bear, but a much greater force inspired her now, one who commanded the cosmos, not merely a bear on a mountain trail.

Trust me in all things, Vickie, no matter how dire.

Vickie nodded.

She held up a palm, which glowed.

There was movement within her body.

"Don't worry, girl. I wouldn't hurt your cubs for all the world."

The entities within Vickie flung themselves against one another and against the walls of her blood vessels, and she breathed heavily, which drew the bear's eye to her cubs. The mama climbed the tree and covered one of them with a paw for protection, as if she would die for them.

You are at a crossroads, Vickie, like the one on this trail.

"What does that mean, Lord? I do not understand."

You must decide to live or to die, not the first death but the second, as the first will come either today or tomorrow, but the second should be your primary concern, as it relies on your name being found in the Book of Life.

Vickie dropped and prayed. "Please, Lord Jesus, be my eternal Savior and fill me with the Holy Spirit and remove any demons from within my body." She caught her breath and looked at the bears in the tree, and then she trusted the Lord enough to close her eyes to the world.

"Please let me know what entities stir within me and how I might rid myself of them, once and for all, for they make me feel unclean."

All in good time. For now, say the Lord's Prayer, which you know.

"I don't know it, Heavenly Father."

She heard nothing but the breeze through the tops of the trees, and she hoped the mama bear would not claw her to death, and if she did, Vickie hoped the cubs would be all right and John would find her body and hide her from the girls so the sight of her bloody flesh laid bare and hideous would not further traumatize them.

The Holy Spirit delivered verses nine through thirteen, as Vickie's mind could not recall them from its recesses in her terrified state.

"Our Father in heaven, may your name be kept holy. May your Kingdom come soon. May your will be done on earth, as it is in heaven. Give us today the food we need, and forgive us our sins, as we have forgiven those who sin against us. And don't let us yield to temptation, but rescue us from the evil one." She slowly opened her eyes.

The bears were gone, leaving only the breeze in the treetops.

Mitch called on Sunday afternoon, once more pleading with Vickie to return, as Nellie's ratings were lower than ever, and he needed her help.

Vickie hung up on him, which had become a pleasure of late.

To ease her mind, she went to Chief and sensed his pain as she gently ran her fingers over the marks on his face. It helped to put things into perspective, knowing how much he'd suffered for his owner.

John entered. "Helping a hurt horse can heal our own wounds."

A squeal mixed with the thunderous sound of hooves reached them.

John shook his head as he turned from her. "Wildfire."

They rounded the corner and watched as he kicked and bit Dash, who tried to escape but failed. Riddle stepped in between them, and Wildfire also kicked him. Vickie rushed forward to the fence and yelled.

"I've had enough of you, horse!"

She pointed at him, and he stopped.

"You think because you got the best of my sister, you can do what you want, but I'm here now, and you'd better learn to behave. Or else!"

He seemed puzzled, but her words had the intended effect.

John approached from inside and kissed her through the fence. He drew back and watched Wildfire, who kept his distance from the other horses. "Impressive," he said, smiling. "Yell at him more often."

She smirked. "I know enough to say he's biting the hands that feed him, and I've had enough of his behavior, rescue or no rescue."

"Like I said, all natural horsewomen scream at their horses."

"You're not funny. You just think you are."

Missy Weldon arrived and asked Vickie to join her on a call.

"Why me?" She gestured at John. "He thinks I'm terrible at this."

"Well, he called me, asking for help with your training, and believe it or not, he says nice things about you." A pause. "Thing is, Vickie, you must learn what neglect looks like and what it does to a horse."

"Oh, I can guess, since people did the same to me."

"Then you're perfect for the job."

At the troubled farm, Ben Hollander said his wife died several years ago, and his grown children were busy with their lives. He and his wife, Martha, used to run a stable in another state, but when she died, he couldn't keep it going, as she was the one with the relationships in the community, and he was overcome by grief and a debilitating disease. Ben saved her horse and moved closer to one of his children, who had little to do with him. Since then, it was the old man and the horse, but the man had little income, and the horse, whose name was Teddy, suffered. Missy said she understood and gave Teddy an examination.

The blood chestnut Quarter Horse was in severe distress.

Missy did what she could and said to call if more problems arose, which was likely. He shook her hand and almost cried as they left.

On the way home, a great silence befell them.

"You know, Vickie, it's a shame a woman with your vast resources wastes them on things that won't matter in a thousand years."

"I'm trying, okay, so stop judging me. I've had enough of it."

"Fine."

When they arrived at Bluecreek, Missy left Vickie alone to think about her future and how many horses suffered in darkness and despair.

Vickie went to Chief's stall and opened his door and ran her hand smoothly across his scarred face, which he allowed. "I'm sorry, boy."

His muscles shrugged, and shivers ran down his back, as if pained.

Her hand followed the ripples, and she spoke soothingly to him.

"I'm here now, boy. Nothing bad will ever happen again."

She went and grabbed a stool and brought it to his stall and sat.

"My father raped my mother, Chief, and she couldn't take it, and so she withheld her love from me and took pills and drank booze, and she called me awful names and said I was devious and sleazy and a monster from the abyss." She swiped at tears as they formed, unwilling to give them the upper hand this time. "Valerie killed herself on the side of the road because I was such a monster." Vickie gestured at the air, and Chief's eyes followed the movement of her hands. "She even wrote a letter to me, which my horrible stepfather, who I thought was my father, shoved across the table on my inglorious eighteenth birthday, informing me he was not actually my father, but a hater of that man and of me, and so I followed my mother's example and took a bottle of sleeping pills." Her eyes rose to meet Chief's. "Have you ever had your stomach pumped?" She shook her head. "Of course not, you're a horse, but let me tell you something, it's no fun." She hesitated, which gave her emotions full sway over her, and she wept. Vickie let the tears flow, as there was little use in trying to stop them. "I was raped, Chief, by a man who asked me the worst question a woman can be asked, and ever since, I've wanted to end my life, every day, and it's all I can do to stay alive, even with John and Katie and Abbie and my friendship with Eudora. It's never enough to make me want to live, but somehow I do."

Chief sniffed the air and stuck his head through the top of the door with his ears pricked forward. His head turned right and then left, as if looking for someone who would never again arrive for him.

The sight broke Vickie's heart.

She stood and rubbed his back and leaned against his coat.

"You loved her so much, Chief, and I'll bet she was a sweet woman."

He looked and called out for her, and Vickie felt Chief's pain.

Her arms stretched across his back, and she hugged him with all her might. He stepped from her in restless agitation, but she held on and would not let go. "I'm not going anywhere, boy. I won't leave you."

He calmed, and she rubbed his neck and sat on the stool.

"I killed my child in the womb because she was inconvenient."

Chief turned, and his nose, eyes, and ears pointed at Vickie as an object of intense interest, and he aligned his body with her on the stool.

He dropped his head, and she rubbed his face and neck.

"I'm sorry to let you down, boy. I'm not good like she was."

He nickered and licked his lips and kept his head near her hands.

"You did all you could to save your owner, even if it meant death."

His head bobbed up and down, as if he agreed with her.

"I chose ambition over the life of my baby, and I miss her so much."

Vickie wept into her hands, and as her body shook, she moaned, but still he kept near her, and his scars became her scars and her pain became his pain, and a bond formed between them, one that might withstand the rigors to come and even a little death would not separate their souls.

FOURTEEN

Psalm 54:7

*For you have rescued me from my troubles
and helped me to triumph over my enemies.*

Vickie and Chief fell behind John and Dash on the waterfall trail. John lingered in reflection on a phone call from Leslie's father. Out of the blue, Roland Carter had ordered John to stay away from his daughter, and since their conversation, John seemed slightly older and less interested in much of anything, most especially romance with Vickie. As they rode the wooded trail, some imaginary ghost haunted him and rendered him afraid. In their history together, his fear had seemed impossible, as his strength endured and his spirit hooked itself eternally into life, refusing to let go. But now she wondered if he might depart from her, much like she had done to him twenty years ago. The notion washed over her like a feverish plague.

She shook off the stress and basked in tiny droplets of sunshine.

The dappled canopy and the soft breeze filled the moments, which had been strung together by the Lord for this day alone. She would ride her horse through them, and the narrow passageway which had intimidated her would now offer contentment, secure as she was in its confines. The voices of water, which once spoke of a brutal rapist, would this morning befriend her and envelop her in tenderness.

John dismounted and stood ready as she arrived.

He took Chief's reins, snapped a rope to his bridle, and tied him to a separate tree from Dash with a slip knot in case of danger.

As they sat, she broached a difficult topic, knowing it might wound.

"Care to discuss the call?"

He smiled and looked away. "Not really."

"They say he's a powerful man."

John looked down, picked up a pebble, and tossed it.

Vickie's eyes found his. "Isn't he?"

A look of agitation broke across John's face. "I suppose."

"Give me more than 'I guess' or 'I don't know.' This isn't high school."

He found a larger stone and hurled it. "Roland and I got along well when I worked for them, and he liked me spending time with Leslie. But now I realize he thought she'd never actually go for a washed-up cowboy like me." He hesitated. "Roland seemed more nervous than mad."

Vickie took in the sounds of the water. They refreshed her.

"Is he part of her cabal?"

John's face brightened. "He's a donor to the party and her campaign. His stud business provides him with elite connections."

She grimaced at the word *stud*.

"His operation doesn't seem very appealing when you call it that."

"Yeah, well, that's exactly what it is. Native Dancer was outcrossed to five generations. Those in the know will pay for his pedigree."

"Does Roland's rejection hurt your feelings?"

"Not as much as yours did."

She chuckled. "Nice segue, and I assume it's why we're here."

He grinned. "You know me so well."

"Lately I wonder," she said. "You seem different."

"My father's death and our conversations about Nicole brought up some things. I've had nightmares, which makes it tough to sleep."

"Will you share them with me?"

"I'd rather not, Vickie. They're personal."

She forced her scrambled emotions into an unusual order, but still her face flushed crimson. "I love you, John. Isn't that personal?"

"You know what I meant. I'd rather deal with this on my own."

"Well, if you want a family with me and the girls, let us in."

"That's just it. I don't yet know what I want, but I'll get there."

His stern attitude baffled her. She grew awkward and insecure.

"I'll say this much," he said, turning, "and I hope it helps you feel better. You've suffered, and I never really understood how much until lately, when I pondered my situation with Garrett and Nicole." He seemed reticent to continue, so she waited. "Not that I was a mama's boy, because I never really had a mother. Instead I had a taskmaster for a father, a man who said I could do nothing right and who blamed me for her death." His admission gave life to her untried senses.

"You were just a little boy. How could he fault you?"

"Garrett condemned me along with her, although he never said it in so many words. But there was distance after the asylum fire."

An unexpected surge of adrenaline rippled through her.

"We are more alike than I ever knew." She smiled. "It feels good."

"It's why I now see you as honorable, and I truly believe you should lighten up on yourself." A pause. "You were defiant back then, and that's what I remembered most about you. Even recently, when we met back in February, I would've characterized you that way. But now I realize you had to be in order to survive the trauma you experienced."

Her eyes moistened, and she swiped at her tears.

"I feel guilty for being alive most days."

She felt like the same breathless girl who went to him at eighteen.

He leaned nearer. "How about this afternoon?"

The glow in his eyes cheered her spirit. "With you, I'm good."

He smiled. "If we're such a happy couple, why did you leave me?"

"I was angry at my family, if you can even call them that, because right now it's the last label I would apply. I thought I'd been granted a new family in Washington, D.C. with Lena and her husband, Richard, and my friends who interned with me. But Lena gave me terrible advice which cost me both then and now." Vickie pulled her legs to her chest and hugged them, as John's appeal intensified her raw feelings.

"We're at the falls together, Vickie, so why now?"

He paused.

"There's something hidden behind what you just said."

"It's a story for another day, so don't make me go there." She lowered her voice, being vague, and a grimness overwhelmed her. She grew wide awake. "I will say this: I'm worried about you and the girls and even Price and Eudora. I'm terrified of the brutality of this fallen world and megalomaniacs like Leslie Carter, who want to rule over us."

John took Vickie's hand and pulled her to her feet.

"I know what you need."

She looked about but saw only rocks and water and soaring trees.

"Follow me down there." He pointed to the base of the waterfall.

They descended the steep trail and slipped behind the pounding cascade. They stood in a pocket in the rock and felt the temperature change and the mist which arose. She held her hand under the cold flow, and the water whispered to her and voices swirled in her head.

"Here's what you do." He screamed into the flood.

She broke into laughter, but her body tightened in apprehension.

John smirked and grabbed her hand. "Come on. It won't bite."

Vickie took a sharp breath and yelled weakly, and her voice trailed.

"No, like this." He turned. "I hate my life! Hate! Hate!"

Her face paled as he turned to her, happy with himself.

"Do you really, John? I thought you loved me and wanted us."

He grew agitated. "I do, but I guess there are things."

"Things? What does that mean?"

"Things I have to work through." He got behind her. "Try again."

"Fine." She leaned in and belted her loudest. "I want to die!"

She turned to him with a questioning look, and he waved her on.

"I want to die! Die! Die! I don't think I can go on living, and I want my parents back, and I hate myself for what I did, and I'll never make it right!" She halted and looked at him in embarrassment and shock.

"Don't worry," he said. "No one hears what you scream but me."

"Why not?"

"The water blocks the sound, so it's like your private confessional. But out here it's only between you and God and His creation."

"Can I do it again?"

John nodded, and she was stunned by his demeanor, as if he'd been here a thousand times and yelled many awful words into the torrent. She emitted a hopeless wail, but left her deepest utterances for another day. Afterward they sat behind the falls and watched the cataclysm.

"The waterfall has collected many voices over the centuries, first the Native Americans and then the settlers who came behind them. It captured their struggles and their victories, their love and their pain."

She rubbed his arm. "You should've been a poet."

Their eyes met, and a new surge ran through her. "I miss Eudora, the friendship we shared years ago." Vickie hesitated. "She shames me every chance she gets, and it frustrates me to no end. She was a big sister when Michelle wasn't, and it feels like Craig's death ruined what we had." Her voice broke off, but there was more to say.

"You two haven't been close for twenty years, so you should stop pretending you and Eudora were like sisters. It's simply untrue."

"What should I do then?"

"Place your focus on the girls and on helping horses who cannot help themselves, just as Missy said." He gazed blankly, as if in reflection.

"What about you? Don't you need my help?"

He leaned in and gave her a kiss. "Yes, I do."

She looked about and noticed the rocks at the base of the falls which carried the cascade of water along a meandering creek bed.

"This spot would be perfect for a water baptism."

"What do you know about it?"

"Not much." She changed subjects. "Why didn't you leave earlier?"

"I worked as caddie for Chris, which is when Carlie grew infatuated with his tour victories and the windfall he might make from a major."

John looked at the creek, and his face grew sorrowful.

"The signs were there, but I swept them to the back of my mind."

She must cheer him up. "One thing is for certain. You bit off more than he could chew with me, and even I knew it back in the day."

"For a while, I considered murder," he said, "but I could never go through with it." His eyes met hers, and smiles broke across both their faces.

A mother black bear and her two cubs wandered to the edge and sipped the fresh water. Vickie tensed and hooked her arm in John's.

He whispered to be still, and the moment enthralled her.

"Do you think we'll get stranded here?" she asked expectantly.

He drew her nearer. "I can think of worse fates."

She gently bumped his shoulder. "Me, too."

John smiled. "We might starve or get eaten by mama over there."

Vickie grunted and slapped his arm playfully as the bears whisked into the woods like phantoms. "Come on. It's time to leave."

Price and Eudora interacted in the side pasture as John watched from the porch. Each had grown closer to the other and to Dash and Riddle, and he envied them, as their desire for life had been reborn. The two horses stood lazily near them, scrupulous in their desire for good grass and convenient company and a sage season of love. His conversation with Vickie at the falls flooded his senses, as did her need for certainty. If he desired her, he must pierce her defiant wall, as she wouldn't lower her guard for him or for anyone else, not even the girls she adored.

Eudora's eyes met his from across the expanse.

She moved away from Price, searched, and went to Riddle.

John walked to the fence and leaned against it, asking Price to ride with him in the flatbed truck to the feed store so they could get supplies. As they piled into the truck, Price seemed lost in thought.

John eased along the driveway and stopped at the road.

He scanned for traffic and glimpsed Eudora, who sat in a glider on the porch and gazed sadly at their departure, as if forlorn.

"Are you two an item?" asked John sincerely.

A scowl formed on Price's face. "It's our business."

"I was just asking."

"And you can stay out of it, because it does not concern you."

At the feed store, Price crossed his arms and kept silent when John gestured toward the entrance. It was a petulant move and unnecessary.

"Suit yourself."

John slammed his door and went inside, where a woman beset him with tales of a troubled horse and of his reputation for working miracles with their feet. She pushed into his personal space, forcing him to step back from her politely but with a firmness which communicated everything.

"You must swing out to my farm on your way home," she said.

John eyed the door as people entered and exited. Two young female clerks chatted nervously with one another and smiled at him, then turned their attention to the next customer as the woman prattled endlessly.

"Ma'am, you haven't told me your name."

She seemed embarrassed. "Oh, I'm sorry. Where are my manners?"

He gave her an arching look. "I don't know."

She burned red at his obvious impertinence. "I am Joan Williams of Little Bee Farm. We raise ponies and honey bees in no particular order."

"Ponies?" He sighed. "I thought you said this was a horse problem."

"Well, it is." A pause. "Do they not count in your view?"

"Sure they do, but the pasture is too wet right now. Move your ponies to another one until the weather clears and the ground dries." Price entered the store as John spoke. "Then move them back in June."

"Will you come by this week?"

"So they've been in a wet field, as I suspected?"

Joan blushed again. "You must understand, my husband died last year and I've taken over the farm. I'm learning and making mistakes."

He considered.

"Since you've had them in a wet field, rot might have set in."

"Please help me, Mr. Breyer. You know what's best for them."

She paused.

"My husband, Ben, loved those ponies, and I can't let him down."

John put a hand on her back. "How about Monday at dawn?"

She thanked him profusely, wiped tears from her eyes, and left.

"It was a nice thing you just did," said Price, who stood nearby.

"I've done nothing yet, and I hope it's not too late for Joan."

As stock workers loaded bags for the feed bin back at the farm, John recalled his boyhood and the many commitments which were cancelled for golf practice or other sporting events. Other more pressing interests overrode John's hopes and dreams and any need he might have for love and affection, even a small bit of warmth. The situation continued unabated into his adulthood, although he grew to be respected in the equestrian world for his knowledge and skill.

Some said he was the best farrier in the county.

As they drove to Bluecreek, Price seemed more upbeat and almost fatherly in his deportment. He quietly observed John for a few minutes.

John could take no more. "Anything you want to say, Price?"

"Only that I appreciate you as a man, and you're good for her."

"Vickie?"

"Yes." Price hesitated. "She needs a stable and decent man."

"I don't know how consistent I am, but thanks."

John turned left down a gravel road and approached a farm. He backed the flatbed close to a red barn and shook the farmer's hand.

"We need two bales of alfalfa."

The farmer nodded, went to his tractor, and loaded the bales onto the truck in a few minutes. John handed him the cash.

On the road, he drove slowly, as the load made the truck somewhat unresponsive and harder to stop and maneuver around curves.

John asked Price to call Vickie and then hand him the phone.

"Are you almost home?" Her voice carried a note of worry.

"We'll be there in about ten minutes. I need you to clear Dash and

Riddle out of the side pasture where Price and Eudora have been playing with them and open the gate so I can access the barn's back door."

"All right. I think I can do that."

He turned into the driveway. "Do it now, Vickie. We're here."

With a gleam in her eye, she shooed Dash and Riddle into the front pasture where they joined the herd. As she worked the two horses and helped them integrate, John considered prayer, as his father's death had caused him to backslide of late. Vickie was a good influence, although her faith still seemed shaky, and she had a temper which tended toward violence. He would learn more about the path she'd taken before committing the rest of his life to her and the girls.

Vickie entered numbers into a spreadsheet as she sat at her desk in the barn office. She found concentration difficult as images of her and John at the falls flashed before her. She should have been more honest, but she held back out of fear of what he might think of her and, more importantly, what he might do with the knowledge. Vickie had grown reserved in her interactions since that April afternoon, which was unlike her, as she created intimacy with listeners for a living. But since coming home and since rekindling her love for John and her hopes and dreams of family, the stakes rose to heights unparalleled in her history.

Price entered and sat silently in a wooden chair opposite the desk.

Her fingers stopped typing. "Yes?"

"I think you've given these horses magnificent care."

"It's mostly been John. He's the one who knows about them."

Price shook his head. "No, ma'am. You bonded with Chief when we all thought he was a goner. Dash and Riddle are like new horses, even more so than Chief, but then again, they didn't have as far to go as he did." He hesitated. "I think it's time you give the others attention."

Vickie sighed. "You're probably right. I'm attached to Chief."

"He needs you, so don't misunderstand. Be there for all of them."

She sank into her chair. "Even Wildfire and Hero?"

"There's nothing wrong with Hero. He's steady."

Vickie flashed Price a look of daughterly disdain.

"Did you come in here to scold me about Wildfire?"

He smiled. "Bond with him as you've done with Chief, and the rest will fall in line. I think they've been standing about, anticipating."

"I fear Wildfire, and you know it." She hesitated. "So does he."

"You're frightened of the girls, too, but you've done well with them, and what you did for Craig and Garrett was amazing. You've been a blessing to everyone who orbits you, especially Eudora and Mary."

"I've done little for Mary, but I'll take your compliment."

"You pushed her to succeed and you've shown her how."

Vickie's nose wrinkled, and she gave her father a wounded look.

"I've spent one day with her, so thanks for reminding me I've let her down, just like I've done with everyone else lately." Her fingers rubbed the top of the desk. She gave her father a suspicious glance and dropped her head into her crossed arms. Her throat felt strained and her lower back throbbed. "I shouldn't be so tired at thirty-eight." Her eyes shut.

"Here's my advice. Combine several activities into one. Work with the horses and ask the girls to help. Travel with Mary on assignment and ask Katie or Eudora if they'd like to join for the day. Make it fun."

"Dad, it's not so simple." Her head lifted. "But I'll think about it."

Vickie sat up and straightened her posture so her back ached less. Somehow she felt less intimidated in his presence and her defenses subsided as her fingers typed words onto the computer screen.

"How's your faith? We haven't spoken about the Lord lately."

She pushed back into her chair and let her hands fall into her lap.

"I've been a believer since I was a girl. Red was a stickler for weekend mass, so we went to church, more to be seen than to worship God."

Vickie stood and opened a file cabinet drawer, placing receipts from the store and the farmer who sold them hay and other transactions into their tabbed sections. She turned to Price. "Why do you care?"

He grew angry, and it showed. "Because I'm your father, and before I leave this fallen realm, I must know you've accepted Christ."

She slammed the drawer. "You want honesty?"

He nodded. "Of course."

"It hasn't been easy having a rapist for a father."

"I know it hasn't."

She interrupted. "Let me finish."

"All right."

"Despite what you did, I've kept my belief in God." Vickie made the sign of the cross on her chest. "But I don't know what He wants. There's very little of value left inside this body. I feel used up and nearly dead."

"I understand, but the only thing that makes anything better in this life is prayer, because it's the only thing that works." His eyes rose to the ceiling. "The Lord is up there, listening, watching, and waiting."

"Waiting for what?"

"For you to be truthful with John."

"I've tried, but the words don't come out right and I freeze."

"You've withheld your abortion from him?"

Vickie's face went pale, and a chill ran up and down her spine.

His voice fell to softness. "Don't worry. It's not my secret to tell."

"If you do, he'll leave and never come back." Her eyes moistened.

"Then start with something else, like your rape."

She grunted. "Oh, that will be painless and wonderful."

"I didn't say it would be easy. He needs you to share it with him."

"Are you kidding? I would be a ball of jelly."

"Then be that for John. He needs your vulnerability, Vickie. You've been an independent woman since you were a girl, and now is the moment to put down your armor and let him be strong for you."

"I cannot do that, Price. You ask too much."

"Please call me Dad or Father. It's what this old man needs."

She swiped at her tears. "I want to, but then I think of Valerie."

"And you feel guilty for surviving your own rape?"

Vickie's dignity concealed her turmoil, but his ferocity upset her.

"What you did left a residue Valerie couldn't shake."

Price reflected for several moments before he offered a response.

He eventually opened his Bible and quoted Psalm 54: "Come with great power, O God, and rescue me! Defend me with your might. Listen to my prayer, O God. Pay attention to my plea. For strangers are attacking me; violent people are trying to kill me. They care nothing for God. But God is my helper. The Lord keeps me alive! May the evil plans of my enemies be turned against them. Do as you promised and put an end to them. I will sacrifice a voluntary offering to you; I will praise your name, O Lord, for it is good. For you have rescued me from my troubles and helped me to triumph over my enemies." He closed the Bible.

"Is that your answer?"

"It's all I have to justify my existence after what I've done."

John stepped into the room. "Is everything all right in here?"

"It is now." Price stood and pointed at the chair. "Sit."

John seemed perplexed and wary, but he complied.

"Care to say what's going on? It seems like you've been fighting."

"Not fighting, but clearing the air," she said flatly.

Price spoke sympathetically as he prepared to leave. "Be honest."

"What's this all about?" John threw her an arching look.

Vickie sat still and then found the courage to respond. "I need to be more truthful with you, as you mentioned at the falls." A pause. "No, you did more than mention. You demanded the truth from me, but I wouldn't give it to you out of fear and out of shame for my many sins."

"We can't go further until I know everything," he said.

"I realize that, but please understand how hard it is for me."

"Do you think I had a good time watching my father die?"

She shook her head. "It was horrible. I was there."

"Yes, and I appreciate your letting him receive hospice here more than I can say, but it left me feeling ashamed and alone and furious."

"I feel for you, John. I really do."

He crossed his arms. "Then let's have your truth."

Vickie peeked through the door to the barn and nodded as she rose and paced about the tiny room, then stood near the file cabinet.

"You know I am the product of rape, which later caused Valerie's suicide. You may also know I've been with a multitude of men."

"I don't care how many men you've slept with, Vickie."

"Because you've had your share of women?"

John chuckled. "Yeah, something like that."

He paused.

"Red and Valerie abused you as a little girl, and you have issues."

"When you see me, do you sometimes see Nicole?"

Mixed feelings ran wild within her as he stared thoughtfully.

"I've always known you were unstable like her. It's why I love you."

"So you're trying to fix me?"

"Maybe." A pause. "I couldn't fix her, no matter how hard I tried."

A wave of emotion broke over Vickie like a tsunami, taking every ounce of her reserves and leaving her desolate and barren and sorrowful.

She dropped to her knees and wept into her hands.

John rushed to her side and gently stroked her hair.

"You're safe, my love. I'm here with you."

She clutched his shirt and pulled herself into his chest and wailed.

He gripped her hard with both arms and hugged her into another world, one mixed with despair and hope. Vickie kissed his neck and tried to unbutton his shirt, but he stopped her. She drew back in shock.

"Why not?"

His lips pursed. "We're not husband and wife."

"Then let's get married this Saturday."

He again seemed perplexed. "It's Tuesday. You expect a wedding by the weekend?" He left her alone on the floor. "I don't get you."

She wiped her puffy eyes and pushed herself against the cabinet.

"There's a wedding chapel in Asheville. It's only an hour's drive."

He sat in her chair at the desk and faced the window.

"Please, John. Talk to me."

He swiveled. "You haven't told me about your rape."

She looked away and wiped her eyes. "I've blocked it out."

"Unblock it for me." He went to her on the floor and held her.

Vickie leaned into his chest and kissed his neck. Again he stopped her, so she buried her cheek into his shirt and let her mind wander.

She whispered, "Logan and I were friends when I first went to Washington. We worked as interns for Lena Lambert, who he later murdered, along with her husband, Richard, who was a kind man. He encouraged me when Lena pushed me into an oblivion, and he became a father figure to me in a way Red could never be in a million years."

"Go on. I'm listening."

"Logan and Mitch Dolan, who later produced my show, were like my brothers, or at least that's how I saw them, but Logan developed romantic feelings, which I dismissed as a crush. You know how first love can be when it's from afar. It hurts more when you're at that age than later in life, when you've had more experiences and more heartbreak. Anyway, I guess he never got over it." Her fingers clutched John's shirt. "Logan left the show and went back to college, and I lost track of him for over a decade. I ran through everyday assignments on my way to the top like a hot knife through butter, and I thought little about it when Mitch said a religious nutcase sought us out for an interview, as he wanted to address the world with a prophetic announcement which we all thought was a bunch of nonsense." Her voice trailed as she reflected.

"And now?"

Vickie let go of John's shirt and once more slid to the cabinet.

"Will you be okay over there?" he asked. "Should I sit in the chair?"

She nodded.

He sat and waited for Vickie to continue, peering like a judge.

"I was hard on him, and before you ask, I don't know why. Perhaps I was angry for having lost touch, or maybe I thought he was crazy, but I humiliated him more than anyone I'd ever interviewed, even dictators who deserved to be deposed for their brutality toward their own people." She bit her lip and looked up innocently at his prodding eyes.

"Should I go on?"

He seemed displeased, and she wondered at his feelings.

"John, please help me. Have I angered you?"

"It sounds like more than a passing crush. You loved him."

Vickie's eyes rose to the ceiling, and she silently prayed for guidance.

Please, Lord, give me the words to say because even I don't know the truth, but I think John might be correct and I've never known it until now.

Comfort enveloped her, and euphoria calmed her emotions.

John waved for her to continue. "You don't have to deny it. Go on."

"As you might expect, Logan didn't take it well, and soon he vanished." She snapped her fingers. "One minute he was leading his organization, which many believed to be a cult, and that's the angle I took with him, but the next minute it was as if he'd never existed."

"Until he showed up out of the blue?"

"Yes. Years later, I was Lena's weekend anchor and her confidante, the only one in D.C. she trusted." A pause. "By then we'd grown close, and I saw her like the mother I'd never known, and it felt good to have both her and Richard in my corner, but the unthinkable happened and suddenly they were gone. When I found out Logan murdered them because of me, I fell into a depression which lingers to this day." Her eyes fell to the floor. "Can we stop now? I'm exhausted."

"No, Vickie. We're just getting started."

She took a deep breath and exhaled. "Fine."

"Did the police suspect you in Lena and Richard's murder?"

Her face flushed crimson. "They had Logan's fingerprints."

"That's not what I asked." He shifted heavily in his seat. "I watched your last broadcast. Nellie Michaels hit you pretty hard on this point."

"Which is?"

"Don't be coy. You know what I'm asking."

"I wasn't sleeping with Logan, if that's your question."

She paused.

"I've slept with many men, but never willingly with him."

"Why not? You were in love with the man."

Vickie felt compelled to turn away, but she could not, as the Holy Spirit encouraged her to search deep within for authentic answers.

"I think it's because of my love for you, John, but also my shame."

"Shame at being a country girl from Addison who wasn't good enough for a bright intellectual man like Logan Meson? Is that why?"

"I felt some of that, yes, but it wasn't the reason." Bested, she pushed into the cabinet. "I did something abominable which ruined me for any man but you, which is quite ironic, because you'll hate me."

"Care to tell me about it? I assume the answer will be no."

"One day, when I'm stronger and when I don't feel like a harlot."

"All right, then walk me through the rape. Where did it happen?"

Vickie tapped her head against the metal drawer. "Enough, John."

"No!" He stood and paced and glared at her. "Give me the truth!"

She held up a palm to appease his emotions. "Please sit."

He complied, but gestured impatiently. "Speak now."

"I was taking a shower in my apartment, which I left sparse because I was rarely there when on assignment or when I worked long hours at the studio. He broke in with a long knife, but it wasn't the first time."

"His first attack?"

She nodded.

"He came out of nowhere one night at the Planar building. I think it was about nine o'clock and I was the only one there, or so I thought."

"But no rape?"

"He seemed intent on terrifying me, which he did, but he slapped my face and shoved me to the floor, which left bruises. He said strange things about a list which contained names of famous people who were evil and in on some kind of nefarious plan, but it made no sense."

They looked at each other for a moment, considering possibilities.

"Did he know Leslie?"

Vickie offered a faint smile. "I'm wondering if there's a connection."

"So when he broke into your apartment, what happened next?"

"He raped me, John. What else do you want me to say?"

"Tell me about it. Did he threaten you with the knife?"

She struggled for the fortitude to go there in her mind.

"He ripped down the curtain and flashed what looked like the biggest knife on the planet and grabbed my hair. I tried to scream but nothing came out, but it set him off and he backhanded me across the face." Vickie grew unsure if John would rebuke her, as he had seen through her defenses, and would have no more manipulation.

"Logan had been working out since our interview, and he was powerful. My back hit the shower wall, and he grabbed my hair again along with my right arm." She held it up and rotated it slightly and grimaced. "It still doesn't work right after he broke it in three places. The pain was the worst I'd ever experienced and I couldn't fight him anymore after that, so I let him drag me into the bedroom, where he slapped me and punched me in the jaw, breaking it as well. He flashed the knife while he undressed and said he would murder me as he'd done Lena and Richard and several other people he despised, but it wouldn't be today if I cooperated, so I checked out completely."

The words flowed from her like a torrent, and then she stopped.

John rubbed his face with his palms. He seemed melancholic.

"I'm sorry. You've suffered more than a human can withstand."

"Do you want to hear about our trip to the quarry?"

"No, but thanks. I heard all about it on your show."

"Marry me, John. This weekend at the chapel."

"You haven't shared the rest with me. The story for another day."

"It doesn't matter to me, so it shouldn't matter to you."

"Then tell me now."

"I know I'm pushing you away, John, but I can't. Please let it lie."

He paced the room and stood over her and pounded the cabinet.

"Even my insane mother was more honest than you."

John bent down to her eye level. "I hate a liar. You must know this."

She nodded and hugged her legs. "You ask more than I can give."

He stroked her hair and then caressed her right arm.

She put a palm to his cheek. "I'll love you forever if you'll let me."

"You say that now, Vickie, but you change like the weather."

The implication sent waves of apprehension through her, and she recoiled at the realization he would soon leave her to raise the girls alone.

"You don't trust me?"

"No, because you don't trust in the righteousness of Christ."

"What does Jesus have to do with us?"

He snorted. "Everything! You don't trust the Lord enough to share every detail with me, without hiding the ones you dislike."

"I dislike all the details and they fill me with a never-ending shame."

She looked up. "Dear Lord, please speak through the Holy Spirit."

Tell him about your visions, my child. He has them, too.

"I just heard a word," she said. "He wants me to share my visions and to trust you not to have me committed to the Scardell asylum."

He smirked. "I'm not my father, and you're not Nicole."

"All the same, I'll sound as crazy as she did."

John arched his eyebrows. "I dream about you sometimes."

Vickie grinned. "I hope so. It's why I want to marry you."

"No, I'm talking about a vision that happens when I'm asleep." He paused.

"You were in New York and you left your apartment and walked the streets to the studio. There was a sound of some sort which affected most everyone on the street, and you fell down to the pavement in a dark alleyway. When you arose, you were a monster after prey."

"I've had those dreams, sometimes while I'm awake." She hesitated. "It's like a movie screen drops in front of me and I watch events which will unfold in the future. When it stops, I feel as if I've gone insane."

"What have you seen since you've been home?"

"I encounter enraged bears who kill Katie or Abbie." She hesitated. "In some visions, I become the monster and terrify the bears."

"Anything else?"

"When I rode with Chief up the mountain, I encountered a mama and her two cubs, who were up a tree. I looked down and my skin flashed effervescent like glow sticks. The mama got so scared, she climbed up the tree after her cubs and put a paw over one of them."

"What do you think it means?"

She sighed. "As a reporter, I have no clue, but after living with Red for eighteen years, I have suspicions about what he did to me as a girl. I have flashbacks to doctors in lab coats and nurses with needles."

"Leslie said the same about the camp, but I thought she was lying."

"I've told Price there's something in my blood. Parasites or demons or whatever you might call them, but they make me want to murder."

"Well, you haven't turned into a werewolf yet or killed anyone, so there's hope." He gauged her faint smile and the distance between them. "You say you want us to get married as soon as possible."

"I do." She smiled at the obvious choice of words. "Sorry."

"And you want to have my child?"

"More than anything in this world. I think it would help us."

"That's no reason to have a child together, Vickie."

His rejection traveled to her core and her senses spun out of control.

"Do you think I would divorce you, John? If so, there's no way."

"Maybe or maybe not, but I need to take things slow for a while."

She interrupted, but he held up a rough hand, which calmed her.

"You have two girls right now who need you. Spend time with them and prove you have what it takes to become a mother for our child."

"And then?"

"If there's time, we'll consider marriage and more children."

Tires crunched on the driveway.

As the couple stood at the barn entrance, Preston Spiro stepped out of a black stretch limousine and onto the pavement. He cast a sneering grin as he gestured to another occupant. Mitch Dolan stepped out and stood sheepishly beside him. They each gazed at the house.

Vickie paced and muttered to herself, thankful for the shelter the barn provided and for the rifle which hung over the fireplace in the living room. Her muscles grew sore, and she felt a pain in the back of her throat. She wanted to run screaming at them with a lead pipe and hit them until they were dead, as it would calm her existence, but it would also put her in harm's way. Vickie mourned as she watched them interact with Katie and Abbie, who greeted them from the porch. Mitch originated from a similar darkness, and Preston had once inspired her, as both men represented aspects of what she lost as a child.

She went to the other end of the barn and stood over a batch of tall grass, attempting to thwart intense cramps and nausea. Unable to resist the welling anguish, she threw up in the grass. She grabbed a rag and wiped her mouth and then marched outside to greet the visitors.

At the car, she slapped both men in the face.

"That's what you get for making me feel like an orphan."

***

Vickie met with Mitch and Preston inside the house while John sat at her desk in the barn office, contemplating what had just occurred between them. Her honesty both relieved and jarred, as she'd been through more than him, but since Garrett's death, his own past roared to the forefront, destabilizing his emotions and his faith in the Lord, much like Eudora. He craved escape from unwanted scrutiny. He roused himself from his bleak abyss and looked about the tiny room.

Pictures of a life spent dedicated to horse rescues and rehabilitation stared reprovingly at him, making accusations against his character.

Jealousy enveloped him as he reflected on her marriage plans with Mitch Dolan which went astray, but a flicker of romantic feeling yet remained, like a pilot light on a fireplace, waiting for someone to come along and push the starter switch to bring it aflame. John knew exactly why the two men were here. They would bring her to Washington, D.C.

Vickie moved in circles John would never know or appreciate, which would forever be an obstacle to their relationship. She and Mitch drifted through life, awash in the esteem of others, while John struggled outside of the equestrian world, as horses were prey animals who spoke through body language and behavior. He blamed himself for his wife and brother's death and for his failed relationship with his father.

His elbows rested on the desk as he examined his options.

He had become an anchor to Vickie and the girls, and he might get them killed if he stayed in town. Leslie would return and she wanted him at all costs, for what reason he could not fathom, as he was a farrier with rough hands and an underdeveloped vocabulary, but she did all the same. Leslie was a woman who viewed love as warfare.

Garrett had insisted he and John take a cross-country golf trip, the type of outing which would bond them as father and son. When John readied Garrett's house for sale, he kept his father's Titleist clubs as a token of his love and an acknowledgment of all which he lost.

Perhaps he would take the trip alone and finally learn the game.

John entered the living room and took a seat beside Vickie on the couch.

She smiled at him and patted his leg and mouthed, "Thank you."

"What will it take, Vickie?" asked Preston in an impatient tone.

Her hand searched for John's. He grabbed her hand and squeezed.

"I am in love with this man and I must think of my sister's girls."

"All right, now we're getting somewhere. We'll set you up in the suburbs." Preston stopped mid-sentence. "What are their names?"

"Katie is fourteen and Abbie is eight. Addison is their home."

"Yes, but soon Reston will be that for them. We will set your two girls up in the finest private school in Virginia, which is nearby."

"They'll hate it there," said John flatly.

Preston grinned. "Not once they become stars of the school."

"You'll see that happens, I assume."

"Not me, but my people. Leslie Carter said she spoke to you both."

"Yes, she was here a few weeks ago. She said others would follow."

"And so we have. I would advise you to listen to our proposal."

John crossed his arms. "All right. Pitch your offer to her."

She stood and paced the floor and turned to John.

"Do you want us to leave?"

He gave her a hug. "Of course not, but hear him out."

"I understand your friend Lewis has become a cameraman."

She turned to Preston with a confused look. "Yes, here in town."

"Why not take him with you to Washington?"

"Are you serious?"

"Absolutely." A measured pause. "And Mary Bishop."

Vickie gasped and put a hand over her mouth.

John stepped forward. "I see you've done your homework."

"It's what we do, son, and I suggest you get out of the way."

John turned to Vickie. A grin had broken across her face.

His feet tied themselves together, and he couldn't take a step.

"Are you planning to leave Addison?"

"Why do you care, John? You said you want to leave us."

"And I agreed to stay for you and the girls."

"For how long?" She gestured sharply. "Did you think I would stay here and wait for your return? You're not a soldier going off to war, but a man whose father died and who now wants to bail on his promises."

He pointed at the barn. "Did our conversation matter at all to you?"

"It did," she said, "but you made things pretty clear at the end."

John went to her and wrapped his arms around her and hugged her tightly. She tried to break free from him but he would not let her, and she surrendered after only a few moments and tears coursed down her cheeks.

"Please don't leave me." Her voice cracked. "I'll die if you do."

His hand brushed back her hair. He placed a strand behind her ear.

"I won't, baby. My heart breaks for all you've been through."

She looked up at him with a child's eyes. "Then you'll love me?"

"Forever."

Preston cleared his throat.

He gestured at Mitch, who sat in an overstuffed chair.

"I was told you would be more accommodating. Leslie said she had broken the ice, so to speak, and let you know your continued rebellion would not hold, as people more powerful than me will never allow it."

John kissed Vickie's lips and drew back from her.

"Is that why no one has been here to kill us since she left?" he asked.

Preston nodded.

"We decided a different approach would prove more efficient."

Katie and Abbie burst into the house, followed by Price. They bounced into the living room and surveyed the new people, and a look of alarm spread across their faces. Price stood behind them and put his hands on their shoulders. "I took them to Missy's for the morning and she made lunch and we played UNO around her table. Missy is good."

"I won two games," said Katie, beaming.

Abbie cast a frown. "I didn't win any of them."

Vickie gave her a pouty smile. "You'll get there, honey."

She turned to Preston. "You see where my priorities lie?"

"Vickie, take the offer and move to Virginia. You'll live longer."

Katie threw a quizzical look at her aunt. "We're moving?"

"No, honey. This man wants me to come back to my former show in Washington, but I was just about to tell him to find someone else."

Mitch spoke up from beyond Preston's position. "Please, Vickie."

"What, do it for you? The way you treated me? That's funny."

"I only followed orders, and I never meant to hurt you."

"What happened to your glorious protégé, Nellie?"

"She failed spectacularly, and Planar's stock is lower than it's been in decades. This is much bigger than you or me, Vickie. Lives are at stake."

"Over television ratings?" Vickie paced the room. "Lena built that show from a simple concept and I was there with her as her intern and later her weekend co-host, but it was always her format and I was only a replacement." She considered. "This is a vast nation full of talented men and women. Can you not find anyone else besides Nellie Michaels?"

"You know it's not so simple, Vickie. We have to integrate new talent into the show bit by bit and it helps if there are soul ties."

"Which you create from thin air, as I have none with Nellie."

Preston shoved Mitch aside. "That's why Mitch failed with her."

"Well, I have none with anyone else in D.C., either, so you're sunk."

"It's why we need you to come back with us now, Vickie."

He paused.

"We must repair our stock price or the company will fold."

She went to John's side. "I'm not going today or any other day."

Preston glanced at the girls. "You must consider their safety."

Vickie marched toward him. "Don't you dare threaten the children in my presence or I will murder you with my father's rifle!"

"You know so little, my darling. What a pity Red had a heart attack before educating you on life's realities, on what is possible for you in this world and what is mere folly, but you will regret this moment."

He turned to Mitch with fire in his eyes. "You, my friend, are fired."

Preston made his way to the foyer and paused. "This isn't over."

"How many ways can I say no to you?" She crossed her arms.

"Look around you, Vickie, and take in the faces of the people you most care about, as they will soon be dead, and it will be your fault."

"Preston, please stop threatening my family or I will hurt you."

He threw open the door and yelled at his driver, who sat in a glider on the porch. The man quickly stood and said, "Yes, sir," and opened the door to the limousine for Preston with a false smile and terrified eyes.

"Take me to the Charlotte airport."

The door closed as the driver glanced at the large house and the group who now stood watching from the covered porch. He tipped his hat and got into the car, but Mitch shoved his way through the melee and descended the steps to the grass. The driver and Preston saw Mitch, and their eyes widened. Preston yelled at the driver, and the car raced down the driveway as Mitch pointed and fired the weapon, sending a bullet into the back windshield.

"What are you doing?" asked Vickie in a high-pitched scream.

Mitch flashed Red's rifle at her, stifling any further criticism.

"Hold on a minute," said John carefully. "Don't shoot."

Vickie held up a palm. "I'm sorry for hanging up on you."

"I don't care about that, but do not follow me when I leave."

He shot the tires on her Ford Expedition and on John's Silverado and then Mitch got into his rental car with the rifle. Vickie ran to him and tapped on the window, pleading with him to stay and talk it out. Mitch said there was nothing there for him and he had no future in Washington. He would murder Preston Spiro and then end his own life.

John glanced at Vickie and then stepped in front of Mitch's car.

"Wait, John! He'll run over you!" She seemed frantic at the notion.

Mitch backed the length of the driveway and onto Route 15.

Price gave John the keys to his old truck, and Vickie thanked him and the couple chased and flashed their lights and yelled for Mitch to stop right this instant, which he finally did, just as he corralled Preston's driver into a concrete column which supported a highway overpass.

Mitch leaped from his rental car and pointed the loaded rifle at Preston as he exited the limousine with his hands raised.

"This will not end well for you," said the smug executive.

"My life is over no matter what I do, thanks to you and Sturgis."

Vickie moved to the other side of the limousine and rested her palms on the roof and pleaded with Mitch to give John the weapon and to turn himself in to the police, as they might go easy on him and allow him to plead temporary insanity. He told her to leave Preston to him.

"Mitch, if you do this, there's no turning back from it."

"Don't you think I know that?"

"You and Logan were my closest friends in Washington."

"So?"

"Please don't lose your mind and die like he did."

Mitch slightly lowered the muzzle. "He raped you, Vickie."

She nodded.

"I'm not like him at all, and I don't appreciate the comparison."

"Stop and look at yourself. Right now, you seem just like Logan."

Mitch raised the muzzle again. Preston glared without a flinch.

"You must want to die, old man."

"If you murder me, you are killing yourself, so what does it matter?"

Vickie eased around the end of the car and moved up behind Mitch.

John called to her, but she refused his warnings.

She spoke soothingly and asked Mitch to give her father's rifle back, as she might need it to ward off the next batch of villains who visited, and she was fairly sure they wouldn't be offering her employment.

Mitch considered, and then he cursed himself for betraying her and for trying to be like those in the political circles he despised. He had lost sight of himself as a man long ago, which sickened him.

"You can run the station alongside my manager, Laura Henagar."

"She won't like interference from an outsider, and you know it."

"You let me handle Laura. We go way back and she is a good friend."

Mitch handed her the rifle, and Preston ducked into the limousine.

The driver hit the gas and the vehicle sped away, slinging gravel.

"Will we see him again?" asked Mitch in a concerned voice.

"No, I think we're officially at the next level."

"Sturgis Faulkner?"

"Either him or Leslie Carter, who clearly works for him."

"Or mercenaries sent to murder us all," said John with a scowl.

Vickie threw him a smile, which he ignored out of anger.

"There's only one man who can save us from this mess," she said.
Mitch pointed at John. "Him?"
She placed her hand on Mitch's arm. "Our Savior, Jesus Christ."

FIFTEEN

Psalm 55:6-7

Oh, that I had wings like a dove;
then I would fly away and rest!
I would fly far away
to the quiet of the wilderness.

June 2008

John tied a piece of wire to Savannah's stall and made a knot, hoping she would stay put, as prior attempts to keep her inside had failed and she was now an escape artist. A butterfly fluttered from the side pasture, and he looked up at the fenced space. The area would give her room to roam, which she would love, but her heart had weakened beyond repair and her foal was due any day. He returned to his work, nailing the end of the wire to a slat of wood on a nearby stall. Savannah would nibble at the knot until she found freedom, and he admired her spirit, as it mirrored his own, a man couldn't fault a sickly mare any more than a woman could stop his own imperfect liberation.

He nodded to the frail horse, a wordless gesture, and then went to Chief, who had grown used to barn life, which once seemed beneficial to his recovery but now seemed neglectful. John would speak to Vickie about Chief during their afternoon session, as she must improve the bay's wretched circumstances before he drifted into the ether.

Laughter caught his attention, and he went to the barn's entrance.

Price and Eudora sat on the porch as they did most mornings, talking about the weather or the girls or cars on the highway, avoiding more difficult subjects while bonding on the surface, a shallowness which would eventually dwindle to mere friendship, and each deserved more at this stage of their lives. John vowed to help move things along before the season dissipated, as often happened with love.

He waved as he sat on the glider and offered them a kind smile.

The front door separated them from John in their rockers and gave them margin to believe their conversation was their own, but as John eased the glider side to side and forward and backward, and the steel contraption squeaked like a mouse, his intentions fell clear and the couple shifted their focus to him and his friendly machinations.

"It's June 6th, which is D-Day." His eyes met theirs.

Price nodded and shrugged. "We must never forget their sacrifice."

The air warmed as sunlight crept across Route 15, and an unknown dog barked off to their right and a bee bounced among the potted flowers beyond the rockers. Sweat arose on John's skin, dampening his collar.

Eudora turned to Price. "Did you serve like Red or Lewis?"

He shook his head. "I was too wild for the military."

"Would you tell me about it? I should know about your past."

John expected Price to relate his backstory, but the older man grew still and stared away at the blue mountains in the distance.

"Funny," John said. "Out here, it's an event when we see a vehicle."

Eudora smiled. "Reminds me of high school, when there weren't as many cars or as many people. Things were simpler then."

John eyed Price from afar, but the grizzled character kept his stoic countenance as he observed the sun-kissed horses in the pasture.

Wildfire stood proud and fierce, with Hero calmly at his side.

Price turned from them and surveyed the land to their left, a strip owned by the power company, and he shifted heavily in his seat.

"See anything over there?" asked John in a gentle voice.

Price glanced at him and Eudora. He seemed alert and on edge.

"Some summers, the wild blueberry crops fail and the bears get hungrier than normal. Grizzlies will dig up roots, but ours come down from the mountain and roam the land over there, looking for food."

"Is that why Red kept a loaded rifle over the mantle?" asked Eudora.

Price threw her a glance. His eyes flashed with contempt.

"It's mostly for freeloaders, like myself."

John chuckled. "And for Leslie Carter's people, whom she claimed would visit death upon us if we refused her agenda. I keep looking, but I don't see her or her assassins. Maybe they'll show up next week."

"Don't joke about such matters," said Price in rebuke.

"You think I'll jinx a good thing?"

"I shouldn't have dragged her on the floor." Eudora's words filled the air with anguish. "But I couldn't watch her destroy Vickie."

John shook his head. "Leslie put something in our coffee. How, I don't know, but she did. Neither of us could move a muscle."

Eudora examined him without looking him straight in the face.

"I could tell, and I hated her for it. She's an evil person."

"She was deadly serious," Price said. "That much I know."

"Then why hasn't anyone followed her?" John waved his hand. "Roland chewed me out on the phone, telling me in no uncertain terms I would not see his daughter again." A pause. "I told him that was fine with me and I wasn't the one who sought her out, but he was adamant."

"Sounds like he also threatened you."

John nodded.

"You could say that, but he was careful in his use of language."

Price considered as he rocked gently forward and backward.

"Roland and Leslie are powerful, and they have friends. I'd tread lightly and hope you never see them again, because if you do, it can only mean one thing. She hasn't given up on you, and someone must die."

"It's why I've thought of leaving Addison."

Eudora gasped. "Then Leslie will have won. Please don't go."

"Why not? She did it to me twenty years ago."

"I know, John, but you were both so young."

"Meaning what? It was okay to run out on me?"

Eudora grew agitated. She put her hands over her ears and stopped rocking. "I can't take this. It's you who will kill Vickie, not Leslie."

John listened to the music of the breeze. He felt like a terrible man for putting an emotionally devastated woman through more trauma, but he must think of the family's safety over his own, and if he was completely honest, the road called to him and he needed time to think.

Price rubbed his chin and eyed John for several moments.

"I understand your need to protect my daughter, but leaving her isn't the answer. Trust me. I know what it's like to lose her love."

John frowned, unable to offer a valid argument other than a hunch.

Eudora turned to him with barely constrained despair.

"Where is she today? Did she go to the station?"

John smiled faintly. "Hardly, but it's where she'd rather be."

He pointed at the barn. "Vickie and the girls are deep cleaning the loft this morning. None of them were thrilled, especially Katie."

"I should help." Eudora's deportment grew ashamed, and she tried to rise from the rocker, but Price put his hand on her arm. She slumped and settled into the chair. Their conversation had drained her.

Price's face lost its color as he patted her knee and spoke lightly.

"Vickie wants to prove she can be a good wife to John. She made the girls help so they can connect with each other while they work."

Eudora threw up her arms. "Over a dirty toilet?"

The two men broke into laughter, but she was unamused.

"I've cleaned my share. It never made me closer to anyone."

Price chuckled, and his manner grew affectionate and playful. Eudora was a favorable influence on him, and it readily showed.

Her hand squeezed his arm. "Please tell me about Valerie."

He stiffened in his rocker, and it stopped. John at first thought he might strike her, as his inner pain seemed sustained and resentful.

Price looked about for a few minutes without uttering a word.

Eudora and John waited for him, each with bated breath, as his next words would carry import. He stopped and started and grew restless, and then his tears flowed. He swiped at them with his paw-like hands.

"Christ is everywhere."

John leaned forward. "He is risen."

"Jesus never will be banished from this realm, although Satan has been given a certain measure of leeway. You can see vestiges of Christ on churches and Christian schools and even in the face of these glorious mountains which go on for fifty miles in each direction." Price gestured at the highlands which loomed all about them and made himself smaller in stature. "Jesus is my life now, but He wasn't when I was a boy."

Price's gruff voice animated Eudora, and she leaned nearer to him.

"We know, and it's okay. Just tell us about it."

He again grew tearful. His shoulders slumped as hers had done.

"I went without as a child, hungry most days and beaten most nights, and then as a young man, human wreckage surrounded me." He hesitated. "Valerie's father, J.T. Malone, set himself up as a kingpin, and he killed men for a six-pack in the early days. It was well known he enjoyed murder and found sport in it. His wife grew ill and died on him, same as happened to many men, both then and now, and his daughter went from being a nice girl to a stripper overnight, as he fell hard into drunkenness, his weak side overtaking the strong." Price straightened his posture in the rocker. "Anyway, her soul grew as wretched as any I'd ever seen, bored housewives or those who walk the streets at midnight, but she earned good money, which kept them afloat during lean times."

"Did she become a prostitute?" asked John with care.

"She was on her way."

"So what prevented it?" Eudora searched for his hand with her eyes, and he gave one to her. She kissed its roughness and held it to her cheek.

"I murdered her father and became the new kingpin."

She let his hand drop. "What?"

His eyes scanned the highway and then rose to the far mountains.

"I struggled with murdering J.T., but his hold on her was too strong for words to break, so I took action which has cast me as a devil."

"In her estimation?"

He shook his head. "No, she understood his death liberated her."

"Whose then?"

Price gestured at the sky. "The Lord's."

"But you've repented," said Eudora pleadingly.

"Yes, but on some level, I'll always be a murderer like Cain, marked and shunned by society. You must understand, J.T. was not the only thug I killed. Others showed themselves to me, and I accommodated their death wishes one by one. Their violence begat my violence."

Her hand went instinctively to her mouth. "How many?"

"I lost count."

John took a deep breath and exhaled. "Did Valerie know?"

"They were wicked men who needed to be dead."

"That's not what I asked."

"Yes, she knew about them. She was glad."

Price pushed himself from the rocker and hopped to the grass.

"I'll take my leave, and you can decide what to do with me."

She stood and wagged a finger. "Price Brewer, you come back here this instant. You will not tell a good woman these things and walk away from her like a vagabond." She put her hands on her hips. "What will you do, jump on a rusted-out boxcar and ride it all the way to Texas?"

"If that's what it takes to rid myself of the guilt."

"You have a daughter who needs you more than she needs air, not to mention the girls who see you as their new grandfather, or John who needs a mentor, both with horses and with life, and then there's poor old me whom no one holds in regard." Eudora quivered with emotion.

"I certainly do," he said.

"Well then, come here and finish." She patted the rocker's arm.

He stomped up the stairs and across the porch and threw himself into the rocker like a toddler who would toss his peas and carrots.

Her eyes fastened on him with an awed expression.

"The shame ate me alive, and I couldn't live with myself, for the type of man I'd become, like some outlaw in a western."

He rose from the rocker and paced the porch in front of them.

Motion to their right caught John's peripheral vision.

Vickie stood at the barn entrance and observed her father.

John leaned forward, hurrying Price. "What then?"

"I told her to leave me and find someone better, but she was so in love, she wouldn't hear of it, and the notion sent her into sobbing fits."

Vickie approached and stood near the edge of the porch.

She listened with crossed arms. Her face contorted as if pained.

John wanted to warn a helpless Price, but the older man's words burst forth over the falls, and there was no stopping his confession.

"I sent the love of my life to Red Morrison, who convinced her to frame me for rape, as he wanted to marry her, and she was with child."

Vickie's face grew horrified. She put a shaky hand over her mouth.

"My son, Tink, was mean from the start, and he enjoyed murder, unlike Vickie, who has a heart of gold, but she doesn't want anyone to know it." A pause. "Tink was the same as J.T. Either God or Satan cut them from the same cloth, and a different one than mine, although I did my share. Anyway, Tink took over as kingpin once I went to prison. I had hoped to keep him out of the organization, but he was bent on doing better than his old man and developed an early taste for robbery and murder." Price's eyes fell on Eudora. "You might wonder about Tink's mother, but she was a prostitute I ran into one night on the street. Jennette was forced to go through with the pregnancy, but she fought me all the way, as she wanted to keep her youth and figure unblemished. After the birth, I named him Tink after my uncle who liked to fix cars and promised to bring money to Jennette for rent and groceries every week. A week later, I went to check on her and the baby boy, as she was hysterical about making ends meet even though I gave her enough for several months. A woman next door said Jennette had left town, and she showed me my son as he slept in a back bedroom. There was little else to do but bring him to my place, although I knew absolutely nothing about being a father to an infant child."

"Did you raise Tink into adulthood?" asked Eudora.

John's eyes flashed restlessly at Vickie. She listened but kept still.

Price shook his head. "I found him a home in Courtland County."

Vickie stepped forward. "You didn't know your son either?"

Her question startled Price, and his eyes flickered, but then he calmed and resigned himself to her knowledge of his sins.

He sat on the steps, and she took a seat beside him.

"I kept tabs on him as he got older, but I wasn't in his life."

"So what happened? How did he join your operation?"

"Tink ran the streets as a teenager and joined gangs, and as he grew into his manhood, he wanted more for himself and saw me as the king."

"One whom he must depose?"

Price's eyebrows arched. "Perhaps. I've never considered that angle."

"I am a journalist, and we seek answers." She glanced over her shoulder at Eudora and then at John. "We all need them, Daddy."

He clutched her knee and wept, and she held his bear-like frame.

"I'm sorry, my darling daughter. I was a terrible man back then."

Her head dipped, and her eyes found his. "You didn't rape Valerie?"

"No, I loved her with all my heart, but I was no good for her."

Vickie nodded her understanding and looked about as Price had done. She took her father's hand. "Why did you go back to prison?"

"The second stint?"

"Yes, the prison released you after twenty years, but you went in for another twenty, and I'd like to know why. Wasn't that one for robbery?"

"We took banks at gunpoint. In the last one, someone died."

She sighed. "Was I to blame?"

John called out from the glider. "Vickie, that's enough."

She turned to him with a devastating sadness. "He went to prison the first time because of Valerie and the second time because of me." Her eyes moistened. "I wouldn't see him, though he tried."

Eudora stood and knelt behind Price and rubbed his shoulders.

"Is this true, honey?"

His head fell low, and he seemed like a defeated boxer. "Yes."

Vickie flung herself onto the grass, and then she turned to John, who came up to her with a loving disposition and hugged her tightly.

Her words whispered soft and wet into his neck.

"He tried after the letter and after I had almost killed myself with the pills, but I couldn't handle him as my rapist father."

"I know, baby. I'm here, and nothing can hurt you now."

John rubbed her hair as she shook in his arms and wailed so loudly it disturbed the horses in the pasture. He turned them so he might get a better view of the porch. Eudora hugged Price on the steps as they cried.

Vickie walked the fence line on the backside of the barn, feeling alienated and solitary even as Katie chased Abbie through the gate and along the trail, their giggles and squeals an indicator of their happiness and the fun of hide-and-go-seek. Vickie might as well have been in the Charlotte airport surrounded by a thousand teeming strangers, head down and depressed and furious, although she should direct her anger at herself. She had wanted nothing to do with her father, the real one, not the persecutor, along with a mother who sent the love of her life to prison for a rape he did not commit and later took pills and drank booze and taunted and jeered at her own flesh and blood, taking her on a joyride for the ages, which ended in a blood-streaked catastrophe.

Vickie let the girls play and entered the house and went straight to Red's office, where she took his picture in her hands and sat in his swivel chair, moving right and then left, wondering if he might come back from the dead and save her like the U.S. Cavalry in an old western.

"I'm sorry for leaving you and for staying away when Michelle was more than you could bear, but you made me feel like an orphan."

Her thoughts fell back to the summer after high school, when her sister had tried to start a colt named Wander. Michelle worked with Wander until he would let her saddle him and then worked with him some more until he let her climb on and off him twenty times. Vickie asked if Michelle would continue until he felt more comfortable, and her sister laughed and said, "Watch this." She climbed on his back and sat there, waiting to see if he might buck, which he did once she applied her heels, a hard and painful lesson Vickie hoped Michelle would learn for life.

Wildfire proved she had extracted little from Wander's teaching.

A portrait of her paralyzed sister on the ground formed in Vickie's mind, which was too much to handle, so she went to the living room and eyed the rifle over the mantle. The ducks and geese were once more on the pond, and it would take only one shot to end her suffering.

There were moments when she felt like a fool in Addison, as she had abandoned her family and her partnership with Michelle twenty years ago, believing Red's hyperbole about her journalistic ability and her charm and her need for fame, as if accolades ever lasted for more than a season. Cable news was a fickle business, and her star had faded long ago.

Vickie sat and put her face in her hands and promised herself she would do better for the girls. They needed her as their mother, and it felt good to know their need was kind and genuine and filled with a longing for family and not manufactured for ratings or money or status. It would never die on the supercilious vine, untended and unwatered and unproductive, but would produce trustworthy fruit for generations.

Price stepped through the door, sweaty from lunging with the horses, and his skin smelled salty, but Vickie minded little, as he was her father and he did an honest day's work without complaint. Red Morrison would no longer carry the title in her head or her heart.

"May I speak with you?"

She threw him a warm smile. "I've been avoiding this conversation."

"It's not what you think."

Vickie gestured at the couch to her left.

He looked himself up and down. "I'm far too dirty."

"I'll feel more comfortable if you're not standing over me."

"All right." Price went to the fireplace and sat on the bricks.

His large, rough hands rubbed against his jeans as he struggled to look her in the eye. She grew wary of yet another grim revelation.

"I'd like to marry again, before it's too late."

Her tight body relaxed, and she unexpectedly broke into laughter.

His face registered her disrespect, and he stood.

She held up a palm, and he sat again, crimson-faced and wrathful.

"Sorry," she said. "Sometimes I laugh when I'm nervous."

"I'd like to think I no longer generate such a reaction," he said.

Her eyebrows arched. "Me, too."

"Eudora is a good woman, as you know."

Vickie recoiled and then looked at him incredulously.

"She's not over the death of her husband. Can you deal with that?"

Price cleared his throat. "I haven't felt like this since your mother."

An image of Valerie in Garrett's arms flashed, and Vickie shuddered. She drew into herself in the chair and hugged her arms.

"I hope our pairing isn't awkward for you," he said with feeling.

Vickie examined him with a cold and disparaging eye.

"She deserves to be happy for once in her miserable life."

Price smiled. "So do you, my darling daughter."

Vickie looked away with a frown. "Stop. I'm not ready for that."

His eyes pierced her soul, and she dared not look at him directly or she might crumple into a ball on the floor, and there had been too much wailing of late. She took a deep breath and allowed the picture of Price and Eudora's future together to settle in her mind. He was fifty-eight, and she was forty-three, a difference of fourteen years, which wasn't an issue at their age, but their life experiences were quite dissimilar, and she had been a battered woman for many years, while he had killed men and served two prison stints, the second commuted for good behavior. It wasn't as if God had made their match in heaven, or had He?

Vickie exhaled, and her face contorted into a grimace, which caused Price to shift uneasily on the bricks as if he wanted to be anywhere else.

She should do something, anything, to relieve their discomfort.

Her eyes sparkled as the notion formed. "Run to town with me."

He gave her a surprised look. "Why?"

"We'll pick up something for dinner. I'm too exhausted to cook."

Price grunted. "Does this news depress you?"

Her lips pursed. "I've been sad all week, so don't take it personally, but I think you should ask her to marry you. You two need each other."

"Thanks, but I'll stay here while you go into town."

She smiled coyly. "No, you'll go with me like a normal father."

He chuckled under his breath and got to his feet. "Fine, let's go."

As Vickie drove her Ford Expedition, she kept quiet and still.

"Cat got your tongue?" he asked.

"Don't have much to say."

He settled into his seat. "John said I don't talk much, and it made him feel strange around me, so I've been trying to communicate better."

"That's nice." She scowled at the roadway as it curved once again.

"It's not good to wallow in depression," he said.

She considered Mitch, who slept in a storage room at the station since his encounter with Preston, believing Vickie would refuse him in her home, which might have been true when she first arrived, but since then things had changed and her attitude toward him had transformed into that of a worried sister. She would stop and check on him and, most importantly, play matchmaker between him and Laura Henagar, that is, if he hadn't ruined his welcome with her by being rude and overbearing, as only Mitch could. But even if he had fouled his chances at the outset, Vickie knew Laura had given herself to her career for too long, and it was high time she knew love with a man who was once as ambitious as she, and it would be just the tonic for Vickie to give the daily operations of her station over to a romantic duo Red would have surely hated.

Price's incessant rambling snapped Vickie out of her reflections.

"I realized John was right, and I'd gotten used to keeping to myself. Now I want to talk all day and share every thought in my head."

"Please refrain," she said. "I can't deal with a chatty Price Brewer."

He laughed.

"All right, but you need to talk."

She threw him a glaring look and turned to the road ahead.

"Be quiet and enjoy the scenery."

A few minutes passed between them, and she pulled her Expedition into a hamburger joint called The Wayfarer, where they knew how to cook a patty to medium, which was a rare feat in these parts, as most places charred the meat inedible. Abbie loved their seasoned fries, which made takeout a hit every time Vickie brought it home, a pattern which had developed with each new visceral emotion she endured.

A father hugged his little girl, scoring yet another one.

Vickie grabbed the steering wheel and shook as the tears flowed.

"What is it, honey? Please tell me." Price rubbed her back.

"I miss my baby, Chelsea. Like you, I never knew her."

She paused.

"I'm rotten to the core." She shook her head. "There's nothing redeeming about me, and I should have been the one who died, not her."

Her fingers clutched the wheel. The pain in her gut and her heart wrenched her into a minor convulsion, and she thought she might die. Her wails grew loud and concerned those who strolled past her vehicle, and their heads swiveled toward her, but she held up a palm which warded off their advances, and then she grabbed the wheel for support.

All the while, Price gently ran his rough hand along her back.

"Let it out, honey. You've suffered with this pain for years."

Vickie turned to him and launched herself at him, and he caught her as only a father could and held her tightly in his arms as she sobbed.

"There, there," he said in a hushed whisper. "It's all right now."

Thoughts of what she had missed with him and with Valerie ran through her mind and tormented her soul, and once more she knew she was about to die in her father's arms, but he held her so tightly and so strongly and with such command, the terrible emotions subsided. She drew back from him and wiped her cheeks and her puffy eyes and looked blankly at the people about them, those whose existence had always been picture perfect and loving.

"I hate them," she said. "They disgust me."

"Don't close up again, Vickie. I know it's raw, but it's real."

She shook her head, and her face grew contemptuous.

Her hand gestured sharply at a group who entered the restaurant.

"There's something evil inside me, and I want to hurt those people."

"They didn't abandon you. It was me and your mother, but she's been dead since you were a girl, and you must let her go."

Vickie turned to him. "I'm sorry I wouldn't see you."

She immediately looked away, as the flood overwhelmed.

Her fingers clutched the wheel. "I'm so sorry, Daddy."

Price reached over and softly squeezed her arm. "I know, but it's what I deserved as a father who was never there for my children."

Her teeth clenched, and her jaw jutted. "I'm just like you."

"You don't have to be. Katie and Abbie are your second chance."

"Once they find out what I did to Chelsea, they won't want me."

His face paled, which she caught from the corner of her eye.

"It's John you're worried about, not them."

She turned to him and studied his features. "Are you okay?"

He recoiled slightly at the question. "It's just my blood pressure."

"From all this stress?"

He nodded.

Her palm tapped the wheel. "See? I'm hurting you now."

Tears coursed down his cheeks. "No, honey. You're saving my life."

He considered and then retrieved a worn Bible from the glove compartment and handed it to her. "Use this until you get your own."

She drew back from his offering. "I couldn't, Price."

"You need it more than I do."

"Gee, thanks." She offered him a faint smile.

"I mean no disrespect. You're my daughter, and I must protect you."

"Is it the one that you had in prison?"

"Yes, and this Bible got me through many terrible days and nights. It kept me going even when I wanted to give up, so I might see you again."

Vickie covered her mouth with one hand, and the other trembled as she took the Bible from her father, the one man she trusted implicitly.

"I'll take good care of it, Daddy."

Tears flowed easily, and she let them, as it no longer mattered if she cried or if she laughed, so long as she was in the presence of her loving father, and perhaps John might be like him. The Bible gave her hope that a rough man who suffered many torments and made many mistakes might learn to navigate this fallen realm and to discern God's purpose for his life, and it filled Vickie with joy to know her father admired and respected John and that he loved her more than he loved himself, the way it must be between a parent and a child. And as she held his Bible against her chest, the Holy Spirit touched her soul and gave her a peace which defied understanding, and sin left her alone.

John sat with the girls on the porch as Vickie and Price arrived with dinner from The Wayfarer. He grew surprised when Mitch stepped from the back of the Expedition and even more so when Mary pulled in behind Vickie's vehicle with Lewis, who had been missing in action for weeks, claiming a hectic work schedule, but word about town was of a brewing romance between him and Mary. It was fine with John, as he held no possessiveness toward her, but in a moment of complete honesty, he would wonder aloud why she chose him, as she was a catch in every sense of the word, and Lewis was a sarcastic troublemaker.

"What's up, old man?" Lewis grinned as he ambled behind Mary.

Vickie exited the Ford with a Bible under her arm and a platter of drinks in her hands. She waited for Price, who carried the bags of food. Katie and Abbie hopped from the porch and ran through the newly cut grass with wide grins on their faces. Katie gladly took the platter of drinks as a gesture of teenage maturity, and Vickie steadied her Bible.

"What took you so long?" Katie steadied one side of the cardboard platter, which had drooped, and then she wobbled toward the porch.

"They came by the station and scooped me up from my makeshift bedroom in a storage room. I was glad they did, because eating from the communal fridge was getting old fast." Mitch gestured at Vickie, who suppressed a grin as he spoke. "She said I could stay here for a while."

The group entered the living room, and each made their way to the kitchen, where the drinks and bags of food were placed on the counter.

"Grab some silverware." Vickie pointed to a drawer near the sink.

"Sure thing." Lewis kissed Mary on the cheek as he met her at the table. Even John thought it reassuring to see him domesticated.

Plates dispersed along with the entrées, each to everyone's liking, and soon grace was said, as there was much to be thankful for and the Lord deserved to be recognized at their table, a practice John had forgotten.

Eudora seemed happier, and every so often she flashed a smile at Price, who returned her warmth with his own glowing countenance.

Vickie addressed Mitch from across the table as he chewed.

"You can stay in one of the front two bedrooms."

He threw her a look of disdain and then held up his can of soda.

"I'd rather not sleep where someone drank too much crapout juice."

Everyone at the table glanced at Eudora, who went pale, but she said nothing and instead cut her meat deliberately and took a bite.

Mitch turned to her. "Was it your husband who died?"

"His name was Craig, and he was a better man than you'll ever be."

"Look, I'm sorry, and I don't mean to offend you, but I hate death."

Eudora gripped her knife and fork and looked straight ahead as she spoke. "Sleep in my late husband's room, Mitch. I have a feeling the Reaper will come for you sooner than later, so you might as well prepare for your casket." She turned and faced him with a dour look. "Maybe you can fold your arms over your chest like a cadaver and pretend you're attending your own funeral." She took another bite and silently chewed.

"You're not a nice woman." He took a sip from his can.

"I've been through too much to be nice. Best you remember that."

Even from across the table, John sensed Eudora's rising temperature.

Vickie gently put her hand on Eudora's arm and turned to Mitch.

"Beats the cot at the station. I had guys come out and move the oak furniture back into each room, so it will be real nice and comfy for you."

"I think I'll go back to the station. At least there, I'm available for work at a moment's notice and at all hours of the day and night, which Laura needs right now. The murders have her staff pulling long shifts."

"Mitch is right," said Mary with a nod. "I've never seen the station so busy, and Laura looks exhausted. We've gotten stonewalled by the police and the sheriff's office. The FBI got here two days ago, but they won't make a statement to anyone, not even the national outlets."

Vickie gestured sharply at Mitch. "Laura needs a break from you."

He seemed astonished, although he must know he was overbearing. "What did I do?"

"You told her she knew next to nothing about running a television station, which, by the way, she's been doing for over twenty-five years." Vickie hesitated. "I thought the two of you might get along, even though she's older, but my plan hasn't worked out very well."

"Laura is disorganized, and she lacks ambition, which you know I can't stand, especially with all the excitement after Roland's death. She needs to be a mover and a shaker like we were in Washington."

"Addison is a mountain village, Mitch, and this will all die down."

He sighed. "I don't know about that. Folks seem plenty upset."

"What happened?" asked Abbie with a naïve curiosity.

"It's not table talk, honey." Vickie's voice carried a cheerful tilt.

John considered Vickie's intention but thought better of it, as the girl must understand what can happen in this brutal world. He leaned over to Abbie. "Some people bought horses from a farm that breeds thoroughbreds for racing and for dressage. You know, where the horses and rider dance about in the arena?" He waited for her response.

She nodded her understanding. "They show it on TV sometimes."

He smiled. "Yes, they do. Anyway, those horses are very expensive, and people who raise them become wealthy, but sometimes all that money creates jealousy, and we think that's why the man was killed."

Abbie gasped. "What was his name?"

"Roland Carter."

John glanced about the table. Price flashed him a look of rebuke, which meant to cease this tack, as it might traumatize the little girl.

"Let it go, man." Lewis had picked up on Price's mood.

"I think she needs to know about these things." Mary's correction and the loving smile she threw at John melted his heart, but it riled Lewis, who shifted heavily in his seat and grew red in the face.

As if scripted and on cue, the doorbell rang.

John and Vickie traded glances.

Each knew who it was without a peek.

She shook her head. "Don't let that woman in here."

Mitch seemed dumbfounded. "What woman?"

John threw down his cloth napkin. "I've got this."

Mitch called after him. "John, what woman?"

Without a reply, John trudged to the foyer, knowing with a certainty which defied explanation that Leslie Carter had returned to torture him.

He flung open the door. "I said we're through!"

The porch was empty. Only the breeze kissed his neck.

John stepped outside and shut the door, wondering if this was a setup and if someone would soon shoot him from a high vantage point.

He scanned the barn and saw no one there, and so he considered.

He hopped to the grass and eased past the line of cars, making his way to the pasture. The smell of perfume met his nostrils from behind, and a feminine arm wrapped around his waist as Leslie sidled up beside him at the railing. She hugged him with the conviction of a villain.

"I thought we'd never be alone again," she said.

"We can't, Leslie. It's over between us."

Her green eyes sparkled as she smiled up at him. "I want you, John."

She seemed so sensuous he could hardly stand it, and her perfume seduced him in ways he thought he'd overcome, and her voice beckoned him into her bed for a night of ecstasy unparalleled since the dawn of fallen man. There had always been something different about her, a pull, a summoning aspect, like a siren from a Greek tragedy who called sailors to their fate through the mist and with voices so alluringly feminine, resistance was impossible. It was in her blood the same as Vickie's held a wrathful nature, but Leslie was crafted for lust, and she was the sexiest woman he had ever known or would ever know, and even though he had sworn off fornication, his will wilted as if made of paper.

He whispered to her. "Why are you here?"

"You know the reason," she said. "My father was murdered."

"I heard the news. Others were also killed."

"Some of his best customers who bought thoroughbreds with the C-allele bloodline. The list goes back two years to when we met."

"What does that mean, Leslie?"

"As I said, you know more than you let on."

Her words confused him. "You think I killed Roland?"

She again squeezed him around the waist. "He stood in your way."

John looked down, and his eyes met hers, and he grew intoxicated.

He struggled to look away from her but could not, so he left his gaze affixed to her gorgeous face, which seemed carved from granite, perfect in its form and in its wanton countenance. "You seem happy he's dead."

She drew him from the fence with her eyes, and he bent down.

Curtains moved in a window which overlooked the porch, and he drew back from Leslie in shock and surprise at his lack of self-control.

"Did you drug me again, Leslie?"

She smiled. "I'll never tell, but you want me so badly it hurts."

He nodded.

"Then have me, and all will be well between us. I am yours."

Her head dipped, and she grabbed his arms, and her neck exposed itself to him. He desperately wanted to kiss her flesh as if she was the first woman and he was the first man and their knowledge of good and evil had been exposed and they would no longer hide from anyone.

The front door opened, and Vickie descended the steps.

"What is this?" She clutched a worn Bible to her chest.

The adversary held onto John's arm as she addressed Vickie.

"I'm here for a funeral. You know all about those, don't you?"

Vickie gave John a pleading look. "Are you with her now?"

He used his right hand to peel Leslie off him and stepped toward Vickie, but she waved a hand and asked him to draw back, so he did.

"You see? Vickie is so easy to defeat, it's amazing. One minute, she loves you, and the next she wants nothing to do with you." Leslie took his hands. "I have loved you since the first day we met, and I've not faltered." She threw a grin at Vickie. "I even had my father killed."

John wheeled and faced the pasture.

His eyes fell on the horses, who grazed lazily near the highway.

"Did you hear what I said?"

He turned to her. "You're just like my mother, a lunatic."

"Perhaps, but she's dead, and I'm here in front of you."

Vickie stepped nearer. "You'll meet the same fate as Nicole."

Leslie caught her meaning and replied without missing a beat.

"You mean I'll be set ablaze in the Lake of Fire?"

"Exactly. You can't win because God will prevail in the end."

"So you say, but we are more alike than you know, Vickie. There are entities within you that are similar to my own, and I wish we could be friends." She hesitated. "You'll need one if I leave here empty-handed."

"More threats? They never cease with you, do they?"

Leslie briefly feigned offense but then broke into a sinister smile.

She turned to John. "It's time you joined my campaign. I wish to announce our wedding to the world, and I have all new advisors."

"Let me guess. The new ones think it's a good idea?"

She shook her head and grinned. "Unlike your precious Vickie, my new people know keeping their mouths shut will benefit their health."

John took a deep breath and exhaled. "Did you kill the others?"

"I did it for us, John."

Vickie studied Leslie, and a thought seemed to take root in her mind, as if there had been an epiphany. She sneered as she spoke. "You did it because you are behind in the polls, and you need him."

She gestured at John.

Leslie shrugged. "A girl wants to win her biggest election."

"You are a cynical manipulator and a cold-blooded murderer."

"A candidate must foment public opinion, Vickie, and you're no different, as you've slanted stories, so the masses believe what you want."

"I never did that. I was bound to the truth, unlike you."

"Bound to the truth?"

The mood grew thick between John and the two women, and he thought Vickie might strike Leslie in anger, but she grew quiet.

Leslie seemed to take Vickie's stillness as acquiescence.

"There are things hidden in your past, even today as we stand here and you speak to me with such defiance, as if you've told him everything and I have no leg to stand on, but we both know there's more."

"I won't let you take John from me, Leslie."

"It would be wise to keep silent and let me have my man."

He turned to Vickie. "I know she's insane, but what does she mean about things from your past? What are you still hiding from me?"

Her eyebrows arched. She didn't want to confess some terrible truth to him, likely out of fear of his reaction, but he also knew his love for her was stronger than anything he'd ever felt in his life and he would die for her, so there was nothing she might say which could harm them.

Leslie took her arm. "Bless our union, and I will keep your secret."

Vickie seemed bewildered. She muttered to herself about a network of spies and asked under her breath how Leslie could know.

She shook off her competitor's hand and paced before them. Leslie turned to John in victory, which seemed sudden and final. "Vickie will give us her blessing, and we will be married in November."

"No!"

Vickie rushed at Leslie and threw her to the ground with such force John thought Leslie might be injured. He glanced at the horses, who looked up from their grazing and eased farther toward the road. Leslie picked herself up and brushed off her clothes, and their roles reversed, as she uttered curses under her breath and Vickie stood by, ready to pounce. "You will regret this day," she said. "Mark my words."

Vickie sneered as she nodded. "You don't scare me, lady."

John reached out, but Leslie shrugged off his advance.

Her beautiful face contorted into that of a grotesque animal. Fangs descended, and she grew larger in stature, as if becoming a reptilian beast from the depths of the underworld, a Rephaim, an undead warrior of renown. She stepped near to Vickie and sniffed at her neck as saliva dripped from her fangs, and her voice, which was now deeper than any man's, assured Vickie that if Sturgis Faulkner hadn't protected her, Leslie would have joyfully eaten her flesh and consumed her blood, as it would only strengthen her resolve to mate with John and to bear his children, and their lineage would help usher in the son of perdition, who would soon make himself known on the world stage, and his signs and wonders would make him a marvel, and the masses would worship him.

John tried to grab Vickie and draw her back, but Leslie turned and shoved him to the ground, which made him feel as helpless as a child.

Her eyes flickered, and he thought she might rip into his flesh with her claw-like fingers, but she wheeled and faced Vickie, who now stood back from her, holding the worn Bible in hand, which she had opened.

She read Psalm 55 with a deep conviction. "Listen to my prayer, O God. Do not ignore my cry for help! Please listen and answer me, for I am overwhelmed by my troubles. My enemies shout at me, making loud and wicked threats. They bring trouble on me and angrily hunt me down. My heart pounds in my chest. The terror of death assaults me. Fear and trembling overwhelm me, and I can't stop shaking. Oh, that I had wings like a dove; then I would fly away and rest! I would fly far away to the quiet of the wilderness. How quickly I would escape, far from this wild storm of hatred. Confuse them, Lord, and frustrate their plans, for I see violence and conflict in the city. Its walls are patrolled day and night against invaders, but the real danger is wickedness within the city. Everything is falling apart; threats and cheating are rampant in the streets. It is not an enemy who taunts me, I could bear that. It is not my foes who so arrogantly insult me, I could have hidden from them. Instead, it is you, my equal, my companion and close friend. What good fellowship we once enjoyed as we walked together to the house of God. Let death stalk my enemies; let the grave swallow them alive, for evil makes its home within them. But I will call on God, and the Lord will rescue me. Morning, noon, and night I cry out in my distress, and the Lord hears my voice. He ransoms me and keeps me safe from the battle waged against me, though many still oppose me. God, who has ruled forever, will hear me and humble them. For my enemies refuse to change their ways; they do not fear God. As for my companion, he betrayed his friends; he broke his promises. His words are as smooth as butter, but in his heart is war. His words are as soothing as lotion, but underneath are daggers! Give your burdens to the Lord, and he will take care of you. He will not permit the godly to slip and fall. But you, O God, will send the wicked down to the pit of destruction. Murderers and liars will die young, but I am trusting you to save me."

As Vickie read the verses, her skin glowed brightly, startling both John and Leslie. The light intensified over the course of the reading until it was difficult to look at her, and, as she closed, her shine faded.

Leslie once more made herself into a ravishing woman, her features soft and inviting and peaceful, but she was now without power.

John gained the strength to deny her. He pointed to her rental car.

"Please leave here and never return, Leslie. I don't want you."

She looked up at him with beckoning eyes, and her finger curled.

"Come with me, my love, and we will take our place on high."

"I don't know who or what you are, but I love this woman."

He gestured at Vickie, who stood her ground.

"You are lucky, John. Yahweh is protecting you right now, but His favor has not stopped me from weaponizing the legal system against you. Although you deny me, I will not harm you today, but I will send you to prison for my father's murder. I have laid many heinous clues which point directly at you as the primary suspect. I own the detectives who took the case and the prosecutor and most of the judges."

"I'm surprised you don't own all the judges," he said.

"That will be rectified soon. Look for it on the news."

"Please don't," said Vickie with desperation. "I beg you."

Leslie strolled to her car and opened the door.

She gave John a heartfelt look. "Won't you come with me?"

He shook his head. "I will marry the love of my life."

"So be it." Leslie gestured. "Ask Vickie about her child."

John gave her a quizzical look. "What child?"

"Ask her." Leslie smiled at him and got into the car.

Sixteen

Psalm 56:11

I trust in God, so why should I be afraid?
What can mere mortals do to me?

Vickie leaned against the top rail and watched a dog bark at a horse she had originally named Breakfast Blend in honor of her morning coffee, but who now went by the shortened moniker, Blend. The cream-colored Labrador Retriever playfully stuck out two paws and pivoted right and then left, and the horse behaved in similar fashion, cavorting in circles, sprinting between the fence at the road and the span which ran alongside the driveway, joyful dog in tow, a dog who three days ago had christened Bluecreek Stables as his home. As the afternoon sun dipped below the far blue mountains, Vickie decreed the retriever Grady, for no reason other than she had once interviewed an old man by the same name who was charitable and decent and wise.

Vickie saw him as the father she never knew, but hoped she might someday earn.

She turned to the house, and her eyes landed on John, who sat on the steps with a watchful gaze. She knew they must discuss Leslie.

At the porch, they sat on the glider. He pushed it back and forth, and it made a friendly creaking sound which reassured her.

John pointed. "The only thing that dog loves more than Blend is chasing balls. There must be a hundred lying around."

She smiled. "I picked up a bunch and put them into a basket."

"That will help. I don't want Price or Eudora to stumble."

Vickie chuckled. "She may be with my father, but she's not old."

"He's in his late fifties, so he's not that old either, but still, "

John stopped his sentence short, and for good reason. Price had seemed lethargic lately, and he said nothing when Mitch challenged Eudora at the table the prior Saturday evening, which was most unlike him when he loved someone and desired to protect them. He gave Vickie his Bible, which she didn't understand even a week later, and he said little to explain his motivation, other than she must know and love the Lord.

Vickie turned to John. "Should we have the conversation?"

He nodded.

"Would you start?" she asked. "I've avoided it all week."

"Alright." His eyebrows arched, and he chuckled. "Who was that?"

Vickie laughed, but each knew it was no trivial matter, there was nothing funny to be found in it, and neither had any idea what to say.

After several moments, Vickie broke the devilish silence.

"How could Leslie transform into someone else?"

"I think she has different DNA from ours," he said confidently.

"Meaning what?"

"It seems plausible she might be of the Rephaim."

Vickie gazed at the mosaic of mountains which reposed beyond the pasture. The mama bear had become frightened when her skin radiated a vigorous light, and the moment confirmed long-held suspicions of entities inside her, asleep until their appointed time. On that day, the entities showed themselves with a ghastly prominence. The mama bear did what all good mothers do: she protected her young, which is what Vickie should have done. Now she wondered if her child would have been a beast, and if death was preferable to life in a monstrous form.

John reached over and squeezed her arm. "Are you okay?"

Shaken from her reflections, she sat upright in the glider.

"I'm guessing you did some research this week."

"After what I witnessed?" He nodded and smiled.

"I've only read the New Testament, but Price said the psalms are the gateway to the Bible, so I read one to Leslie, and it seemed to work."

"I'd say so, since you sparkled while reading and your light weakened her, but the Lord's Prayer is a better choice, in my opinion."

"Would you recite it? I haven't heard those words in a long time."

John recited Matthew 6:9-13 from memory. "Our Father in heaven, may your name be kept holy. May your Kingdom come soon. May your will be done on earth, as it is in heaven. Give us today the food we need, and forgive us our sins, as we have forgiven those who sin against us. And don't let us yield to temptation, but rescue us from the evil one." He gestured with his hands. "When I was a boy, my father took me and Chris to church every Sunday, and at the beginning of the service the congregation always stood and said the Lord's Prayer, which confused me, because I didn't know it very well and I felt ashamed."

"You know it now, which is what counts," she said more cheerfully.

"It's the prayer Jesus instructed his apostles to pray, as He knows what we need before we do, so we don't need to ramble on, but your recital of Psalm 55 caught Leslie by surprise and likely saved our lives."

Vickie's eyes narrowed. "Does the Bible mention creatures like her?"

"A portion of God's divine council, spirits referred to by the lower-case elohim in ancient Hebrew, departed from their heavenly estate and mated with the daughters of men. Their offspring became known as Nephilim, which is a plural word translated as giants in the Greek Septuagint, but there was another word used in the Masoretic Hebrew text and in the Dead Sea Scrolls, which was Rephaim. The Bible contextually grouped the Rephaim with the Nephilim, meaning it described them as giants. However, in the surrounding region, the term Rephaim held other connotations besides giants, such as a messenger of the underworld or healer, as in someone who mended using the dark arts. It's important to consider all aspects of the term, because the giants were eventually cleared from the land, along with the inhabitants of cities who supported them, but rather than liberate, God commanded His chosen ones slay them, men, women, and children, and there's a singular reason He devoted them to destruction."

"They had different DNA?"

John smiled. "They were corrupt beyond repair, and there was no living with them in the land which was set apart by God."

She considered.

"You said they eventually cleared the Rephaim from the land."

"The task wasn't complete until King David, as some remained along the coastal plain in what later became known as Philistia, or the land of the Philistines. If you recall David and Goliath, then you know them. Goliath had brothers who were as colossal and mean as him."

"I didn't know that." Vickie pushed the glider as she pondered. "So, if I understand, you're saying there were offspring of the fallen ones who might not have been giants, but they had tainted DNA, and their slighter size probably made it easier for them to hide in plain sight. If the Israelites hunted the giants to extinction in the Holy Land, maybe some of the lesser Rephaim left and integrated into the tribes of Europe?"

"I think it's possible, and it might explain Leslie Carter."

Vickie pursed her lips, and her fingers clutched the side of the glider.

"Did you sleep with her?"

He shook his head. "Thankfully, it never happened."

"Then why is she so in love with you?"

"I don't know, and it's never made much sense. We worked together for a time and she showed interest, but despite her beauty, there was always something about her which made my skin crawl, and I declined."

Vickie sighed. "It's a strange world God created."

"No, it's a fallen world, and it's our fault. We must do better."

She let the comment pass without a response, as she had tried.

"If there were giants on the earth before the Flood, how did they survive all that water? How could there could be giants on the earth afterward?" Vickie's mind painted a portrait of larger-than-life Nephilim swimming in the raging seas, where even the birds had no place to land. Maybe it's why God sent the waters to cover even the highest mountain peaks, as it was necessary to drown the giants. They may have possessed special powers like the superheroes of modern comic books, those who could fly or listen through walls or jump over metalline skyscrapers in Manhattan. "It seems so confusing."

She slumped and sighed loudly.

"It might help if I clarify the falls from grace," he said, "because there were three. First, Adam and Eve listened to the words of the nachash in the garden on the mountain, which was called Eden, and they ate the fruit of the Tree of Knowledge of Good and Evil, which opened their eyes to pride and wrath and lust, the latter leading them to cover themselves in shame. Second, there was the Flood, precipitated by the spirits who left their estate and mated with human women. Third, which in some ways is the most relevant, is the Tower of Babel event, where God grew furious at the idolatry of the people, so He disinherited them and gave them over to a group of spirits from His divine council according to geographic boundaries. Those territorial spirits later turned from God as the others had done prior to the Flood, and they corrupted humanity in the same way, resulting in another round of Rephaim, some of whom were giants." A pause. "The Lord confused the languages at Babel, which caused the territorial spirits and their worshippers to fight against one another in a series of perpetual wars, which is why we haven't had another Flood, but since the Age of Enlightenment and the Industrial Revolution, knowledge has increased and, with the invention of the Internet and as English becomes the world's common language, cabal forces plot their rebellion. Leslie seemed like she despised the Consortium, but she's one of them."

Vickie shifted indignantly on the glider and suppressed a sigh.

"Those spirits must have seen what went on before the Flood, and they had to know what God would do if they rebelled, so why do it?"

His brows flickered as he stopped the glider. "It's never made much sense to me. All I know is they fight across centuries and to the death."

Vickie hugged her arms to her as she realized why those spirits went against the Lord. "They rebelled for the sake of rebellion."

She looked out at the peaceful horses and then shut her eyes.

"Am I also a Rephaim? Please be honest, John."

"Leslie said you two were similar, but you are nothing like her."

Vickie threw up her hands in frustration. "What then?"

"That I don't know, and we may never learn the truth."

She nervously paced the porch in front of him.

"Didn't Leslie love Roland? Why would she murder her father?"

John shrugged. "Maybe she wasn't his daughter."

Leslie had said the Morrison bloodline ran similar to her own, which let Vickie off the hook, as she was a Brewer by relation, but what about Katie and Abbie, who were products of Michelle and Tink? The prospect of their salvation being lost was more than Vickie could bear.

John patted the glider, interrupting her thoughts.

"Please sit and tell me about your child."

A corner bin held a plastic chucker and several squishy balls. She went over and grabbed the wand. "Let's play for a while."

He sighed. "Alright, but you can't put me off forever."

They hopped to the grass and went through the gate to the pasture, and Vickie chucked the ball for Grady, which he loved. When he grew tired, he laid at Blend's feet, who munched on grass and wandered about, forcing Grady to move with him. Apart, they were timid, but together they were strong, much like Vickie and John, who needed one another, more so now than ever before, as forces aligned against them.

John guided her to a section of fence which paralleled the driveway, where no one could hear, and then he drew back and held her at arm's length. His rough hand raised, and he gently ran his fingers through her hair, and she melted before him, her trembling visible and intense.

"I had an abortion." Her eyes fell to his shirt.

He cupped a finger under her chin. "I thought as much."

"Logan raped me and, "

"You aborted his child." John stroked her hair, and she let him.

Logan had a desperate need for Vickie to die with him at the quarry. His death wish carried over to her, and many nights since then, she dreamed of going over the edge and joining Chelsea, so little and pure.

Acknowledging her sin, she turned abruptly, but John overtook her.

"It's not like you got rid of your child because it was inconvenient."

She made herself look away. "It was a difficult, "

"A madman raped you, and delivery under those circumstances would be unthinkable, not that I would force a woman otherwise, but you know what I mean." He struggled, which seemed sweet.

She would not dare tell him the truth, not the fullness of it. Although she had made strides in her pursuit of honesty, this was a bridge too far, as John would certainly leave over her transgressions.

"I didn't abort my child because of the rape. That happened later."

He sighed. "The rape or the abortion?"

"It's complicated."

Their bodies separated, and he grabbed the fence rail, likely to ease his mounting frustration. "Okay, uncomplicate it for me."

"When I first came to D.C., I worked as an intern."

John kept still and silent. He wanted simple answers, but there were none to give, as everything had been a blur and still was in her mind.

"I said I was with a lot of men. Please don't judge me."

"I know, but you also said you worked incessantly in those early days and your only outlet was spending time with Mitch and Logan, who were like brothers." John turned and eyed the house. "Was it Mitch?"

She shook her head. "It was Logan who took me to the clinic."

John drew farther from her and grunted. He gazed at the herd.

Vickie stepped toward him. "Please don't leave."

"Why shouldn't I, Vickie, when all you do is lie?"

"How did I lie? Please talk to me."

"You said you never slept with Logan before the rape."

Her lips pursed. "I said I never willingly slept with him."

"What? He raped you when you were eighteen?"

She nodded and mouthed the word yes.

"Wow, and you said nothing about this to me or anyone?"

"There was nothing to say, really, because he thought we were on a date and believed he deserved gratification at the end of the evening, but to me, he was a brother and we were out having a good time together."

There was no denying John looked uncomfortable. He frowned and gestured for her to continue, but she waited for his features to soften.

"After Logan forced himself on me, he felt ashamed and begged me not to call the police. When I said I was pregnant, he offered to take me to the clinic, and then he was kind and even paid for the procedure."

John picked at the top of a fence post as she spoke.

"So you forgave him, and that was that?"

"He left after the abortion, and I didn't see him for years."

"Until the interview," said John impatiently.

"I guess there were pent-up emotions which erupted."

"And he went ballistic, thinking you were debased like him."

"Something like that. He expected us both to die in the quarry."

John again watched the horses. He seemed mesmerized by them. He turned to her. "So whose child was it?"

"Someone you don't know, a guy I met on my first night in D.C."

"At a bar?"

Her nod sent a rush of pain through her heart. "Yes."

The lie was horrific, and she would pay for her deception, but it was all she knew to say. If John left her over this, she would surely die.

Price and the girls ventured outside to the porch, followed by Lewis and Mary, who had slept in a guest room since last Saturday night.

"I want all of you to see this." John cast a strained smile.

Vickie's eyes widened in apprehension. She felt his muscles tense.

He placed his rough hands against her cheeks and kissed her deeply in front of the group, even Mitch, who had just stepped onto the porch. Vickie closed her eyes and let the moment happen undisturbed by the opinions of others, as this man was hers and hers alone, and she loved him with all her heart and soul, even if she couldn't yet reveal herself to him. Maybe she would someday, after she gave him a child.

Price and Eudora clapped, and the others did likewise.

Lewis stuck two fingers in his mouth and whistled.

John addressed the porch. "I love this woman, and I will marry her!"

More whistling and more cheering.

Her worries fell to sheer bliss.

The following Saturday afternoon, John asked Vickie to accompany him to dinner at a steakhouse by a rippling mountain creek and to dance at LuLu's Hall, but she was reticent to spend an evening with so many of Addison's most popular citizens. They knew her now as a national embarrassment and would condemn her twenty years away from home, her refusal to nurse Michelle after her accident and to console Red, the town's favorite son, or so it seemed to Vickie while growing up under his control. Worse than all the above, people knew she had balked at adopting the girls. It would prove an unforgivable sin in their eyes and in Vickie's, but she had begun a reclamation effort with Katie and Abbie, and they responded in kind, as they needed a mother as badly as she needed a child. She was thankful for their love and that Leslie had not revealed Vickie's innermost secret to the good brothers and sisters of Addison, for if she did, they would shun her. John wonderfully and completely disregarded her feminine insecurities, and his masculine strength calmed her frazzled emotions, which would otherwise churn as they entered LuLu's and made a beeline to the crowded dance floor.

The ordeal went better than expected, and soon she settled into the flow. Everyone gladly reconnected with her, and she even shared a deep and meaningful kiss with John in front of what felt like all of Addison.

Golden-haired Rachel Daniels threw Vickie an icy glare and then pouted at a table. The couple shared another kiss in the poolroom in the back, which teemed with shooters most nights, but during the dance sat empty. The dimly lit room kept them from Rachel's prying eyes, but knowing she might walk in any second elevated their adrenaline levels.

They later took a break outside on the steps, where John shared more about grace and truth, as she must confess her sins to the Lord.

When she balked, he said she must also confess to those she had wronged, and then she might expect God's grace to follow, as He dealt only in honesty. Vickie agreed, but still her secret kept itself hidden.

Another hour passed, and they left LuLu's and their new friends.

On the way home, they sang along with country songs on the radio, the oldies and the latest hits, and the number of verses Vickie knew surprised her. It heartened her to know she was no longer a city girl.

John parked in front of the house and eased around the Silverado. He opened Vickie's door, and she beamed and said she wished they were married, and he grabbed her and kissed her with every ounce of strength he possessed, as she was his one true love and had been since they first met, when their souls momentarily left their haphazard course and bonded in friendship and love, and they first thought of children.

He led her to the barn where they checked on Savannah, as her milk vein had formed from behind her belly and her tailbone dropped and her rear muscles relaxed for foaling. Savannah's heart was weaker than ever, and her chances of making it through delivery were slim.

Earlier in the afternoon, a worried Vickie had walked Savannah in the side yard, and the mare's gait was good, so John persuaded Vickie to go to LuLu's, but during dinner she called Missy repeatedly with pestering questions and asked Katie to check on Savannah in her stall.

As they stood in observation, Savannah seemed uncomfortable on her right side, and her breaths came out in shallow snorts. She struggled to rise, which made Vickie grab John's arm, and then flopped onto her left side. Her breaths seemed pained as her eyes finally met theirs.

John stepped inside the stall and looked underneath her belly.

"There's wax on her teats, which is a sign."

"Do you think it'll happen tonight?" Vickie peered after him.

"Could be. Guess we'll sleep in the barn."

Katie and Abbie approached. "Can we sleep out here, too?"

He and Vickie traded glances.

"It might not be wise." John ran his hand over Abbie's head.
He looked at Katie. "She's too young for this type of thing."

"So am I," Vickie said. "If you think her heart will fail."

Abbie gasped. "When she has the baby?"

"Yeah, kiddo. Missy will be here soon to help, but Savannah's heart has been weak for a long time, and Missy doesn't think she'll make it."

Abbie sat on a hay bale and dropped her head low.

John left the stall and bent down in front of her.

"See? That's why you should be inside the house."

Abbie shook her head. "No, I have to be out here with Savannah."

"Why, sweetie? You can't save her."

"God can."

He shot Vickie an impatient look, and she came over to them.

"The Lord can perform many miracles," she said, "but He won't save Savannah tonight because He wants to have her all to Himself."

"I don't care. I have to be with her when she leaves us."

Vickie's brow furrowed. "To say goodbye?"

"So I can stop her pain with my hands."

A wave of emotion broke over Vickie, and she swiped at her tears.

She stroked Abbie's hair. "It's fine with me, honey."

At the dance, Vickie had mentioned the change in Abbie and how when she first met her, she saw the girl as oppressed by a demon or perhaps even possessed, but since Katie shared the Gospel and they prayed together on their knees in sincere supplication, the eight-year-old took on a reformed persona, and a light shone from within her, which was both joyous and healing. Anyway, who knew about such things? Maybe she could help after all. The family would need all it could get.

"Thanks," said Abbie pensively. "I sense her pain."

Vickie turned to Savannah and then back to Abbie.

"Now? She hasn't gone into labor yet."

"Her heart. It hurts her, and she doesn't know how to stop it."

Vickie sat beside Abbie on the hay. "How do you know?"

"An angel is in there with her, and he tells me how she feels."

Vickie again glanced at John. "Is the angel nice?"

Abbie nodded her reply. "He said Savannah asked for me."

She went to the stall and gazed at the mare with kind eyes, and then she ventured near Savannah, who lay on one side, and she stroked the mare's coat and relayed soothing words from the angel. Vickie followed and sat against the wall, and as John kneeled near Savannah's head, he sensed some scene from Vickie's past must have come rushing back, because she wept to herself. She looked up at him with innocent eyes.

"I don't like this world most of the time, especially tonight."

"Me, too," he said. "We never really get over childhood loss."

"Or failing to help those we loved," she said.

"You're thinking of the teenage girl, right?"

"Helen Dunstan. I was selfish, and she died."

"Well, you're anything but selfish now, and it shows."

Vickie wiped her tears. "Thanks. That helps."

Savannah grunted and her head lifted, as if she struggled to breathe, but John noticed a protrusion at her rear and realized the foal was coming right then and there, which was a surprise because he and Missy assumed the delivery would occur later that night, as was customary, but in Savannah's weakened condition, she must need the foal out as soon as possible. It made John both happy and sad, as he dreaded the rest.

Price and Eudora leaned into a corner, and Mitch stood at the stall's doorway as Vickie and the girls crouched and sat about Savannah's head while John positioned himself at her rump. Abbie rubbed her and said loving things, and John knew Savannah's time on earth neared its end.

A truck door slammed outside the barn, and Missy soon appeared.

"John, what are you doing with Savannah in there?"

She looked at the side yard. "You should've moved her."

Vickie gave John a sheepish look. "Missy told me, but I forgot."

"It's my fault," he said. "I spaced on it, and I'm an idiot."

Missy surveyed the stall. "Can you remove these pieces?"

"If I have to, but the posts are load bearing, so I'd rather not."

Price cleared his throat. "We can fashion something to brace it."

The foal pushed its way out as Savannah grunted and strained.

"Come on, girl. You can do it," said Katie pleadingly.

She seemed worried, as did John and Vickie and everyone else, including Missy, who had seen births a thousand times, but this was different, as the Reaper would likely visit afterward, and the impact of a horse's death could not be overstated. They were majestic and powerful animals with a caring heart and a playful intelligence, and losing even one before its time seemed such a grievous mistake, but the Lord had sent an angel and a family to be with the mare in her last moments.

Savannah had raised up slightly on one side, but as more of the sack exited her rear, she fell flat, and she kicked out with all four hooves.

Abbie put a hand over her mouth. "Is she dying?"

"No, honey," John said. "She's pushing more comfortably."

"Okay." Abbie took a heavy breath and exhaled.

The foal dropped out, and John cleared the sack from its mouth and nostrils so it could breathe easily. "Like this?" He looked up at Missy.

"You're doing fine." Missy again glanced at the side yard.

"I'm sorry I messed up," he said. "It was dumb of me."

"Death is hard," she said in a pained tone. "I never get used to it."

Both foal and mare grew exhausted as each struggled to breathe.

John wasn't sure what to do next, so he turned to his cousin.

"It won't be long." Missy turned her face as the tears coursed.

Katie openly wept, and John knew it was from the joy of birth and the tragedy of death, but at least the family was there for foal and mare.

The foal wiggled and squirmed, and John asked Katie to take off the rest of the sack so it might stand. She complied, and the foal struggled.

"Hey, he's a boy." Katie turned to the group with a faint smile.

The foal raised his head and his body into a sitting position, and Savannah raised her head to look at him, mother and son exalted in love.

Savannah's head lowered to the floor, and her breathing eased.

"No, don't go," said Vickie in a pleading voice. "It's too soon."

Eudora covered her mouth. "I can't take this."

Price wrapped his long arm around her shoulder and squeezed, and she leaned into him and wept. He whispered to her as he watched.

Abbie sat up. "The angel told me to lay hands on Savannah."

"What, honey?" Vickie turned to the girl in surprise.

Abbie placed her palms on Savannah's coat and muttered to herself, and then she spoke Psalm 56:12-13 aloud. "I will fulfill my vows to you, O God, and will offer a sacrifice of thanks for your help. For you have rescued me from death; you have kept my feet from slipping. So now I can walk in your presence, O God, in your life-giving light."

After a few moments, the dam got up and stood near her foal, and she encouraged him to rise alongside her, which he did, and it seemed like a miracle, and it certainly was, as Savannah had been about to take her last breath. At Missy's insistence, John led them to the side yard.

She grew amazed. In even the speediest cases, it usually took at least twenty to thirty minutes before a foal could stand, much less walk.

When they reached the middle of the yard, Savannah licked her foal and rubbed her face against his and nudged her body near to him so he might know his mother. She encouraged him to nurse, which he did, and she stood tall and proud of her offspring, as he seemed strong and sturdy and fine, and she gave him her colostrum, instinctively aware it was the most important meal of the foal's existence, as it was packed with life-saving antibodies which fought against infection and provided healing elements. She continued this for the next thirty-six hours, until her colostrum turned to milk, and then she gave him a motherly lick before God took her home. On the night of the foal's birth, Abbie had heard from an angel who showed himself to her in the stall and in the side yard, and both dam and foal walked fifty yards of their own accord, and Savannah lived much longer than expected. It was for this reason Abbie named the foal Miracle, and all knew it to be true.

Missy stayed with the family for three nights, as she didn't want to go home, which reminded her of the recent miscarriage. Savannah's passing was too much to withstand on her own, so her husband, Lee, joined her at Bluecreek. Her tiredness and irritability showed as John sat with them at the kitchen table over coffee. He felt guilty for bringing Savannah to the farm in such a condition, as she was a tragedy waiting to happen, and he shouldn't have been so cruel, but he was angry with Vickie for her belligerence and had wanted to force harshness on her.

Vickie ran her hand over his shoulder as she passed by him and sat.

"I know you're hurting, but she lasted longer than we thought."

"You were right to name the foal Miracle," said Missy in an agitated tone. "It was a miracle we got the dam out of the stall and into the side yard. If Savannah had died in those tight quarters, you cannot imagine how horrible the situation would've become, especially for the girls."

Vickie cast a confrontational look. "John knew what to do."

"What, take down the front wall and the load-bearing posts?" Missy waited for Vickie to consider the question. "How would a tractor get close enough to scoop up her body? Would you split her into sections?"

"Of course not." Vickie gulped her coffee with renewed indignation.

Missy leaned forward as her mug slammed the table. "You didn't give him my message. It would have cost him a great deal in this town."

Katie approached, with Abbie trailing. "Everyone makes mistakes."

"Oh, so you're on her side now?" Missy gave her a wounded look.

Katie grabbed a chair and sat. She smiled at Vickie with warmth.

"Vickie is our mother now, so yes, I suppose I am."

The word seemed to wash over Missy and cause her pain.

She turned to Lee. "Let's go. I don't need this abuse."

He gave them an abashed look. "Sorry, but our miscarriage has her on edge." He turned to her, but she slapped his hand and scowled.

"Don't tell them about my problems!"

"It's our problem, Missy, and they already know."

"How?"

"You told John and Vickie the afternoon Savannah died."

"I don't remember that, so you must be lying."

"Missy, you were very upset. We all were when she passed."

"Lack of sleep makes it hard to remember things." John headed for the coffeemaker but then wheeled. "She'll be much better tomorrow."

Lee slid out of his chair and gently took her by the hand.

"Come on, honey. Let's get you home and into bed."

"There's too much to do and too many animals to see."

"I'll handle those until you get some sleep and feel better."

Her eyes fell to the floor. "Am I so terrible?"

He cupped a finger under her chin, and his eyes met hers.

"You're my wife and I love you, but it's time for us to grieve."

Missy's eyes moistened, and she clutched his shirt. "Alright."

John considered how she must be feeling and thought of Vickie in the clinic so many years ago, scared and insecure about her decision, knowing it would end her baby, so faultless and trusting in the womb, a life never to be lived and a regret which would consume her forever.

He glanced at her, and she looked at the wall and wiped her eyes.

As Lee corralled his weepy wife to the car, he apologized for her outburst. Missy had been told having a baby was impossible, but she was determined, as she wanted one so badly it hurt. They had tried IVF, which they thought had worked until a miscarriage ended it.

"Stop telling people, Lee. It's not fair."

"They are family, and they should know what you're going through." Lee held her hand as she got into her seat and turned. "Thanks for understanding. Missy can be a handful, but she's in pain."

Vickie's eyebrows arched. "Takes one to know one, but sharing her pain is the only way to get over it. Trust me. I know all about it."

Lee's eyes narrowed. "You should heed your own advice."

Vickie seemed taken aback. "Sure, I guess you're right."

"Tend and befriend as women usually do." He gestured at John. "We men become introverted and withdrawn, which is unhealthy."

"I have the same feelings as her sometimes. It can be really hard."

Missy looked up. "What do you know, Vickie? You never had a child, and you never set up a nursery or dreamed of cribs and diapers and play dates and first day of school and prom and watching her walk down the aisle on her wedding day." She wiped her eyes. "You know nothing."

Lee swung the car door shut, which further inflamed Missy.

"I take it you also lost a child?" He waited for Vickie's response.

"Yes, years ago, when I was just out of high school."

"Well, I don't know your circumstances, but it doesn't matter."

He walked to the driver's side and opened the door.

"I'm sorry for your loss, Vickie."

"Yours, too," she said.

He gazed at the road and then turned to her. "Do we ever heal?"

She shook her head. "No, but you learn to live with it."

He took a breath and chuckled. "Guess it's better than nothing."

Lee got into the car and waved as they drove toward the highway.

SEVENTEEN

Psalm 57:2

I cry out to God Most High,
to God who will fulfill his purpose for me.

Vickie awakened in the night and tiptoed through the hallway, cracking open Katie's bedroom door. Her comforter had tangled itself into a knot, but she seemed asleep, so Vickie gently closed the door and eased down the hall to Abbie's room. The little girl was the picture of peace as she slept amid the gleam of a nightlight near her closet, helpful as it was to ward off any monsters who might spring out and attack her in the wee hours. Vickie wanted to sit beside Abbie and ask her about Michelle and about Savannah, and mostly about laying hands and soothing angels, but she withheld her queries until later. Losing the sweet Appaloosa mare had kept the family in a gloomy mood all week, and the girls had huddled together, offering faint responses when prodded, as anyone would when confronted by death.

She slipped on her boots and stepped onto the porch, mindful of bears who roamed about in the darkness, then made her way to the barn.

Chief eyed her, and she knew her training must recommence, as she had withdrawn from the horses. It was unfair to them and to the girls and even to Price, who picked up her slack, as was his custom and his fatherly duty. This last notion drove her to stand in front of Chief's stall, where she gave him an inquisitive look and rubbed his neck.

"He doesn't want your apology."

The voice from behind startled her, and she wheeled around.

Katie stood with arms crossed, glaring.

Footsteps sounded from the lane, and Abbie soon joined them.

Vickie sighed, realizing she must have interrupted their sleep.

"What does he want, a carrot?"

Katie smirked. "You're not funny."

Abbie looked up at her sister with widened eyes. She tugged on Katie's t-shirt and shook her head. When Katie turned to Vickie with renewed zeal, Abbie again tugged and mouthed the word *no* to her.

"All right," said Katie in an agitated tone.

"Should I offer you an apology instead of Chief?"

Katie recoiled. "Me?"

Vickie nodded.

"What for?"

"I'm sorry about Savannah. I know she was your favorite."

A look of sadness fell over Katie, which broke Vickie's heart, as it replaced the defiance in her spirit that every independent teen carried.

"Like you said, she was a tragedy waiting to happen."

"Still." Vickie hesitated. "It doesn't make it any easier."

The teen's boot kicked at the dusty floor. She wiped away a tear.

Abbie brushed by Vickie and peeked into Miracle's stall.

She grinned. "He's sleeping in the hay."

Vickie shrugged and again tiptoed, this time to spy on the foal. She and Abbie leaned forward and peeked into the stall, marveling at Miracle's perfect form. Katie sat by herself on the feed bin and read her Bible.

At such a young age, she had witnessed too many painful scenes.

Vickie watched the sleeping foal, but the portrait of Katie alone nagged at her. She had done the same as a teen, but without a Bible.

She tapped Abbie on the shoulder and put a finger over her lips as a signal to be quiet, then led her to the feed bin and lifted her to the top. Vickie smiled at the little girl and then drew near to Katie, who perused a page as if in contemplation. Vickie knew better, Katie hurt so badly, and in places she thought were forever locked. Vickie knew her agony, as it went far deeper than the loss of a sweet Appaloosa.

"Will you talk to us?" she asked kindly. "We love you, honey."

Katie looked up with a blank face. "I think there are parallels between the three temptations of Christ and your life in Addison."

Vickie gave Abbie a flat stare, as if what Katie had said was absurd.

Abbie giggled and covered her mouth. Katie took a breath and went back to her Bible, but Vickie put her palm on the page and met her eyes.

"I'll play your game if you'll let me. How are they the same?"

She removed her hand, and Katie placed a bookmark in her Bible.

"In the first one, the Holy Spirit led Jesus into the wilderness, where He fasted for forty days and nights. Satan appeared and told Him that if He was the Son of God, the stones would turn into bread, but Jesus referred to the Exodus, where the Israelites wandered in the same wilderness for forty years. God fed the hungry people with heavenly manna."

"How does this apply to me?"

"Well, you were cut off from your job because of what I told Mitch, and when you came here, you were hungry for a real life, but you thought there was no food. It was here all along, provided by God."

Vickie considered this.

"Have the scales been removed so I can see?"

Katie smiled, clearly pleased with her pupil's discernment.

"It's been slow, but you're getting there."

"All right, so what about the second temptation?"

"Satan said that if Jesus was the Son of God, He should fling Himself from the highest point in the temple, as the angels would surely catch Him. Jesus said not to test the Lord, as the Israelites did at Massah."

Katie paused.

"The Israelites had seen the parting of the Red Sea and were fed by manna from Heaven, but when they ran low on water at Rephidim, they questioned God's power and authority and were ready to stone Moses. Then the Lord told him to take his staff and strike a rock."

"What happened next?" asked Abbie intently.

Katie gave her a warm smile. "Water flowed in abundance."

She turned to Vickie, and her expression darkened.

"Satan tempted Jesus to prove His powers, and you tried fiercely to prove yours in cable news and again after you came home to Addison. You rode with Reggie and Mary and tried to figure out the kill buyer operation, which had been going on in Western North Carolina for years, but they had yet to meet the great Victoria Morrison. She knew better than anyone how to stop those ignorant yokels. Am I right?"

Vickie's lips pursed. "That's not fair. I cared about the horses."

"John cares about them. You only think about yourself."

"Not anymore, Katie. Now there's you and Abbie to consider, and Price and everyone else, not to mention John, whom I have always loved."

"Why do you still call your father Price?"

Vickie drew back from her. It was a low shot after Savannah's death.

"I don't know. Maybe I'm not ready to call him Daddy."

"Have you ever?"

"In private, but not in front of everyone else."

Katie's eyebrows arched, and she sighed.

"In the third temptation, Satan took Jesus to Mount Hermon, where the fallen ones came down to earth in the time before the Flood, and offered Jesus the world if He would kneel and worship him."

"How did Jesus respond?"

"He told Satan to get out of there; it is written that everyone must worship the Lord. This also parallels the Israelites, who turned from God and were removed from the land and placed into exile in Babylon."

"Are you telling me I should leave?"

Vickie reflected on the Morrison bloodline. Could Katie be a wicked Rephaim sent to cause dissension and to disrupt Vickie's daily walk with Christ? She paced in angry confusion as the girls watched.

Katie hopped down and squeezed her arm, stopping her movement.

"I'm saying do not stray from the Lord as Satan would have you do. He tempts us the same three ways every time. First, we believe, like Adam and Eve, that we are being denied something we deserve, like you and your precious slogan, 'the face of cable news.' Second, we respond to a challenge to our status by proving our power, like the fallen ones did when they descended to earth at Mount Hermon and sought to change human DNA before the Flood, and like you tried to do when you moved back here and tried to show how great you were as a journalist. Third, we turn from God at the slightest hint of trouble, just as the adversary persuaded the Israelites to do, which led them to exile, and just as you would like to do now, after sweet Savannah's death, but she was always going to die, just like every one of us will die."

"That's quite a speech. I'm surprised you didn't rehearse."

"Unlike you, I don't have to practice. I speak from the heart."

Vickie's heart thumped rapidly. She grabbed the edge of the bin and slumped over it, wanting to curl into a ball like the sleeping foal.

She raised up. "Why are you so angry with me?"

"You allowed Savannah to come here, knowing what her death would do to us, and you paid her hardly any attention. Then you forgot to tell John about the stall. If she had died in there, they would've cut her into pieces, and that I would have never forgiven you for, no matter what you said or what you might have done to make up for it."

"You're right, Katie. I was distracted by things that happened."

"And the dance."

Vickie felt her self-worth under attack. "Yes."

"But more importantly, your abortion." Katie threw her a look of disdain. "Bet you were hoping that one never saw the light of day, huh?"

Vickie sat on the feed bin and hung her head low. "You're right."

"Is that all you have to say? Our mother is dead, and you wouldn't help her, even when she was paralyzed and our grandfather was crying his eyes out every night in his office. Then we find out you killed your own baby in the womb, as if you were too cool to care about anyone?"

Vickie scooted off the bin and threw up her hands. "Yes! Yes!"

She turned to Katie in anger. "You're right about everything!"

"I know I'm right. That's why I said it."

"Does it make you happy? Are you having fun at my expense? Do you not think I've stayed up nights in misery for the last twenty years, wishing I could somehow bring back my beloved Chelsea?"

Katie flinched. "Chelsea?"

"That's her name, if you must know."

Abbie gasped. "You knew she was a girl?"

Vickie took a deep breath and exhaled. This was going to be the worst moment of her life, or perhaps the second worst, as the absolute epitome of horrible would occur when she told John about their child.

"There were complications with the saline abortion, which was widely used in those days." Vickie steeled herself by leaning against the feed bin, as she hadn't planned to have this conversation in the middle of the night, just after Savannah's death, but Katie was adamant, so she must. "Chelsea was technically born alive, so the doctor knew her sex. He took her from me, and I waited in a very large room with the other girls. It was then I gave her a name, and for a moment I hoped she might live, because I regretted what I had done to her, my lovely child, but then he came back and she was dead."

"And someone like you thinks she can be our mother?"

"I want to try, Katie. It's the best I can say right now."

The teen spat out her next words. "Are you leaving?"

"What?" Vickie grew uneasy. "I'm not going anywhere."

"What about John? He seems agitated when he's not making pronouncements about marrying you and kissing you like a fiend."

Vickie chuckled. "Colorful, but that's one way to look at it."

"Is there another way?" She turned to Abbie. "We need answers."

Vickie squeezed Katie's hand as a gesture of her love, then turned to Abbie and asked for her hand. The little girl gave hers gladly, and they formed a circle in front of the bin. Vickie pulled them tightly to her and swore an oath to never leave them alone, no matter what, and they believed her because she spoke the truth to them, which was all.

Thursday morning, Vickie lamented her lack of sleep as she entered data into a spreadsheet in the barn office, hoping a lightbulb might pop on in her head as it had done for Michelle, who knew more about horses than Vickie ever would, except for the fierce one who killed her.

Her fingers paused.

She glanced about the room and again considered the Morrison lineage. If Michelle was a Rephaim with entities in her blood, it might explain Wildfire's aversion to her, as by all accounts he seemed to take an instant dislike. But then again, Katie and Abbie caused no such reaction in him, and he seemed to like them more than anyone else in the family. Vickie rubbed her face and ran her fingers through her hair. It was all so confusing, and there was no one to see about the matter and nobody to ask honest, probing questions. Her eyes fell on her father's Bible, which caught dust on her desk, unused since Leslie's menacing visit.

Her senses flashed with alarm as a notion struck her.

The girls had been unaware of her abortion, but John knew, as Leslie had hinted at Vickie's lost child before she left. Neither Katie nor Abbie were on the porch, and it was later when Vickie confessed her abortion to John. This meant he must have told them without asking her permission or without having her present for the conversation, and it felt like a betrayal. Katie had confronted her with a mixture of distrust and hurt and condemnation, all of which were warranted based on history.

Price cracked open the door and gently knocked, interrupting her pondering, but the sense of treachery unleashed something in her and she responded sharply, abandoning the facade of politeness. As in the past, she found a perverse pleasure in the challenge of uncovering the truth from those who would seek to hide it from the world.

Pity the same defiance didn't apply when she looked in the mirror.

"Yes?" She wore a look of irritation as she resumed typing.

"I need to ask a favor." He sat in the chair opposite her.

"Price, I'm tired and I have yet to catch a second wind. I don't have the energy to handle a problem, so handle the situation yourself."

"I thought you would call me Dad or Daddy or Father. Something."

She looked away and sighed. "I don't feel like it after what you did."

He shook his head as if genuinely surprised at her immaturity.

"I asked the woman I love to marry me. For that, I won't apologize."

"And everyone celebrated, including me, but it made me wake up in the night and I went to check on the girls and then Miracle." She ran her long, sensitive fingers along the tabletop, right and then left, just as she had done in her Washington apartment. "Katie confronted me in the barn about my abortion, and the worst part is Abbie was right there beside her, young and impressionable, and she will probably hate me for life, just like Katie does. As far as I can figure, the only other people who knew about Chelsea were you and John."

"You finally told him the truth?"

Vickie's back pushed into her chair. "Not all of it, but enough."

He flashed her a look of disapproval, and she knew what it meant.

Her eyes flickered. "So you didn't tell them?"

His eyebrows arched. "I did not. Your secrets are your own."

"Then it must have been John. But why would he do it?"

"You'll have to ask him."

She reflected.

"John told me about the Rephaim and the Nephilim, how they were similar, but the Nephilim were the giants who roamed the land of Canaan and were eventually cleared from Israel." She let Price consider her words and then continued. "Leslie mentioned cabal bloodlines, hers included, and said the Morrisons were of an ancestry which traces back to that time. She showed herself to us as a Rephaim, or at least it's what John called her, and she bragged about killing her own father and those clients of his who bought horses from Roland since she first met John. It's all some sick and twisted game to her which I'd rather not play, but since she left our farm, I've been wondering if Katie and Abbie have something inside them which might keep them from receiving salvation. I know it sounds crazy after we witnessed Abbie lay hands on poor Savannah, whose heart hurt her so badly, but I love those girls and I cannot bear to see them lost to the Lake of Fire." Her eyes moistened, and she swiped at her tears. "Daddy, help me make sense of this because I'm in over my head and I wonder if I'm also a monster." She rose from her chair in tears and went to the filing cabinet.

Vickie turned to him. "I don't really know anything anymore."

Price went over to her and drew her close. "You are no Rephaim."

She looked up and wiped a tear. "You know about them?"

"I've read my Bible just like John. It's all there."

She drew back from him. "Do you think they're lost?"

He guided her back to the desk, and each resumed their seats.

"Katie seems to have the gift of discernment and a desire to learn the Word at a deep level, which is an unexpected but glorious development and, as her mother, I would encourage her to continue in her studies."

"Of course."

He held up a palm. "Abbie is on another level, and I've yet to fully comprehend what God has in store for her, but I suspect she's a healer."

"Like one of those 'be healed' frauds who shove people down?"

He chuckled. "No, the real thing, and I don't mean some type of witch who gets her powers from the pit of Hell, but an apostle of God."

Vickie again ran her fingers through her hair and sighed.

"If she's a Rephaim, that makes no sense. He wouldn't use someone with a corrupted bloodline. It's why He cleared them from the land."

"Oh, you know so much now that you've returned to the Lord?" He gestured. "It's a common problem with new Christians. They think they know exactly what God is doing or can do, but He's limited by nothing. Jesus died on the cross and was resurrected and ascended to Heaven, which removed Satan as the ruler of this world, so nothing is out of reach if God wills it and makes it so through the Holy Spirit."

Her head bent and her eyes fell to her hands. She studied them, as they had guided her along with her two feet to stardom and also to murder. What right did she have to judge the Morrisons or God?

She looked up at her father. "I'm sorry. It was presumptuous."

"Honey, I'm only making a theological point, but it doesn't mean I have the slightest idea about the Morrisons, other than Red was misguided, and I think by now you would agree with me, but I am grateful he allowed me to live in the trailer, as it brought us together."

"I feel the same, and I hope he was saved when he died."

Price nodded and smiled. "On that note, would you do me a favor?"

"What favor?"

"I need your permission to train a horse for Eudora, which I'll present as a wedding gift. An older man taught me a lot about training horses while we were in prison, and I'd like to use those skills for her."

"Which horse, Dash or Riddle?" Their eyes met in affection.

"She's fond of Dash, but I want to train Ocean, the liver chestnut."

Vickie's eyes rose in puzzled astonishment. "She seems so distant."

Price nodded.

"That's why I want her. She needs someone who cares."

"Don't we all?" Vickie looked away and then glanced at him.

"Yes, we do," he said warmly.

She admired his longing to help both horse and woman, and Ocean was the perfect choice, as she had a presence but kept at arm's length.

"It's a travesty to let her drift into the ether, as she's been doing."

"I felt the same once about Eudora."

Vickie smiled. "After so many years of abuse, you saved her life."

"So, it's settled?"

She nodded her agreement. "I've thought of Eudora as my big sister since high school, so I want her to find happiness, and I can't think of a better match for you in your old age." She grinned as he feigned offense.

They went to the round pen, where Price showed her things he'd learned at Baldwin Correctional. She was scared of making a mistake in his presence, but he was an excellent teacher and he helped her learn with more gentleness and patience than John had ever displayed.

Her father knew how to get the most from a horse and he kept his cool under pressure. As a result, she gifted him his favorite horse, Riddle, which made him proud. The moment reversed her gloomy mood, and she no longer felt like an orphan child but a blessed woman with a loving family and a protective home to tend.

Eighteen

Psalm 58:1

Justice, do you rulers know the meaning of the word?
Do you judge the people fairly?

Vickie and John rode with Mary and Lewis in the news van on Monday morning. She surrendered her role as journalist, but she would pay her knowledge forward before giving herself to the horses. Price and Eudora joined the adventure for the first half of the day, which filled the six-seat van with a cast of colorful characters, each with their own idea of what made a story relevant. The van stopped at the kill buyer barn where a drug runner had brandished a gun, the memory excited them but also served as a reminder of candidate Leslie Carter's looming presence, which was on the cusp of widening to nationwide once she took the governor's chair in Raleigh. On that terrible day, sinister cabal factions would unite under one banner, and a bitter reckoning would find the once-renowned Victoria Morrison.

Lewis idled the van as Reggie had done.

Vickie turned and observed Price and Eudora in the third row. His usual crimson face had paled, which concerned her, but she kept it to herself.

"I look at the dilapidated barn and I think of my son."

Eudora reached over and squeezed his arm.

"He was no good," she said. "You couldn't have changed him."

"Tink was my son, and I should have tried harder."

Mary repositioned herself in the front passenger seat, and her eyes met Eudora's. "I'm glad we don't have those issues. I love you, Mom."

"What brought this on, honey? Are you all right?"

Mary's brow furrowed. "Why wouldn't I be?"

"I don't know, but you seem distracted lately."

Mary turned to the road and flicked her hand. "Let's go."

Lewis grinned and shifted the van into gear. "I aim to please."

They passed hilled strip malls and valleyed vacation rentals and billowed service shops, all pocketed along the roadway, which curved and meandered and rose and fell. As the van approached Addison's business district, Lewis made a right-hand turn onto Highway 52.

John addressed Lewis from the middle row, his voice agitated.

"Any issues with your leg as you drive?"

Lewis shook his head. His squinted eyes were lit with a twinkle of mischief. Vickie enjoyed his willingness to spar with anyone.

John crossed his arms and gazed through the side window.

Vickie put her hand on Lewis's arm. "It wouldn't kill you."

His eyes met hers in the rearview mirror. "To do what?"

"Be a little more friendly to the man I love."

He shot a glance at John. "Big boy can handle himself."

John kept his good nature, but there was a distinct hardening of his eyes as he leaned forward. "Next time we stop, let's find out."

Lewis grinned wider. "Fine by me, boss. Haven't fought lately."

"Me either." John grew more animated. "Boss."

He gestured as the van approached a foreclosed restaurant.

"Pull into that empty lot and we'll see what's what."

The van slowed, which alerted Mary, who spoke sharply.

"Keep going. The gate is a mile ahead on the right."

Lewis grunted and did as he was told. The van sped up the hill.

"Where are we going?" Vickie asked.

Some of the anger in the van evaporated, leaving only curiosity.

"There's a woman who lost her husband to the recent murders. She's given her statement to the police, and a reporter interviewed her, but he wasn't thorough, and I think she's holding something back." Mary hesitated. "I also believe she wants to speak her mind."

Vickie's head tilted. "She'll be called crazy if she does?"

"Or worse. The police might think she was involved."

At the gate, Mary jumped out and entered the code. She quickly resumed her seat, hoping to keep the internal climate cool and calm.

The gate groaned to life and slid from left to right, and Lewis eased through. He pressed the accelerator, and the van marched up an incline, its engine announcing their presence. He quickly located a sharp left-hand turn, and they ascended the mountain. The van leveled as it rounded curves on a single-lane road which seemed suited for a golf course.

"This place is like a national park," said Vickie with wide eyes.

Mary stared at the directions on a wrinkled piece of paper.

Her face seemed strained and frightened as her head swiveled and the ground fell away from the lane on the right side, providing a marvelous view through random openings in the trees. They passed a house with a statue of Jesus in the middle of the rising yard, and suddenly the asphalt ended and there was only gravel ahead, which caused Lewis to stop the van and turn to Mary in confusion.

"Are we on the right road?" He peered up the way.

Her voice conveyed worry. "I don't know. The directions said nothing about this." Her hands trembled, and it seemed she might cry.

He rubbed her shoulder and ran his hand along her neck and back.

"Honey, we'll be all right. Don't worry."

She wiped a tear. "I'm trying."

"That's my girl."

Mary's eyes dulled as he squeezed her leg, and the journalist in Vickie grew alarmed at the danger. There was something Mary wasn't telling them.

Lewis coursed along the gravel as the lane curved left and then right, and again the ground fell away from them in stark fashion. Mary's fingers clutched at the top of the door and the dashboard. She glanced at Vickie and gave her a watery smile, which seemed forced.

The van once more found asphalt and Lewis drove up yet another steep incline and past a house on the left, then drove straight into a driveway. He parked behind the homeowner's car, and everyone relaxed.

Lewis pried Mary's hand from the dashboard and kissed it in front of the others. She wept for several moments before composing herself.

"What's wrong, honey?" asked Eudora from the back.

"Nothing, Mom. Leave it alone." Mary swiped at her tears.

She collected herself and exited the van. The owner's silver Honda sat under a deck which doubled as a carport. Mary strolled beside the vehicle and knocked on the side door. She turned and shrugged.

A minute passed, and she went up the stairs to the deck. Her boots thumped as she traversed its length and found the front door at the midpoint of the house. She rang the bell, and again, there was no answer.

Vickie got out and stretched her legs beside the van. She noticed two bear-proof trash cans and beyond them a tiny open area, where a large propane tank signaled a generator. Vickie wondered if they often lost power as she peered into the thick woods which ascended another twenty feet. A portrait of the mama bear and her cubs painted itself in her mind. Their three ghosts climbed the wooded hill and waved to her.

She called herself a lunatic for seeing images which were not there, and then she thudded up the steps to the deck, amazed by the landscape to her left, which stunned her above and beyond anything she'd seen around the world. The view surpassed the side of her mountain, which arose from behind her farm, as there were no obstructions here.

Mountains ran from every direction and formed a series of chains which linked themselves in elegant majesty, rolling one after another, merging into the distant horizon. The beautiful scene must be a mirage, as there could be no place on earth this incredible. The farthest mountains blended so spectacularly into the celestial that the eye and the mind were each fooled momentarily into doubt, but then the clouds shifted and the eye finally made the rugged outline a reality.

She gaped rather than gazed, and so she closed her mouth. Her hands squeezed the cedar railing as she continued her rise to the deck.

"I don't think anyone's here," said Mary from up ahead.

"It's okay."

"No, it's not. I'm here to interview this old woman, but apparently I got my wires crossed." Mary gestured with the paper. "Jessica was supposed to be home, but she's not, and I don't know what to do."

Vickie was taken aback, as she'd never seen Mary this upset.

"What's the matter? It's not like you're about to get fired."

Movement sounded from inside the house.

Vickie gave Mary an eager look. "See? Someone's here."

The door cracked open a few inches. "Yes?"

"Mrs. Harper, I'm Mary Bishop from the television station."

"Oh, yes. Where are my manners?" She opened the door with an abashed bearing. "I didn't sleep well last night, and I was taking a nap."

She stepped out to the deck and pointed to the furniture.

"Have a seat. Those swings are really comfortable." Jessica put a finger to her lips. "I think we put them in around 1984."

Large chains screwed into the rafters above the deck held the two wood-framed swings in place, and thick cushions rested on each seat and stood vertically in the back, the two working together to entice would-be victims into their clutches. One swing reposed parallel with the house and looked out to the mountains, while its partner occupied the corner and faced the driveway. The arrangement seemed cozy enough, so they plopped onto the swings, Vickie taking the one which respected the spectacular mountain view, as Mary and Jessica had claimed the one in the corner. A gray fire pit with lava rocks and wheels and a hidden compartment underneath for propane sat in front of Vickie, and at her left rested two vacant rockers. Her eyes drifted to the cedar shingles which sided the cabin-like house and the sturdy posts which held the deck in position. She quickly calculated the number of balusters which supported a top and bottom rail, discerning there must be over one hundred. Whoever built this mountain home took great care and clearly fashioned it with love, and the many joyful memories called out to her.

If she could only have a home like this, devoid of all corruption.

"I got into a habit of sitting here years ago. In the cooler months, when the leaves are off the trees and the sun's angle changes, the light hits you square in the eyes. It's one of Jim's regrets that he didn't think it through." A pause. "Mine is not having him here with me right now."

Mary's brow furrowed. "I'm sorry for your loss."

Jessica patted her knee. "Thank you, dear. It's been difficult."

Mary traded glances with Vickie, who encouraged her.

"I'd like to know more about your husband."

"And his death?"

"Yes, ma'am. That, too."

Jessica surveyed the mountains as if in deep reflection.

"We loved it here and used the house as a getaway from his breeding operation. Thoroughbreds were everything to Jim, and at first I loved raising them, but over the years he grew more ambitious, and his success only fueled a stronger desire, which became an obsession with winning the Triple Crown." She hesitated. "Jim bought Enchanted River from Roland Carter, thinking the horse had Native Dancer's genetics, and River, as I call him, shows real promise, even though he's only a colt."

"Did your husband have enemies in the business?"

"The detectives asked me all these questions."

Mary nodded. "Yes, ma'am, and I don't mean to be insensitive, as I know you're tired of all this and want it to go away."

"So why are you troubling me? There must be an angle."

Mary turned to her friend. "You know Vickie Morrison, I assume."

Jessica nodded, and her eyebrows arched. "She's a Brewer."

"Yes, I am," said Vickie firmly. "Through and through."

"Good. I like a straight shooter." Jessica sighed. "Have you retired?"

"I'm in Addison to stay, but I wanted to help Mary this morning."

"Interview a broken-down old lady like me?" Jessica chuckled as she tapped her chest. "I haven't been a formidable opponent in decades." Her eyes drifted again to the mountains. "But there was a time."

"I'll bet," said Vickie with reverence. "Did you know Roland?"

"Roland courted me when we were in high school. He was quite the athlete in those days, and all the young girls thought he was their ideal man, you know, the one we dream about in our bedrooms at night."

Vickie's mind flashed a picture of her and John at the same age. They had been in love, but Garrett wanted his son to have nothing to do with her for reasons she wouldn't understand for decades, and so they snuck dates when they could. Their teenage romance was bound to implode under such conditions, and Vickie wasn't surprised when John ended their relationship, saying he wanted to stay friends. She accepted his terms and said hello to him in the hallways and smiled in class, but her emotions raged and she cried herself to sleep most nights, as he was the love of her life, and suddenly he was with Carlie Hill.

Mary squeezed Jessica's leg. "But Jim Harper won your hand."

The portrait of their wedding returned Vickie to the conversation.

Shaken by her losses over so many years, she kept still and silent.

"Yes, and we dreamed of leaving everything to our sons, which is why we moved up here a few months before his murder. His once vigorous health had gone downhill, which no one knew but me and his doctor. He claimed he wanted to retire, but it was only true because he was tired all the time, much like I am today, and when Roland offered him Enchanted River, he jumped at the chance. Jim left me alone during the week, tending the colt. He said it was only temporary."

"The detectives said Jim was murdered in front of the horse and there was blood everywhere, as if a wild beast had attacked him. Could it have been a bear?" Mary retrieved a notebook and flipped it open to a page. "This quote says wildlife management was called in to investigate."

"They found no animal tracks or scat or any other sign," Jessica said.

"Was River injured in the attack?"

Jessica shook her head. "Not physically, but emotionally."

Vickie leaned forward. "How so?"

"River hasn't been himself since it happened, and we chalked it up to his youth, but weeks have passed and he isn't getting any better."

Vickie considered.

"I've helped my father, who trains horses, and folks around the county know my friend, John, as a farrier, but he also has a reputation for rescue and rehabilitation. He brought a herd to my farm and they're all doing well." She caught her breath. "I say this to offer an alternative for River, only for a time, until he feels better. I could work with him, and we even have a foal named Miracle. The two might bond."

"Thank you, dear, but we'll handle things at our facility."

Price approached and took a seat in a rocker. John took the other.

Mary looked at the steps. "Where are Lewis and my mother?"

"Eudora wanted to have a talk with him," said John flatly.

"Uh-oh. That can't be good."

The group laughed, and even Jessica understood the significance.

Vickie pointed to Price. "This is my father."

Jessica gave him an amused look. "You are exactly as I pictured you."

Price stopped rocking and smoothed his shirt.

"I wasn't always a Christian man, but I found Jesus in prison."

Vickie interjected. "He and John are guiding me through the Bible, and I've learned a lot, especially about the Old Testament."

"Except John is wrong about the Rephaim," said Price abruptly.

"What do you mean?"

"They were all giants, and no more Rephaim walk the earth."

Vickie traded glances with Jessica, who eyed Price with suspicion.

"Daddy, I know what I saw, and John saw it, too. She changed."

"To whom do you refer?" Jessica seemed keenly interested.

"It will seem crazy."

"Try me."

"Leslie Carter and John were once together, and she wants him back for political reasons, as she believes he can help her campaign. She's made several threats of murder and even claimed responsibility for her father's death and the murder of all his recent clients, including your husband." Vickie allowed her words to register. "While she stood in front of us at my farm, she changed into some kind of creature. She grew fangs and her skin took on a scaly texture, and her eyes seemed like those of a serpent. Leslie became stronger than any natural woman and threw John to the ground as if he was a rag doll, and I thought she might murder us." Vickie gestured at Price. "Luckily, I thought to bring my father's Bible from the house, and I recited Psalm 55."

"Did it help the situation?"

"Vickie glowed as she read," said John in a definite and final tone.

Jessica settled into the swing and stared for what seemed an eternity.

"From inside her body?" she asked.

"Yes, and when Leslie saw it, she became human again."

"Leslie has visited us twice, making dire threats each time. She's a demented individual who murders those who stand in her way, even her own blood, if you believe Roland was her father." Vickie glanced at John. "Neither of us is sure she's a Carter, but we have little proof."

"Would you like some?" asked Jessica with a sly grin.

Price took a deep breath and exhaled. "All this talk seems like bottled insanity, and you both clearly had a break from reality in the moment."

His body tensed as Mary's had done, and he seemed pale.

Jessica left her swing and joined Vickie. "I don't know many details, but Jim said there is something more to the Carters than meets the eye."

"Like what?"

"He said they are part of a cabal who runs the world, and it's why the Carters have the best racing horses, as the upper echelon grants the family anything it wants in return for information. I never went along with Jim's rants because it all seemed so fantastical, and I suppose I was too grounded to see anything supernatural, even though I've always claimed to be a Christian woman who loves God and I regularly attend church, but the pastors don't teach us about these things and so we are unprepared." Jessica took a breath. "Now I realize Jim was right."

She paused.

"If the offer stands, I'd like to send River over to you."

Vickie was floored, as she meant what she'd said, but never thought Jessica would give her a thoroughbred with such prized genetics.

"Are you sure? I'm not a professional, at least not yet."

"She has a way with horses," John said. "Vickie senses their pain."

"Well, that's exactly what River needs, so it's settled."

Jessica asked if the group could eat breakfast, and each appreciated her generous nature. Eudora and Lewis took up the rockers on the far side of the front door. Their conversation seemed endless, and each saw themselves in their counterpart. The differences in their gender or age or experience made little difference. Vickie envied Mary, as John and Price didn't have the same relationship, which hurt.

When Jessica ventured inside, Mary took her place.

"I need to ask you something, since you've been so honest lately."

"Okay." Vickie's internal alarm bells sounded.

"Do you regret your abortion?" Mary realized her words were direct and might be construed as unkind. "I mean, as it related to your career."

Vickie shifted heavily in her seat. "What happened?"

"Remember my old boyfriend, the one with the job in Atlanta?"

Vickie nodded.

"Ryan popped into town about a month ago."

"A second time?" Vickie glanced at Lewis. "With him in your life?"

Mary averted her eyes, unable to withstand her mentor's scrutiny.

"And you got pregnant?"

"Yes." Mary covered her face and peeked through her fingers.

Her childish nature infuriated Vickie, as she should grow up. Vickie craned her neck, and her eyes fell on Lewis and Eudora. He threw them a cordial nod and a grin, but Vickie grimaced and turned from him.

"Do they know?" she asked in a bitter tone.

"Lewis does, but not my mom. It would kill her."

"Mary Bishop, I could strangle you." Vickie got up and paced furiously for several moments, and then she stood in agitation at the railing and scanned the skyline. The never-ending flow of mountains dipped and rose, and the clouds which both encircled and floated above the green peaks broke apart in patches and descended into cool blue recesses, calming the flawed mentor. She once more sat on the swing.

"I'm sorry, Vickie. You taught me better, but I blew it."

"What will you do?"

Mary pursed her lips. "Probably get an abortion."

"Like me?"

"Like you."

Vickie glanced at Price and John, who each squirmed in discomfort.

"Did either of you put her up to this?"

Both men shook their heads.

"It was my idea," said Mary innocently. "I need your advice."

"Sounds to me like you've decided."

"I suppose I have."

Vickie's fingers clutched the cushion as adrenaline rushed through her, giving her the courage to continue their taxing conversation.

"If you seek my opinion and my approval, I think you should have the baby. I chose ambition over my child, and there isn't a day that goes by without the memory backing up on me, and I often wish for death." Vickie's eyes moistened. "When I was in the Caribbean, I almost did it."

"You shouldn't talk like that," said Price in rebuke. "She might take you seriously and think it's the right thing, just like your friend Helen."

Mary stiffened. "I would never do that, Price, so don't worry."

"Good." He rocked slowly and with great tension.

"What's gotten into you, Daddy? Are you against me now?"

"I'm growing tired of your lies, and so is John."

John sat upright upon hearing his name. "Don't bring me into it."

Price gestured sharply. "You know she hasn't told you everything."

"Yes, and I'm giving her space to figure it out. She'll get there."

"No, she won't, John, because you're enabling her deceit."

"What does that mean?"

John turned to Vickie. "What is he talking about?"

Blood flushed her cheeks, and her thoughts scrambled. She hadn't planned to be put on the spot by her father so outrageously and with no warning whatsoever, but she could think of little to say in response.

Vickie blurted the first thing which sprang to mind.

"Logan asked me a horrible question, remember?"

John sighed. "You've changed your story, so not really."

Vickie steeled herself. "Would I rather be raped or murdered?"

She paused.

"It's what he asked me, and there was no other choice."

Price glared at her, even as the question brought a tear to his eye.

Her walls reformed, encapsulating her in safety, and no one, not even her father, could penetrate her defenses. She would win, because she was the great Victoria Morrison, who always got what she wanted.

John took his time as he contemplated her admission.

"So, you feel bad because you chose rape over murder?"

"I feel more than bad, John. I should have let him kill me."

Price gasped and caught himself. He stood and leaned into the rail.

"Why would you say that, Vickie? One is better than the other, even though both are awful to contemplate, but at least you're here now with me and the girls." John's eyes rose to Price. "He needs you, too."

Price wiped his tears. "If I had been in your life, you wouldn't have left Addison, nor would you have been raped. If I was a father and not a gangland thug, my Valerie would be alive, and so would my son."

Vickie nodded. "As a Morrison, I think Michelle was meant for Washington, not me, but Red couldn't send her down that path."

"Then I brought about your sister's death as well," Price said.

"No, it's the fallen nature of mankind, as the Knowledge of Good and Evil tempts our flesh toward malevolence unless we follow Christ."

"When you are sincere, you are decent," said John with feeling.

"Then why does my honesty make me feel ashamed?" she asked.

Jessica brought a plate to Price, but he wouldn't eat. He instead stood at the rail and peered into his own abyss, as if mesmerized by what might have been and what had been lost. Vickie held her plate and watched him, and she barely nibbled as his countenance worsened.

She put down the plate. "Daddy, are you all right?"

His right hand gripped his left arm, and he began to sweat.

"Oh, my God." Eudora leapt from her rocker. "Price!"

Lewis followed her and grabbed Price's left side while John took the right. They lifted Price and carried him to the van. Mary apologized to Jessica for the trouble they had caused. Vickie stood frozen in place near the swing, watching as the father she hardly knew struggled for life.

"You'd better go with them, honey." Jessica gave her a worried look.

"I can't." Vickie swiped at her tears. "My feet won't move."

The van door slammed. John called out to her.

"Go be with him while you still can." Jessica stepped near to her and rubbed her arms. "Once they're gone, there's no getting them back."

Vickie stifled her need to collapse into Jessica's embrace, as she longed for a mother who might soothe her with kind whispers which said everything would be all right, but Valerie killed herself and lost herself to perdition, and this stranger could not assume her post.

Her boots made an angry racket as she plodded along the deck.

"I can tell you more about Leslie Carter," said Jessica in a loud voice.

Vickie stopped and measured, and then continued to the van.

Eudora prayed as Lewis sped along the highway after scooting down the mountain and through the gate in record time. Mary craned her neck as she checked on Price and her mother, and then Vickie and John.

John held Vickie's hand as her head hung low. She had pushed her father into a heart attack since their first day at the farm, as her need to be right won out each day, but soon it would lose the war for love and restoration. She was more a beast than Leslie Carter, as she had a choice, while Leslie was born of a corrupt lineage, long ago damned.

They reached the county hospital, which sat atop a hill and faced the highway like Addison's other strip malls. Lewis slammed the brakes at the ED and raced to help Price exit the vehicle, accompanied by John, who was forced to let go of Vickie's hand, although she struggled to keep him with her in the seat. She said no, no, no when he pulled away from her, but then she covered her eyes and wept, and then she watched her friends help Price through the hospital doors, and the scene quieted.

A police cruiser parked behind the van. Officers stepped out.

Their presence caught her attention, and she opened the door and followed a few steps behind, knowing something was amiss, as their intensity of purpose was immediate and pressing and undeniable.

The officers waited for attendants to wheel Price away on a gurney.

One turned to John, who stared at the still-swinging door.

"Are you John Breyer?"

His face grew ashen, and for an instant Vickie thought he might have his own heart attack, for he must know why they were there.

"Yes," he said reluctantly. "What's this about?"

The officer held up a writ.

"Mr. Breyer, we have a warrant for your arrest for the murder of Roland Carter. Turn around and put your hands on your head."

John complied, as there was little choice, but he seemed dazed. Neither he nor Vickie had believed Leslie would ever be so bold.

The officers placed John in the back of their cruiser and left.

Vickie took a seat in a far corner of the crowded lobby.

She observed the others who gathered about her in the lobby, searching their eyes for any flicker or restless flash. There must be Rephaim in her midst, as she sensed their presence, and they seethed with a gnashing desire. Her shoulders slumped as she settled into the uncomfortable chair. She should pray, but the Lord would demand she speak the truth to John, which was something she would never do unless he went to prison for murder and had nowhere to run, but even then he could deny her visits, and so she vowed right then and there to keep the truth eternally hidden, even if the Lord withheld His grace.

Friends rotated in and out until late afternoon, when Vickie sat with Eudora and the girls. She was half-awake but unable to rest in her stiff seat. Red's death had decreed her as the matriarch, but she felt more like a degenerate known for vulgarity and promiscuity. Katie read her Bible and made notes in the margin, and each time her aunt cast a sidelong glance, Katie flinched, as if aware of the overbearing examination. Vickie longed to hold her father's worn Bible in her lap, but she wouldn't open it with Price's chest spread open on the table. Nothing about this event seemed remotely fair, so she grew defiant, even as Eudora rocked back and forth and hummed to herself and said in a kind voice he would live.

The surgeon approached.

A quick assessment told Vickie her father's surgery had ended, and it took longer than expected and was decidedly arduous.

She rose to meet her adversary, the one who would deliver the day's awful news to an unsuspecting public, this time the once-great Victoria Morrison, known far and wide as the raven-haired purveyor of doom.

"Hello, I'm Dr. Erin Williamson." She extended a slender hand.

"How is my father?" Vickie studied her eyes for any portent.

Katie and Abbie wore looks of concern as they stood nearby.

Dr. Williamson cast a wan smile. "We found two blocked arteries which required coronary bypass, which is why the surgery took so long." She seemed relieved as she rubbed her moist forehead. "We moved him to ICU, where you'll be able to visit him soon, but I must warn you, it won't be a pretty sight for a while. Our staff inserted a tube in his mouth and throat to help him breathe, and we'll monitor his heart rate and blood pressure for the next twenty-four hours. You'll likely notice other tubes, which were inserted into his chest and bladder. Those are to remove bodily fluids which build up, and although they may look strange or scary, they are there to help him." Dr. Williamson's eyes were patient and caring as she observed Vickie's reaction to so much information at once. "Your father also has two IVs, one in each arm, so don't let those alarm you. It's a precaution and per ICU policy."

Vickie sat and ran her fingers through her hair as her head fell low and her eyes scanned the tile floor. She was thankful her father was still alive, but the harshness in his rebuke had stirred the entities inside her.

Dr. Williamson sat beside Vickie and put a kind hand on her knee.

"Please call me Erin."

"All right."

Vickie looked up at her nemesis in careful observation.

As a healer, did she have the eyes of a serpent or any other sign of otherworldliness? The answer was a firm no, which sent an onrush of insanity through Vickie's veins like the most expensive designer drug on the market. Her thoughts scrambled themselves and her emotions rolled and tumbled and screamed.

"What happens next?" she asked.

"When he's ready, we'll move him to another unit."

Vickie sat motionless, as if considering intently and trying to fasten upon some rogue idea. She summoned the strength for questions, as the Lord had allowed more time with her father, but not nearly enough.

"For how long?" asked Eudora, holding her peace no longer.

Erin's eyebrows arched, as if the question related to insurance.

"It's not about the money," Vickie said. "We just need to know."

"I must warn you both, anything can happen and there aren't any guarantees, but for now, his prognosis is good and he should be here for about a week." Erin let the words linger for a moment. "He may be grumpy for a while because it's hard to sleep with ICU staff entering and leaving at all hours. Even after we move him to a regular room, the area around his incision will be very sore. Recovery can be painful as he breathes and coughs deeply so fluids don't accumulate in his chest."

Eudora leaned forward. "To avoid pneumonia?"

Erin nodded.

"Here's the roughest part, which is why I saved it for last."

Vickie sighed. "Oh, no. This can't be good."

"We'll get him up and walking as soon as possible, which he will not like, but we must get the blood flowing and rebuild his strength. Eating regular meals will help in this regard. That and your encouragement."

Vickie paled at the enormity of the situation and the road ahead. She looked at her best friend, whose eyes watered, and then she squeezed her hand. Eudora had come to love Price, and it was nice to see, even now, in this terrible moment, when all seemed lost. Something good might be derived from his pain and their suffering, if such a thing were possible.

"And then we can take him home? Please say this has an end point."

Erin smiled. "Yes, but he'll need anywhere from six to twelve weeks of recovery time in a place which is well suited for round-the-clock care. Before he leaves, a hospitalist will interview you to ensure a good fit."

"We're covered there. I allowed two friends to receive hospice in my front bedrooms earlier this year, and there were no problems."

"I will be with him night and day," said Eudora presently.

"Great, then we have a tentative care plan."

Erin stood. "Are there any more questions?"

"When can I see him?"

"Oh, yes, sorry. I'm distracted and tired." The doctor considered for a few moments. "Let me check on his progress and then I'll come back."

"Sure, that's fine. I may get something to eat in the cafeteria."

Erin smiled. "The food here is better than you might expect."

"Meaning I should get used to it?"

"Yes, you should." Erin smiled again and went on her way.

Vickie thought of John in Addison's metro jail, and she wished he was there with her, as hospitals had become their special place.

He would hold her hand and tell her things would be just fine.

The girls lost all pretense of formality or independence and huddled about her in the aisle, continually arguing and shifting positions.

Katie looked after the doctor as if wishing she'd asked questions.

Abbie leaned into her sister and elbowed, which incited a reaction.

"Stop!"

"No, you stop!"

Vickie had no clue what to say, as Price was her father, not theirs, but he was once the de facto patriarch after Red's death, and now the ball had been thrown into her court, but leading a family was absent from her résumé, much like being someone's mother or wife. Love in all its forms was for other people, those who grew up in normal households where trustworthy adults structured daily activities and bedroom doors were unlocked at night, as there were no villains in their midst.

"Can I tell you about Mom?" asked Katie.

Vickie looked up from her pondering, shocked at her revelation.

Red had tried to force himself on her when she turned fourteen, and when she fought back, he seemed hurt and disappointed and treated her unfairly from that point forward. She counted it as a primary reason he sent her to Washington in place of his own daughter, but now she realized Michelle had taken her place at the tender age of twelve.

How did she know such things, and why were they hidden until now? The indicators were everywhere, but she ignored them, choosing her new life over the old, fresh suffering in place of legacy torments, even after Michelle wrote about her pregnancy not once but twice, and then there were phone calls which went unanswered. When they did speak over the phone, their conversations were stifled and bland. Vickie's problems in D.C. superseded all else, as work had been her true god.

She vowed to revisit Michelle's grave and apologize for her failures.

Vickie turned to her niece. "You miss your mom, don't you?"

"Every day, especially now, when someone I love might die."

"Please don't say such a thing." Eudora seemed taken aback.

Vickie glanced at her friend and sighed. "He's my father."

"He's the man of my dreams who helped me endure while Craig beat me senseless and yelled curses at our daughter. I won't sit here in this lobby and listen to either of you say he's going to die. I simply won't have it!" She got up and paced the hallway and then went outside.

Vickie's voice trailed as she tried to call after her.

She understood Eudora's jealous mood all too well, as she was also possessive of her father, and it was only fair, since she had gone a lifetime without knowing him and in the span of one morning almost lost him.

"Price is our grandfather," said Katie, seemingly unaware of what had transpired between the two women. "The same way you are now our mother. I'll never forget our mom, though." Katie settled into the chair and her shoulders slumped. "We've seen too much death."

Vickie sighed heavily. "Yes, you have."

"Mom cooked dinner for us most nights, and Grandpa Red said he liked whatever she made, but he especially loved her hamburger and potato casserole. When she first tried it, she didn't get the potatoes cooked well enough, and they were firm like when they're raw, but we could eat them and it was so good Grandpa Red ate too much and there wasn't anything left for lunch the next day, and so he asked her to make it for dinner that night, which she did, and she cooked the potatoes better the second time." Katie's eyes watered as she remembered. "The funny thing is, he knew John was coming over to work with Hero the next night, and he asked her to make it again, which she gladly did."

"The same dish three nights in a row?"

Katie smiled. "John said the potatoes were great."

Vickie nodded.

Michelle had been every bit as determined to make her father proud as Vickie, but she went about it in different ways, using cooking and horses and children to make a good impression, as he was all to her.

It must have been difficult to reconcile his horrific abuse, especially with two daughters in the same house. Perhaps Tink helped her in some strange way, as he was a rough character and Price's son, and he likely intimidated Red, but then he died and Michelle was left to her own devices, a single mother forced to deal with her hideous father.

Vickie cursed herself for staying gone when Michelle was thrown. Her sister needed her more than ever, and she must have been so scared.

Abbie looked up and met her eyes. "I can't picture Mom's face."

"What do you mean? She was beautiful and had long, dark hair."

After what Michelle endured, the least Abbie could do was remember what she looked like. There were pictures of her all over the house! The idea of her being forgotten by her daughter, young or not, infuriated Vickie and made her wish to cry or yell or hit someone.

Katie elbowed Abbie. "Mom told you about Tink, remember?"

"Yes, but her face is fuzzy in my memory, like she wasn't real."

Vickie was growing increasingly resentful of the situation.

"Well, she was, and I know she loved both of you with all her heart."

Michelle's image fluttered through her own memory until her spirit faded into the ether, and then Vickie fought the urge to curl into a ball.

"I love Mom," said Abbie, "but I don't remember her."

The way the child spoke, choking back her tears, stimulated Vickie's anger, and she reacted. "Mine took pills and wrecked her car and left me alone to fend for myself, so in my book, you got lucky."

Katie held Abbie's hand and walked her around the line of seats and stopped. "You know, Abbie is only eight, and she needs a motherly woman who loves and encourages her, but instead she's got a defiant big sister in an adult's body, which she doesn't need, and neither do I."

"Really? Have you seen my father? He happens to be lying in there after heart surgery with a bunch of tubes sticking out of his body, and I barely know him, since he wasn't around when I was growing up and neither was my suicidal mother, but still in your estimation, I shouldn't be defiant, even though it's exactly what has gotten me through every terrible moment in my otherwise wasted life."

Katie sighed and then sat again.

"Look, we will always be Michelle's daughters, especially me, because I knew her much better than Abbie, but our mother is dead and she's not coming back. We need a mother to replace the one we lost, but we need to know with certainty you will love us as if we're your own children." She hesitated. "We're not dumb. We know you and John will get married and you'll have a baby, and we don't want to be discarded when that happens. I swear we won't cause you any problems."

Vickie broke down in tears and went to the water fountain.

Katie followed her and stood still, tapping her foot.

"Were you serious the other night in the barn, or were you just placating us after Savannah died because you knew we were sad?"

Vickie turned and gave Katie a sarcastic chuckle.

"It's a big word, placating, and don't act like you aren't scared out of your mind right now. I've been where you are, and I know the truth."

"Will you answer my question and quit stalling?"

"You don't want me as your mother," said Vickie flatly.

Katie looked back at Abbie and sighed. "Yes, we do."

"I'm not worthy of motherhood. Don't you know anything? If you girls knew how overconfident I was on assignment, how cocky, how arrogant, how haughty, and the mistakes I made in the field and in my personal life that got people killed, you would want anyone besides me."

"We don't care about the past. Only the present."

"Katie, you're not listening. If you knew what I've done, you would never accept me as your mother or even want me in your world."

"We talked about your abortion, Vickie, and we forgave you."

"You don't know everything. There's a lot more."

"So tell me, and we'll work through it together."

Vickie glanced about her. "Here and now, in the hospital?"

Katie nodded. "It's as good a place as any other."

Vickie headed toward the elevators as tears again welled in her eyes.

"Where are you going? Don't leave us alone!"

"I'll be in the cafeteria."

Katie ran to her and grabbed her sleeve. "Why?"

Vickie shrugged her off and almost hurled an expletive, but she calmed herself. "I need a drink so badly I can taste it." She turned to Katie with a sneering grin. "Who knows? Maybe they sell bourbon."

As the elevator doors closed, Katie's reply stung her.

"You're not cool, Vickie, so stop trying so hard."

The steel box descended, and the words hung in the air like a perfect truth. She had never been cool a day in her life. Not one single day.

She sat alone at a table as children performed a skit on the other side of the room. Parents and staff clapped, and their faces registered joy.

It was so long since Vickie knew such an emotion, she'd lost track of what might have triggered it, what day or event or relationship, and then she considered the night at LuLu's and their kiss in front of the town.

John must be worried sick in his jail cell, wondering if a court might convict him of a crime he didn't commit. Vickie would have to find an attorney, someone who won every case and money wouldn't matter, only the prospect of returning the love of her life back into her arms.

Erin stood in line for coffee and noticed her, and then approached.

"Your father has stabilized and is in a room in ICU. You can see him if you'd like." She hesitated. "Just remember, it won't be a pretty sight."

"Will he be able to talk to me?"

"Not right now, and he'll be very tired."

Vickie nodded.

The small crowd cheered from across the room.

"They're performing for an elderly gentleman."

"Is he sick?"

"No, it's his wife. That's all I can say."

"I understand. It seems we're all in the same boat."

"Yes, and eventually, it will be us."

Vickie's eyebrows arched at the reality of Erin's comment.

"Seems like his spirits are good, thanks to the kids."

Erin sipped her coffee. "Yes, it's something."

She turned and then paused. "Come see your father."

"I will." Vickie's eyes averted to the kids. "In a while."

"Take your time, but I think he'd like to see you."

Vickie sat for a while after Erin left the cafeteria and even clapped along with the old man and the parents, and then she got up and walked to the elevator, unsure what she might say to Price. She had gained a certain amount of adoration for him, which was hard to process because of so many years of hatred and bitterness, all the times she'd withdrawn from friends and family. Even now she wanted to run away, but it would only make things worse for her and everyone else in her life.

She entered his room and sat beside him. Her eyes fell on the bed.

He breathed through a tube, which made conversation impossible, but his eyes said more than his words, and it was enough, as she was his loving daughter. Price lamented taking the blame for rape, but since he was a dangerous man who Satan tempted toward theft and murder, he allowed Red to have Valerie. He didn't expect to be framed for rape when Red discovered she was pregnant, but he went along with it.

After his stint in prison, he tried to reach out to Vickie, but she wouldn't see him. Distraught, he joined Tink on a heist, which got someone killed and Price sent to prison. All this she knew from their talks and his apologies, but he signaled a strong desire to communicate with her telepathically or through his eyes. She kissed his forehead.

"It's okay, Daddy."

He stiffened, which caused him pain, and she soothed him.

Vickie mentioned her mistake with Chelsea and said she hid her grief from John, who must never know or he would leave her alone.

"It's why I haven't told him, Daddy, so please don't hate me."

His eyes pleaded with her to offer her truth and accept God's grace, but she would not, even if it cost her everything, including her salvation.

She regretted trusting Red and mistaking who he was and for failing to lessen Michelle's agony. Price felt much the same about Valerie and Vickie, as he left both mother and daughter to die unwanted.

"I know how you feel about me, Daddy, so don't struggle so much."

Vickie considered.

The old man's wife might soon die, despite her desire to live.

This was a woman who was loved, and so she must fight where others couldn't and go on to make the world a better place.

There was motion from the doorway, and a deep voice spoke to her.

John entered and stood underneath a flat-screen television which had mounted itself near the ceiling and now cast competing images.

Vickie found the remote and clicked off the distraction.

Under normal circumstances, she would run to him, but this was no ordinary day, and she would not leave her father's side for any reason.

"What are you doing here?" she asked.

"I don't know, honestly."

"What does that mean? They arrested you for murder."

"Yeah, and then a guard pulled me out of lockup. The prosecutor dropped the charges like it was all some big mistake." John ran a rough hand through his hair and sighed. "I have no idea what's going on."

Vickie breathed heavily and exhaled. "One thing is for sure."

John took a seat. "What's that?"

"Someone is sending us a message."

He shot her a straight glance, which seemed accusatory.

"But why? What have you done?"

"Clearly it's Leslie Carter." A pause. "Yet again."

"Maybe, but if she's part of a network who put her up to running for governor and who covers for her crimes, there are more people to consider." He gestured at Price. "He was right about one thing earlier."

Vickie tensed.

His tone indicated he would say something awful.

"What's that, John?"

"If he'd been around when you were a girl, none of this would've happened. If you ask me, he's a weak man who should've loved you and your mother enough to change, but instead he bailed on his duties."

John's eyes fell on Vickie's Bible, which she had placed on a table.

She tried with all her might to change the subject, as he would condemn her with his scripture reading; that much was certain.

"Is Eudora downstairs with the girls?" she asked.

"Yes, she is." He gave her a reproachful look.

Vickie searched for a proper reply. "She loves them."

"As you do, right? Or do I presume too much?"

"Of course I do, John, but right now I must focus on my father."

He went over and opened the pages to Psalm 58 and then he recited verses 3-11. "These wicked people are born sinners; even from birth they have lied and gone their own way. They spit venom like deadly snakes; they are like cobras that refuse to listen, ignoring the tunes of the snake charmers, no matter how skillfully they play. Break off their fangs, O God! Smash the jaws of these lions, O Lord! May they disappear like water into thirsty ground. Make their weapons useless in their hands. May they be like snails that dissolve into slime, like a stillborn child who will never see the sun. God will sweep them away, both young and old, faster than a pot heats over burning thorns. The godly will rejoice when they see injustice avenged. They will wash their feet in the blood of the wicked. Then at last everyone will say, 'There truly is a reward for those who live for God; surely there is a God who judges justly here on earth.'" He closed the Bible and glared at her with condemnation.

"How dare you?" His bleak and furious expression momentarily silenced her. "After all we've seen together and after what we discussed with Jessica Harper, you would call my father a serpent?"

She considered.

"You would accuse me of having fangs like Leslie Carter?"

"All I know is that man is a murderer." He pointed at Price. "And you killed your child in the womb, which I now realize probably would have been just like you, a sinner who lies at every opportunity and goes her own way, who refuses to listen to advice, and who disappears like water into sand, but now you have no more weapons, Vickie, as your career in the news business is finished and it's never coming back, and as I stand here and watch Price with all those tubes coming out, I think of those he murdered. I think of your mother and I think of Michelle."

Another realization washed over Vickie.

"You knew about Red's abuse?"

"Yes, she confided in me."

He paused.

"After Tink died, there was no one else."

"Did you sleep with her, John?"

"We grew close for a while, if that's what you're asking."

"It's not, and you know it. Did you?"

He sighed. "Yes."

She left her chair and ran toward him. "Get out!"

"I'm speaking the truth, but you can't handle it."

"Go walk the halls, John, and don't come back until you can show my father respect." She gestured sharply at Price. "The man lying on that bed has changed, but you don't want to see it for whatever reason."

She reflected.

"Maybe you're mad at Garrett for dying or at Price for not dying. I don't know which, but right now I don't want you in my presence." Her eyes flashed toward the hall. "Go! Get out of here!"

"Fine, but I won't change my mind about your father, the snake."

Vickie waited for John to leave, and then she turned to Price.

His finger lifted, and she clasped his hand.

Price's eyes said more than his words ever could.

They said John was right: she should leave this ruthless man alone.

"I don't care what you or anyone says, Daddy."

She kissed his hand as tears coursed down both their cheeks.

"We're going to make a go of this family, with or without him."

Price cast an imploring look, but she paid him little heed. Vickie had failed her sister and her daughter and even Logan Meson, who might have been saved if she witnessed to him about Jesus instead of hating him so fiercely. She would become the matriarch of this makeshift family, and she would devote her remnant years to raising the girls and rescuing needy horses and giving refuge to all who needed one.

In her home, bedroom doors would swing wide and no monsters would ever enter, and an enduring love would tear down the thick vines of greed and envy and wrath, and the dark ice of pride would warm and grow light again as charity and kindness and patience shone brightly.

Nineteen

Psalm 59:1

Rescue me from my enemies, O God.
Protect me from those who have come to destroy me.

John lurked about the house after Vickie left with the girls and the others shifted between the station and the hospital. He was a man without a country in her eyes, and he wasn't sure how it had happened. One minute they were blissful, and the next they avoided one another in the hallways, a notion that had seemed impossible only two weeks earlier.

John peeked through the window into the narrow backyard with its round pen and shed and path, the latter leading to a fork: one way up the mountain and the other to the falls. He pictured a modest wedding off to the left, just in front of the gate. The lane led directly to the back door, offering access for food and drinks and bathroom breaks, and a sailcloth filled with gleaming friends and lyrical anthems and elegant style would foster joyful memories.

A wedding might have saved their relationship, as it had been on shaky ground from the start, but after his arrest, he could not hold his peace. John had spent a lifetime under the thumb of one overbearing father, and he wasn't about to live under another, especially a murderous thug like Price Brewer, the one whom police should have shoved into a cruiser, fingerprinted, photographed, and then thrown into a group cell with thirty other men, all of whom would rather rape and pillage than work.

John cracked open the back door and stepped into the yard. His eyes rose to the blue sky, and his skin felt the heat and humidity growing. The early morning mist had ascended above the highest points of the mountain range, leaving warm summer air in its wake.

Out of idle boredom and boyish curiosity, he opened the shed door and peeked into the shadowy cavern, which was mostly filled with yard tools and gas cans, all resting comfortably on a concrete floor. He ventured inside and clicked on the light. The shed's interior was more expansive than he might have imagined, but the floor was filthy with grime and mounds of dead bugs. To his right sat a tarp covering an unknown object, and when he raised the plastic, the dust made him turn his head and cough. When he wheeled to face the problem head-on, he was shocked to find a weight bench and a set of free weights stacked neatly on a metal tree.

John grabbed a broom and swept the floor, thrilled at his good fortune, he hadn't lifted weights since his arrival at Bluecreek. He stretched his taut muscles and soothed his aching bones, then went back into the house for a quick change into workout clothes.

As he returned to the shed in a t-shirt and shorts, the sun hid behind ominous clouds and lightning grumbled in the distance. He stopped in the grass and felt the breeze pick up and smelled the petrichor, which had delighted him since childhood when he watched the rain with his mother. John considered the horses in the pasture and rerouted to check on their vulnerability. They stood about and munched grass and occasionally glanced at the highway, but seemed unperturbed by the weather.

He sat on the porch and waited. No one was home to ask, nor would they be soon, which felt odd, as he didn't relish being alone. He could leave the horses in the field, Wildfire was a handful, and the storm might shift, but a mature man would make a better choice. He opened the gate to the side yard and guided them into the barn, each choosing a stall. He fastened their doors and looked up at the gray sky and felt the wind, which now whirled about him.

Inside the shed, he found another tarp that rose to the ceiling. John removed the cover and discovered a power rack meant for weight lifting. Red's stubborn insistence on buying the very best of everything impressed him yet again, free weights were superior to machines, and a power rack allowed Olympic-style lifts to be performed safely. He inserted steel hooks at position number twenty-five on the rack and placed an Olympic bar on them, then loaded one hundred thirty-five pounds on the bar and stood under it. He did a set of front squats as the storm raged both inside and outside, within and without, and he felt a beckoning to leave Vickie and the girls and take up life in a calmer locale, somewhere tropical, where fathers did not get sick and die and all women told the truth about love and loyalty.

John ran through back squats and overhead presses and bench presses and back rows and deadlifts and behind-the-neck presses and curls and triceps extensions, preoccupied by restless thoughts and sorrowful reverie. His relationship with Vickie was unlucky, both in the past and in the present, and there were too many complications.

He finished the workout and sat in a camp chair at the door.

Vickie Morrison lied. It was the foundation of her personality and had served her well for twenty years in the cable news business, but it was a showstopper for a marriage, where truth and openness meant everything to romance.

John reflected on his affair with Leslie Carter, and he wondered if she really was Rephaim. Was Price correct? Had their kind been eradicated from the face of the earth, or had their lineage survived through the millennia in various forms, mixed with the DNA of God's creation?

If she was Rephaim, would Jesus save her if she repented, or was she corrupted beyond any hope of salvation like Pharaoh or Og or Goliath?

Thunder sizzled and cracked as it broke the sound barrier. A boom shook him, snapping him out of his self-imposed trance, lost as he was in self-pity. His fingers clutched the arms of his camp chair, and he pondered moving farther back from the doorway but decided it was up to God. He would test his faith as the Lord had tested him.

The storm ended outside but continued within John as he left his chair and surveyed the property for damage. He happened upon a tall cedar that had split as a sapling into three massive verticals. Lightning had ravaged one of them, and it now blocked the gate. He looked about the farm and sighed, thankful he had put the horses into the barn but irritated at the obstacle course of his life.

It's always something, Lord, and I'm exhausted.

He heard only the cicadas, which resumed their rattle from nearby oaks, and the vroom-vroom of katydids as they looked on in amusement, he was a merry clown of the highest order, and they had the right.

John circled back to the shed and retrieved a brand-new chainsaw from a box, which Red must have purchased not long before his death. He found a can of fuel mix and filled the port, then marched out to the tree. While he cut, John considered Leslie, and his mind drew a portrait of a medieval dragon who blew fire and menaced villagers.

He finished and returned to the shed and cleaned the saw as Garrett would have expected, then eased his truck around so he might collect the logs for burning in the secondary pasture across the highway, all the while feeling depressed and angry and bewildered. He threw the cedar logs into the truck bed and fought the urge to go to Vickie and apologize and ask her forgiveness, as he had likely overreacted due to his father's death and Leslie's metamorphosis and Price's theological rebuke, not to mention his murder arrest and the dropped charges.

Life was stranger than fiction, but no one else noticed, which harkened to his hours with Nicole in the dayroom of the state mental hospital, where inmates floated about the visitation table and leaned in and made awful faces as he sat with his poor mother, who soon departed from him. It was then he discovered this fallen world, which should have been faithful and hopeful and loving, was a terrestrial asylum. Only no one else understood it but a lunatic and her son, each longing for a realm without steel mesh on the windows and freakish imps who wore unholy sneers.

He drove the truck across the road and opened the gate and dumped the logs into a pile at the center of the field, then returned to the house, secure in the knowledge he had done his duty. He would wait a few days for the logs to dry before burning the pile. Grady met his truck as he parked, which improved his mood.

His boots stepped onto the porch as a car entered the driveway. John sat on the glider and assumed someone had the wrong address. He grew surprised when an attractive young woman exited the Camry with a purposeful countenance. Her face seemed familiar.

"Hello, I'm Nellie Michaels." She extended her hand.

He shook it with suspicion. "What's this about?"

Her smile waned, and her arm dropped to her side.

"Could we share a cup of coffee?"

While in jail, a guard had escorted him through several steel doors, and upon entry into the group cell, an immediate slamming sound from behind confined John with murderers and thieves and perpetrators of every crime under the sun, mankind had advanced little since the days of Solomon. He had lain on a top bunk, hoping for bail, but no one came to get him, which felt like yet another of Vickie's betrayals. When the jail set him free, a cab was parked at the door. He got in and asked the driver who had paid the fare, but the cabbie only shrugged and said it was someone else's business. With each passing mile, John grew more furious and hurt and intent on inflicting damage on everyone in his path. Now, with his goal attained, he was alone.

He settled into the glider and eyed the young woman who stood before him with what he was certain were nefarious intentions, and made a snap decision to hear her out.

"I just cut up a pile of logs." He gestured at the field across the road.

Her eyes remained on him. She smiled coyly, unwilling to budge.

"I'm too dirty, so we'd better sit out here."

Nellie glanced at the house. "I'd like to see the kitchen."

"It's like any other."

She gave him an imploring look. "I promise not to be a bother."

He sighed and then stood. "Fine, but we need to go around back."

Nellie followed him, and soon they were at the table as he made coffee. He turned to her. "I assume you know my name?"

She nodded. "John Breyer, and your father recently passed."

He recalled Leslie's first visit. "You won't put anything into my drink. If that's your angle and if you're working for Leslie Carter, you can leave." Her gaze remained fixed on him, as if he were a zoo animal of intense interest, and her face took on an eerie presentation that made her seem partially inhuman. A tingle ran up and down John's spine, but he suppressed it, reminding himself that Jesus had His hand on this situation and whoever this woman might be, she could not kill him.

Nellie seemed taken aback by his declaration. Her cheeks paled.

"I wouldn't hurt you, John, no matter what Vickie might say."

He handed her a mug and took a seat across the table.

"But you destroyed her on national television." He hesitated. "Then you stole the show from underneath Vickie, the show she built."

"Yes, I did those things out of resentment and jealousy, and I hope to repair our friendship in the near future. But that's not why I'm here today, speaking with you." Nellie seemed unwell as she shifted heavily in her seat and dark circles formed beneath her reddening eyes. "I'm sorry."

She leaned over the table. Her head fell to her arms, and she wept.

John wasn't sure what to do, so he filled a glass with water and handed it to her as he removed her coffee. She wiped her tears and gulped the water as if she were so dehydrated she might die of thirst.

He stood watch for a few moments. "Should I call someone?"

Nellie regained her composure as best she could and shook her head.

"Okay, well then, what's the matter? I don't know why you're here."

"Me either, if I'm being honest."

"Did you drive a long way?"

She smiled faintly at him. "I flew here in a private jet."

"From Washington?"

"No, from New York. Powerful forces demand Vickie's return."

"I thought when Preston fired her, it was final."

"Since you mentioned Leslie Carter, you know there are those who operate in darkness, a cabal with an unbelievable reach, known to some as the Consortium. I work for a man who controls global media."

"Did he place Leslie in the governor's race for political control?"

"We leave nothing to chance, John. Failure is never an option."

"This man who owns you, what is his name?"

"Sturgis Faulkner. He will soon be here, so you have little time."

"For what, dare I ask?"

"To run."

John took a deep breath and exhaled.

"If this man wanted to murder me, I'd already be dead, so I'm going upstairs to take a shower. Look around in the living room if you'd like." He gestured kindly. "The couch is soft if you're tired and need a rest."

She smiled with warmth. "I may take you up on your offer."

Upstairs, he hurried into the shower, but once inside, the water felt good, so he took his time. There was little Nellie Michaels could do to him now, and he might not be around much longer anyway.

He buried his fears and dressed himself in jeans and a polo shirt. As he neared the stairs, he noticed her behaving strangely. Nellie stood in front of a bookcase and peered at a photograph, and he immediately got the sense she was there for Vickie rather than him.

She took the frame and removed the picture, studying it for what seemed an eternity as he stood silently at the top of the stairs. She wiped more tears and pocketed the photograph. He wondered about the reporter but then recovered his senses, she was likely there for an exposé and would overcome her feelings of guilt at ruining Vickie's life.

John started to speak a kindness in hopes she might alter her malevolent plans but paused when she leaned over an arm of the couch, as if in pain. Nellie's behavior alarmed him, she was far too young to have health issues, and there seemed to be something terribly wrong with her.

It would be just his luck if she died on his watch.

John thudded down the stairs, observing her as he went.

"Are you okay?" he asked.

Nellie lifted herself with effort. "No, I don't believe I am."

She lay on the couch and fell unconscious.

Vickie took a break on Friday morning to work at the station, as it gave her an excuse to avoid John. She left the girls with Eudora, who sat with Price in his room. Over the last two weeks, Vickie had stayed with her father every night, barely getting any rest, and during daylight hours, she escorted him along the corridors. His age and the nature of the surgery had lengthened his stay, but he would soon be home, so he encouraged her to take time for herself at the television station she dearly loved.

Laura entered Vickie's office and sat opposite her.

"I'm sending a crew to cover a home invasion, if you're interested."

Vickie's fingers typed fast on the keyboard, and she spoke in a monotone over her shoulder. "I'm in, but I have to finish this story."

Laura smirked. "I'm sure it will keep."

Vickie found it impossible not to return Laura's disarming smile.

"I like to finish what I start."

An intern stuck her head inside the door. "Someone's here."

Both Vickie and Laura turned.

The intern shrugged. "Some man in a limousine is out front."

Again, both women moved in unison as they peeked through the blinds.

"I've got to see this," said Laura mischievously.

Vickie gave her a playful shove as they walk-raced to the front, but who met them made her shudder and caged her like a trapped animal.

Sturgis Faulkner extended his hand. "Hello, Vickie."

She shook it lightly and let her arm fall.

"I had hoped we might discuss your future," he said.

There was a possessive fury in his voice, hard and ruthless.

"I'm doing well here, Sturgis."

His smile grew sinister, and his eyes communicated everything.

She turned to Laura, determined to save her from his wrath, and she wished she'd remembered her Bible, but it rested securely with Price.

"I'll take a drive with him. We won't be gone long."

Laura seemed concerned. "Are you sure? I can call John."

Vickie squeezed Laura's arm and sent her friend to safety.

As they lazily roved the countryside, Sturgis gazed at the scenery, seemingly mesmerized by the mountains like a tourist on vacation.

"Will you talk to me?" she asked. "Am I about to die?"

He broke into laughter. "No, my dear. I'm about to offer you a job."

His contemptuous tone sparked her anger, as his words seemed insincere, like everything spoken by cold and calculating men.

"Well, in that case, save your breath."

He directed the driver to the William Blake mansion, which had just been renovated. She looked forward to seeing its grand interiors, as they were said to be the epitome of Gilded Age design, but then her phone rang. She turned from Sturgis and huddled near the window. "Yes?"

"Hey." John hesitated. "I know you don't want to hear from me."

"What's going on? Are the horses okay?"

"Yeah, they're all fine, but someone is here, and she's sick."

He seemed agitated and nervous, which was unlike him.

"Slow down, John. Tell me what happened."

The limousine entered the gate and meandered down a lane to the manor, with its profusion of dormers jutting in all directions, its bay windows designed for watching the morning sun, and its Elizabethan gables that framed the home's one-hundred-fifty-foot length. She counted five chimneys, two on each end and one in the middle of the gambrel roof. Some windows were stained like those of a majestic cathedral.

John's impatient breaths interrupted her stargazing and recaptured her focus. "Are you there?" she asked, hoping he could handle the issue.

"Yeah, but I'm not sure what to say."

"Me either, John." A pause. "Who is at my house?"

"Nellie Michaels."

The name struck Vickie like a bullet.

She cringed and held up a finger to placate Sturgis, who smiled.

"Why is she in my home? Did you bring her there?"

He grunted. "Of course not, Vickie. Why would you think that?"

"I don't know, but maybe it's because you slept with my sister."

"Look, this girl is far too young for me and, "

"It didn't stop you with Mary Bishop."

"It sure did."

"You were never with Mary?"

"I've already told you I declined her offers."

"Meaning she approached you more than once?"

"She did on a regular basis, but I politely said no each time."

"Why?" Vickie glanced at Sturgis. "What's wrong with Mary?"

"She's never been you. I thought you understood this."

"I'm not sure what to believe with you anymore." Vickie's mind raced as she searched her recollections. "What about Rachel Daniels?"

"She's closer to our age, but I wasn't with her either."

Vickie gasped as the truth dawned on her.

"Michelle was the last one?"

"Yes, after her, I changed my ways. Are you happy now?"

Vickie wasn't sure if she would ever be happy again. John had violated a long-standing trust, and he knew it when he did it, and she couldn't bring herself to forgive his transgressions and might never do so, as Michelle was both precious to her and hated, and she was off-limits.

"Fine, so what is Nellie doing there?"

"Right now, she's lying unconscious, and I'm about to call 911."

Vickie turned to Sturgis and placed her hand on the receiver.

"Nellie Michaels is at my farm, but something is wrong with her."

Sturgis asked for the phone, and she gave it to him.

"Hello, Mr. Breyer?"

He listened to John's response and then continued.

"Listen to me. There is no need to call for an ambulance."

Sturgis directed the driver to leave for Bluecreek Stables.

After he concluded his conversation, he handed her the phone.

Sturgis reassured her Nellie would be the picture of health once he administered her medicine, as she must not have taken her required dosage. The journalist in Vickie smelled a story. Things did not add up.

"Why is a twenty-year-old sick with major health problems?"

Sturgis patted her knee like a child. "All in good time, my dear."

John stood at the window as a limousine parked in the driveway. Nellie stirred and looked up at him with youth and innocence, and then she grew alarmed as the sound of slamming doors met their ears.

"Who's here?"

She struggled to sit up and then eased against the couch's arm.

"Vickie and this Sturgis character." He turned. "Want to run?"

"You must help me stand, John." Her eyes pleaded with him.

John sighed.

He went to her and grabbed her hand.

"Please, not so rough." She wobbled and leaned into him.

A miserable torment broke Nellie's firm countenance as her palm fell flat against his chest. She was a beautiful woman, even while in distress, but he felt no attraction to her. Nellie must surely be a shapeshifter like Leslie Carter. He was right in his deduction about the Rephaim. They walked the earth, blending with humans in plain sight.

As the door opened, she drew back and collected herself in dignified fashion, her eyes laser-focused on Sturgis, who gave her a look of fatherly disapproval. Vickie seemed reticent and lingered at the threshold of her own home, her face registering every thought and emotion.

More sounds needled inbound from the driveway as brakes squealed and doors shut, and then hard footsteps landed on the porch and men with boxes appeared in the foyer. Sturgis waved them toward Nellie, and they opened their kits. She melted onto her knees as their stone-cold faces menaced her into submission. One took her arm forcefully and removed her blouse. John started to interject, but Sturgis threw him a look of warning, so he held his peace for the first time in weeks. The medic checked her blood pressure and listened to her chest and back with a stethoscope. Streaks became noticeable on her torso.

As John looked closely, they formed into scars that ran vertically and horizontally and in swirls all over her skin, and he wondered if her reptilian scales might soon appear. It was then he grew frightened.

Several shots were administered, which gave her the strength to stand. Color returned to her face, and the scars buried themselves.

She slipped into her blouse and buttoned it with lowered eyes.

The medics packed their kits with precision and set them in the foyer. They returned with pistols drawn, as if expecting to murder.

Sturgis waved them off dismissively, for which John was grateful.

Vickie shifted her weight but kept silent. She glanced at John but soon diverted her eyes, and it became clear she suspected him of a betrayal, much as he had suspected her. The chasm between them widened and their love waned. With all they had seen together, they should be closer than ever, but the lies and the lack of trust and the petulant unwillingness to pray for one another took its toll. In that instant, he knew she would soon leave him or he would leave her.

It was merely a matter of who said what first and who picked up the keys, and little mattered other than freedom and solitude and clarity.

Sturgis directed the medics to help Nellie to the limousine.

Outside, John and Vickie stood several feet apart as they watched the group cross the grass. Sturgis took Nellie's hand as she sat in the limousine's backseat and then carefully shut the door.

He gestured at the men. One of them drove her vehicle, and the other followed in the black van. Sturgis turned to Vickie and smiled.

She walked over to him, and John followed.

"Should I leave you two alone?" he asked, assuming the answer.

Sturgis shook his head. "I'd like you to hear this."

Vickie cast an involuntary look of concern at her nemesis.

"What's wrong with Nellie?"

"She has a rare condition which we must treat or she will die. Miss Michaels is perfectly aware of this, as she's suffered since girlhood, but there are days when she refuses her medicine like a spoiled little child."

He gave them both a cheerful smile, which seemed the opposite.

"Her intention was honorable, as she meant to provide you with news of a most urgent nature." He turned to the car and then faced them with a sad look. "It seems your good friend Raul has been killed."

Vickie gasped, and her hand went to her mouth.

Her voice rose an octave. "What?"

John had never heard the man's name, and he grew wary.

"Who was he to you, Vickie?"

She flashed him a restless squint but refused to answer.

"Did you murder him?" She glanced at the car. "Or did she?"

"It was not our doing. As you know, heroin is rampant on the islands, and the homeless can be vicious when given a reason. It seems there was a dispute over a young woman, and the other fellow took his revenge with a knife." His eyes flickered. "I'm sorry for your loss."

Vickie paced in the grass as tears coursed down her cheeks, which she at first tried to hide but then gave up, as her misery was too heartfelt. She fell to her knees and wept bitterly and sorrowfully and unreservedly.

John stood his ground, unwilling to console her.

"Why did you send Nellie to tell me?" Vickie looked up at Sturgis.

"She wants to make amends with you and ask for your return."

Vickie snorted and swiped at her tears, then fell onto her palms in the green grass. She let out a mournful wail, which devastated John, as he knew it was born of love. Then she stood and wiped her hands on her jeans and gave Sturgis a sneer. "I highly doubt she wants that."

"Well, ask her yourself in New York."

Vickie recoiled.

"Sturgis, I have a life here now, and I cannot leave my girls."

"You won't leave Katie and Abbie, nor your father?"

She nodded.

"Bring them with you to New York. We will select the finest private school for your girls, one that will guarantee their future, and your father will enjoy a lavish lifestyle only the kings of Europe have known."

Vickie turned to John with teary eyes.

"What do you think?"

"You should consider this a fork in the road," he said flatly.

"Meaning I might travel a different path than ours?"

She paused.

"Is that what you are planning, John?"

"I don't know, Vickie. It's not like we've gotten along lately."

"You wouldn't marry me when I asked you," she said. "It hurt me."

"Knowing you loved a man in the Caribbean hurts me, Vickie."

She took a breath and exhaled. "We didn't have an affair, if that's what you're implying. We were good friends, and he loved another."

"I see it in your eyes, so stop lying, and it's why we've struggled."

"Fine, I could have loved him. Is that enough for you?"

"And once I thought the same about Michelle, so we're even."

Sturgis drew nearer.

"Children, let's stop arguing." He placed a gentle hand on both of their backs. "It seems you two could use a break."

John shrugged him off and drew back from him.

"Talk to me, John." She went over to him and met his eyes.

"If you want to go to New York, I won't stop you."

"Is it what you want?"

"I don't know, but I thought about our wedding this morning before the storm blew down half a cedar tree in the backyard. I could picture a tent, a band, a huge crowd of people. Happy conversations filling the air along with the clinking of glasses and music and dancing."

"That works for me," she said. "But is it what you want?"

"I don't think you're done, and fame is calling again."

She frowned. "That's not fair, John. I've changed."

"Well, there's only one way to be sure, and it's New York."

"What if I don't ever come home?"

"It's a chance we'll have to take."

"And the girls?"

"They'll follow you anywhere. I know that much for sure."

Vickie considered.

She turned to Sturgis. "Will you promise not to hurt John if I go?"

"My dear, we are not monsters. He will be perfectly safe."

Her eyes met Nellie's, and there seemed to be a connection.

"All right, I'll go, but only for a tour, and then I'm right back here."

"It's all I ask." His eyes flickered. "Once you meet your own kind, you won't wish to leave. Those who work for me have a certain quality."

"Which is?"

"Like the two of us, they must rule the world."

Twenty

Psalm 60:9

Who will bring me into the fortified city?
Who will bring me victory over Edom?

Vickie entered the barn and whispered her goodbyes to Chief and Miracle as John stood nearby, pretending not to listen or care. Waves of emotion had built his resolve to keep his distance, but he disliked growing old with no wife or children, and she was his first love, no matter how many times they argued or declared otherwise. Chief strutted in his stall as she spoke softly, and Miracle grew delighted in her presence. John thought of Savannah more than usual, as parallels between Vickie's departure and the mare's were hard to miss, both made John's heart flutter and haunted his dreams. Vickie was strict with her heart of late, as she found forgiveness difficult once wronged. The intentionality made little difference in her estimation; any penetrating wound pierced like an arrow and caused her great distress.

Mary found Vickie, and her focus quickly diverted to John.

"Why are you here?" she asked excitedly.

He looked up from saddle cleaning.

"Working. Nothing else."

Buoyant and giddy, she made mocking eyes at him and then drew near to Vickie and touched her arm. "Your old show just called me."

Vickie stiffened. "And?"

"They say Nellie is transferring to New York like you predicted, and they need another youthful face, only one with more experience than a glorified intern, to use your expression." She eyed her mentor, waiting for a sign, and her voice rose. "They want me in D.C. yesterday!"

Vickie took in the information silently and with a grave air.

She turned to John. "How should I respond to this?"

"Why ask me?"

"You have all the answers."

He snorted. "Hardly."

Vickie smirked and addressed Mary. "Have you considered Lewis?"

"He'll be my cameraman, just like here in Addison."

"And the baby?"

"We talked, and he wants a child." A pause. "So do I."

"The old boyfriend? Will he be in the picture?"

Mary shook her head. "He's gone for good."

Vickie's lips pursed. "Shocker."

"Look, I'm sorry I can't be like you, but at least they want me."

"Oh, you're exactly like me. That's what I'm worried about."

Mary squeezed Vickie's arm. "Will you support my decision?"

"To saddle Lewis with Ryan's baby or to take a job in D.C.?"

"Both, equally."

"Preston Spiro will not like his new star being pregnant, and Mitch won't be there to run interference for you. It will be a rough ride."

"I'm up for it, Vickie."

"Oh, so now you're a big girl," she said flatly.

"I want to be. Can that be enough for now?"

"I suppose, but now I'm worried about you. And the baby."

"And Lewis?"

"Him, too."

Lewis entered the barn and crept up behind Mary. He put his hands over her eyes, and Mary turned to him and fell into his firm embrace.

They were obviously in love, and John longed for the same.

Vickie glanced at him and tossed her hair over her shoulders.

"Congratulations are in order, since you'll soon have a wedding."

Lewis grew puzzled. "We haven't discussed marriage."

"Then you'll do that very thing today. It's an order."

"We have time, Vickie. Stop being such a mother."

"No, Lewis, you don't." She paced the floor as they watched her, dumbfounded. "Washington is a pit of vipers, and it will eat you alive in about ten seconds if you don't have a strong foundation of love."

She paused.

"Trust me. I know of what I speak."

Mary gave him a coy look. "What do you think? Should we?"

He took both her hands. "There's no time. We have to leave."

Vickie stepped forward and grabbed both of their arms.

"Don't overcomplicate it. Find a wedding chapel the first week."

Lewis grinned at her. "Yes, ma'am."

After they bounced gladly into the house, Vickie approached John in the corner, as both knew he would not come to her for any reason.

She gripped her bag tightly in her fingers and stared at him.

"Will you talk to me, John?"

He ceased wiping the leather and looked up at her.

"What's there to say? You're going, right?"

She gently set the bag at her feet. Her eyes moistened.

"I love you. Do you not know it by now?"

Her words washed over him, and a lump formed in his throat.

John eased around the saddle, went to her, and kissed her deeply.

He drew back and asked how things got so messed up.

"I don't know, but I hate it," she said.

Her head bowed, and she slumped into him as if all hope was gone.

He pushed a strand of hair behind her ear. "Me, too."

Vickie wiped her eyes. "It's our pattern. We start out great, and I think we'll last forever, but then we end up like poor Savannah, lost and alone." She gave a desperate laugh and shrugged in mock resignation. "It's what I loved about Raul. He was born in cartel country and lost his family, but he fought those monsters and found a better life."

"It's what drew me to Michelle after she lost Tink, which she'd hidden so carefully from everyone. But then when she told me about the abuse, her relationship with her children amazed me all the more. Most victims can't stop hating their abuser long enough to become a parent."

Vickie's fingers clutched his shirt. Her body molded to his.

"I want to hate you for Michelle, but I can't. You were there for her, and I wasn't. Now that I've thought about it, I'm glad she had you."

He grabbed her hands and kissed them lightly.

"You can't imagine how scared she was after the accident. It hurt her more than words can express when you wouldn't come home."

"She must have thought I didn't love her."

"You didn't."

Vickie yanked herself from his grip and slapped his face. He stepped back. Fury turned his cheeks blood red, and he raised a hand but then stopped himself and threw the saddle against an empty stall.

Tires crunched on the driveway. Her limousine had arrived.

He calmed himself in ways she could not, as her wrath, when ignited, could be uncontrollable. Her eyes flickered, and she suddenly seemed possessed by a diabolical spirit, sinister and ghastly.

She grabbed her bag. "So long, John Breyer."

"Wait!"

He rushed forward, spun her around, and grabbed her shoulders.

"Isn't there anything I can say to make you put down that bag?"

"I may forgive you for sleeping with my sister, but I will never forget what you just said." She looked at the driveway and steeled herself. "I must investigate this offer, as it could mean a great deal to Katie and Abbie's future. I've known Sturgis since I was a girl, and he was Red's most valued friend, so I will trust him to keep his word."

She walked to the barn's entrance and then wheeled.

"This might be just what we all need."

John snarled, uncaring of her reaction. "No, Vickie. You only care about yourself. It's always been that way. You look out for number one."

He held up his index finger, which seemed clownish, even to him.

She smirked and marched to the limousine as if it was her birthright.

He again rushed at her, this time with greater vengeance.

"I've half a mind to sue for custody of the girls."

Vickie dropped the bag. "What did you just say?"

John gestured at the house and the pasture and the barn.

"Katie and Abbie need to be here at Bluecreek with the horses and their new grandfather, not in Babylon." A pause. "You'll grow tired of them and then you'll send them to a boarding school, which they'll hate. Don't take those girls from the only home they've ever known."

"You would actually challenge me in court?"

"I would."

She tried to slap him, but this time he caught her arm and threw her onto the grass. She rolled like an athlete and landed on her knees.

The driver pulled his pistol and pointed it at John.

"Come with me, or this man dies."

Vickie's face went pale. She stood and brushed off her jeans. The car door slammed with her inside, and John was once more on his own.

***

Her shoulders slumped as she settled into the leather seat, and her eyes shut as she drifted onto the island of St. Christina, where Raul took her hand and led her from Irene in the encampment to a tent in the jungle. There he laid her on a blanket, the sand soft underneath. As he made love to her, the humidity glistened their skin, and their bodies slid and rose and fell and pressed until man and woman knew great heights unparalleled. Then he fell beside her and eyed the ceiling.

"You must commit to him, body and soul," he said.

"I only want you, Raul. You are a murderer like me."

"Yes, and I am dead."

She rolled, and his eyes bulged. A sneer crawled across his face.

Vickie jolted as the jet banked. She found her senses as she peered through the tiny window at the majestic skyline, which seemed to go on forever in one cascading expanse of buildings and roads and bridges and tunnels, all crammed and stuck and folded into what passed for order.

Her hands braced as wheels touched and skidded on the runway.

"Miss Morrison, we are now at La Guardia. A car awaits outside."

A steward opened the door and gestured for her to descend to the tarmac, where a limousine greeted her with a sinister warmth.

The car ventured southwest on I-495, crossed the East River, and then turned onto FDR, passing Freedom Plaza. On 34th Street, she passed barber shops, condominiums, beauty spas, restaurants, and a sense of dread washed over her as she passed a Masonic Lodge, which glowed as if beckoning her forth. Then her skin gleamed as it had on the mountain, and she grew frightened of this place, even more so as the limousine passed an occult bookstore which displayed tarot cards on a table out front. Some bore angels, which also glowed and then flapped their bright, beaming wings and left their abode to join her journey across town. They entered the backseat and flew about her with toothy smiles which portended doom. They brushed her hair with their slender fingers like playful imps, and the terror rose higher in her than she had ever experienced on assignment or as Logan broke her into a million pieces which were never put right. These entities connected with those inside her, as the appointed hour, once merely a prediction, was now at hand. As the limousine entered the deck at Planar, she wished to run and hide and never show her face in this fallen realm.

A guide led her to a private elevator and an undisclosed floor, where Sturgis met her with a handshake and a smile. His staff scurried about, eyeing her as they passed, and Vickie wondered after them, as their looks seemed more intense than curious. He led her into an office and announced her presence to the room, saying work had ended for the day and each should ready themselves for a meeting in chambers.

At the sound of his voice, she lifted her head and listened.

His tone had become caustic, stirring a dormant shame.

"Why are you meeting in chambers?" she asked.

"Come with me, and I will show you the opulence of this city."

She followed him into an exquisite office which overlooked lower Manhattan, and they gazed across the skyline to the east and south.

"Central Park lies north of our location. I have an apartment for you there." He jingled keys, and she took them. "Consider it home."

"Is it furnished?"

"With the finest of everything." A pause. "I know your tastes."

She nodded.

"You've known me since my childhood, so I'd hope so."

He stepped forward and clasped her shoulders with force.

"Trust me to provide what's best for you."

"Is there enough room for the girls? I won't leave without them."

"There are three bedrooms, one for each of you, and you will walk them each morning to a renowned school. In the afternoon, you will pick them up and ask about their day." He allowed the visual to register and then continued. "This is only for starters. I will show you a mansion in Montauk, which was owned by a movie producer who grew isolated."

"A beach house?"

"Yes, but larger than your home in Addison."

Vickie hugged her arms, unable to comprehend such extravagance.

"What's more, if you perform well, there will be another home, a farm in Southampton, where you will foster Native Dancer's offspring."

"And if I must travel?"

"Elegance will meet you everywhere you go." He gestured at the city. "Your feet will step on those who get in your way, and your mouth will know only five-star delicacies, and your eyes will see only beauty. This province and all within it will be yours for the plunder."

"So, for clarity, I'll get a nice house?"

He chuckled.

"Yes, my dear. Men will strain their backs for you, and women will serve at your feet, and the masses will know your words, as you will become my head of propaganda. We will condition a global audience to accept the rise of the son of perdition, who will soon rule the world."

"Why me when you could get anyone else?"

"All in good time, my dear." He waved a hand. "For now, we go."

Macabre demons encircled her, emissaries for an antediluvian spirit, greater and more troublesome than modern intellectuals might conceive. They pushed her toward a steel door, which slid open, and she entered a cylindrical chamber lit by candles on the outermost periphery.

On her right and left, a demon took position as her guard.

From behind, Sturgis escorted a translucent woman, whose gown and hair fluttered in a breeze which had only manifested in the ethereal but which could be seen in this dimension. Her crystal form glowed as Vickie's had done, and then the woman ascended to the ceiling, where she hovered above, simmering and seething and gnashing like a lion who would devour. Staff members were dressed in scarlet robes of silk as they entered through a door at the far end of the room. Their feet padded across the floor, and it dawned on Vickie this was a pagan ritual.

She turned to Sturgis. "What is this?"

His eyes flashed about restlessly. "We have plans for you."

The group, composed of men and women in equal measure, split into two parts with a lane through the middle, and each chanted.

"Please don't sacrifice me, Sturgis. I didn't care before, but I have a home and a family, and I don't want to die here. Please, I beg you."

He gave her a laugh. "No, my dear. You will not die today."

Terror gripped her. "Surely not Katie or Abbie?"

She looked about for them, scanning the faces of this group.

"Your family is not here," he said. "I sense your thoughts."

"What do you want from me? Please let me go home!"

He turned and addressed his staff, who ceased their chants.

Vickie retraced the steps in her mind, reflecting on how she got to this moment. Only a few weeks before, things seemed blissful and good.

"Your queen has been prophesied, and you awaited her arrival with patience and diligence. Today, I present her to you in might and glory."

Each man and woman placed their palms on the floor, worshipping

Vickie as a goddess. A sense of foreboding broke over her as the spirit of death descended from the ceiling, exciting the entities inside her.

They cried out with wrath and lust and pride, and the envious hatred of a thousand generations commanded Vickie to murder.

"Behold your priestess!"

The men and women chanted fervently, and their voices grew louder until the combined sounds might deafen, but she could not lift her hands to her ears as the spirit rooted itself in her entities and controlled her movements. She was diabolically possessed, as the priest had feared.

"Lilith has descended, and she lives inside your priestess!"

A cocoon of anguish enveloped Vickie, weakening her resolve to live, just as she had almost given up on the balcony in the Caribbean after Raul left. She wished to cry out to the Lord, but the spirit who called herself Lilith threatened Raul in the underworld, who lay broken in love and sweat and agony and whose existence was at the mercy of a wicked accomplice. It could not be true, as Jesus had died on the cross for all our sins and Raul repented of his bloodshed and accepted Christ as his Savior, but Vickie's many lies coalesced within her, and she was torn between feelings for Raul and for John. She understood lucidly her utter confusion, but she could not break free of the conflict which raged within her, binding her in chaos to the malevolent Lilith.

Sturgis left the room, and she fell to her knees, as there was barely any energy left in her body. She almost crumpled into a ball, but she knew if she did, the chanting staff members would rise and kill her.

He entered at the far end, now dressed in a scarlet robe which seemed darker and more blood red than the others. As he approached her and the guarding demons to her right and left, the men and women arose from the floor and kept themselves at attention. Then he stood in front of Vickie, taller than she had remembered him only minutes before. His eye color changed from brown to yellow, and his face transmuted. He shook off the robe, revealing scales which formed over every inch of his muscular body. The men and women behind him did likewise, revealing themselves as reptilians of a more impressive stature than when she first saw them. Their eyes gouged her soul, and Lilith commanded her to murder, murder, murder, which became a horrifying mantra in the shadowy corners of her psyche, wearing down her resolve for anything but the Reaper's cold embrace.

Sturgis turned and kissed her passionately with his reptilian eyes.

His clawed hand found her shoulder, alarming and shivering her. "You will soon become my wife like the daughters of men, both before and after the Flood, and you will bear a son, the man of perdition, who will reveal himself in a future decade and be worshipped as a god."

Vickie's skin glowed brighter than ever, and the group bowed to her. The Lilith spirit within grew more jealous and prideful and enraged.

Terror ran rampant, and she thought she might faint, which delighted the taunting and jeering spirit. Vickie's mortal flesh was weak and pathetic and unworthy of such a deity, but in the absence of another candidate, her form would have to do, disgraceful as it was.

She found a tiny bit of courage and begged for respite.

"Please don't sacrifice a victim in front of me. I cannot take it."

"Oh no, my dear, it is you who will do the deed, not us."

Her eyes looked up from the floor and met his.

She tried to defy him with words, but Lilith choked her speech.

Sturgis waved forward a woman who retrieved a long knife and disrobed, revealing her nakedness. She seemed vulnerable but unafraid.

"Commence," he said.

The woman cut her arms and legs, running the knife along the length of her skin, and blood flowed from her into a puddle.

He nodded, and the woman stepped back from the blood. Her skin grew scales, healing her wounds. Now all were Rephaim, and Vickie thought herself of a tainted line. She wept into her trembling hands.

"Do not worry, my dear. You are not yet one of us."

"What am I?"

"You are of Moravian lineage, the original Protestant reformers. Since the 1400s, Lucifer has sought to eradicate your bloodline from the earth, as it is good and decent and kind, each of which we despise."

"You're wrong. Something has always been wrong with me."

Her skin glowed effervescently, and the group murmured.

Vickie considered her daughter and her desire for Mammon.

She knew the fame of the masses, who might once again sing her name as his staff now chorused for their goddess. She wished for her father and his Bible, worn and well used, and she reflected on John, how angry he had become, much like Lilith, who now controlled her flesh.

"Since your girlhood, we have defiled you with parasites, so you might one day bear a child for Lucifer's throne, as the son of perdition must be half Rephaim and half transhuman. Our order made many attempts before your birth, all of which proved unsuccessful, but great scientific advancements will soon allow for fulfillment of our prophecy." He hesitated. "You may wonder if Red was involved, and the answer is yes, that is, until he balked at using Abbie, which prematurely ended his life. I advise you to avoid his mistake, as others will suffer in your stead."

He nodded sharply, and a door opened.

Two men brought Nellie into the room. They removed her robe, revealing her naked body, and forced her to kneel in the blood. Lines and swirls and welts had formed on her skin, and the width and breadth of them made Vickie gasp, as they were everywhere and they were deep and they were ancient. She wondered if Nellie might be an experiment gone wrong and perhaps it was why Sturgis sought her death.

The creature with the knife offered it to Vickie, and she took it.

She weighed it in her hand as Lilith excited her entities.

"End her life," Sturgis said. "You were each bred for this moment, and once you do, we will celebrate your entrance into our order."

Lilith screamed obscenities and commands at Vickie.

You must take this woman's soul, as she stole your career!

She debased you on live television! Your humiliation will not stand!

I will grant every wish, every desire, every want, but you must obey!

Vickie's life transitioned into more than she could have possibly imagined since her shaming at Nellie's hands, as John and her found family and the horses had given her validation, and even Mitch turned a corner, which was miraculous. She wondered after Red and his refusal to allow Abbie's continued defilement, which likely saved her at his own expense, and in that instant, she knew he had repented for his heinous sins, and Jesus forgave him as He would forgive her if she would only speak the truth here and now and forevermore, no matter the cost, holding nothing back from anyone, including John, who loved her.

The tenderness in Nellie's pleading expression steeled her resolve.

Vickie raised her head. "I tried to kill my unborn child while she was still in the womb, my precious Chelsea, through abortion."

She glared at Sturgis. "That is the only murder I will ever commit."

Nellie's eyes lanced Vickie's heart as she flinched at the words.

She would become a figment of the imagination, a faded memory, fleeting and worn and flickering like magic, and Nellie would burn.

"God in Heaven," said Nellie in horror, "please save my soul." Her eyes raised again to Vickie. "I don't know Him and He doesn't know me, but please help me if there's an ounce of humanity left in your bones, for I have been misled and I hated you and I sought my revenge."

Murder her, as I command! Murder her where she kneels!

Vickie shook her head. This gruesome ordeal must cease. She cried out to God, asking for His grace, as she had spoken truth. He gave her the Lord's Prayer from Matthew 6:9-13. "Our Father in heaven, may your name be kept holy. May your Kingdom come soon. May your will be done on earth, as it is in heaven. Give us today the food we need, and forgive us our sins, as we have forgiven those who sin against us. And don't let us yield to temptation, but rescue us from the evil one."

The doors burst open, and a mighty wind rushed into the room.

Swaths of fire gathered at the ceiling without scorching it.

The wind pinned Sturgis and the other Rephaim to the walls. Blood from the floor hurled itself at them and scalded their scaly skin.

Fire descended, and they cried out as the flames consumed them. When only Vickie and Nellie were left, she helped the wretched girl stand. The wind and the flames continued, blowing open each door in their path, consuming the wicked who were given over to depravity.

Vickie stopped and put the robe over Nellie, who shook with fright.

"Tonight we'll stay at the Central Park apartment."

"What then, Vickie?"

"Tomorrow, I will open a Bible and share the Word with you."

Nellie squeezed her hand as tears coursed her cheeks.

"No one has ever done that," she said.

"Well, honey, it's high time they did."

Vickie slept on a king-size bed and got up often to check on Nellie. Eventually she drifted into a semi-comatose state and found herself on the streets of New York, where many were tainted by parasites at the behest of government, recasting their body chemistry, zombifying themselves. Now they sought Christians to devour, believing the light of God shined in them, which they sought for themselves as recompense.

At eight o'clock, with Nellie sleeping soundly in her room, Vickie took a risk and went out for groceries. She found a Christian bookstore and purchased a leather Bible and waited for the clerk to inscribe it. She carried the Bible and the groceries proudly back to the apartment, and as she unlocked the door, Nellie cried out in panic from her bedroom. Vickie ran to her, and for the next ten minutes, she rocked Nellie in her arms and soothed her with kind words which Nellie had needed to hear since girlhood but which were rarely expressed.

When her tears dried and she found comfort in Vickie's presence, they went to the kitchen and sat at the table, where they read the Word.

Vickie knew not how to help Nellie other than to share what others had taught her, namely the three falls from grace, the Nephilim and the Rephaim, and the supernatural birth of Israel, which portended the coming of a Messiah who would be baptized and venture into the wilderness to reclaim those who were disinherited. He would then minister for a time and cast out demons and feed the masses and explain the intricacies of the Most High's plan of redemption in parables so people might understand. Then He would die for the sins of mankind, taking the place of animals which were sacrificed for our transgressions. The Messiah would allow His crucifixion on the cross and His body to be cast into a tomb for three days, and then He would ascend from the

Mount of Olives to Heaven, where He would sit at the right hand of Yahweh until His triumphant return in the clouds.

Vickie caught her breath, hopeful her paraphrase of the Bible in minutes would not fall on rebellious ears. To her surprise, Nellie listened and wanted to know more. As Vickie made breakfast, she sat on the couch and clutched the Bible and considered all she had heard.

Tears welled in Vickie's eyes, and she wiped them with a towel.

After they ate, she asked Nellie for the Bible, but Nellie gripped it with her fingers, and Vickie hoped she would not worship it as an idol.

"Would you do me a favor and turn to Psalm 60?"

Nellie shook her head, and her eyes moistened.

"I don't know where that is."

"Can I help you, honey?"

Nellie laid the Bible in front of her and put a palm on the leather.

"Can God fix what's wrong with me, my scars, and my weakness?"

Vickie nodded.

"I cried out to Him at Planar, but He hasn't healed my body."

"Maybe it's your soul He will restore, and then the rest will follow."

"I will love Him if He will love me, but I need to see evidence."

"Of His love?"

"Yes."

Vickie sighed. "It's a daily walk, and we don't get instant answers to our questions or quick fixes for our problems." A pause. "Parasites live inside my body, and they make a perfect home for demons, which is why Lilith possessed me so easily. I was terrified and prideful and angry, the right ingredients for diabolical oppression and possession."

"But you said a prayer, and He saved our lives."

"Yes, and for that, we must be grateful. And also faithful."

"Is Lilith still in you, Vickie? Please say no."

"I don't sense her spirit now, so I think she's gone from me."

"Can she come back someday?"

"I would assume so, but it's the same for anyone else. If we invite demons into our lives, they gain authority to take residence inside us."

Vickie rubbed a hand on the table and then squeezed Nellie's.

"Will you come home with me?"

"To Addison?"

"Yes, to live in my house. I want you to know a genuine family."

Nellie held the Bible against her chest and considered.

"You think I have no family?"

"I wouldn't wish to presume, but if you had known love, I doubt you would be so wrathful and so ambitious, as those are signs of a dark past filled with horrible traumas." Vickie waited for Nellie to respond, but her new friend kept still. "I'd love to hear your story sometime."

Nellie put the Bible on the table once more but kept a hand on it.

"A wealthy family from Connecticut adopted me. I never knew my father or my mother, but my adopted parents gave me everything my heart desired because they felt bad for my having to endure so many surgeries and so much physical pain, and for that I consider them a true blessing. But they died in a fluke car accident when I was twelve, and the order confiscated me from a foster home and made me study you."

"Me?" Vickie tapped her chest lightly.

"Along with other subjects which I was forced to learn or die a bloody death. Sturgis didn't hold the utmost position in the order, so you shouldn't feel too comfortable with him gone. He claimed the leader's title, and many saw him that way, but there are others behind the scenes who hold raw power, and they wield it from atop a distant mountain in a land you'd never suspect, like Addison, North Carolina."

Vickie smiled. "Can't be my town. We only care about horses."

Nellie returned her smile faintly, and then it vanished.

"You are still so naïve, Vickie, even after all these years."

"You're referring to Leslie Carter?"

"Among others. She is merely a foot soldier in their order."

"So who runs things in Addison? Do you have an org chart?"

"I believe Jessica Harper knows some of those answers."

"Jim Harper's widow? Mary Bishop and I just interviewed her."

"I'm aware, and it's why she's now dead."

"What did you say?"

"You heard me." Nellie hesitated. "Your questions got her killed."

Vickie left her chair and paced the room. Not another victim!

She wheeled and faced Nellie, looking for a better response.

"Why did Sturgis use you? That part I don't understand."

"He had his reasons."

"Which were?"

"It's a story for another time, Vickie. For now, I am tired."

"Nellie, I need more information. I thought we won the fight."

"We're just getting started," said Nellie with a sad countenance.

"Will they come after my family in Addison?"

"Absolutely, if you refuse them again."

Nellie paused.

"They saw me and Sturgis as expendable, but you are not."

"I'm no Rephaim, so what can I possibly mean to them?"

"As he said, they've groomed you since childhood, and they won't stop until every one of them is in the grave. That's the way it is."

Nellie put her head on her arms and shut her eyes.

"I'm very tired of this world, and I'd like to leave it."

"No, Nellie, you must stay with me. I won't lose another friend."

"Let me go, Vickie. You are the fierce warrior, and I am a weakling."

"You're much stronger than you realize, honey, so let me help you."

Nellie's eyes opened slightly. "How?"

"Please let me read Psalm 60. It won't take long."

Nellie sighed and then slid the Bible to her and shut her eyes again.

Vickie turned to the right page. She eyed Nellie briefly and then began, hoping it might have the intended effect and wouldn't scare her.

"You have rejected us, O God, and broken our defenses. You have been angry with us; now restore us to your favor. You have shaken our land and split it open. Seal the cracks, for the land trembles. You have been very hard on us, making us drink wine that sent us reeling. But you have raised a banner for those who fear you, a rallying point in the face of attack. Now rescue your beloved people. Answer and save us by your power. God has promised this by his holiness: 'I will divide up Shechem with joy. I will measure out the valley of Succoth. Gilead is mine, and Manasseh, too. Ephraim, my helmet, will produce my warriors, and

Judah, my scepter, will produce my kings. But Moab, my washbasin, will become my servant, and I will wipe my feet on Edom and shout in triumph over Philistia.' Who will bring me into the fortified city? Who will bring me victory over Edom? Have you rejected us, O God? Will you no longer march with our armies? Oh, please help us against our enemies, for all human help is useless. With God's help we will do mighty things, for he will trample down our foes."

Vickie closed the Bible and did her best to explain the text. "Yahweh had Esau and Lot clear the Rephaim from the Canaanite lands of Moab and Edom before the Israelites passed through on their way to the territory known as the Promised Land, and He will do the same for us if we surrender and work His perfect will, as we have our own Rephaim to clear."

Nellie sat up in her chair. The Word had recaptured her interest.

"I have no idea what He wants from me. I'm worthless."

Vickie rose from her chair and hugged her former nemesis and told her never to say such a thing, for she was anything but worthless to God and to Vickie. If she would only come home to Bluecreek, they would learn about the Lord together, and she would find healing.

There was a connection Vickie could not explain, but she would not hide her feelings or lock them away, as they were motherly.

"Alright, but only until I figure out what to do with myself."

Vickie chuckled. "I'm still trying at thirty-eight."

Nellie wept as she kissed her mentor's hand. "I'm so sorry."

"For what, honey?" Vickie bent down and met her at eye level.

"I was angry with you, and I tried to destroy your world."

"But you didn't end me, because I'm still here."

When she put a hand to Nellie's hair, the younger woman drew back, as if no mother had touched her in such a way, which her mentor found unforgivable, as every child should be loved from the heart.

"Red left me more money than I could spend in this lifetime, and I would like to open my home and my family and my station to you."

Nellie cast a woeful look at Vickie, as if the older woman's kindness was pure and her own sins far too wicked. Vickie started for the kitchen, but Nellie tugged at her arm like a little girl and held out the Bible.

"Please read to me. Something from the Old Testament."

Vickie instead flipped to John 1:1-5. "In the beginning the Word already existed. The Word was with God, and the Word was God. He existed in the beginning with God. God created everything through him, and nothing was created except through him. The Word gave life to everything that was created, and his life brought light to everyone. The light shines in the darkness, and the darkness can never extinguish it."

She handed the book to Nellie.

"This Bible has your name inscribed on the cover just like your name is written on the heart of Jesus, and all He asks of you, Nellie, is to allow His name to be written on your heart eternally."

Nellie held her Bible against her chest. "Can I live with you?"

"I thought you'd never ask." Vickie smiled and readied for home.

Twenty-One

Psalm 61:4

Let me live forever in your sanctuary,
safe beneath the shelter of your wings!

July 2008

Vickie gave Nellie space to roam, both in her bedroom and about the property, as she must find a spot to call her own, much as Vickie had done. Nellie must decipher something fresh and painful and wise each day, and while there was life yet within her, there was hope of finding the meaning so often robbed by a servitude to sin. Her story was more commonplace than most would allow, having faced the enchantments of malevolence head-on and survived. For all Vickie had encountered throughout the world, her experience in New York was the most frightening, as the wicked spirit of Lilith descended upon her. For a split second, she considered using the knife as commanded, but Nellie's wounded eyes besieged the castle of her heart, and a motherly knowledge stole over her, forcing her keen defiance.

She observed her ward, who stood with the horses in the pasture, running her hand along Wildfire's back, a sight to behold, as he only let a few trusted souls into his space. Then Nellie leaned against him, and Vickie wanted to call out and tell her to be careful, but the herd gathered about her and loved on her and asked for her love. The sight gladdened Vickie's heart. She turned and marched to the porch, where she sat on the glider, watching Nellie with her eyes but drawn in her mind to her problems, most of which correlated to John's departure.

Her eyes drifted to the clouds which passed overhead, and she prayed for strength. Once he learned what she had done to their child, he would pry her from his heart and toss her out like yesterday's paper. But even if he left her alone for life, she must deliver the news to him.

Eudora had brought Price home from the hospital, establishing herself as his primary caregiver and disallowing unauthorized intrusions into his regimen. Vickie despised the change, as Price was her father and he almost died after a lifetime spent apart, which still hurt her terribly. She had wanted to be with him longer in his room, but Sturgis took her from his side, and now she feared she might have lost her father's love forever, as his focus was now on Eudora, who did not deserve it.

Vickie hugged her arms amid the heat and humidity and listened to the cicadas and the katydids. Then her arm draped along the glider's length, and she wondered what John might do with his afternoon.

Nellie left the horses and crossed the field, her eyes on the grass before her, and Vickie hoped she was unsure rather than sad.

"How are you holding up?" she asked as Nellie sat beside her.

"I've slept more in the last few days than I did for ten years."

"Has it helped your pain?"

"Some, but I'll need more injections if I'm to feel normal again."

"What are they?"

"Monoclonal antibodies." She paused. "Don't ask where they get them."

"I think I can guess."

Nellie's eyes found the distant mountains as her shoulders slumped.

Vickie lightly rubbed her neck. "Cheer up."

"Why? I'm never going to be the same, and you know it." Her voice was cold and exact and tragically honest.

"No," Vickie said. "But you'll be better inside, where it counts."

"You'll soon grow tired of me."

Vickie sat up straight and wrapped her arms around Nellie. "Honey, I meant what I said. You will live here with me forever."

Nellie shuddered into Vickie's embrace and wept into her blouse. "The cabal took me from the only home I'd ever known and trained me to hate you and to destroy your career, which I did with relish."

Vickie drew back from her and cast a confused expression. "Was it so easy to hate someone you didn't know?"

"You have no idea."

Vickie sighed, and her eyes followed Nellie's to the horizon. "All right, then tell me why, so I can stop being so confused."

"I'm not ready to talk about why, so instead I'll tell you about my adopted parents." Nellie hesitated. "I was a sick child from birth, and my parents didn't want me, so William and Nancy Michaels took me and loved me and provided medical care from the start, which went on for years. You cannot imagine the number of surgeries I've endured to look like this, especially in the face and neck, and even so, the injections are required to keep me from looking forty years older than I am. My skin scars and burns and peels without those shots, and the pain is so intense I cry out both day and night. There is no refuge from my misery."

Vickie squeezed her arm gently and with feeling. "I can't imagine what you've been through, but I'd like to help."

Nellie considered. "The others don't seem to want me here, which I understand."

"They will in time. I'll let you in on a little secret. When I first arrived, no one wanted me here, either, not even Katie and Abbie."

"Katie must have, since she called Mitch and got you fired."

"Yes, but she was standoffish and rude, and sometimes she's still that way to me, even though I've tried to show her and Abbie love. Eudora was angry over past hurts, and John assumed I'd leave within two weeks."

Nellie looked at her in wonder, as if she was an ever-changing puzzle. "Ironic you're still here, and he's leaving town."

"I'd like to stop him, but I don't know how."

Vickie conjured a picturesque shipwreck in her mind, one which would land them as a couple on a deserted island in the Pacific, the kind with sparse sailing traffic, forcing them to work through their problems.

"Did he give you a reason?" Nellie's voice rose with the question.

"He thinks I'm withholding the truth from him, which I am."

Nellie's eyes raked over her in blunt condemnation. "About your abortion?"

Vickie accepted the implied rebuke, as Nellie's mother had thrown her away the same as Vickie discarded Chelsea, and it was only fair to resent any mother tormenting her child. But what she didn't realize, and what Vickie wouldn't share, at least not today, is that her own mother did the same. Only Valerie aborted herself, which was worse, as her abused and neglected daughter would chase her approval to the grave.

Nellie's thin fingers tensed in her lap, and it seemed her dismay grew worse without an answer, so Vickie left behind her recollections.

"John knows I had one when I was eighteen, thanks to Leslie."

"But it's not the whole story?"

Vickie took a heavy breath and exhaled. "He doesn't know Chelsea was his child."

Nellie seemed distressed by the grim revelation, and her already pallid face went completely ashen. Her chin jutted, and her fingers clutched the arm and the seat. She drew back from Vickie, pushing into the corner of the glider like a small child escaping a wild beast, which is exactly how Vickie saw herself. It was all the worse knowing her new friend saw her in such an unsympathetic light.

"Will he accept you once he knows?"

"No, I think he'll disappear and never come back again."

"Then it's critical you tell him before he leaves Addison."

"Why? He's going regardless, so what's the point?"

"You know why, Vickie. Be honest with him."

Vickie chuckled sarcastically. "My father would agree."

"So will you do it?" Nellie hesitated. "Please say you will."

"If it means that much to you, come with me."

Nellie's eyebrows arched. "Me?"

"I'd like the moral support, if you're up to it."

Nellie glanced at the door, as if expecting someone to come outside at any moment. She gestured sharply. "What about your family?"

Vickie sighed. "They're caught up with Price's recovery."

"Shouldn't you be? I thought you two were on good terms."

"I suppose we are, but I feel like I let him down."

"Because you left for a tour of Planar?"

Vickie nodded.

"But you rescued me from certain death. What have you told him?"

"He only knows you came home with me after losing your job and you're sick with some kind of disorder. Otherwise, he thinks you're the same woman who outed me on national television." A pause. "There's more to it, as my unwillingness to tell John the truth of my abortion has weighed on him, along with our disagreement over Leslie as a remnant Rephaim." She released her frustration with a sigh and gazed at the road.

"I think you should have a long talk with Price and let him know what we've seen and what you did for me in that chamber in New York." Nellie seemed dejected as she turned to Vickie and made eye contact. "Maybe he and the others would accept me if you did."

"I will after the holiday. Tomorrow is the Fourth of July, and I've planned something special. We'll have a picnic at the falls, and in the evening we'll go downtown and watch the fireworks at the fairgrounds."

"You won't miss your chance with John?"

"He has many admirers in Addison, and he'll want to say goodbye to them before he leaves. We'll probably run into him."

Nellie reflected on the opportunity and then smiled. "I'll do my best to keep up with you, but without my injections, I can't promise much." Her eyes welled. "There's more I wish to say."

"I know, honey, but wait until you're stronger."

"The hour might arrive sooner than you think, but rest assured, Vickie, you won't be equipped for my tale. It's an impossibility."

Vickie saddled Nellie on Dash, as he was the easiest horse at Bluecreek. She had made a promise to Price, which she disregarded after his heart attack, so to ease her feelings of daughterly betrayal, she took Ocean, the distant mare her father wished to train for Eudora but now could not.

They reached the gate, and the early damp gave way to warmth. The air about them grew humid but golden. Vickie rubbed her hand along Ocean's neck, soothing the mare as they passed through. She listened to the crickets in the grass and the birds in the trees on each side of the trail, who warned them of a beastly presence, but Jesus called her into the light, her days of mourning having ended. Only He could evict the descended Lilith from her flesh and return her to the foot of the cross, and so she went forth as both servant and sword-bearer.

Nellie struggled to stay in her saddle, which worried Vickie, but she said little other than to pass the time and cheer her prodigal companion.

She dismounted at the high bank over the creek, glad to be near water, and led Nellie down the steepness to the falls, where they stood behind the onrush, entranced by its majesty and the mist of the air and the coolness on their skin. Vickie reached out and touched the water and brought some to her face, and Nellie mimicked her movements.

"This place is amazing," she said.

"I thought so when John brought me here."

"Hadn't you been here as a girl?"

Vickie nodded. "Those memories had long since faded, but he rekindled them."

"I wish someone would do that for me."

Vickie squeezed her arm. "I'm trying, honey."

Nellie gave her a sullen look. "I know, and I'm sorry for being sad."

"It will work out." Vickie splashed more water. "You'll see."

"I wouldn't be so sure if I were you."

"What does that mean?"

"The Consortium will kill everyone around you to make a point."

Katie and Abbie were two innocents, caught up in a dark intrigue.

Vickie longed for the love of her life, as he handled himself well in a crisis, and his rough and bold touch elevated the fervor of her resolve.

She left Nellie alone and went up to the horses and gave them each a pail. Then she brought down the food. On the way, she spotted the mama bear with her two cubs, and her feet stopped on the trail.

The mama stood and made eye contact, and Vickie returned her gaze. The bear turned with her cubs and continued along the creek.

As Vickie descended, she beamed, and her heart gladdened at the exchange. Once she had been afraid, but now she was fearless.

She reached the spot behind the water and looked for Nellie, assuming she had continued around the bend to the other side of the creek, but then she heard a whimper and looked to her left. Nellie had hidden herself within a crevice which extended twenty feet into the rock at ground level. Vickie dropped the basket and kneeled at the opening and beckoned her out, but Nellie curled herself into a ball and would not budge, so she crawled on her knees and rubbed Nellie's arms and spoke soothingly to her. She braced a shoulder against the low ceiling and tugged on Nellie's arm, and a rock shifted above her as she pushed against it. Her curious eyes searched in the dim light, and then her fingers picked at the outline of the rock, loosening it from its position.

It dropped and thudded on the hard ground, which frightened Nellie and sent her scampering for the opening. Vickie remained behind and peered into the nebulous hole but saw only murk, so she returned the rock to its sculpted position. She crawled to her companion and said they should head back home and shower and rest for the evening.

As they climbed to the horses at the top of the falls, Nellie stopped to catch her breath, and her eyes swept over the beautiful gorge.

"I love this place, although it scares me," she said.

Vickie turned. "I'm sorry, honey. I underestimated your fear."

"How could you know? I was a ruthless lion as your protégée."

"Did the injections make such a difference?"

"Yes, they affected me physically and emotionally, and when I look back, even spiritually. When I took them, I was filled with hatred."

Vickie reflected. "Perhaps it's the nefarious source that caused your fury."

Nellie's eyes moistened. "To think I benefited sickens me."

Vickie nodded and spoke with a melancholy bitterness. "And knowing I caused some part of it makes me want to die."

She took the waif's hand and kissed it, and the pair climbed the hill.

At the top, Nellie turned to her with a grim countenance. "Have you figured out my identity, who I am to you?"

"I think so, but I'm not ready to say." She looked about as Nellie had done, bridling her emotions. "It's unbearable to contemplate."

"It was harder to live." She wiped her eyes. "I hurt."

Vickie pressed onward to her horse, one foot before the other, suppressing an urge to fling herself over the ledge and onto the rocks. Once Nellie spoke the words aloud, they would ring authentic, and there in that instant, all life on earth would end, as there could be no further acceptance, no rolling up the sleeves and getting to work, no archaic and unhelpful tradition to carry one through. Only a fall into the gutter and the scrounge for clay and worms and darkness, and the slashing of the Reaper's scythe across her neck would suffice, as a mother who murders her child knows well, and she counts the seconds until death.

<hr>

At the fairgrounds, people gathered and mingled and waited, eyes alternating between the night sky and one another, and smiles abounded. The light show began with a dazzle and a spark and expanded into a crescendo, which transfixed the focus to the blues and oranges and reds and the offshoots which went in every direction and the sound which reverberated off the tin roofs of the wooden sheds nearby. Vickie held Nellie's hand gently so as not to hurt her delicate bones, which had decayed, but it was little matter on this wondrous night when a love might be reborn between teacher and pupil.

Her eyes found John in the crowd, and her heart melted. She longed to run to him and beg him to love her for the rest of their lives.

Rachel Daniels stepped into the frame, sinking Vickie's hope. She laughed with a cheerful delight, and at first glance Vickie knew she was now in his life in some fractious capacity, and so she hated her with the fervent passion of a thousand suns. Her entities stirred, and she wanted to run at Rachel and bash her teeth with a lead pipe.

When he noticed Vickie, his lips twisted thinly into a smile. He nodded faintly, and his eyes flickered nonchalantly while inside her heart was breaking under the immense pressure of their separation. It was then he turned from her and walked away with odious Rachel.

As if a character in a masochistic play, Missy approached with fire in her eyes and a stern rebuke in her bearing, and Vickie braced for impact.

"I want you to know something, Miss High and Mighty." She eyed Nellie, who shifted her weight, partially because of fear but also from pain, and Vickie calculated the distance to the car. "Are you listening?"

Vickie nodded, unwilling to offer Missy a verbal response.

"You were supposed to go with me when I checked on the neglected horse, remember? Well, you didn't, and so you lost the lesson because the horse couldn't take any food and I had to put him down." She let the words register. "You've been missing in action ever since you returned from New York with this monster." Missy gestured at Nellie. "It's one thing to avoid your father, as he has Eudora, and I hear you two were fighting when his heart gave out, but you will not abandon those girls."

"I know, and you're right, but I've had, "

Missy put up a palm. "I don't want your excuses."

"All right."

She eyed Vickie like a criminal. "I hear from John you had an abortion."

Vickie traded an awkward glance with Nellie. "Yes, but it happened a long time ago."

"What you did blows my mind, Vickie. I had a miscarriage after working on our nursery for months, and I would give my life to bring a child into this world, but the Lord, in His wisdom, took my baby." She wiped her eyes and cleared her throat. "Anyway, I know why you're so worked up over this wretch, and I must say it sickens me to watch."

Nellie would not let this woman put her down any further. "I may be a wretch, as you say, but I'm no girl," she said.

"I don't care if you're the president. You're nothing to me."

Nellie looked away and said, "Fine."

Missy returned to Vickie. "You want to know the way I see it?"

"Of course, Missy. I've always valued your opinion."

"Here it is, and I doubt you'll like it." She crossed her arms. "You got careless and messed up with that young girl, Helen Dunstan, the one who killed herself in her car, and now you want a shot at redemption."

Vickie sighed. "Maybe that's where it started, but not anymore."

"What then? Why do you care so much about her?" Missy quickly continued. "You have two girls tonight who need a mother."

"I know they do, and I want to be that for them eventually, but, "

"Eventually? What are you talking about? The time is now!"

Vickie thought Missy might hit her, as her cheeks burned red.

Missy pointed a finger as her annoyance boiled into rage. "I'm only going to say this once, so you'd better listen good. If you don't drop what you're doing and attend to your family, you will lose them forever, and then it will be time for the great Victoria Morrison to leave this little town, which is filled with good folks who are already wondering why John feels he must leave us rather than you."

Missy wheeled and stomped through the crowd to Lee, who took her arm and led her to the car as he chided her for such an outburst.

They made a good couple, and Vickie thought they should try again, as a baby with an innocent grin and a powdery smell might take the sting out of Missy's miscarriage. At least those two had the option.

"I'm sorry," Vickie said. "She gets excited sometimes."

"Was she correct? Am I just another Helen Dunstan?"

"You and Mitch tried to ruin me, so I was angry with you both for a while, but then my life changed for the better after I spent time here in Addison and with the girls and the horses, and obviously with John."

"It doesn't explain your interest or why you saved me."

"I felt a connection to you for years," said Vickie reticently.

"Why?"

"I wanted to see it as helping an intern the way Lena helped me."

"Was there more to it?" Nellie tugged her sleeve. "Please say yes."

"Yes, you rooted more deeply into my psyche from the start." Vickie looked about as the tears formed. "A mother knows her own child."

"Then stop playing games and tell me about your abortion."

Vickie took a step back. "You ask too much, Nellie."

The crowd dispersed, and Nellie went to a bench and sat. "I need to hear the details," she said.

Vickie stroked her leg so as not to hurt her. "Okay."

She took a gulp of breath and blurted her first sentence. "I was told I was the product of rape at eighteen, and it helped explain why my mother hated me so much and why she killed herself rather than raise me as her daughter. It was then I learned my father was in prison for his second twenty-year stint, and the man I thought was my father was just a mean man who blamed me for everything which had gone wrong." She caught her breath and continued. "I took a bottle of pills and almost died from the overdose, and when I got out of the hospital, I ran to the summer camp where John worked as a counselor. I took a horse out to the overnight camping area and slept with him in his tent. It was the best night of my life." She reflected on their moment of bliss, and a deep peace washed over her. "Anyway, he was with a girl named Carlie, and I assumed he wouldn't lower himself to date me, even after we shared a special night together." Vickie hesitated. "His father, Garrett, wouldn't let him see me in high school, so it wasn't a ridiculous assertion, and, as I said, he had a girlfriend."

"I understand, Vickie. You were in a painful situation."

"D.C. seemed like the answer, but it was worse as I was under the gun and worked constantly as Lena's intern, and I thought of Mitch and Logan as newfound brothers, but then Logan raped me after a harmless date." She fell mute as the words formed in the air which did not wish to be said, but she must speak them aloud or there could be no more hope. "The rape happened just after I learned I was pregnant with you."

Nellie's eyes teared. "You finally see me as your daughter?"

"I do, but I don't understand how you survived."

She leaned over and stroked Nellie's hair as tenderly as possible. "Honey, how did you live after the delivery? The doctor came out to the room where I laid in sweat and blood. He told me you were dead."

"How would I know such a thing? I was a little baby."

Vickie gasped at the portrait. Her hand covered her mouth.

Nellie considered for several moments. "Logan raped you twice?"

Vickie tensed at the memory. "Yes, he did."

Her heart hammered against her ribs. She thought she might faint.

"I'm amazed," said Nellie simply. "And I'm sorry."

"For what, honey?" The apology took Vickie aback a little.

"I should have died like you wished. It would've made things easier."

Vickie wrapped her arms around Nellie and wept, but she would not let herself fall apart as she must hold strong for her daughter's sake. Nellie was frail of mind and body, and she might finish what Vickie had started. The notion was unfathomable, and so she held her dearly.

She kissed her child's forehead for the first time and then drew back from her and spoke lovingly. "We should go home so you can rest."

After putting Nellie to bed, she went to her bedroom and opened her Bible and read Psalm 61:1-4. "O God, listen to my cry! Hear my prayer! From the ends of the earth, I cry to you for help when my heart is overwhelmed. Lead me to the towering rock of safety, for you are my safe refuge, a fortress where my enemies cannot reach me. Let me live forever in your sanctuary, safe beneath the shelter of your wings!"

Vickie closed her father's Bible and curled into a ball and wailed into her pillow, unable to stop herself from shuddering and shaking.

There was little good about her as her path had run straight toward fortune and glory, and a sea of misery surrounded her. She saw the ceiling bubble, and an entity appeared, sneering and grinning with pride, and she knew Lilith would descend once more and take up residence.

John was right to leave her. She was vile and wicked and treacherous.

The door cracked, and Abbie stuck her head inside the room. Her eyes rose to the ceiling, and the bubbling intensified. She rushed to Vickie and touched her arm.

"Are you okay?"

Vickie rolled, and the girl's innocent eyes, which had widened in terror, told her she was bound to a foul demon, and the revelation sent her reeling once more, as it's what she had always known about herself.

Abbie left the room. Her feet padded down the hall.

In a few moments, Katie trailed Abbie to the bed. "What's going on here?"

She shook Vickie with measured force. "Please get up and talk to us."

Katie's words broke over Vickie, and she wailed more loudly.

Abbie shut the door so as not to alarm the entire house.

Katie seemed unable to see the demon as she climbed beside Vickie and chided her for scaring them and told her with authority to get herself out of bed, but her rebuke changed little in Vickie's disposition, as her entities stirred, readying themselves for animation. A radiant light appeared at the ceiling and a red mist formed on the floor, and Vickie feared herself as all voices dissipated into oblivion along with her will.

Vickie hugged the pillow and thought of Raul in the underworld, and she hoped to join him so they might wallow in their sorrows. Abbie tugged on Katie's sleeve and begged her to do something fast.

Katie picked up Vickie's Bible and removed the bookmark. She read verses 5-8, and her voice raised as she went. "For you have heard my vows, O God. You have given me an inheritance reserved for those who fear your name. Add many years to the life of the king! May his years span the generations! May he reign under God's protection forever. May your unfailing love and faithfulness watch over him. Then I will sing praises to your name forever as I fulfill my vows each day."

The teen begged Vickie to cheer up, but she could not.

Katie read the Lord's Prayer from Matthew 6:9-13. "Our Father in heaven, may your name be kept holy. May your Kingdom come soon. May your will be done on earth, as it is in heaven. Give us today the food we need, and forgive us our sins, as we have forgiven those who sin against us. And don't let us yield to temptation, but rescue us from the evil one." The words of Jesus cast the demon from their midst, quieting the room as God's grace enveloped them, warding off unwieldy spirits.

Vickie sat up and wiped her eyes and her nose. She held out her arms, and Abbie climbed onto the bed and fell hard against her in love and desperation. Vickie hugged both girls tighter than she thought healthy, but it didn't matter because they were hers and always would be, and for that she was grateful to the Most High.

Twenty-Two

Psalm 62:1

I wait quietly before God,
for my victory comes from him.

Valerie drove erratically in the dream, weaving in and out of traffic while in Addison and then edging to the shoulder on the outskirts. She waved her right hand as she jeered at her daughter, who sat cornered against the passenger door. Trees and weeds and asphalt whizzed by at speed, and then suddenly Valerie stopped the station wagon and wobbled around the hood in flailing intoxication before ripping open her child's door. Her ravenous fingers dug into Vickie's scalp as she dragged her from the hot and sticky seat to the pavement, where the tiny bits of gravel dug into Vickie's tender skin, lacerating her in places. She dropped her daughter like unworthy refuse and stood over her in rough bitterness, then left the great Victoria Morrison alone to decipher her path without the confidence of a mother's love.

Vickie startled awake in sweat and tears, knowing she had done much the same to her own daughter and that for it she must pay a heavy cost. She went to the kitchen and poured a glass from their well. The clean, pure water made her feel physically better but did little to lighten her mood as her emotions ran rampant. A paralyzing anxiety gripped her, and she instinctively looked at the ceiling but saw no spirits gathered there. She returned to her room and sat on the edge of her bed, attempting to blank the grim portraits from her mind.

She tossed and turned for the next half hour, her neck hurting against the stack of tall pillows, which for some inexplicable reason she insisted must remain, even though their height proved burdensome every night. Vickie checked the clock whose face proved an enemy, as the hands pointed to two o'clock and the witching hour approached.

She was a mother to her sister's two orphans and to a daughter she had vowed to destroy. Nellie once wished her dead, on the face of cable news if not in actuality, and the shift in family allegiances over the next few weeks would prove as erratic as Valerie's driving on a summer day. Just as when she was a girl, Vickie alone must discern a path forward. She flung back the covers, dressed, and descended the stairs.

On the porch, she sat on the glider with a flashlight at her side and slipped on her boots. The night was cool and wet, the crickets chirped in the grass, and the birds were silent in their perches.

In the barn, she rubbed the leather of Michele's saddle and thought of her accident, her paralysis, and her death after a year. Abbie must have thrown her hand to her mouth as she gasped at her mother's condition, and Red must have assured them he would make things right when there was no affecting such an outcome. Katie must have known her world had turned upside down, clever as she was. Red had a wickedness about him, and he might have killed Vickie if she exposed him to unwanted scrutiny. His contacts likely covered up his crimes, but he seemed repentant in the eyes of Sturgis Faulkner, who lamented the loss of a friend and cohort. Perhaps it meant Red had turned to the Lord on the eve of his death, and the notion restored a last remnant of hope as Vickie's mind shifted its attention to the curious rock at the falls.

She pulled Chief from his stall and placed a pad and then Michelle's saddle. As disfigured misfits, it was high time the world saw them for who they were, and she would shine Michelle's light evermore as Missy demanded. Horse and rider drifted through the gate, and she considered the old man and his neglected horse. She understood all too well her own selfishness. Vickie would do better and try harder, and others would see how much she cared. The news received on her eighteenth birthday had ruined her youthful spirit, as it confirmed all she had ever known about herself, the mistake who should have never been born. It was the same feeling now shared by Nellie, her beloved daughter returned.

Katie felt the same, and the burden erected heavy defenses against the world, as a fortified heart protected against shame and fear.

Soon Abbie would do likewise, and the notion broke over Vickie as she neared the falls, along with a fiery determination to help.

She soothed Chief and tied him with a slipknot, then descended the steep decline with flashlight steady in hand. Once behind the rush of water, she crawled into the crevice and pried out the sculpted rock.

As before, it fell with a thud. Without allowing herself a moment's hesitation, she reached into the gloom. Her fingers felt a tight edge, and her mind discerned it to be paper, then an envelope. She retrieved it and dropped it beside her, then felt again and found a burlap sack deeper in. Her hand snagged the bag and dragged it against the edge of the abyss. Her hands trembled as she pulled the string and opened the sack. Inside, she discovered a bottle which contained a reddish liquid. Vickie wasted little time and opened the envelope and read the letter it contained, which was from Red as she had suspected. His words were a salve for her wounds which had never healed, as he offered his sincere apology for his malevolence, both toward her and Michelle, whom he wronged to an unimaginable degree. He said they parted as father and daughter upon her death, as she found the courage to forgive him at her agonizing but heartfelt end.

He would not let the Consortium have Abbie, as he loved her and Katie dearly and wished to do right by them in ways he could not with his own two daughters. He begged Vickie's forgiveness and said the cylindrical bottle contained an elixir formulated against the parasites, and once consumed, they would trouble her no more. Without a thought or a care, she removed the top and downed the liquid, then pressed her back into the rock wall behind her, her palms pushing against the ground. Soon a great pain washed over her, and she convulsed and grew fearful. She crawled toward the opening, but the parasites within her cried out in torment, and then she stopped and vomited a batch from her body. The parasites glowed, lighting her face and the tiny cavern and the falls which sparkled and crackled and spoke the voices of a thousand years, captured within and without, unutterable until now.

The light dimmed, and the parasites disappeared.

Vickie was now exhausted, so she crawled back to her spot near the hole where her adopted father had secured her future, along with his own destruction. More comforted than ever before, Vickie slept.

Vickie returned home the next morning and led Chief to the side yard, where she gave him hay from a round bale that had arrived the previous week. Contentment found her as she watched him eat, and for the first time, she saw herself as a horsewoman. She turned toward the house and, to her surprise, saw a car parked in the driveway. Out stepped Leslie Carter. Without her father's Bible, Vickie felt helpless.

She steeled herself and marched to the porch, bypassing Leslie.

Her nemesis followed, and Vickie didn't bother to leave the door open but let it slam. Leslie caught the door and continued her vigorous pursuit. Unsure of the right path, Vickie went for the loaded rifle. She took it down from the mantle and pointed it at Leslie.

"John isn't here, so we have no business," she said.

A sinister beam passed between them, as if Leslie probed Vickie's insides, searching for what she knew to be there but could little detect.

"They're gone," said Vickie loftily.

"How so?" Leslie threw her an arching look.

"Red left me a letter and an antidote to your poisons."

"Did his weak missive plead for your forgiveness?"

"Yes, but his message was heartfelt rather than cynical."

"Frame it however you like. He was your father, not mine."

"No, he wasn't, but he was a man who repented in the end."

"Why follow his example when we offer so much more?"

"Which example, Leslie? The one where you murder for sport?"

Leslie grinned, and her eyes flashed restlessly, preparing for an attack.

"An invocation of Christ's name is no free pass through this world."

"Perhaps not, but it is a place to begin, and I will follow His perfect example and accept His death on the Cross for my sins."

Leslie considered.

"You may lower your weapon. My appearance has not changed, and I have no intention of ripping out your throat, if that's your concern."

Vickie complied, as the rifle had grown heavy in her arms.

"I should warn you, Vickie, if you shoot me and I die here today, I will become more powerful than you can imagine, as I will transmute into a disembodied spirit who roams the land in search of a new body. You might have a care, as yours could be the one I choose, or perhaps young Abbie." Her eyes turned yellow as they again probed for clues. "I see you've told your daughter the truth about her identity."

"Yes, it was time. Sturgis expected me to end her life in New York."

"You did not follow instructions, which is a pity, as it would have been just the initiation you needed to join our order, and I would have been forced to give John over to you, much to my consternation."

"He is leaving town, so have at him. I'm sure you will try."

"My time with him is over. Lucifer will soon send another."

Vickie reflected on Leslie's words; a name popped into her head. "Rachel Daniels?"

"A journalist to the end and a good one, if I might say so."

Vickie raised the rifle. "Why are you here, Leslie?"

"Alas, to say goodbye. My campaign will shift into another gear over the coming months, and I will introduce a new lover to the world."

"New?"

"I must have something to show for my trouble, don't you think?"

"You say it like you and John were once lovers."

"Did he say otherwise?" Leslie's voice was monotone and superior.

"You know he did. Stop playing games and leave."

Leslie's eyebrows arched, and she shrugged in amusement.

"It would seem John is the game player here, not me."

She paused.

"Why do you think I fell so hard for him? For his country charm?"

"I had hoped so, and it's what he said to me."

Leslie turned and headed for the door, then wheeled around.

"You fill your world with lies and liars, Vickie, but I will set you straight once and for all, and you should listen to my words because they will impact your life." A pause for effect. "John and I shared passionate encounters, and as I am a Rephaim, our lovemaking infected him, and he will never be the same man you once knew, even though he's tried hard to find him. But once DNA is changed, it does not suddenly revert."

"Are you saying he's now like you, a Rephaim?"

"Not exactly like me, but he is no longer fully human."

"What does that mean for him? And for us?"

"Once he leaves here and searches within himself, he will access more of his brain than he knew possible, and he will grow stronger and perform tasks with greater ease and efficiency than other men."

Vickie took a seat at the table and set the rifle on the floor.

"What did you do to him, Leslie? He was perfect as he was."

"Far from it, which is why he hid his time with me, as I'm sure he hoped to find himself within your relationship, and it's why I left."

"You knew he wouldn't," said Vickie flatly.

"He couldn't. His DNA is no longer the same."

Vickie put her head in her hands and wept.

When she looked up again, Leslie Carter was gone.

In the evening, Vickie slipped outside and eased across the grass, hoping to leave before anyone detected her exit, but Nellie had watched from a window and rushed after her, begging her to ride along. She knew where Vickie must go next and wouldn't allow her to go alone.

They exchanged few words on the highway, and soon Vickie's Ford Expedition entered John's driveway and parked behind his Silverado.

She gave Nellie a hopeful look. "Here goes nothing."

"Good luck."

Vickie took her daughter's encouragement and marched steadfastly to the door and rang the bell. Her anxiety spiked and her heart raced.

He opened the door and threw her a scowl.

"Yeah?"

"Could I come inside? I need to talk to you."

He glanced over his shoulder. "Now?"

Vickie could hardly stand the sight of him without falling apart.

She nodded. "It won't take very long."

"Fine." He flung open the door and stepped aside.

Boxes sat atop other boxes, and clothes piled themselves on the table.

"Are you going somewhere?"

He sneered at her. "You know I am."

"But when?"

"Tomorrow, if you must know."

She looked about, and her eyes grew moist.

"Are you selling your house?"

He nodded.

Tears flowed, and she wiped them, as she didn't want to break down so soon, but the finality of his tone was too much to withstand.

"Have you sold Garrett's house?"

"And his company." He surveyed his surroundings. "Soon this will be gone, and I won't have any ties left in Addison. Bet you'll be happy."

"No, I won't, John. I wish you would stay and fight for me."

He sat on the couch with his hands on his knees and grunted at her.

"It's too late for all that, Vickie. We had a chance, but it's gone."

"There are things you don't know. Things I'd like to say."

He held up a palm.

"Save your breath. Leslie stopped by here earlier."

"Did she tell you we talked?"

"Of course. Now you'll scream at me and call me a liar, right?"

Vickie paced for several moments and then knelt in front of him.

She put her hands on his and gently squeezed.

"Why did you say you never slept with her?"

"Because you wouldn't understand the pressure I was under to conform to a wealthy woman's expectations, not to mention Roland's, which were crushing to a country farrier who comes from nothing." He sat back and settled on the couch. "Garrett's company made money the last ten years or so, but for a long time, we were broke. It was hard."

"And then she showed up and demanded you come with her."

"When her dealings with the cabal came to light, I ended it."

"She changed you, John. You aren't the same man I used to know."

"Which is why I'm leaving town, and it's why we're through."

Vickie paced again. "Then why lead me on?"

"Because I wanted it to work as you did, but I've grown tired of the lies, both on my end and yours. It seems all we have are half-truths."

Vickie took a seat in a chair opposite him. "It's why I'm here."

"You want there to be honesty between us?"

She closed her eyes, feeling utterly miserable, and reopened them.

"Yes, now and forever."

"Then tell me about Raul, what he meant to you."

The question took her aback. "Why ask about him?"

"Tell me you don't think about Raul or see him in your dreams."

The door opened and Nellie entered the foyer and stood at the edge of the living room, reticent to enter but clearly needing to participate.

"Come in, honey." Vickie pointed at the chair to her left.

"Honey?" He eyed the younger woman with suspicion.

"It's a long story, but I intend to help her."

He sneered at Nellie for several moments, and her face reddened. "Whatever."

He gestured. "You were saying."

"I see Raul in my nightmares. It's not a happy portrait."

"It proves one thing, Vickie. You save your love for wicked men."

He spoke so viciously. How could she ever think him decent?

"Wicked like you are now?" she asked, shifting blame to him.

"I suppose, but I wasn't always this way, and you gave me up."

Her mouth opened in dismay, as he should be over her betrayal.

"I came home, John, and I've loved you every day since."

"And when I argued with your father, you told me to leave."

Vickie grunted. "That's unfair. I was mortified by what you said."

He turned to Nellie. "Why exactly are you here?"

His countenance was grim as he confronted the former nemesis, and whatever spark of hope remained inside Vickie extinguished. Her only clear course was to save her daughter from the lies of the past and give her a sense of dignity in the present. "John, you should know she's, "

Nellie waved off her mother, unwilling to go there.

"I'm here for moral support," she said with pained authority.

"Is what Vickie has to tell me so horrible?"

"Yes, I believe it is. For you, anyway."

"Fine, then let's get on with it." He turned to Vickie. "Go."

She grew flustered and fidgeted. "You're putting me on the spot."

He stood. "Look, I have things to do before I head out, so, "

"I aborted our baby when I was eighteen!"

She blurted the words and then covered her mouth.

John's probing eyes searched Vickie. Her head dropped in shame.

"What did you just say?"

"You heard her," said Nellie with feeling.

His eyes flickered, but he withheld a response.

Vickie stifled a mournful howl that arose in her throat. She repeated what she had said. "I aborted our baby when I was eighteen."

"I don't believe you. It was a guy from a bar."

"It's true, John." She choked back her tears.

"Logan took me to the clinic, and I went through with it. There were all these other girls waiting in a big room for the saline to take effect, and I waited with them, but then I went into labor and delivered right there on the covers. Someone went for the doctor, and he took her away from me, and when he came back again, he said she was dead."

She turned to Nellie. "I'm sorry you have to hear this."

"She is a grown woman," he said in a bark, "and she's seen worse."

"Yes, she has." Vickie's voice trailed as she nodded her agreement.

Nellie found the strength and the courage to stand.

"Do you love her, John?"

He fumed at Vickie and paced, refusing to answer the interloper.

"I asked you a question. Do you love this woman?"

"What does it matter, Nellie? She killed our child!"

"Vickie is relatively young. You could try again."

His hands wrapped around his head as he shook off her words.

"No! No! This cannot be happening," he said tearfully.

He turned to Vickie. "You really did this to us? To me?"

Vickie nodded, and her eyes found the floor again.

"I hoped for a moment our child might live. I named her Chelsea."

"But she didn't live, now did she, because you killed her!"

"Yes, and ever since that terrible mistake, I've found it difficult to breathe, and I wish every day for death, but he won't come for me."

"Who won't come for you, Vickie?"

"The Reaper."

"Just great!" He threw up his hands. "Now you've lost your mind."

A sensation of intense sickness swept over her, and the torment of their reunion and her father's heart attack and the pressure to raise Michelle's daughters and her own daughter's return overwhelmed her.

"If you leave now, I will lose my sanity, just like Nicole."

He grabbed a pillow and almost hurled it but stopped himself.

"That's a low blow, even from you!"

"I'm not being mean," she said, "and I'm not kidding."

He squeezed the pillow hard and let out a wild yell.

She covered her ears as the worst would come next.

"I hope you die, Vickie, and as soon as possible."

"That's a terrible thing to say." Nellie glared at him.

He turned to her. "Oh, really?"

He seemed to take pleasure in the younger woman's challenge.

"Vickie deserves credit for being sincere with you, John."

"Nellie, you're a jealous failure who enjoys ruining lives because you can't stomach being front and center. Make trouble somewhere else."

He pointed at the door. "Get out, the both of you!"

"Please don't." Vickie swallowed her sobs. "There's more."

Nellie stood. "No, Vickie. It's time we left him alone."

She took her mother's hand and helped her to her feet.

The two women made eye contact, and Nellie shook her head.

She whispered into Vickie's ear. "Don't say anything else."

Vickie reached out her hand to John, but he turned his back.

"What will you do when you leave us? Will you marry Leslie?"

"Whatever I do, it will be for me and no one else," he said.

Nellie squeezed her mother's arm. "We've said enough. Let's go."

Vickie cried out in torment. "Please, John. I love you!"

He wheeled, and his voice took on a sinister tone.

"I don't love you, so get out of here and take her with you!"

His last words broke Vickie's soul into a million tiny pieces, and her form crumpled into a mess. Nellie helped her to the car as best she could, but there would be no tomorrow, as the Reaper approached.

As the Expedition rolled along country roads, Nellie wept in the passenger seat. Vickie's eyes darted to her, but she kept her own distress bottled, as the first word uttered in agony would unleash a flood.

"He will never want me." Nellie choked out the words.

"You don't know that, honey. Give him time."

"There's too much water under the bridge." Nellie clutched at the window as if trapped in a grievous cage. "It will be too shocking."

Vickie gently squeezed Nellie's leg. "Please don't give up."

"Don't you understand? I've waited a lifetime for my father."

"You have my love, Nellie. Can it be enough to fill the void?"

Nellie's eyebrows arched. "Doubtful."

"Why not? Am I not giving you what you need?"

"You tried to end my life, Vickie. I can forgive, but never forget."

The wintry knowledge twisted inside her, and she felt a remnant of parasites burn and toss and tug at her, desperate to gain firmer ground, striking at her with chilly, faint glimmers of injustice, mostly incurred by her against others. They screamed foul obscenities, accusing her of murderous intent, even now, many years later.

"John would have raised me as his daughter, and you know it."

Vickie's fingers latched onto the wheel, which she gripped for dear life, knowing her daughter's words were the truest she'd ever heard.

A truck eased beside them, and at first Vickie thought it might be John. Her spirits lifted, if only for the briefest of moments, but then she realized it was a stranger who glowered at her as if he wanted her dead.

His steering wheel turned sharply, and his truck powered into their lane. Vickie swerved to her right and almost ran off the road and down an embankment, but she wrested control and pulled over as the truck disappeared around a bend in the road, leaving them once more alone.

"Oh, God, please take my life! I cannot handle this world!"

Vickie flung open her door and stumbled to a rock wall, where she threw up against it. The vomit splattered all over her jeans and boots.

Her eyes rose to the heavens. "I'm a lost sinner, Lord Jesus!"

Nellie followed her in the darkness and hugged her tightly, begging her not to do anything drastic, as she needed her mother.

"What can I do to help you?" she asked tearfully.

Vickie shook her head. "I don't know."

She looked at the sky and begged the Lord to forgive her. She said the Lord's Prayer and asked Jesus to be her eternal Savior. She repented of her sins and asked Yahweh to remove any unclean spirits who were within or without and to send them to the abyss. She asked God to fill her with the Holy Spirit and to heal her.

Her gut rumbled and then burned again, and she fell to the rock and vomited. This time she shivered with a glorious and joyful release.

Another pile of parasites glowed, illuminating their faces.

When they reached Bluecreek, Price stepped to the porch, accompanied by Eudora, who held his arm and wore a scowl on her face that matched his. Nellie helped Vickie from the Expedition, and father and daughter looked one another up and down, discerning the other's wretchedness, knowing with certainty it was greater than their own.

"I see you have graced us with a visit," he said.

Vickie smiled at Nellie and gently broke free from her grip.

"I'm here to stay if you'll have me. I'm sorry I left your side."

"I suppose it makes us even, since I left yours as a girl."

Katie and Abbie spilled out to the porch, followed by Mitch.

"I'm glad you're all here." Vickie pointed. "Please sit for a minute."

The group complied with her wish, but Nellie stayed at her side.

Mary and Lewis turned from the road and eased up the driveway.

Vickie waited until they had parked and joined the others. Mary wore an anxious expression, and her words burst forth from her lips.

"We were almost killed in Washington!"

"What?" Mary's declaration aroused old fears and doubts in Vickie. She turned to Lewis. "Are you both alright?"

He shook his head. "Barely. They shot out our tires."

Mary could not refrain from interjecting. "We had gone to dinner and were on the way to our apartment. When the tires blew, the car swerved into a reservoir and flipped upside down. I was scared to death!"

"Is this true?" Vickie's eyes again diverted to Lewis.

"Yeah, unfortunately. Water rushed in from every angle."

"If Lewis hadn't had a tool on the glass, we would have drowned like Jessica Savitch." Mary hesitated. "Was someone sending us a message?"

Vickie glanced at Price on the porch, who sighed.

"It sounds like it," she said, placing her hand on Mary's arm.

"Are they coming to kill us? What should we do?"

"Pray for our lives," said Vickie with authority.

She looked about her and was thankful for home and family.

"From now on, we will pray our way through everything."

"Even if they come for us?" Nellie's face clouded with fear.

Vickie made direct eye contact with both women.

"Dependence on God is all we have left, which is how He likes it."

She went to the porch, hoping her brave proclamation would hold, as she was prone to worry and there were more battles to fight.

"Everyone sit. I have something to say that will shock you, but it's the best news I've ever had or ever will have, and I must share."

TWENTY-THREE

Psalm 63:6

I lie awake thinking of you,
meditating on you through the night.

Chief sauntered along the wooded trail, dutifully aligned with Vickie in resignation, as John's departure had torn a hole in her heart. Horse and rider came around a bend, and when the fork presented itself, she pushed her right leg inward and raised her left hand. Chief went left, ascending the mountain with an abnormal gait and a lack of coordination. She grew alarmed but continued higher, as the summit called her name, beckoning her forth. Vickie had to get her former flame out of her mind and focus on her family, the mountain would help her see clearly the horizon of her life.

She dismounted at the lookout near the top and let Chief graze on weeds and grass, but only after inspecting them for Johnsongrass or milkweed. She congratulated herself on her awareness of such natural poisons.

Clouds danced and looped and swirled, and a helicopter made loud noises before revealing itself, then flew on a vector toward parts unknown.

Her horse seemed unbalanced as he stood nearby, and sweat covered his coat. She rushed to Chief and asked him what might be the matter, waiting for him to tell her through their senses, bonded as they were in empathic communication. But he said little other than that he felt unwell.

She walked him down the mountain. The journey took far longer than normal, and her feet and ankles hurt. She grew thankful the path led down rather than up, in their condition, they wouldn't make it very far. She spoke soothingly to Chief, telling him all would be just fine and he shouldn't worry because Missy would be there soon. But in her own mind, she feared the message she must deliver when they arrived back at Bluecreek. She would not make the same mistake as John, rather than placing Chief in his stall, she would put him in the side yard, where he'd eaten from a bale for two weeks and seemed merry in spirit.

At the gate, his head tilted, and he stumbled. She grasped the rail. Tears coursed freely from her eyes, and she fell to her knees.

"Don't do this to me, Chief. Not now, when I'm so alone."

He shifted and leaned against the fence, and she stood quickly.

"Come on, boy." She opened the gate and led him through and into the barn, where her boot heels clicked and his hooves clopped wearily.

She pushed the slat at the end of the runway and ushered him into the side yard and over to the hay. There she asked him to eat something, anything that might reverse his weakness and send him in the right direction. But he stood there with a droopy mouth and vague lameness, and it was at this point Vickie grew terrified. She could not lose him, for if she did, it would only confirm the worst of her apprehensions.

She went to the end of the yard that faced the road, hoping for an improved signal on her phone, and fearfully rang Missy's number.

Once done, she snapped the phone shut, along with her chances.

There was the desire for a new and better reality than what she'd forged in Washington, but she killed everything she touched, it had always been the case, as her mother would testify, along with Nellie and Logan and Helen and Savannah and a host of others. She would forever be a beast. Her eyes swiveled toward Chief and, as suspected, he looked lousy. She put her hands over her eyes and uttered the awful wail she had swallowed in John's living room, and her world fell to darkness.

Missy led Chief in a circle and noted his feeble form. After several minutes of this, she sighed and unhooked his lead and stared at the bale.

"How long has this been here?"

Vickie withheld a response.

"I asked you a question." Missy pointed angrily at the hay.

Vickie took a heavy breath and exhaled, knowing she had made a mistake but unsure what it might be or how bad Chief's injury was.

"A couple of weeks, I think, but it's just a guess."

"Was it delivered while you were in New York?"

"What does it matter? Tell me if my horse will live!"

"So you realize this is serious," Missy said, "which is a start."

Vickie suppressed a sob. "Yes, of course."

"Fine. Then I will give you my diagnosis, which is preliminary, I must take blood and run it through the lab to be certain, but I've seen this before and it seems straightforward, especially with this fouled hay."

Vickie peered at the bale. "Did it rot after being outside?"

"No, but it's infested with opossum droppings."

Vickie stepped near the bale and kicked at it with her boot. Some flakes fell atop the pile that had provided nourishment for her horse.

She looked up at Missy in agitation. "Please be straight with me."

"Equine Protozoal Myeloencephalitis. That's the scientific name."

"What does it mean? Speak English."

"We call it EPM, and it causes severe debilitation and, sometimes, death." Missy let her words register. "He may have a seizure."

Vickie wheeled and threw up her hands and paced the fence line.

"That's just wonderful! I've killed the best friend I ever had!"

Missy called after her. "Yes, you may have done that very thing!"

Vickie spun around to yell an obscenity but stopped herself.

Instead, she sat against the lower section of a post and cradled her face in her hands. As her pulse beat in her throat, she shed awful tears. Missy took blood and stomped to the gate and opened it wide.

She paused. "I hope you're happy with yourself, Vickie Morrison."

Vickie's eyes rose to Chief, who stood in a wobbly manner.

"How can you say such a thing? I love him more than my life."

"You're a monster who burns those around you to a crisp!" Missy calmed herself. "Why not do all of us a favor and get out of Addison?"

Vickie grunted sorrowfully. "And go where? This is my home."

Missy's eyes flashed to the house and then back at Vickie.

"I really don't care. Anywhere but here with these good people."

She paused.

"I'll come back tonight with anti-parasite meds, and in a couple of days the lab will confirm my diagnosis. But don't worry yourself over there on the ground, because before I go, I'll stop at the house and leave instructions for Price. He and Eudora will see Chief gets what he needs, and the girls will gladly help keep your horse alive a while longer."

Vickie wiped her wet eyes. "Will he die, Missy? Please say no."

"There's a strong chance, so you'd best get your mind right."

With the last question hanging in mid-air, Missy stomped to her truck.

Vickie waited for the engine sounds to fade on Route 15, and then she pulled herself up and leaned against the fence, unable to look at Chief.

His potential demise sent shockwaves through her spirit. She snuck a glimpse at his atrophied form, and his sadness pounded her heart. The prospect of her own death entranced her soul, which sought escape from this realm. She thought of what John would say, and the tears flowed. She clutched the rail and fell over onto it, then yelled, "No!" and rushed through the gate and toward the house, where she flung open the front door and thudded her way to her bedroom. Once inside, she slammed and locked the door and fell onto her bed, boots and all.

Sleep caught her in a powerful embrace, and she drifted to a world of Caribbean skies and sandy shores and the darting and twirling of pirate fish. There would never be a reawakening or a recovery or a rebirth.

Red's loaded pistol reposed in a drawer, summoning her awake.

John struggled with painful memories as he left the tiny clubhouse and marched to the driving range, which sat next to the tenth hole. A group of men played the ninth green as he dropped his bag into a rack and spilled his basket of balls on the turf. He eyed them suspiciously, as they seemed intent on having a good time, something he could not bear in his paranoid and reflective mood. Some might call him nostalgic or even paranoid, but depression and anger had gripped him, and he would battle against all forms of inane pleasantries.

He took a six iron from the bag and gripped it loosely, trying to recall what the greats had taught him in various books. He'd read them in place of his father's instruction, but little worked, and he became a frustrated golfer like most of the men who played the game. But unlike them, his father was an excellent student of golf and his brother a professional with a major under his belt and enough advertisement money to last for decades, so John had quit the game he might have loved and did not play for fifteen years.

He recalled the two kinds of swings: the two-plane version in which the golfer stood upright and yanked down on the club with the arms and somehow contacted the ball at impact, and the flatter one-plane swing in which the player brought the club in a circle on the backswing and used only the legs to power through the downswing, allowing the arms to go along for the ride, as Ben Hogan used to write prolifically.

John's hands seemed like those of a mannequin as he tightened his grip on the handle, unable to remember the proper method. His shoulders fell out of alignment with his hips and with the direction of his shot, and the result was a slice out to the right. When he tried several more times, his slice ceased and his hooks started, careening the ball hard left like a missile.

The four men laughed and drove their electric carts like proud schoolboys as they approached the clubhouse. One called to the others and turned for the door, but then he wheeled and faced John as he struck a ball poorly and without an ounce of skill or any measure of precision. The man's eerie presence gave John pause.

He turned to the sneering man. "Do you need something?"

"You played baseball, didn't you?" He hesitated. "I can tell."

The man's accusing voice stabbed at John through the air.

"Why do you say that?"

He shifted his weight and gestured. "Because you're trying to hit a home run with every shot. All power hitters do the same thing."

"Well, I never played baseball or any other sport."

John was keenly aware of the scrutiny, which embarrassed him.

"Whatever you say, pal. Lift the club up high like this, "

The man illustrated what he knew to be the proper method.

John grew furious. "Look, I'm not using the two-plane swing, pal, but the one-plane. My father was a golf teacher and my brother won a major, so I don't need any advice or tips or anything else from you."

He surveyed the other sneering jerks who snickered to one another. "Get lost before I take this club and wrap it around your head."

The man's face flushed crimson, and he stiffened.

He looked back at his cohorts, who shook their heads.

"I was only trying to help." The man put his hands on his hips.

"Maybe you didn't hear me. I said get out of here." John spoke slowly, and his feet took him toward the man. His hands held the club in a menacing fashion, and the ground between them closed rapidly. The man's face turned pallid, and he turned and scooted down the path to his cart, where he stomped on the accelerator. The cart passed John and then stopped at the tenth hole. The men spilled out of their seats and looked toward the road, rather than at the crazed lunatic.

The men hit terrible shots but did not take a mulligan. Instead, they drove down the fairway and picked up their balls and moved to the next hole, leaving John free to continue on the range.

An older man observed his next few shots from the covered deck of the clubhouse. He presented differently from the others, as he seemed a refined gentleman who was sympathetic to John's plight. He stepped down to the grass and introduced himself as Franklin Young, a retired golf pro and former player on the tour. He invited John to hit a few more balls so he might advise him properly. John initially declined, but when prodded, he complied, there was something about the man.

"I see the problem," he said. "You're allowing the face to roll over, and the club gets stuck in the backswing before reaching the top, or it makes it to your shoulders but in the wrong position. Thus, your body has no choice but to sway to the right, moving you off the ball."

"What does all that mean?"

"It's why you're falling backward on the downswing."

"And hitting bad shots," said John flatly.

"Precisely." He hesitated. "Now then, let's check your grip."

John showed Franklin the method he'd learned from Ben Hogan's instructional book, *Five Lessons*, and it was met with approval from the older man, as he appreciated Hogan as the finest ball striker in history.

"Again, I see the issue. Your index fingers are activating as you bring the club away from the ball, even when you try to avoid it." He wriggled his thumbs. "Ensure these are left of center and use them to pull back."

At first, it felt awkward, but then John got the hang of it and his backswing felt much more stable at the top. He shoved his right leg forward to initiate the downswing, and the ball sailed left and curved back to the middle for an excellent power fade, landing on target.

"Do it something like that," said Franklin with a devilish grin.

John frowned. "It won't last. Everything works at first."

"And then it doesn't?"

"Right." John looked at the clubhouse. "I haven't eaten since yesterday and I'm hungry." He shook Franklin's hand. "I appreciate the session, but it's time I got something for lunch." His hand dropped.

"Before you leave, I'd like to offer a nutritional bar my company recently developed. It has all the healthy ingredients and will keep you playing longer. We're testing them on golfers and noting the results."

"Sure, why not?" John took a bar from the man.

He grinned as he ripped it open. "Won't kill me, will it?"

Franklin laughed. "Surely not, and it might help you play better."

When John took a bite, Franklin waved a hand. "Hold on."

He asked for the bar, and John gave it to him.

"This one is highly potent. Too much might be harmful."

"Too much of what?"

"Invigorating ingredients."

Franklin paused.

"They will help you think more clearly than ever before, but too much at one time could be lethal, as you're not yet used to such things."

A rush of enthusiasm and vitality overtook John, and at first he thought the man might have poisoned him. But then his senses took on greater function, he heard more sounds and saw more sights.

"I suggest we begin again, with the proper grip and alignment."

"Alright."

Little by little, John's energy levels rose, and he hit shot after shot. Then he played a round, and his ability to judge chips and putts improved. His pitch shots flew high and landed softly on the green.

John fell to his knees, as his victory seemed hollow without Vickie. He wanted to run to her and apologize for his anger and bitterness, but he was now a Rephaim and would not infect her with his iniquity.

"Come with me. I wish to explain myself to you."

Franklin drove the cart to a pavilion and parked.

He gestured, and the two men sat at a picnic table.

"You may have wondered who I am and why I chose you."

"It must have something to do with Leslie Carter."

"To an extent, it does. I've been sent to you as a guide, not one for golf necessarily, but it was a place to begin a new and lasting friendship."

"Are you with Leslie now?"

"Oh, no, I'm far too old for her, as I originate from another era."

John sized up the older man. "Born during WWII, by chance?"

"Older," said Franklin, chuckling. "From before the Flood."

John stood. "Look, I don't have time for this nonsense."

Franklin sent a bolt of current through John, freezing him in place and draining his spirit, forcing him to slump over the table.

"There is more to the electric universe than you can imagine, and you could have any woman you desire if you align with me. The people in your life have never appreciated your talents, John, but I am the one who does, and I will give you the world if you will only worship me."

John ground out the words between his teeth.

"I don't know who you are, but please let me go."

Franklin shook his head. "I cannot do that, at least not yet."

He leaned over John. "You see, I have your mother, Nicole, safely in my care. She enjoyed Ouija boards and séances and tarot."

An invisible weight sapped John of his masculine power and held him in place. "My mother never did any of those things."

"Oh, but she did when she was a teen and a young woman."

"She must have repented somewhere along the way."

"No, I'm afraid not, and it cost her sanity and her soul."

"And her son." John's voice faded, losing its edge.

"Precisely."

"What do you want from me, Franklin? I'm no one."

"We have plans for Vickie Morrison and for you. She will lead our propaganda network, which will do far more than present slanted news coverage, and you will assist a young singer with immense talent but little direction who will become an influencer of epic proportions."

"I will do no such thing. I have horses to rescue back home."

Franklin grimaced as if pained and ran a finger through John's hair.

"You left it all behind and hit the road, remember?"

"I can go back. They'll take me in."

"The good mountain people of Western North Carolina?"

"Yes, that's right. You mock them, but they have grit."

"They will have much more when I'm done with them."

John spoke through a choked voice. "Is that a threat?"

"Oh, yes." A pause. "I'll leave you with one more piece of advice."

The devil peered at John through fiercely intelligent eyes, which glowed with a brutal inner flame, remote and insolent and magnetic.

"I lost your father because of your meddling, but I won't lose you."

Franklin's cool, aloof presence infuriated John, which the ghastly fiend seemed to enjoy, as if anger enlivened him, which, of course, it did.

"You showed your hand today," John said. "I'll never join you."

"I am here to serve notice, as I know your Achilles' heel, which I will use."

Franklin patted his shoulder and left him alone with his thoughts.

Minutes passed, which felt like hours.

John's strength returned, and he raised up in alarm.

He drove toward the parking lot, hopeful for a return to normalcy, and his eyes caught the motion of a graceful deer in a grove of redwoods. He stopped the cart and looked about for several moments, wondering if the fiendish man might return and murder him. Then he eased to the trees and entered the tall canopy, but the deer had disappeared.

A golden-haired woman turned from him in shyness, and he rushed forward and called out to her. He spun her shoulders and stepped back.

"It's so good to see you, John."

Her slender form beckoned to him as she curled a finger.

He frowned. "Hello, Rachel."

Twenty-Four

Rachel Daniels accompanied John from his wooded course in Mill Valley south across the Golden Gate Bridge and through San Francisco, all the way to Monterey, where she knew of a more private venue than his father's favorite, Pebble Beach. She gestured excitedly at the turn, and they drove an elongated driveway through manicured grounds to the Binghamton Green clubhouse, fashioned as it was in ornate marble. She promised this course would prove a welcoming environment and a proper warmup for his blossoming game and, even more to his surprise, she insisted on being his caddie for the day, eschewing the normal caddie assignment proffered with the fee, and spoke of majestic high and wide outcroppings with fortified donjons.

Off they went, slender golden-haired beauty carrying his rented bag, which weighed a ton, draped over her shoulder, and nervous golfer, fresh to the life and unsure of his manner, hoping against all hope his newfound swing would stay with him for one final round.

At the first tee box, he hit a line drive that fell softly to the fairway on a five-hundred-yard par five, with three hundred yards to the green.

He remembered his swing thoughts and hit a wood off the sloping turf, skipping it slightly, but the ball kept under the billowing wind. John turned to Rachel and asked her to give him the bag, but she would not, which made him frown again as they descended the hill and ascended the less steep grade to his ball. He sized up the shot, knowing it must make the green if he were to make par, and turned to Rachel.

"What do you think?"

She dropped the bag and huffed for a moment.

"I'm not used to this," she said.

"I know." He smirked. "It's why I should carry the bag."

Her face contorted in offense. "I have it under control."

"Fine." He looked about, enjoying the scenery. "So?"

"So what?"

"What club should I use? It's one-sixty."

"How on earth should I know? Why you play this game is beyond me." She fumbled through the assortment of irons and wedges and woods and handed him a putter. "Here, try this. I've seen it on TV."

He took a deep breath and exhaled, then broke into a grin.

This would be a fun and entertaining day.

John grabbed an eight-iron and stroked a shot to one foot.

"Wow, that was amazing," she said, almost dropping the bag.

He grabbed it and steadied it for her. "Watch out, Rachel."

"I'm trying." Her face flushed. "You humans make things hard."

"What does that mean?"

"Nothing."

She slung the bag over her shoulder and walked ahead of him.

He let the comment pass, but it created an awkwardness he found difficult to shake, as her lustrous radiance seemed otherworldly.

John sunk his putt, and they continued to the next hole, which graded up marginally from the tee box but bent midway to the right, and a tree stood next to the wide fairway at the downsloping curve.

"Nice obstacle," he said, frowning.

"You can get past it." She smiled at him.

As promised, his shot landed pure, and as they walked toward it, he broached the subject of her appearance amid the redwoods and the deer.

Rachel withheld a response but guided his next two shots with the wisdom of a much older woman, and he birdied the second hole.

At the third tee box, she dropped the bag, and they surveyed the spectacular scene, as finally the sea showed itself just past the rocks.

The green reposed across a great expanse atop a high bluff, and the wind blew in off the ocean with tremendous force from right to left.

"I've seen holes like this on golf broadcasts. The trick is to hit the ball toward the water on the right and let the wind blow it left."

"John, I love you."

The declaration came seemingly from nowhere, but it must be stated, for it was the reason she had appeared before him, and he must choose. Franklin Young knew well how to get at John, as she was the perfect age and her feminine form was unmatched and her countenance was sweet and loving and without guile, but he sensed something eerie and abstract about her, which was difficult to fathom or explain.

He lined up his shot with an iron, and it sailed right, then left.

As they walked down the slope to the green, she spoke again.

"I love you, and I want us to be together forever."

"So you've said, both here and at your farm."

The breeze blustered and whipped her hair about her neck.

John tapped his ball into the hole and sensed it was all too easy.

"Franklin sent you, right?"

She nodded.

"Yes, but I am here because I honestly love you, and I have given up everything I know and hold dear to be in your human arms."

A bench called to John from the rocky outcrop just off the green.

He gestured, and they sat. John gazed out to sea as he reflected.

"Do you have parents?" He turned to her in earnest, and his eyes found hers. "I never thought to ask before today, but I assumed."

"Most do," she said. "Who would own such a farm at my age?"

"Right, but I'm guessing the Consortium actually owns it."

"Yes, although I run the Consortium in Western North Carolina."

John chuckled.

"You find me amusing?" Her face grew serious.

"Maybe not." His expression changed along with hers, as it had communicated too much. "How old are you, Rachel?"

"In human terms, twenty-five, but I am far older in reality."

John grew frustrated with the lies and half-truths.

"Stop speaking in riddles. Who are you, and what do you want?"

"As I've said since last year, I want you, John. That is all."

"What have you given up for me?"

"Everything." She sighed and looked at the horizon.

He took her arm and squeezed hard. "Tell me!"

"Please stop, John. You're hurting me, and I don't like it."

She tugged, and he let go of her arm, and she rubbed it.

"You hurt me." Her face grimaced as she pouted.

"Is pain an unfamiliar experience for you?"

"Yes, but since I am now human, it is my life."

He drew nearer, and she flinched slightly, but he put a hand to her golden hair and used his finger to place a strand behind her left ear.

"I need honesty from you, Rachel. Please give it to me."

Her eyes moistened, and she wiped a tear.

"I am the Nymph of the Mountains, and I have watched you grow from a boy to a man in those hills and valleys, and I admire your deep fondness for horses, as they are spiritual animals who never deserve mistreatment but frequently receive it, and I have sensed your internal struggle to find yourself in the midst of great family turmoil, and I have often wept for you and your poor mother, who reached out to us in agony but was given no solace for her trouble, and I wish to make amends for her death through my eternal love and motherly affections."

"That's quite a speech."

"It's from the heart, John." A pause. "Please don't mock me."

"All right, fine, but it sounds like you belong with Nicole."

"In an asylum?"

"Yes, exactly. She often said similar things."

"Nicole's human mind could not comprehend the electric universe, but she wanted to learn all its secrets, and so they were given to her."

"Which drove her insane," he said flatly.

"Yes, but I am of the nachash, and I will replace your mother."

"You've taken human form?"

"Yes."

Her guarded admission made it seem she had been hurt by his refusals, as they offended her pride but perhaps deepened her love.

"For how long?" he asked.

"One human lifespan, but I retained my powers before today."

"Meaning you left them behind to be with me?"

"I made a deal with Franklin, who wishes for our union."

"So now you are a normal woman in every sense?"

Rachel nodded.

"With one exception. I am to become a singer."

John reached over and stroked her warm, sunlit hair.

"With your guiding hand," she said, "I will sing for the masses, who will conform to my messages of love and freedom and inversion."

"So you'll lead them to the fires of perdition?"

Her demeanor grew more intense, and her adoring gaze swept over him. "The world is in the midst of change, John, and we must change with it, as Internet platforms are emerging which in the next decade will provide for enormous upheaval. Music and online social interactions will place ideology foremost in the minds of the masses, opening them to our guidance, as we push them toward a new spiritual awakening."

John stood, as their conversation had grown worrisome.

"Look, Rachel, I might be a Rephaim, but I'm not against God."

"He doesn't love you like I do." She stood and drew near and rubbed his chest and pulled herself nearer to him. "I've traveled so far, and I've given up so much for this one chance to know real love."

His eye caught a replica of a castle keep to his left, and then he looked about them, as it seemed they had the course to themselves.

"Where's everyone else? This place should be packed."

"Binghamton Green is owned by the Consortium."

He gave her a sidelong glance. "Of course it is. I should've known."

He drew back, and she smiled and took his hand.

"I would like to show you something, if you'll allow it."

His lips pursed at what seemed like a bad idea.

"All right," he said reticently.

Rachel led him to the keep and opened the door to a shadowy room, tiny as it was and filled with dust and cobwebs and various garden implements. She burst forth into the space, pulling him along with her.

"Come on."

As they entered, the door closed behind them.

"Do you trust me, John?"

"In the pitch of darkness, not so much."

"Then we must have illumination."

A light flicked on, and the space transformed into a grand castle, filled with all the most elegant and modern accoutrements. Franklin descended a set of steps that rose to the top of the keep. Formerly narrow like those of a lighthouse, now they were wide and carpeted.

Franklin said hello and sauntered over to a piano that sat near a roaring fireplace. He played a classical melody, and Rachel joined him.

She sang beautifully, befitting her charm, and John was at once reminded of the song of the sirens who tempted sailors to their fates.

He went to a window that overlooked a jagged cliff and the rocks below, and lamented all he had lost, the worst being love.

Franklin ceased playing. "What's the matter, my boy?"

His eyes were sharp and assessing, and his expression fierce.

"I am now a Rephaim," John said, "but I long for God's grace."

He paused.

"I didn't know what I had in Jesus until I lost Him."

Franklin studied John thoughtfully for a few moments.

It seemed the hands of time had quickened their pace.

"The Most High has forsaken all Rephaim and will not catch you if you fling yourself over the edge and onto the rocks, where the sea consumes all."

"Colorful image," said John dryly. He wrung his hands and paced.

"It's no mere metaphor. I will catch you if you fall, but you must worship me," Franklin said. "It's all I ask and a small price to pay."

"You want a lot more than my worship, but you won't admit it."

"I have set aside earthly tasks for you and for Vickie. This is true."

He turned to Rachel. "As for this splendid mountain creature, I have lifted up many a soul from obscurity to fame. I will do so for her."

Rachel went to John and wrapped her arms around his waist and asked him to kiss her deeply, which he did, and they found themselves on a gilded bed at the top of the keep, surrounded by a multitude of red roses. A terrible sorrow washed over him as their bodies blended and molded harmoniously on the massive four-post bed, and red petals dropped from the roses wherever they were found in the room.

Franklin stood at their feet as passion enveloped John.

"Consummate your love, and all will be made possible."

The dread inside John worsened, and his soul cried out in fear.

He drew back and rolled over and stared at the flowered ceiling.

Rachel rubbed his chest and kissed his neck, unwilling to let him go.

"Another rose approaches, and soon her last petal will drop."

John sat up straight. "Is it Vickie?"

"No, it is Nellie Michaels, and you must refuse her call."

"What call?"

"No matter." Franklin smiled benignly, as if dealing with a fool. "She will beg for your love, but you must turn her away. Once done, I will cast her to the depths of the ocean, completing a long-awaited task."

John sat on the edge of the bed and considered.

His eyes rose to Franklin. "Who is she to you?"

"Nellie has tempted Vickie toward the Most High."

"And you wish to see her influence removed?"

"Precisely."

"You won't break my bond with Vickie, no matter what you do."

Franklin gestured at the luminous Rachel, who seemed dejected.

"Why must you hurt this lovely creature who is your twin flame?"

Rachel's cheeks flushed at Franklin's revelation.

"What do you mean, twin flame?" John asked.

Franklin smiled. "I am a guiding spirit of the elements, and I have bound your soul to Rachel, as she is bound to you. There is a spark within me which I now bestow unto you. I will change your restless nature into calm, your sloth to diligence, and your dark prison to light."

"You didn't answer my question."

"No matter how many centuries pass, you will find her or she will find you, either in youth as you frolic or as adults who meet accidentally on a train or in an elevator, and an electricity will flow between you."

"You are a liar. Rachel is no more human than this castle."

She spoke in a wistful voice. "Be careful, John."

He lingered on Franklin's words and then turned to her.

"Careful with what?"

"Franklin has immense authority, and he never lies."

John turned sharply around. "Much like yourself, I assume."

She shook her head. "No, I have given up my powers for you."

"So what do you want with Nellie Michaels?"

As she responded, he drank in the sensuality of her feminine body.

"We must follow Franklin's instruction and divert her from Vickie." She searched for the right words to persuade him. "Nellie's influence has angered Lilith, which we must never do under any circumstances, as she merely wishes to guide Vickie down the proper path, one of light rather than darkness, knowledge over superstition, and an evolution of humankind into spirit beings who possess a divine power."

"You are both insane," said John in disgust.

Franklin looked at him with amusement. "Perhaps, but you will throw Nellie to the rocks, ending her life." A pause. "No one will miss the poor girl, as she's been an orphan from the very beginning."

John recoiled and went to the window.

"Don't worry," said Rachel, moving beside him. "I will take their places in your heart, and as a loving couple, we will have all we desire in this realm as we lead the masses to depravity and ruination."

"Why do you include Nellie? I only love Vickie."

Rachel glanced at Franklin, who shook his head.

"No matter," she said quickly. "Slip of the tongue."

John sighed. "Why would you want to align with Lucifer and lead the masses astray when you will be destroyed by God in the end?"

Rachel's face took on a sinister look, and her eyes glowed red.

They now stood atop the keep, overlooking the Pacific Ocean.

A fireball passed brightly overhead and landed in the sea, miles from shore, and a tidal wave pushed toward them with awesome force, but she raised a hand and the wave subsided. "Some of us, those who left Yahweh's divine council after the Flood, honor our ancestors who are chained in the gloomy underworld, known as Tartarus in the Greek, and wish to see the world burn and all souls within it consumed."

Her hand fell to her side, and fire exploded from the window on the ground floor, pushing out to sea with a menacing growl.

"You will be included in that fire," John said, "as God unleashes His fury on the Day of Wrath and the elements melt with a fervent heat."

"Perhaps so, but I have been given a rare glimpse of humanity's capacity for love, born of our fallen state and a desire to return to the garden on the mountain. I offer you a chance to know such a life."

John once more fell sad and disappointed at his many mistakes.

"Although you are now a woman, you misunderstand me."

"How so?" She drew near to him, her body filled with new life.

"As a man, I cannot know bliss without a true romance."

She rubbed his arm. "And I will be the twin flame you adore."

"It must be genuine, and I must feel it in my own heart."

He paused.

"I will never love another besides Vickie Morrison. I am bound to her for eternity, and I will roam the earth until God's triumphant return, lamenting my sins and awaiting His wrath upon my wicked soul."

A wild surge of grief ran through Rachel, paling her cheeks.

"Please reconsider," said Franklin urgently. "You know not what you say in this moment, as your words penetrate deeply into her heart."

"She must find another, as I am taken."

"There is no other. If you refuse her, she will most surely die."

"Today?"

"Yes, you must choose Rachel over Vickie. It is her only hope."

John turned to her. "I am sorry, but I do not love you."

"Please, John." Tears coursed down her cheeks.

Her beauty manifested as her blue eyes sparkled and her golden hair shined and her perfectly shaped form beckoned to him. She had been constructed for this purpose, of that he was certain, but it was no use.

"I must decline your offer, as I cannot love anyone else."

She turned to Franklin in a desperate panic.

"I have watched this man for decades, and I know his mind and his heart. He always rebels when confronted in this manner, and it was a mistake to do so." She addressed John again. "Please accept my apology. We have forceful natures, but we are used to getting what we want."

"Save your breath, Rachel. I will never love you."

She sighed and took his arm, and her voice dropped low.

"In time you will."

Her soft, bewitching eyes and her refusal to accept his answer angered him, and he reacted unkindly. He shook her by the shoulders and yelled at her as she tried not to hear him, turning her sensuous chin and wrinkling her nose and laughing as if the quandary pleased her. "I will never love you, Rachel! Get my words through your evil head!"

She laughed faintly and then caught herself, and her eyes widened.

"Please, John. You cannot do this to me. I've sacrificed so much."

He let go of her shoulders, unaware of any risks.

"I'm sorry if it's hurtful, but I cannot spend my life with you."

Rachel shrieked and then dropped to a ball on the floor in tearful sobs. Her body writhed, and her form glowed in a pulsating light.

Franklin tried to reason with him. "You are giving up your chance to be with a spirit of great esteem who has given up her powers for you."

"Here's what neither of you understand. I will never accept a spirit or a woman who would willingly corrupt Vickie's two girls."

"The girls must also join us, so they can take their rightful places in my kingdom. There are many tasks ahead and little time to waste."

Carlie and Chris flashed before John, bonded in laughter and love, and their images infuriated him. Franklin said to let his hatred flow.

"They deserve your curses, as does your mother."

John turned from the devilish man and the portrait painted before him, and he reflected on Garrett's love for Christ at the end of his life.

He wheeled. "I am my father's son, and I forgive him, along with my mother and my brother and all others who have hurt me." A pause. "My DNA has been corrupted by Leslie, and I am a pitiful shell of a man."

He dropped to his knees. "But I forgive her, and I ask the Lord for His grace and mercy and to use me in some small measure for His will."

My son, recite the Lord's Prayer from Matthew 6:9-13.

John complied gladly and unreservedly. "Our Father in heaven, may your name be kept holy. May your Kingdom come soon. May your will be done on earth, as it is in heaven. Give us today the food we need, and forgive us our sins, as we have forgiven those who sin against us. And don't let us yield to temptation, but rescue us from the evil one."

Franklin called out in agony and then vanished into thin air.

Rachel remained whimpering on the floor amid dust and cobwebs.

She looked up. "I would have loved you for the rest of my life."

"I'm sorry, but I will never turn my back on God or on the girls."

She picked herself from the floor. "Then so be it."

Rachel brushed past him and out the door, and it slammed shut.

He went after her, calling her name to little avail, as she reached the edge of the high cliff and flung her body to the wind and the sea.

John reached the spot and looked over the side, wincing at her mangled form below, and suddenly the waves rushed forth and swept her forward into the rocks, crushing her further as she looked sadly at him, and then her eyes shut as the cold Pacific waves swallowed her whole.

He dropped to his knees and reached out in sadness, wishing he could have saved her from such a fate, but knowing it to be impossible.

A voice called out to him from over his shoulder.

"John, please don't follow her! I am your daughter!"

"Nellie?"

He turned as he stood. "What did you say?"

Was she another nymph sent to lead him into darkness?

Nellie approached, but he held up a palm.

"Stay back. I warn you."

"I cannot do that."

Nellie took another step, and his foot found the jagged edge of the cliff, and a few rocks loosened and fell to the roaring waves, which, like Franklin Young, roamed about, looking for those they might devour.

"You are my father, John, and as your daughter, I ask for your love." Her hands extended, and she gave him a look of supplication. "It's all I've ever wanted, and I've dreamed of this moment since I was a girl."

"I have no daughter," he said with feeling. "Chelsea is dead."

"I survived, barely, and with many hardships, but I am *her*."

Twenty-Five

Psalm 65:3

Though we are overwhelmed by our sins,
you forgive them all.

Vickie dreamed of a vast desert and a mountain of stones piled one atop the other, so she ventured forth and picked her way to the peak, where a cloud of fire descended. The spirit of Yahweh spoke to her from a flaming bush and told her to remove her boots, as they were tainted and would defile this holy place. She complied, still unsure of her surroundings, as a great multitude from the valley, those who had sent her on their behalf, called out from their worship of a golden calf, saying she must hurry, as their time in this realm grew shorter by the hour and soon His wrath would arrive. She looked to Yahweh and asked for His merciful grace, which He freely gave her, but He said she must forgive those who hurt her and, most importantly, she must forgive herself, as all souls outside the garden have eaten and fallen.

Price knocked on her bedroom door, startling her awake.

He cracked it open, sending shards of light into her eyes. She held up a hand amid the foul odor of sweat and uncleanliness and sin, then rolled over, unwilling to listen to his sweet fatherly calls for life.

An hour later, he returned, repeating the process, but this time he ventured to her bedside with a chair and stared at her in the darkness.

"I know where you are," he said. "I spent years in this place."

Her exhaustion existed on a level never before reached.

"I doubt it."

He read from Matthew 11:28-29: "Then Jesus said, 'Come to me, all of you who are weary and carry heavy burdens, and I will give you rest. Take my yoke upon you. Let me teach you, because I am humble and gentle at heart, and you will find rest for your souls.'"

She listened as he recited the verses, staring at the ceiling.

"Daddy, I killed Chief like I kill everyone."

"Honey, Chief isn't dead any more than you are."

"But he will be dead, just as I am now dead to this world."

"You're ready to die?"

She flashed an angry look at him.

"As soon as I get my hands on the pistol, which you stole from me."

"I couldn't let you take the easy way out, and for that, I will never apologize." He flipped his Bible to Matthew 10:16. "'Look, I am sending you out as sheep among wolves. So be as shrewd as snakes and harmless as doves.'" He closed the book and gazed at her in the dark.

She chuckled bitterly. "I'm the wolf who devours the sheep."

"No, this world has eaten you alive since your girlhood."

"Are you the wolf?"

"I was, but now I hope to be the Good Shepherd for you."

She rolled over, leaving her father behind, traveling to some distant shore, as this was no longer her home, she had destroyed all she loved.

Her mind drifted to another world, this one different from the burning mountain. She met a man who gave her strong drink, which captivated her mind and soul, and then he led her deep inside a shadowy cavern lit by torches along each side, the air cool and dry.

They reached a room with walls one hundred feet high and stopped.

A gray-haired man appeared from the gloom with eyes aglow.

"Hello, Vickie."

She withheld a response as shivers ran along her spine.

"I've waited for this moment since you were young," he said.

"All right."

His bright, beaming eyes calmed, and he took on an air of gentility.

"I spent time with your mother just before her death." He hesitated for effect. "She was most sad to leave you, but joyful for my embrace."

His words piqued her attention, as he knew they would. She looked intently at him in silence, trying to read the outcome of their encounter.

He smiled. "Don't worry. Valerie is safe in my hands."

Vickie hugged herself. "Why am I here?"

"I tested your twin flame, and he passed easily."

"Twin flame?"

"Yes, you and John were meant for one another and have been joined many times over the centuries, but each time tragic circumstances interfere with your union, war or plague or the death of a child in the womb. I offer to recompense your misery and bring the two of you into perfect harmony, as he still loves you."

"How did you test him?"

"I offered him another, a woman of my creation, a figment of his imagination, exquisite in every category save one. She wasn't you."

"Why would you do this? You must want something from us."

"I want exactly what I asked for in New York: the death of your daughter, Nellie. Once done, I will join you with John, and as a couple you will mentor Katie toward a career in the music industry. She has artistic talents yet undiscovered, but soon she will take the world by storm. Katie will arise as my creation, a tempest of chaos, as she will lead the masses to accept my messaging and to worship me as their god."

"You are insane."

He laughed. "John said the same at first, but he came around."

"John Breyer would never accept you."

"You forget, he is now a Rephaim, and as such, has fallen in line."

Vickie considered.

The older man greeted her in a businesslike manner, conducting himself as a man of distinction, but he was merely a common thug.

"I want nothing to do with your wicked schemes, especially when they involve Katie or Abbie, and I will never again hurt Nellie."

"Oh, no?"

Vickie shook her head. "My daughter has suffered enough."

"You lie in bed while she has disappeared," he said accusingly.

Vickie shuddered at the condemnation in his voice. His thin nose rose and the lines on either side of it thickened, and he looked injured. Vickie detested him and would not be done in by his machinations.

"Nellie must find her own way, which may not be with me."

"That's right." His eyes sparkled. "She has joined my cause."

Hands found Vickie's shoulder and rocked her slightly, bringing her out of her cavernous dream. She rolled over to discover Abbie in tears.

"Please wake up."

Katie entered the room and switched on the light.

"It's time to get yourself out of bed, Aunt Vickie."

The teen's chiding tone angered her and inflamed her indignant rebelliousness. Who was this girl to judge her or tell her what to do?

"Let me be." Vickie rolled over and hugged her pillow.

"I've been doing all your chores, but the horses need you."

"Get Eudora to help," Vickie said through the pillow.

"She's busy taking care of Price and all of us."

Vickie removed the pillow. "Is my father okay?"

"Yes, but you are causing him stress, which he cannot handle."

Katie paused.

"He gets exhausted and has to lie down on the couch."

Tears formed in Vickie's eyes. Even in her despair, she hurt people.

"Who are all of us?"

"Me and Abbie and Mary and Lewis and Mitch and Laura."

Katie paused.

"Missy has been over to see Chief and stayed for dinner."

"I'll bet she has. Probably demanded potato casserole."

Katie's brows drew together in a hurt and confused expression.

"No one has made it since Mom died."

Vickie sat up and reflected on Michelle's paralysis and death and the ungrateful selfishness of her caustic sister in Washington, D.C., who refused to take a moment from her busy career to sit beside Michelle's bed, and the utter irony of Michelle's daughter sitting beside Vickie right now, in this moment of agonizing sorrow. It was too much to bear.

She cradled her face in her trembling hands and wept.

"Please don't cry, Vickie. Chief will be all right."

"How do you know?" Her voice choked through sobs.

"Missy said so earlier today."

"I don't believe you." Her eyes found Katie. "You'll say anything."

"I promise," Katie said innocently, "and I wouldn't lie."

"Fine." She swiped at her eyes. "Do you like to sing?"

Katie was taken aback by the question. "What?"

"Would you sing me a song?"

"Why, Vickie? You're not making sense."

Abbie tugged on Katie's sleeve. "Tell her."

Katie gently pulled away from her sister. "Stop."

Vickie's eyebrows arched. "What does Abbie want you to say?"

Katie frowned. "I do like to sing, but by myself in the barn."

She threw a frustrated glance at Abbie, who rolled her eyes.

"Katie is always humming or singing something when she works."

Vickie nodded and considered her dream.

"Does Katie have a pretty voice?"

"It's like an angel," Abbie said, smiling. "But she's shy."

"I see."

Vickie threw herself onto the bed, more confused than ever.

She rolled over. "Turn out the lights when you leave."

"Please, Vickie." Katie spoke with a sense of urgency. "Get up."

Vickie waved off the girls and hugged her pillow like a man.

Katie opened the door at eight o'clock, bringing a bowl of hot soup and a kind word, as she knew enough at her age to take a different tack when the original plan had failed. Her love was on display as she set the bowl onto a tray and helped Vickie sit up in bed, then stood over her while she ate every last bite, even the crackers, and drank two glasses of water.

"Do you need to go to the bathroom?"

"No."

"Are you sure? I haven't seen you use it lately."

"Leave me alone."

Vickie shoved the tray, but Katie caught it. The bowl and spoon and plastic glass fell to the oak floor with a bang, and Vickie turned to the bed, covering herself in the grim stench of urine-soaked sheets.

She soon grew agitated at Katie's incessant need to place the items back onto the tray and set it in the corner, then sit and stare at her.

"I love you, Aunt Vickie. Please come back to us."

"Let me guess." A pause. "You don't bite?"

"We don't, and we forgive anything you've ever done."

"Well, I do bite, and if you don't get out of here, you'll find out."

She left the room with the tray, and Vickie relieved herself on the sheets. The urine ran quickly over her legs, and the liquid felt warm.

This must have been what happened with Nicole, first a descension into clinical depression and, after a while, schizophrenia. Vickie had already experienced hallucinations of strange, devilish men, so it was simply a matter of time before the dam broke in her mind. She had read about the connection between mental patients and the occult, and she wondered if her experience in New York or her association with Leslie Carter qualified her for such a label, but neither likely helped her sanity.

She drifted, careful to keep to a shallow slumber, as a return to the cavernous depths of her previous dream terrified her, not so much because of fear but the attraction to the older man's charm and his power. In her weary state, she might succumb to his seduction.

Katie burst into the room, disrupting Vickie's repose.

"What is it this time, you little brat?"

"It stinks in here. I mean, it really stinks!"

"Then leave me be."

"How can you stand it, Vickie?"

"I'm lying in it, that's how."

Price appeared at the doorway with a concerned expression.

"My Lord, it's terrible in there. Has she bathed at all?"

Katie shook her head. "I don't think so."

She pointed at the bed. "She's lying in her own filth."

He stepped into the room. "I need to get her up."

Katie stepped out of the way, and her face brightened.

Price moved forward, but then his hand pressed against his chest and he paused. He moved back a step and leaned against the door frame.

"I can't do it in my condition." His eyes met Vickie's. "I'm sorry."

Her half-shut eyes closed, and she rolled over to face the wall. There would be no redemption tonight, only the longing for death. Sooner rather than later, the Reaper would find her, as she had left the smell of death for him and, like an attack dog, he would sniff her out.

"Do you need help?" Katie asked worriedly.

He waved a hand. "No, sweetheart. I'll be all right in a minute."

Katie brought over a chair from the corner, and he sat.

Vickie sensed his pain but also his mood as he considered.

"I'm proud of you for helping your aunt. It really helps her."

Katie sighed. "I don't think I'm doing much other than feeding her, and most of the times I come in here with a tray, she won't eat a bite."

"Keep trying," he said. "Eventually you'll get through to her."

Vickie rolled over, feeling the wetness about her legs, enjoying her own filth, as it was all she deserved, she had earned every awful sore which would soon cover her skin and every infection which would further sour the room. She was a monster, and they should suffer.

"I want Red's pistol."

He gestured. "Please, honey. Not that again."

"Where is it?"

"Don't do this to the girls."

"Please, Vickie." Tears coursed down Katie's cheeks.

If they wouldn't give it to her, she would find it herself. It was the one thing worth getting out of bed for, and it was high time she did.

She flung back the covers, and Katie gasped.

Vickie pushed past her, moving more quickly than she'd expected, but Price stood and blocked her with his body and his rough hands.

"You're weak, old man. Don't make me shove you down."

He took a deep breath and exhaled, then grabbed her hair and dragged her back to the bed. He threw her down into the muck and let out a whimper as she landed, then covered her again with the sheet.

Price sat in the chair and wept into his hands for several minutes.

Katie put a hand on his shoulder, and he squeezed it.

He turned. "You should leave. I will watch her."

Katie shook her head. "I want to be here."

"It's too much for a young lady to see." He wiped his eyes.

"I don't care. She's my mother now, and I won't leave her side."

The words pierced through Vickie like a dagger to the heart. Michelle would have given anything to get out of her own dungeon, but Vickie locked herself there willingly and forced those about her to cry.

"Where's Nellie? She should be here with her mother."

Katie smirked. "I have no idea. She rode out to the falls by herself, which made no sense because she was so weak, but she wouldn't let anyone go with her. Then when she came back, she put Dash in his stall and packed a bag. The next thing you know, she's gone in a cab."

"She took one last look before leaving me," Vickie said.

"Nellie will be back, honey. I'm sure of it."

"No, Daddy. My daughter left because she hates me." She curled into a ball and shook, then let out a mournful wail. "My beloved Chelsea came back to me and I tried to reach her for God, but I failed."

She paused.

"My baby left me because I tried to kill her."

"Recently?" He sat up in the chair.

"Twenty years ago, when she was inconvenient."

Price wept into his hands again. "Please stop, Daddy."

His weakness made her despise him, which made her ashamed.

"Let me help you, my darling daughter. Please get up."

"I'll help you get into the shower," Katie said presently.

"If I go to the bathroom, I'll grab a razor."

Price stood and took a wobbly step, but he reached the door.

He looked back at Vickie, who turned and stared at the ceiling.

His form caught her peripheral vision as he departed the room.

Two hours later, the door opened yet again, and Missy stuck her head inside the room. She quickly retreated and made a guttural sound. She collected herself in the hallway, then entered the room and sat in the chair by the bed with a Bible in hand. Missy opened it but could barely make out the words, so she switched on the nightstand lamp, which blinded Vickie's eyes. She rolled over and faced the wall and wept.

Missy shifted in her seat and closed her Bible.

"Please, honey, don't do that. I can't handle you this way."

"Then leave like everyone else."

"Is that what you want, for us all to stay in this awful bedroom?"

"No, I want to leave this world."

Missy reflected.

"Is this why the young teenage girl killed herself?"

Vickie wiped her eyes. "Yes. I told her how I felt."

"Your mother wanted to leave, and she did."

"Are you saying I should crash my SUV?"

"No, honey." Missy cleared her throat. "I don't know what I mean."

She opened her Bible to Psalm 65:1-8: "What mighty praise, O God, belongs to you in Zion. We will fulfill our vows to you, for you answer our prayers. All of us must come to you. Though we are overwhelmed by our sins, you forgive them all. What joy for those you choose to bring near, those who live in your holy courts. What festivities await us inside your holy Temple. You faithfully answer our prayers with awesome deeds, O God our savior. You are the hope of everyone on earth, even those who sail on distant seas. You formed the mountains by your power and armed yourself with mighty strength. You quieted the raging oceans with their pounding waves and silenced the shouting of the nations. Those who live at the ends of the earth stand in awe of your wonders. From where the sun rises to where it sets, you inspire shouts of joy."

She closed her Bible and waited, but Vickie made no sound.

Missy placed the book on the nightstand and walked to the end of the bed. Then she climbed between Vickie and the wall and snuggled up close to her and hugged her tightly and gently stroked her hair.

"I got the lab results, and Chief will survive."

Vickie tucked her chin and burst into sobs. She clutched Missy, who hugged her again and said she was sorry she went ballistic on her, but her miscarriage had indwelled an anger and a despair she'd never known.

"Lee and I will try again, and so will you, honey."

"With who? John left me, and so did my daughter."

Missy pushed a strand of hair behind Vickie's ear.

"He just went to cool off for a while. He'll be back."

"How do you know?"

"John is my cousin, and I've known him since we were kids. He loves the mountains and the horses and you too much to leave for good."

She paused.

"Not to mention Katie and Abbie, whom he adores."

"I tried to kill his baby, and he will never forgive me."

"Yes, but she came back alive and ready to love you. How, I don't know, but God surely works in mysterious ways, as His will is perfect."

Vickie sniffed the putrid air. "They have each other now."

"Meaning they don't need you?"

"Yes."

"Honey, neither this farm nor this family will work without you. Think about it for one second. If you leave us and there's a funeral and they must somehow move on from your death, they will be devastated, and I don't think any of them would recover from the pain of your loss. Bluecreek would be sold, and Katie and Abbie would have no home."

"You could take them like you did before I got here."

"For a while, but the courts would step in eventually."

"It doesn't matter. Another family would be better than me."

"What about the horses? You've made so much progress."

Vickie laughed in bitter self-condemnation. "Sure."

"I'm serious, and I should have gone easier on you, but I assumed you were full of yourself." A pause. "I had no idea what went on inside."

"No one ever has, Missy. They only care about results!"

Vickie's shout reverberated off the walls and caused Missy to pull back slightly, which gave Vickie license to roll over and shut her out. But Missy held on, so Vickie fought harder, but still Missy wouldn't let go. Then Vickie elbowed her in the face and she recoiled as blood flowed from her nose, and then Vickie faced the Bible on the stand.

Missy climbed from the bed, uttering curses, and went to the door.

She opened it and turned. Her hand fell, and the blood ran unabated. "You know, Vickie, you don't have to hurt everyone."

When Missy closed the door, Vickie reached for the lamp.

Once more, the smooth envelope of darkness found her.

Twenty-Six

Psalm 66:1

Shout joyful praises to God, all the earth!

The plane banked and readied for descent onto the runway. Nellie had conversed with a theology student who sat next to her for the entire flight, which suited John well, as he was lost in his own thoughts and wished to be left alone. The pilot asked all passengers to prepare for landing, and flight attendants asked everyone to turn off electronic devices and buckle their seatbelts. The interruption seemed to jar Nellie and shift her focus to John. He turned from her and peered through the tiny window at the clouds, which grew larger by the moment. Then they passed through them, and he sensed gravity take hold of the airplane, which banked a second time. She placed her hand on his arm and asked if he believed her, but he withheld a response. She wiped a tear from her eye and turned to her new friend, saying not to mind her father, as he had much to consider and disliked air travel.

Nellie Michaels was a liar, so her untruth did not surprise him.

In the baggage area, he stood apart from her and waited for his bag while looking about the lower level. Nigel Farrell approached and made small talk, which did little to endear him to John, who had put out the vibe to stay as far back as possible. But the young man either missed the cues entirely or followed his own agenda, no matter how many feathers he might ruffle. In many ways, Nigel reminded John of himself.

John's blue duffel appeared, and his hand grabbed it as he turned.

Nellie stood in front of a bench near the exit. He went over to her, and they sat and shared a moment of silence as Nigel grabbed his two bags. The young man made his way to the exit and then stopped.

"I couldn't help but pry into your affairs, sir."

Nigel put his bags at the far end of the bench.

"I noticed," said John, frowning.

"Your experience at the golf course has piqued my interest, and I wonder if you might share more detail for my dissertation? You see, I'm almost done with my Ph.D., and your story would be most helpful."

Nigel stared at him as if the request was made every day.

"I've said enough on the subject. Maybe some other time."

Nigel nodded.

"Understandable." He took hold of his bag. "Good day to you."

Nellie blurted her words. "I have something to share."

Nigel let go of his bag. "What might that be?"

"My mother tried to abort me twenty years ago, but I survived."

"You mentioned her on the plane. Haven't you reconciled?"

"For a long time, I hated Vickie Morrison, and I wanted to destroy her, but then a powerful group who used me for their purposes decided to sacrifice me in front of her in a terrifying chamber in New York."

Nigel sat beside Nellie and squeezed her arm. "I'm so sorry."

Her chin dropped slightly. "Thank you."

"Vickie never mentioned it to me," said John sharply.

Nellie shook her head in confirmation. "She wouldn't."

John looked about, defying her sentiment and her demand to be taken seriously, as if she'd never been a member of the Consortium.

"If you are now so taken with Vickie, why ambush her in front of millions on national television? If she is, in fact, your mother, I mean."

"Vickie knew me right away when I left hints." She gave him an exasperated look, as if he was in the wrong. "Why can't you?"

"Because I was responsible for her abortion, and our child is dead."

Nellie reached out and rubbed his arm. "No, I am right here."

"It can't be." A pause. "Babies don't survive the procedure."

"Some do," said Nigel helpfully. "When God has a purpose for them." He pointed to her scars, which ran vertically and horizontally about her neck. He gently asked her to lean her head forward, which she did, and he lifted her hair in the back to reveal more scarring. "These are wounds consistent with saline abortions. I'm sure she had a horrible time of it in childhood and must have endured many surgeries."

He let her hair drop to her neck and smiled at her.

She returned his smile. "The only thing which really helped were daily injections, but cabal antibodies originate from awful sources."

"So you said at Bluecreek." John hesitated. "I'll get to the bottom of this when we get there. Vickie will not lie about it any longer."

"My mother is done with lies. Of that, I am certain."

He grunted, but inside he sensed Nellie spoke the truth.

"Vickie defied Sturgis Faulkner when he demanded she take a knife and cut my throat. He wanted her to complete what should have been done in the past, or so he said, and the others were all too ready."

John shifted on the bench. "I'm guessing he disliked her defiance?"

"Very much. Any of them would have gladly murdered me."

"So why didn't they follow through? It would have been easy to take the knife from her and do the deed, you being a fragile waif."

"Vickie called on Jesus, who told her to recite the Lord's Prayer."

Nellie reflected.

"A bright light flashed, and all the people and the demons were swept out of the room just like that." She snapped her fingers. "Then Vickie guided me out of the Planar building and to her apartment in Central Park. I was very ill and didn't think I could make it, but she helped me."

"Did she take you to a doctor?"

Nellie shook her head. "I already knew what was wrong."

"You missed your daily injections," said John flatly.

"Yes, for quite a while." She hesitated. "But I slept for many hours until I was well enough to sit with her, and she read me the Bible."

"Did her reading help?" asked Nigel intently.

"Oh, yes, and for the first time, the verses made sense to me."

"That was the work of the Holy Spirit, guiding your mind."

John stood and looked about the airport and considered.

He turned to Nigel. "Do you have somewhere to be?"

"Nowhere more important."

John offered the younger man a half-scowl and gestured.

"Fine, then you'd better tag along. I have a feeling we may need some help." He started walking and then wheeled. "Are you good in a fight?"

"I can hold my own."

"Good, but you haven't seen what we're up against."

"I have the Most High, which is all that matters."

Another scowl, this time full and deep. "I knew you'd say that."

<hr />

On the way to the farm, John detoured to downtown and parked on Main Street. He walked along the sidewalk, with Nellie and Nigel in tow, and entered Simpson's Fine Jewelry. Nigel peeked over his shoulder as he browsed, irritating him, and Nellie pointed to the rings she loved.

"Are you sure?" asked John, holding one up to the light.

Nellie looked at him in amazed wonder. "This is so exciting."

She bounced gleefully, which seemed rare for her, and nice to see.

John handed the ring to the owner and asked him to box it.

"Certainly, sir. Would you like the box wrapped?"

John turned to Nellie. "I don't know about these things."

She grinned and drew over to the owner and handled the purchase.

John scanned the open roadway on Route 15, silently thinking over what he might say when he and Vickie locked eyes. Nellie made a sound to his right and began to quiver, catching his attention. Nigel leaned forward from the backseat and asked if she was okay, rubbing her arm.

Her hand gently found his, and she patted it lightly.

"I'll be alright once I tell John what I did."

"Oh, boy."

John squinted as his eyes rose to the clouds overhead.

He shot her a glance. "Let's have it."

"After you left, I was jealous and defiant. Vickie and I had found a section of the falls where one could crawl in and pry out a rock, and in the hole, there was a bag with a vial of healing water, which Vickie took. Then she threw up a batch of parasites, and they lit the space."

She had spoken very quickly but stopped to catch her breath.

"Go on."

"When Vickie fed Chief some bad hay, and he got sick, it made me mad, because I understood how neglected and abused he must feel. And when she holed up in her room and wouldn't come out, even for me, I decided to get even." John shot her another glance, and she looked away from him and spoke to the window. "I went there and found a second bag, which contained a letter like the first one, but it was meant for Abbie. Red wanted to help Abbie heal herself if the cabal ever took her for experimentation. He knew he was about to die at their hand."

"Let me guess," he said sarcastically. "You drank all the water."

"Yes." A pause. "And now I am ashamed."

"So what was Abbie supposed to do, suffer and die for your pride?"

"I know, John, and I wish I could take it back."

"But you can't, Nellie. None of us can revisit the past."

"Do you have any regrets about me?"

"I might, if I believed your story."

They drove in silence until he turned into the driveway. Once parked, Katie and Abbie came out to meet his truck and hugged him.

"It's so good to see you." Katie wiped a tear. "Vickie is really bad."

He looked down at Abbie. "Has she frightened you?"

Abbie nodded.

"She fought with Grandpa Price in her bedroom."

"Physically, like an actual fight?"

Another nod.

"What for, sweetie?"

"She wanted Grandpa Red's pistol."

Nellie interrupted. "John, please ride with me to the falls."

He turned to her in disgust. "What, again?"

"Yes." She hesitated. "I know there's another one for you."

"You saw it?"

"No, but there has to be. God wouldn't let things end this way."

"I'm not going anywhere with you."

She drew nearer, but he brushed past her and thudded up the steps to the porch and into the house. He flung open the door, and Price called to him from the couch in the living room, but John said nothing.

He stuck his head into Vickie's bedroom, and the horrible stench overwhelmed his senses, forcing his retreat into the hallway. He turned to the girls, who approached as he shut the door, masking the foul smell.

"How in the world did this happen?"

"John, please come to the falls with me." Nellie stood behind Katie and Abbie and threw him an imploring look. "It will help you."

He grew furious and went to the living room, where Price sat.

"I heard Chief was sick from bad hay. Is this true?"

Price nodded.

"Yes, he was, but Missy thinks he'll be alright."

"So why is Vickie still in her room? Has she bathed at all?"

Price took a heavy breath. "She's very depressed."

"Over the horse?"

"And you and her daughter and everything else, including me."

"Why didn't you do something about it? You can't let this fester and become full-blown mental illness. Trust me. I know all about that one."

"I know you do, and I've tried to help her every day."

John turned to Katie. "Tell me what happened here."

"Like Price said, we've all tried to help her, but she won't get up."

A portrait of his mother flashed before him, as did her fiery death.

"No one has reached her, John, and she's honestly lucky to be alive because Price cracked open the door when she had fished the pistol from the drawer and held it in her hands. She had opened the cylinder to check for bullets, and in the split second he watched her, she shut it."

Katie paused.

"Price rushed over to her and grabbed the pistol, and they fought."

John sighed and turned to Nellie. "If you really are her daughter, "

He stopped himself before completing his sentence.

"It's why you've got to go to the falls," she said in desperation.

"We'll go, too," said Katie reassuringly. "Anything to help."

He considered the dark hallway and made his choice.

"All right. Let's go."

On the ride, Nigel almost fell out of his saddle several times, and John wondered why he had agreed to lead this ragtag bunch of misfits, when what he should have done was force Vickie out of bed and back into her life. Somehow he understood she would not move for him any more willingly than she would for the rest of her family, who also loved her.

He hoped the falls would offer a solution.

They tied the horses and descended the steep drop to the water.

Once there, Nellie crawled inside the small cavern while he and the others watched, and then she called him to join her. He said no at first, but then she begged, and so he uttered a curse and crawled beside her.

"You've got me in here. Now what?"

"Help me find another bag." Her fingers felt along the rock.

He grunted and placed his palms on the ceiling and the sides, finding nothing but solid surface, and so his fingers tried to pry open every crack, but it was little use, as Red had only left two for his girls.

Nellie gave up and curled into a ball and wept.

He crawled out to the falls and stood. "Come on out, Nellie."

Her face appeared, but it looked pale, and her eyes were red.

"I should have died," she said, looking up at him.

"What?"

"If I hadn't survived the abortion, I wouldn't have become Vickie's protégé, and I wouldn't have betrayed her, and she would be okay."

"If Vickie was still in D.C.," he said, "she would be miserable."

Nellie crawled forward, and John heaved her to her feet.

"Like she is right now?" asked Katie.

He turned to her and smiled. "Point taken."

Nellie put a hand to her brow. "I suddenly feel unwell."

To their left, from around the bend, Leslie approached. She wore a business suit, but every few steps, her form shifted to reptilian, and then, a few steps later, shifted back again. Her eyes were yellow and her mouth formed into a sneer, and she walked with grim determination.

Franklin appeared to their right, from the other side of the bend. He wore a gray coat and a blue turtleneck and seemed dressed for a fall class at a university. The mountains came alive with the song of the nymph.

Abbie's eyes rose to the blue sky. "This makes God angry."

"How do you know that, honey?" John put a hand on her shoulder.

"He talks to me and tells me things and asks me to heal people."

"Like you did Savannah?"

She nodded.

"He says I have much work to do and I'm smart for my age."

"You certainly are," John said, looking about and wincing.

Nigel gave him a restless glance and then held up his Bible.

He turned to Psalm 66:1-4 and read. "Shout joyful praises to God, all the earth! Sing about the glory of his name! Tell the world how glorious he is. Say to God, 'How awesome are your deeds! Your enemies cringe before your mighty power. Everything on earth will worship you; they will sing your praises, shouting your name in glorious songs.'"

The song of the siren ceased, and the air took on an eerie aspect, as if a great storm would soon drop from the sky and wreak unholy havoc.

John looked to his left. Leslie had stopped in her tracks.

To his right, Franklin had done the same.

"I thought we were past all of this," he said under his breath.

Franklin offered a faint smile. "My condolences for your darling Vickie. It seems she has given herself over to madness, much like your poor mother, and like Nicole, she lies in her own feces and urine."

"You drove her to insanity," said John fiercely.

"Yes, that's it. Let go of your rage!"

John turned and looked at a horrified Nellie.

"I must share a piece of truth with you, John. You are not a Rephaim, but you were tainted by Vickie's parasites in your teens, as was your daughter in her misbegotten birth, which is why she must die."

"Why not take me in her place?"

"Oh, no, we have plans for you and Vickie, and even for your girls."

He looked at Nellie with shimmering eyes. "You must ease your parents' suffering and end your pitiful existence once and for all."

"Will you help me?" she asked sacrificially. "I lack the bravery."

Katie called out. "No, Nellie! Please wait."

Nigel stepped nearer. "I know we recently met, but I had so hoped we might get to know one another and for you to accompany me back home to Britain. I'm sure my family would love you very much."

Her eyelids fluttered in confusion. "You don't even know me."

"That's just it." A pause. "I think I do."

Leslie took a step, but he held up his Bible, ceasing her progress.

"It's a simple matter, really," said Franklin. "We want Nellie's soul."

"And then?" John's eyes rose from the rocks to the devil.

"As she is your daughter, you will feel remorse, a human emotion which escapes me, but in your shame and sorrow, you will join Vickie in her foul-smelling state of living death, and as twin flames, you will descend into utter madness. It's high time you followed your mother's path, John." He hesitated. "Rather than take your life in a fire, I will lift you up as a couple and send you on a new journey, more to my liking."

"But we would be insane. How would we function?"

"With my help, of course. You will be invited to the best parties, and you will cavort with the finest people, and you will be stimulated by the most wicked atrocities ever devised by mankind, which will elevate you and keep you on the right path, one which will usher in my kingdom."

John considered, as this was his third temptation, and only Jesus Christ could resist such persistence, and the entities within him cried out for justice, as they had been denied for so long and they hungered for blood and for fame and for riches, and Nellie stood in their way.

He caressed her golden hair. "I'm so sorry."

"No, please don't," said Nigel with feeling.

She turned to her new friend. "It was very nice to meet you."

Nellie put her hand on John's arm. "Please do as you will."

"I must get back to Vickie," he said ruefully.

"I know," she said through choked tears. "My life for yours."

She smiled wanly. "That was the bargain, wasn't it?"

"I suppose it was."

Franklin raised a palm, and an electric force shot through the air and took hold of the entities inside John, and adrenaline rushed through his bloodstream to power them. He gripped her arms and prepared to throw her into the onrush of water, which would take her down to the rocks below and shatter her frail bones in a matter of seconds.

His mind declared no, but his muscles obeyed.

Nigel saw what he was doing and tried to pry away John's hands, but the young man was not strong enough, and Nellie cried out for John to complete the task which should have been done so many years ago.

Leslie became reptilian and hissed her approval.

Katie and Abbie were thrown down, and they crawled behind the chaos and hid themselves in the cavern where the bags had been kept.

John struggled with Nellie to the falling water and leaned back her head until the flow rushed inches from her hair, and she gave him a look of love. Images from his life flashed: first his brother's shadow, which had always loomed large, and then his wife's betrayal, which kept him from knowing a real family, denying his dreams of safety and peace.

Something wicked was inside him, pushing him to kill her, the same entities which once controlled Vickie more than she controlled them. But now she was home in her bed, oppressed by the same madness which had enveloped his mother, never letting go, and death in a fiery inferno was her only release. He would not let it happen again.

He thrust Nellie behind him, and his body flew forward and into the waterfall, which took him gladly and threw him down onto the rocks.

He heard sounds but felt little pain as he bounced and careened into the pool below the falls and submerged to its raging depths. A second later, he surfaced at one side, pushed there by the rush of cool water.

John's body was broken in several places, and a bone stuck out of his lower leg, a compound fracture which was sure to get infected, incurred as it was out here in the middle of nowhere, a haven for bacteria if one ever existed. He heard yells and footsteps, and soon his group surrounded him in the water and dragged him onto the bank.

The fractured lower leg remained submerged, and his knee bobbed up and down. He was thankful the excruciating pain had not yet set in, for when it did, he would scream bloody murder and then pass out. Nellie leaned over him, her body also soaked, and she wept.

Katie turned to his sister. "Ask God to do something!"

Abbie took her sister's cue and stepped into the water and raised her hands to the sky. "Dear Heavenly Father, we come to You in humble supplication and ask for Your blessings and Your forgiveness and Your healing." She pointed. "This man has repented for his sins in Your holy presence, and you aided his escape from evil. Once again, we ask You to work in his life, so he might carry out Your perfect will, helping Aunt Vickie to recover, and saving horses destined for the awful kill pens."

John bit his lip and leaned into the dirt as the pain came on faster than expected. He felt about for a stick and put it in his mouth.

"Dear Lord," he said. "Please take me and save my daughter."

Nellie's chin raised. "You finally acknowledge me?"

"Yes." He stroked her cold, wet hair. "And I love you."

She wept for joy as she put her head on his chest.

Abbie pushed through the pool of water and laid hands on his arm, which healed. She asked Nellie to move and put her hands on his stomach and said a prayer, and he sat up slightly and retched to one side.

Parasites glowed on the bank to his right, and then their light faded.

"Thank you, Lord."

John wiped his mouth and splashed water against it.

The clouds parted and light shone down on him, and a voice spoke.

"You are not a Rephaim, as your DNA was not altered, but you were infected with parasites like your beloved Vickie."

"Why was I told otherwise, Dear Lord?"

"Lucifer is the father of lies, and he surrounds his followers with deception, and soon I will give the entire world to his strong delusion."

John looked down, and his fractured leg was healed.

He slid away from the water and tried to stand on the bank.

"Please be careful, John!" Katie held out a hand.

He looked up at the sky. "Dear Lord, you are astonishing!"

Katie raised her arms to the heavens and began to sing, and her sweet voice sounded like an angel. "Amazing grace, how sweet the sound! That saved a wretch like me! I once was lost but now I'm found! Was blind but now I see! 'Twas grace that taught my heart to fear, and grace my fears relieved. How precious did that grace appear, the hour I first believed! Through many dangers, toils, and snares, I have already come. 'Tis grace hath brought me safe thus far, and grace will lead me home. When we've been there ten thousand years, bright shining as the sun, we've no less days to sing God's praise, than when we'd first begun."

God's voice spoke to Abbie. "Place your hands on Nellie."

Abbie complied, and Nellie's face colored, and her eyes cleared.

"She will be healthy each day of the year—except Hallow's Eve."

The Lord paused.

"On that night, Nellie will grow ill with sores all over her body, and her hair will fall out. Her legs will not carry her, and her skin will peel until she cries out in despair, but you will read My Word to her, and she will be soothed in her spirit, which does not require the flesh to be made whole." A pause. "In this manner, you will be reminded how you turned from Me and how you tried to murder her in the womb with saline and how her skin peeled and her blood boiled and she cried out."

"Yes, Lord." John gave Nellie a sad look. "We will never forget."

At long last, he was forced to choose his daughter's life over his own selfish pursuits, and in so doing, he realized Vickie suffered at his hand, as he had picked Carlie over her for status, which broke her pure heart.

Twenty-Seven

Psalm 67:2

May your ways be known throughout the earth,
your saving power among people everywhere.

John stepped onto the porch and sat beside Price on the glider as Nellie and the girls went inside to rest from their ordeal at the falls. The afternoon sun set the grasshoppers buzzing in the field, and the horses stood in the shade as the day grew hot on their coats. The steel glider creaked in time with its movement, front to back and side to side, and the road invited cars that rarely passed. The power lines to their left rose higher than the trees. John leaned back and settled into the seat as a breeze kicked up and the air smelled like rain. He considered mentioning the weather, but offhand comments wouldn't pass muster after so many unexplainable experiences, and with a woman in her bedroom who had given up on life and everything within it, including her father, the man she loved, and her daughters. The thought made John wince.

The screen door opened, and Nellie slipped out quietly, bringing them each an iced tea. She seemed happier and healthier than ever before, and it was little wonder after the Lord had spoken words on her behalf. John thanked her, and an arc of color broke across her cheeks.

John placed his half-empty glass on the small table to his right. He must plunge into the depths of conversation and come up again until all was settled between them. He spoke without looking at Price.

"I guess it's about time I showed you something."

"What is it?"

"Just a minute." John paled as he fished through his jeans pocket and produced the diamond. It took about everything he had to keep still. "I thought it only proper to ask Vickie's father for her hand."

Price squinted and held out his palm. "Well, let's see it."

John handed over the ring, and Price studied it against the sunlight. "It sure sparkles, and I'll bet it set you back a little."

"Or a lot." John smiled, and they both chuckled.

Price handed the ring back to John.

He sighed, crossed his arms, and looked about the property.

"Do you think you can get through to her?"

"I plan to try."

Grady the dog meandered through the pasture and the herd, then started toward the house. He sauntered slowly up the slope but turned and investigated as Wildfire eased nearer to the highway.

"It's not what I asked you."

"I know, but it's not the real question."

"What is?"

"Am I prepared to do what it takes?"

"Well, are you? It won't be a pretty sight."

"When I go in there, my mother will be fresh on my mind, and I'll tell you what, I will never let another woman I love go out like that."

"She had schizophrenia, right?"

"Yes, but first it was a deep depression like Vickie's."

"My daughter has heard voices and seen wicked visions."

John drew a napkin from the table and polished the ring.

"Lately I've seen things that defy explanation, and I believe they're a test of faith." He pecked angrily at the diamond with the napkin.

Price reflected.

"When I had my heart attack, I saw a glimpse of the demons who populate Hell, how they claw and scrape over one another like crabs."

"It must have been terrifying, especially while in limbo."

Price nodded.

"I was very glad to see Vickie when I woke up, but it's also why I've been wary of getting into any altercations with her. I'm not up to it."

"I know, and I don't blame you for having a heart attack."

Price looked meditatively at the horses in the field and the dog, who interacted so easily with them, and his voice took on an air of benevolent invitation. "What I'm asking is for you to go in there and do whatever it takes to bring her back from the pit of Hell. But it won't be easy, and she might not want to live another day, so she might end her life." He wiped tears from his eyes. "If she really wants to die, we can't stop her."

"If she dies, you won't last a week," John said after a pause.

"It won't bode well for you either."

John nodded.

"Probably not. I was a wreck without her in California."

"Tell her what you just told me. It might make a difference."

"I'll make one promise, and that's to love her the rest of her life, no matter how long it might last. And I'll love her even after her death."

Price put his face in his hands and sighed heavily without speaking a word. He collected himself and sat up straight, then patted John's knee.

"It's one of the many reasons I'm proud of you."

He stood, looked about, and took a deep breath.

"Now please go in there and wage a holy battle for her soul."

John had been holding the ring in his palm.

He pocketed it. "So I have your blessing?"

The two men smiled at one another as thunder faintly growled.

"You do."

John waited for the extended family to arrive, then gave them instructions as he paced in the living room. When he was convinced they understood his plan, he left them and went to the hallway. He paused and steeled himself for the painful journey ahead.

He opened the bedroom door, surprised to find Eudora sitting with a Bible in her hand. She looked up at him and smiled with warmth.

He nodded at the two windows across the room.

"Why aren't those open? The smell in here is awful."

"She wouldn't let us, and it's a hundred degrees outside." Eudora hesitated. "It's Vickie's house, so we have to honor her wishes."

His lips pursed. "Won't be for long if she keeps this up."

John went over to the windows and opened them.

"I was just about to read Psalm 67," she said. "Do you mind?"

"By all means." He sat on a trunk that held old record albums.

"May God be merciful and bless us. May his face smile with favor on us. May your ways be known throughout the earth, your saving power among people everywhere. May the nations praise you, O God. Yes, may all the nations praise you. Let the whole world sing for joy, because you govern the nations with justice and guide the people of the whole world. May the nations praise you, O God. Yes, may all the nations praise you. Then the earth will yield its harvests, and God, our God, will richly bless us. Yes, God will bless us, and people all over the world will fear him."

Vickie had rolled over and faced the wall. She did not stir.

Eudora closed her Bible and gave her friend a sad look that seemed to last an eternity. "Craig was sometimes like this," she said.

"I'm sorry, Eudora. I never knew."

"It was hardest on Mary." A pause. "Keep the girls in mind."

"I will, but they've already seen enough for three lifetimes."

"Perhaps, but at some point, it's going to back up on them."

He knew she was right, but had to focus on the task at hand.

Standing, he asked her to pull her chair into the hallway.

She complied, and he grabbed the lamp and nightstand and placed them farther down the hall, so they wouldn't be in the way. Mitch and Lee were to follow behind him and remove the soiled mattress.

John positioned them and returned, then shut the door so he might speak with Eudora in private. "I spoke to the others in the living room and asked Mary and Lewis to bring her some new clothes. I doubt hers will be salvageable at this point." He took a heavy breath. "This won't be pretty, just so you know, and it will probably be very hard on Price."

Eudora nodded.

"Like I said, I dealt with Craig more times than I can count."

"So you know what happens next," he said matter-of-factly.

"More or less, as I'm sure you do, because of your mother."

He sighed. "I blame myself for both of them."

"You can no longer help Nicole, so put all your efforts into Vickie."

He leaned against the wall and pushed into it with his fists.

"I'm not sure how to fix her any more than I could my mother."

Eudora put her hand on his arm. "I think you know everything about Vickie there is to know, and you love her with all your heart."

He turned to her with watery eyes. "Will it be enough?"

Her eyebrows arched. "That's not for me to say, John."

Eudora paused.

"I was angry with Vickie Morrison for a long time, but she was my friend, and she's loved you, and she's been hurting deep inside. None of us ever really understood her until now, and so we're here."

"Yes, we are."

"And we will do whatever it takes." A pause. "So will you."

"If she leaves us in the end?"

"Then we'll stand over her grave and know we did all we could."

Tears coursed down his cheeks, and he looked away to hide them.

She rubbed her hand up and down his arm. The rush of emotion overwhelmed him, and his shoulder pressed into the wall as his face fell into his hands. He shook as he softly wept, knowing she might not make it back to him, as once down the path of insanity, rarely did people return.

"Don't do that here, John. Save it for later, when it's done."

He collected himself. His hands instinctively swiped at his tears. His voice barked a sharp command. "Take care of Price, as I said."

She nodded and smiled. "I will."

His hand found the doorknob, and his voice choked.

"Don't let the girls come anywhere near us."

There was a brief moment of silence as she considered.

He turned to her with fierce eyes. "Did you hear me?"

"They've seen too much death," she said. "It stops today."

Eudora wheeled and marched toward the living room.

He cracked Vickie's door and entered, then lay beside her on the bed, snuggling close and draping an arm over her body. She stirred slightly, as if asleep, and he pondered his next move. The stench in the room seemed less powerful than before, but he must soon take action.

"Did you come here to taunt me?" Vickie asked in a whisper.

"No, honey."

"Then why?"

He ran a strand of hair behind her ear. "Because I love you."

She chuckled sarcastically. "Right."

"It's time to get out of this bed. I'll help you get a shower."

Vickie curled herself further into a ball like a child.

"Don't you want to see Chief? He misses you."

"Chief is dead."

"No, honey. Missy helped him, and he's just fine."

"She's a liar, just like you." A pause. "It doesn't matter, anyway."

"Why not?"

"I'll soon be dead, and you all can have this world."

He gasped and caught himself, as it would do her little good.

"I want to help you get better. Will you let me?"

"You left me alone, John, and you said you didn't love me."

"I never said any such thing." Her accusation sparked his ire.

"You don't want our daughter, either, the one I tried to kill."

"Well, you're right about that, but I made up with Nellie, and now we're in a good place. She found me in California and brought me back here to help you. We saw some strange things at the falls that are hard to explain, but with Katie and Abbie's help, we got through them."

"I've been hearing voices in my head. They tell me to kill myself."

"I know." He hugged her tight, breathing through his mouth to avoid the remnants of the smell. "It was the same with my mother."

"A man spoke to me in a dream. He said you were with Rachel."

The words washed over him. Franklin must have approached her and driven her to the brink of madness, which John must now repair.

"I've met that man. He's the devil who sent Rachel to test me."

"He said that, too, and he said we'll fall to insanity together."

"I'd rather be sane," John said, smiling.

Vickie remained still and stoic, so seriousness returned to his face.

"Get up with me and let's fix this."

She clutched at her covers like a terrified child.

There were afternoons spent with Nicole when the light bent itself around the curtains at five o'clock and shone on the wallpaper's flowery patterns, and despair transferred from her to him as she forced him to stay. He stood and opened the door and fanned the room, allowing better air inside. Then he steeled himself again and ripped the pillows from underneath her head and tossed them into the hallway.

"Stop, John!"

"You will get up right now!" He yelled through gritted teeth.

His rough hands jerked the covers off her, and he recoiled at the mix of urine and feces about her lower body and the noxious stains on the sheets both above and below. The smell that had been partially blocked was now front and center and incredible. He went to the end of the bed and removed her boots and socks and drew back, as small sores had formed on her feet, and he could only imagine her backside.

John rubbed a hand gently over her foot, and she winced.

He must carry her to the bathroom.

She wouldn't walk on her own.

He held one end of the covers and for a split second debated what to do with them. Then he grabbed at the other end and pushed it toward the middle and balled up the covers and threw them into the corner. He opened the door and yelled toward the living room to come get them. A crescendo of footsteps thudded toward him as he turned back to his pitiful Vickie on the bed. Missy and Nellie grabbed them.

"Be strong, John." He wasn't sure who said the words, as the full picture of his beloved made him want to take a knee and weep, but he held strong and gathered her up, uncaring of the foulness on his clothes. He took her into his arms like he should have done when she first arrived. She moaned and tears coursed down her cheeks, and her head fell back against his chest. The frailness of her body beckoned to his desire to protect and his fatherly need for justice and his undying love for her. With moist eyes and a stern chin, he moved her through the doorway, yelling at the others to make way, and he carried her scarred body down the hall and turned right, bumping her against the frame.

"You're hurting me." Her voice seemed weak but imploring.

John set her carefully in the tub and ran warm water.

"Go find someone else," she said. "I'm not worth it."

"I need you to stop talking." He washed his hands with soap.

Activity behind him caught his ear, and he craned to see.

Missy ducked into the bathroom. "Her mattress is an unbelievable disaster. Lee and Nigel are struggling to carry it down the hall."

"All right." He smiled faintly. "We're not going anywhere."

Her eyebrows arched. "Do you still want what you asked for?"

"Yes."

Missy gave him a desperate look and then left him with Vickie.

"Want what?" Vickie's eyes rose to his.

"It's not important." He took the shower head off its base and changed the setting to full blast and sprayed her with warm water. She held up an ineffectual palm, but he brushed her aside and ran the wand up and down her form several times. Then he turned it on the tub, so the filth that came off her would run to the drain. He dropped it and gestured at her clothes. "Let's get those off so we can bathe you."

She settled into the tub, as the fight had gone out of her.

"Do whatever you want. I don't care."

"I want you clean, Vickie. That's all I ask."

"I'll never be clean of my sins, John. Don't you realize the truth?"

"That's not what I meant, and you know it."

"It should be." She looked about, half dazed. "I'm defiled."

He lifted Vickie to her feet and unbuttoned her blouse, and let it fall in a dank wad. Then he unsnapped her jeans, which had soaked up a large amount of bodily fluids and would go directly to the landfill.

He pulled them down, and the sores on her feet paled in comparison to those on her legs. He cursed her family for allowing this to happen, although he knew they had tried to help her and possessed no real understanding of mental illness, as they had not dealt with it in life.

Missy opened the door and placed the requested item on the counter. He turned, and the look on her face when she saw Vickie said more than a thousand words, but his savage expression forced her to go.

"I won't let you leave without a fight," he said to Vickie.

He removed her soiled undergarments with one hand and tossed them to the door, and with the other, held her still. "Do you hear me?"

Vickie spat in his face and sneered. "That's for leaving me for such a horrible woman and then blaming me for the last twenty years."

John spat in *her* face, and she flailed, as it was unexpected.

"And that's for killing my child and giving me no say in the matter!"

He sprayed Vickie, and she wiped her face.

"Nellie isn't dead," she said abruptly. "She's in the other room."

"How do you know?"

"I heard her voice earlier. A mother knows her own child."

John turned and groped for the shampoo bottle.

"Here." He handed it to her. "Use this!"

She took it from him and grinned like a schoolgirl.

"When did you get so forceful? Such a big, strong man."

He crossed his arms. "Do it, Vickie. I'm not kidding."

She tried to open the top but couldn't, so he helped her.

He lathered her hair, and her head bobbed along with his hands. Once done, he left the shampoo in and went for the bar of soap.

Vickie looked past him at the counter, where the pistol reposed.

"Are you going to shoot me, John?"

"Don't tempt me." He took the soap and lathered every inch of her body, even her feet and toes, but he saved the worst parts for last.

"Those are for you, as it wouldn't be right for me to do them."

"I'm not cleaning them," she said with a sly grin.

John had gained a little ground with her, but she was falling deeper into her abyss, and he might have to call for a psychiatric evaluation, which would involve the police and cause a scuffle in the house.

"Please, Vickie. We're not married."

She took the soap with a gleam in her eye. "Oh, so now you're a moral man who always does right by his woman? That's too funny."

"I'm *trying* to be him. Is that all right with you?"

Vickie washed her privates, which calmed his nerves. She likely had a severe infection that would require antibiotics, but the measure would have to wait for another day, once she regained stability.

He stepped forward and sprayed water on her head, clearing out the shampoo and the grime. Then he washed off her shoulders and the rest of her body, thankful this part was over, but still dreading the rest.

"Oops. Somebody has to potty," she said in a child's voice.

Urine ran between her legs, and she shrugged naughtily.

John grew furious at her lack of care for herself and for him and for the girls, not to mention her father and the rest of the family who loved her. At least Nicole had the excuse of being mostly unloved. He cursed under his breath as he washed her legs with the soap again. Then he felt a hard blow to the head and recoiled, realizing she had hit him with the metal sprayer. Blood ran from his scalp as she cackled with glee.

"You're crazy!" He went to the mirror and squinted at his reflection.

"I told you I'm not worth it, John. You should have listened."

After a minute, the blood stopped, as the cut was shallow.

He held up the pistol. "This is Red's, and it's loaded."

She eyed him and it suspiciously. "So?"

"If I give it to you, will you shoot yourself?"

Vickie glanced down at the tub, noting the flow of water.

"I might," she said, looking up at him.

He retrieved a knife from his pocket. "How about this?"

"Only if it's sharp. Red always warned me a dull knife was a dangerous knife. He said to me, 'Vickie, never own a dull knife.' I always thought it was odd advice to give a daughter. Don't you agree?"

She was testing him, but he wasn't sure of her purpose.

His eyes clung to hers, pondering her reaction and her next move.

"Like everyone else, Red assumed you wanted to live."

He held up a tube of toothpaste and squeezed some into her mouth, then gave her a toothbrush. She complied and then spat into the tub, and her eyes rose in defiance. "No, he demanded I live for *him*."

"Okay, fine." A pause. "It doesn't mean you should die now."

"I hurt people, John. I'm a monster—I tried to kill my own baby."

He had no response, as it was true, but there was forgiveness.

"You don't have to beat yourself up for your sins, Vickie. Once you have repented for them, the Lord forgives, and you can move on."

"Raul is dead, and I am too, inside, where it counts."

The insolence in her voice was blatant, and it pained him.

"Did you love him more than me?" John asked angrily.

She seemed surprised by the question. "What? No."

"But you did love him?"

"More than anyone I'd met since you."

"You still have *me*, Vickie. I'm not going anywhere."

"That's great, John. I have you now that you're a Rephaim."

She paused.

"Should we kill everyone here and then really go mad?"

He smirked. She had always thought herself quick-witted.

"I was never a Rephaim, but I was tainted by your parasites after our night in the tent. So was our child, who grew up just as wicked as you."

His revelation washed over her, paling her already ghostlike cheeks.

"Red left an antidote in a vial," she said. "But I drank all of it."

Vickie gave him a dejected look. "I'm sorry, John."

"There was another vial, but Nellie used it for herself."

Vickie reflected.

"It was for the best. She deserves to heal—if anyone does."

"And so do you, Vickie. Please let me help."

426

"But you're still tainted, and there's no cure."

"When we were at the falls, we saw the devilish man from your dream, and he tried to tempt me with a mountain nymph who we knew briefly as Rachel, but I refused his offer and his command to kill our baby girl, the one we both now cherish, and then I almost died."

"Obviously you didn't."

His countenance brightened. "A voice broke through the clouds, and a light shone on us at the base of the falls, in the round pool of water."

He paused.

"The Lord spoke to Abbie and told her to lay hands on me."

Vickie's eyes sparkled with recognition.

"Does this mean you're back for good?"

"I won't leave you again, Vickie."

Her eyes watered, and then she burst into tears. She fell to her knees and wept over his blessed renewal. He knelt and held her as she wailed into his chest and her wretched body shook. He hoped she wouldn't have a stroke in her feeble condition, and so he wept along with her.

"I'm sorry for killing our baby, but you sent me away when you knew I loved you with all my soul, and I had no one else to love me."

He drew her wet body nearer. "It's all my fault, Vickie. I chose Carlie because I wanted my father's approval, and he never liked you or wanted me to have anything to do with you. For some reason he said he liked her, and it was all I knew to do, because nothing else worked."

Vickie wept harder and wailed even louder, and he grabbed her hair and pulled her chin around and kissed her lips and her cheeks.

She drew back from him. "I was raped, John."

"I know, honey, and I'm so sorry."

"That man raped me twice," she said with contempt. "And you did it to me as much as he did, because you sent me to Washington just like Garrett and Red and Michelle and everyone else in Addison."

He pulled her close and kissed her neck and whispered in her ear.

"Can you forgive me for all the damage I've caused?"

She melted to his touch and gave herself over to him.

"Yes, a thousand times, yes!"
He pressed into her mouth and kissed her deeply.

After John bathed her again, he put her in a robe and led her to the front bedroom where Craig died and helped her dress in new clothes.

Mary had bought several outfits from the feed store along with boots, and as requested, she dropped by Sylvia's and picked out a dress.

He called in Nellie and the girls to help with Vickie's makeup, and she asked why there was so much fuss made over a worthless heap, but no one paid her words any mind, as she was their mother and they loved her. Katie and Abbie even insisted on putting antibiotic cream on her legs and feet so her sores might heal more quickly, which made her cry.

Satisfied with her cleanliness and her appearance, more for her sake than anyone else's in the family, he shooed everyone away from her and led her to the porch, where Price rose from the glider in happy tears.

"I'm so glad to see you up and about," he said in a choked voice.

"Me, too." She smiled but still seemed in a fog.

John led her down the steps, and she stumbled once in the grass, but he caught her and held her firm and told the girls to get back, as he had his woman under control, thank you very much, and he always would.

"I'm not sure about this," she said as they neared the barn.

"I am."

They walked through the wide doors and along the runway, and her hand trembled in his, but he squeezed it and spoke with kindness.

Vickie tensed as they stood in front of Chief's stall.

The horse licked his lips and nickered and pawed the ground.

John opened the stall door, and Vickie rushed to Chief and fell against him and begged him to forgive her, which he merrily did.

While she steadied herself against her horse, John took out the ring.

He knelt on the runway and called her over and held it up.

Her eyes glistened as her hand covered her mouth.

"Vickie Morrison, I have loved you since the first moment we met, but I could never tell you how I felt until today. You are my sun and my moon and my stars, and I have never felt so close to anyone in my life."

He glanced sheepishly at Nellie and the girls and shrugged.

Nellie gestured for him to hurry and beamed at him.

John turned again to Vickie, and she wobbled slightly.

"Will you marry me?" A pause. "Please say yes."

A flood of tears cascaded down her cheeks, and crimson color returned. Her entire body trembled, and her hands went to her face.

"I thought you'd never ask," she said in adoration.

"I wasn't sure if I ever would, but I was a fool."

He went to her and put the ring on her finger.

She held up her hand and studied the diamond in the light.

"It's so beautiful, John. I love it with all my heart."

"And I love you with all of mine," he said.

"I know you do."

He smiled. "So is that a yes or a no?"

"Yes! A thousand times, yes!"

Epilogue

Psalm 68:1

Rise up, O God, and scatter your enemies.
Let those who hate God run for their lives.

September 2008

Two months of proper courtship came and went, the kind they should have had from the beginning, and finally the hot August sun gave way to the cool and gentle breezes of late September. Her wounds healed, both within and without, and she worked daily with the horses, improving past her sister's skill level. Then Vickie tried the unthinkable: she worked with Wildfire and Hero.

Now she rode Wildfire in a procession as the family trekked along the trail on their way to the falls, decked in white and carrying their Bibles. A wedding would soon begin, which would make all the pain of the past disappear in a flash of light and love and laughter. Afterward, John and Vickie would take the loft over the barn so they might have privacy. There were children on their horizon, or so they hoped.

Ultimately, it would be up to the Lord in Heaven to decide, but until He gave His blessing, they would try and try and try again. Their intimacy was long delayed and forever negated by a world which would tear them down, but they had survived more than most, bonded in love and grace. Now they would share another virtue: humble sincerity.

No more lies would cross their lips, as there was nothing left to hide. All had been exposed, the worst of the worst, but their love prevailed, and now they were holy, set aside by God to perform His perfect will.

After the wedding ceremony and the joyful shouts, Price stepped from the grassy bank and into the sunlit pool. He opened his worn Bible and read Psalm 68:1-15, his enunciations reverberating off the walls, even above the whispering voices in the water, those which cried out for peace in the land and revival before judgment might fall upon the people.

"Rise up, O God, and scatter your enemies. Let those who hate God run for their lives. Blow them away like smoke. Melt them like wax in a fire. Let the wicked perish in the presence of God. But let the godly rejoice. Let them be glad in God's presence. Let them be filled with joy. Sing praises to God and to his name! Sing loud praises to him who rides the clouds. His name is the Lord, rejoice in his presence! Father to the fatherless, defender of widows, this is God, whose dwelling is holy. God places the lonely in families; he sets the prisoners free and gives them joy. But he makes the rebellious live in a sun-scorched land. O God, when you led your people out from Egypt, when you marched through the dry wasteland, the earth trembled, and the heavens poured down rain before you, the God of Sinai, before God, the God of Israel. You sent abundant rain, O God, to refresh the weary land. There your people finally settled, and with a bountiful harvest, O God, you provided for your needy people. The Lord gives the word, and a great army brings the good news. Enemy kings and their armies flee, while the women of Israel divide the plunder. Even those who lived among the sheepfolds found treasures, doves with wings of silver and feathers of gold. The Almighty scattered the enemy kings like a blowing snowstorm on Mount Zalmon. The mountains of Bashan are majestic, with many peaks stretching high into the sky."

Price caught his breath and looked about for a moment, then proceeded to verses 16-21.

"Why do you look with envy, O rugged mountains, at Mount Zion, where God has chosen to live, where the Lord himself will live forever? Surrounded by unnumbered thousands of chariots, the Lord came from Mount Sinai into his sanctuary. When you ascended to the heights, you led a crowd of captives. You received gifts from the people, even from those who rebelled against you. Now the Lord God will live among us there. Praise the Lord; praise God our savior! For each day he carries us in his arms. Our God is a God who saves! The Sovereign Lord rescues us from death. But God will smash the heads of his enemies, crushing the skulls of those who love their guilty ways."

Price received a word of encouragement from the sky above, as the Lord was pleased with his reading, and then he read verses 22-35.

"The Lord says, 'I will bring my enemies down from Bashan; I will bring them up from the depths of the sea. You, my people, will wash your feet in their blood, and even your dogs will get their share!' Your procession has come into view, O God, the procession of my God and King as he goes into the sanctuary. Singers are in front, musicians behind; between them are young women playing tambourines. Praise God, all you people of Israel; praise the Lord, the source of Israel's life. Look, the little tribe of Benjamin leads the way. Then comes a great throng of rulers from Judah and all the rulers of Zebulun and Naphtali. Summon your might, O God. Display your power, O God, as you have in the past. The kings of the earth are bringing tribute to your Temple in Jerusalem. Rebuke these enemy nations, these wild animals lurking in the reeds, this herd of bulls among the weaker calves. Make them bring bars of silver in humble tribute. Scatter the nations that delight in war. Let Egypt come with gifts of precious metals; let Ethiopia bring tribute to God. Sing to God, you kingdoms of the earth. Sing praises to the Lord. Sing to the one who rides across the ancient heavens, his mighty voice thundering from the sky. Tell everyone about God's power. His majesty shines down on Israel; his strength is mighty in the heavens. God is awesome in his sanctuary. The God of Israel gives power and strength to his people. Praise be to God!"

Price closed his Bible and rested in place.

Vickie and John went out into the water to meet her father, and each gave him a heartfelt hug, both for performing the wedding and for offering them wise counsel. Price handed John his Bible and turned.

"This family has known its share of pain and suffering, but we have come together on this fine September day to honor Jesus Christ, who died on the cross for our lost souls. We accept Him as our Savior, now and eternally, and are baptized in this water, washing away our sins."

Price took Vickie's hand and smiled warmly as the sun lit her hair. She had healed the sores on her body and in her heart, and those attached to her soul, the entities from within and without who would lead her to self-destruction. With one hand at the small of her back, her father dipped her in the cool, refreshing water. Instead of the voices of the past, she heard only the call of Christ, who strengthened her.

John would go next, and the rest of the family would follow.

The ancient elohim who fell to Mount Hermon, known as Bashan, and became territorial spirits of renown, including the Nymph of the Mountain, would no longer bother Vickie Breyer or anyone in her family. The human authority granted to them by sin had been removed by the truth of her words and the grace of the Most High.

Her eyes rose to the top of the falls, and she wondered after Rachel Daniels, who took human form in hopes of knowing love but fell like the petals of a rose into the abyss of time, cracked on the rocks, broken in spirit and in flesh, forever sentenced to wander the earth in chains.

Vickie's shackles were forever undone by the power of a love so lovely born, that of forgiveness over hatred, even of oneself, and a yearning for the child once missed and scarred and beaten but now found. A wretch from the wilderness who both saved and was saved herself, the fires of perdition having no sway, as faith now ruled her.

Like her daughter, Vickie would take the best from her parents and let go of their faults. She revealed her own malevolent sins, both in her heart and in her actions, hiding nothing from herself or the Lord, as He saw all before our birth, even our murder of His only begotten Son.

Afterword

Jesus suffered alongside you. He wept when you wept. He loves you with an eternal love. He receives your truth, trades grace for your pain, and offers a peace that surpasses understanding—a peace born of being fully known, and still fully loved.

The scriptures within *Love So Lovely Born* are only a beginning. Let them point you to the Lord's Holy Bible, for *faith comes by hearing, and hearing by the Word of God.* There is supernatural power in His Word. Within it are the pieces of a greater story—one that leads to the cross. To the empty tomb.

To life everlasting.

Jesus is the light of the world.

He will guide you on your way.

Acknowledgments

A special thanks to all those who helped make this novel a reality.

Your helpful assistance in navigating the many revisions, the never ending edits, and the painstaking proofreading process was invaluable.

Any remaining mistakes are most certainly mine.

About the Author

Ken Fulmer has worked for a number of years in the computer field as a network engineer. Since college, he has dreamed of becoming a writer.

A father of one daughter and many pets, he lives with his wife in the rolling hills of North Carolina.

Love So Lovely Born is his second Christian romance novel.

Visit www.kenfulmer.com.

Author Q&A

How would you describe your writing style?

Great romances carry a sense of adventure and the characters seem our best friends, people we wish to spend time with day after day. My novels promise the discovery of Christian romance, which develops slowly over many chapters and the restoration of broken family bonds which have caused deep emotional wounds and now seem insurmountable. Along the way, characters will overcome their pasts and learn the Lord's purpose for their lives as they help those more vulnerable than them.

How does place influence your writing?

My favorite stories offer unique settings with fascinating characters who populate the pages. Many of my novels will take place in locations within the United States, such as Western North Carolina, but others will drift across the sea to Europe, Asia, and other lands.

Our family loves the rolling hills of the North Carolina Piedmont.

We also enjoy the flatlands of the Sandhills, the sand swept houses of the Outer Banks, and the panoramic views of the Blue Ridge mountains.

I will set many stories within the confines of this wonderful and varied state. It's more than our home. North Carolina is our great love.

Is this Vickie Morrison's story?

The story tilts a bit in his direction at the start, but as the plot progresses past the midpoint, John Breyer emerges and takes center stage.

As the exciting conclusion nears, their fates are intertwined.

Who is your favorite character in this novel and why?

The characters usually take on the breath of life during my writing process, and today I am partial to both Vickie and John. I also appreciate Katie and Abbie, not to mention Nellie, Price, Missy, and all the wonderful horses.

Will these characters appear in another series?

I may revisit one or more characters in a short story or novella.

Do your story ideas come from real life or from your imagination?

An idea may originate from personal experience or from an article or a documentary. Sometimes the narrative unfolds quickly in my head, while at other times, it's a methodical process of developing a simple concept into a complex tale filled with interesting characters and places.

Each story is a journey for the reader, but also for the author, and even with a solid plan or outline, the plot often deviates in unexpected ways.

Do you write to a schedule or only when inspiration arrives?

Early morning is my best time, as then my creative urge peaks.

I admire those who write in an ad hoc fashion and do it well, but as an obsessive-compulsive person, planning is in my blood, which translates to the creation of several reference documents at the start of my process.

What is your most passionate life pursuit?

I find writing for the Lord to be my most meaningful calling.

During my elementary years, I used action figures to create stories, and as I look back now, the process seems to align with what Freud termed our *Prehistoric Wish* (i.e., what we most loved to do as a child).

I diverted from the land of imagination while working in the business world, and the opportunities afforded by my career have been a blessing.

It's been a thrill to explore a creative vision once more and I hope to fulfill the Lord's calling for my life by introducing others to the Most High through the psalms, which are a special gateway to the Bible.

I also enjoy quality time with my family and our pets.

What is your next project as a writer?

In my historical novel, *What Remains of Eden*, characters will grapple with their fallen natures, the desire for redemption, and with trusting in the righteousness of Jesus Christ. This story will be a departure, as it will be a bit more graphic--not to glamorize sin, but to show its destructive effect on our lives.

Reading Group Questions

1. Why did Vickie refuse to come home for twenty years?
2. Why did Helen take her life?
3. What did Raul see in Vickie Morrison?
4. Why didn't Ron and Julie sue Vickie over Helen?
5. Why didn't John take the girls from Missy's farm?
6. Would the courts have separated the girls?
7. Was Wildfire a dangerous horse?
8. Why did Garrett Breyer dislike Vickie?
9. Did Vickie have any obligation to help John rescue horses?
10. Did Red love Vickie at all?
11. Was Vickie right to leave and never come back home?
12. Why did Valerie go along with Red's plan?
13. What impact did Vickie's mistakes have on her life?
14. What made Vickie upset at Missy's farm?
15. Why was Vickie mean to Mary Bishop?
16. Was Vickie conflicted over her past career choice?
17. Why didn't John ever get married?
18. Did John and Vickie treat the rescue horses well?
19. Was Price a decent man from the beginning of the novel?

20. Why did Chris and Carlie betray John?
21. Did Vickie do right by Craig Bishop in the past or present?
22. What was the reason Vickie chose to stay in Addison?
23. Why did Vickie and John argue repeatedly?
24. What caused the horses to misbehave at times?
25. What happened to the neglected horse?
26. Why wouldn't Leslie take John on the campaign trail?
27. Why did Vickie open up about her traumatic past?
28. Why did Vickie wish to save Savannah so desperately?
29. Did the dance go as expected? Better or worse?
30. Why did Garrett help Valerie but mistreat her daughter?
31. Was Price to blame for Valerie's downfall?
32. What did Vickie learn from Valerie, good or bad?
33. Why did Mitch react so violently to Preston?
34. Why did Vickie care about Mitch after his betrayal?
35. Why didn't Leslie Carter have the family killed?
36. Why and how did Nicole die?
37. At what moment did Vickie and John bond in love?
38. Why was Nellie so angry with Vickie?
39. What dark secrets were revealed upon Nellie's return?
40. How could kill buyers be so heartless toward horses?
41. Did Red have remorse before his death?
42. How did Rachel Daniels figure into the story?
43. Why did Rachel desperately seek love?
44. What did Franklin hope to gain from Vickie and John?
45. What led Vickie and John to break up?
46. What caused John's Christian reversal?
47. How did Vickie finally reach Wildfire and the other horses?
48. Did everyone in the extended family live at Bluecreek?
49. Did Nellie and Nigel marry and have children?
50. What became of Lewis and Mary and Price and Eudora?

ALSO BY KEN FULMER

Wild Forest Rose